The Orphan Girl

Lindsey Hutchinson

W F HOWES LTD

This large print edition published in 2019 by
W F Howes Ltd
Unit 5, St George's House, Rearsby Business Park,
Gaddesby Lane, Rearsby, Leicester LE7 4YH

1 3 5 7 9 10 8 6 4 2

First published in the United Kingdom in 2017
by Head of Zeus Ltd

A CIP catalogue record for this book is available
from the British Library

ISBN 978 1 52885 109 1

Typeset by Palimpsest Book Production Limited,
Falkirk, Stirlingshire

Printed and bound by
T J International in the UK

MIX
Paper from
responsible sources
FSC
www.fsc.org   FSC® C013056

CHAPTER 1

Lily Rae's fingers gripped the edge of the table as she shuffled her way around it.

'You touch me and I'll scream my head off!' she rasped.

'Scream away, my little one, there's no one around to hear you,' her tormenter replied as he followed her around the dining room table, an evil grin spread across his face.

'You stay away from me! I'm warning you!'

He laughed. '*You're* warning *me*? Whoever do you think you are? Lily, you are a maid in this fine house and I am the master!'

'You are not the master!' the girl yelled. 'You're the master's son, and when I tell him what you're . . .'

He cut across her words with a hint of sarcasm in his voice. 'He won't believe you! It will be your word against mine and who do you think he will believe?'

Lily's heart plunged in her chest. He was right in what he said of course. Her breathing came in short rasps and her heart hammered. Rallying herself again, she yelled, 'I don't give a bugger! You just get away from me!'

As he threw back his head and laughed again, the girl saw her chance and ran around the table.

In a flash he kicked out at a dining room chair and Lily collided with it, falling heavily to the floor. Desperately trying to get to her feet cost her vital seconds in her bid to escape. Then suddenly he was on her.

He dragged at her long skirt and pulled her backwards. She tottered, trying to keep her footing, but her weight was too far back on her heels and she fell again. As he lunged at her, she brought her knees up and kicked out with her booted feet. She caught him a glancing blow to his stomach but it was not enough to drive the wind out of him.

He threw himself on top of her and pinned her to the floor. She struck him hard with her bunched fists as she tried with all her might to shift him. She saw the evil grin spread across his face as he realised her strength was waning. She slapped him as hard as she could, trying to wipe the smirk from his face.

'Get off me! Get off me now!' she yelled.

With renewed vigour, she fought like a wildcat as she endeavoured to throw him off her. A sharp slap to her cheek stunned her but only for a moment and then she was kicking, scratching and biting in an effort to free herself. Dragging in a great breath, Lily screamed until she thought her lungs would burst.

'Nooooo! Get off me! Leave me alone!'

A hefty punch to the side of her head left her

dazed; her senses reeled and suddenly all the fight drained out of her. She realised he was lifting her skirts and tearing at her underdrawers as she tried to gain control of her senses once more. Her breathing laboured and she saw black spots before her eyes. Her hearing was muffled and she shook her head to clear it but all she felt was blackness surround her and she knew she was going into a faint. Then she felt a searing pain which instantly brought her senses back into focus and realisation dawned – she was being raped by the master's son!

Hours later in her tiny box room at Ryder House in which she worked, Lily sobbed as she bathed her bruised body. The cracked mirror showed the bruise beginning to form on her cheek where he had punched her. The most private parts of her body were torn and burning. Soaking the cloth in the cold water from the bowl on the dresser, she held it between her legs. Wincing, she repeated the process again and again until at last the soreness turned to numbness.

Lying on her side on her small bed, the wet cloth held in place, Lily finally gave way to her misery. Silent tears ran down her cheeks as she thought about what had happened to her. She felt dirty, a dirtiness that no amount of scrubbing would erase. She had been abused against her will; her virginity stolen. A sob caught in her throat as she closed her eyes to the feeling of disgust that wrapped itself around her. The tears ran like a river as great heaving sobs racked her body. Lily knew she would never be the same again.

She'd had no warning that this might have happened. There was nothing that told her what the master's son had on his mind, otherwise she would have ensured she stayed out of his way. He'd given her no cause to believe that he was anything other than a spoilt young man.

She knew she could say nothing about the debacle to anyone – who would believe her? She was just the maid after all.

Her thoughts swirled and it suddenly occurred to her – if he'd done this once, he might try to do it again! Her resolve began to stiffen; there was no way on God's green earth that man would abuse her again. Then another thought struck, what if he had made her pregnant? Lily shuddered. She knew the old wives' tale about not being able to get pregnant the first time, and she dismissed it as nonsense. If the act had been performed then it was always possible a pregnancy could occur. What would she do if that turned out to be the case? She had very little money, not near enough to seek help. Besides, women had died trying to get rid of unwanted pregnancies.

Watching the moon cast its glow on scudding clouds through her tiny window, Lily knew if she found herself to be with child, she would be dismissed from her work. Then what? With no job, no money and an unwanted child growing in her belly, where would she go? How would she live? Would she end up in the dreaded workhouse?

'Please God, not that!' she whispered into the empty room.

Then, realising she was meeting trouble round the corner, she settled her mind to priorities, the first of which was to stay as far away from the master's son as she possibly could.

Sebastian Ryder had laughed as he'd left the maid on the dining room floor. He had enjoyed knowing he had been her first. He didn't care that he had spoiled her for any other man. Or that she would probably never be in a position to marry now, and have a family of her own. He'd laughed again thinking it may be that she might in fact have a child – his child. His father would dismiss her if that proved the case, but it would be months before it would be known for sure. He could take his pleasure many times with her during that time.

Riding his horse across the heath to the town to meet his friends, Seb felt the joy of being young, healthy and most of all – rich. At least, his father was rich, but Seb wanted for nothing. His mother doted on him and spoiled him, which allowed him to do exactly as he pleased.

As he rode over the scrubland he thought about his parents. His mother was a soft touch and he could twist her around his little finger. His father was either at work as a buyer and seller of anything he could get his hands on, or he was at his Gentlemen's' Club in the town.

Their house was on the outskirts of Wednesbury set in the centre of the Black Country. The town itself was dirty and drab; the coal dust from the collieries coated every building, which even the rain couldn't remove. Only the surface dust could be washed off, which would run down the cobbled streets like a black stream.

Bringing his horse to a walk, in order to enjoy the sunshine, Seb thought again of his lifestyle. Free to come and go as he pleased, he often sought out the company of his friends in one or other of the taverns in the town. There they would drink themselves senseless and he would climb onto the back of his trusty steed. The horse would find its own way home and so deliver him safely to sleep off his stupor more often than not in the stables.

Life was sweet and now he could take his physical pleasure at home yet again rather than having to go to some bawdy house and pay for it. He thought again about Lily Rae and how she had struggled to fight him off. She was strong, there was no disputing that, but not strong enough. The familiar stirring in his loins made him smile; would she fight as hard next time? Or, would she accept what she might consider to be her fate? That would hold no pleasure for him, he liked her wild side; it was that which set his blood on fire. Yes, he planned to enjoy the young maid for many months to come. Spurring his horse to a canter, Seb laughed out across the wasteland.

'Lily Rae, I'll be coming for you again very soon!'

As she lay in the darkness of her room, Lily had heard the familiar sound of the horse returning to its stable. Fear and anxiety held her in its grip before she realised he would most likely be out of his head on drink. No doubt that drunken sot would lie there and wake with a headache like a beating drum. Good! He deserved everything he got and more.

Her mind moved in pictures following around the rooms of the house and the possible places she could find herself trapped. Places she needed to avoid at all costs when the master and mistress were out. The cook was the only other person there, and she would be no help at all. Rarely sober, it was a wonder anyone was fed at all. No, Lily knew she was on her own, it was up to her to keep herself safe.

The task was a huge one; her duties meant she was often alone. She cleaned the rooms, lit the fires when needed and . . . changed the bed linen for all. She would have to go into *his* bedroom. The thought filled her with dread. She would have to clean his room at night whilst he was out with his friends. It meant changing her routine, but at least it would keep her safe.

Slipping quietly out of bed, Lily took her chair and wedged the back firmly beneath the door handle. Now she could get some sleep knowing *he* couldn't get into her room.

However, once back in her bed, sleep evaded her. Tears ran freely again as her mind relived over and over the horror of what had befallen her that day. All night she lay awake desperately trying to decide what to do about her dreadful situation.

The morning dawned and the cracked mirror showed a reflection of the walking dead. Cold water splashed on her face, Lily felt no better than she looked. Donning her black skirt, white blouse and pinafore, her white mob cap pinned securely onto her dark hair, she walked carefully downstairs. Aware Seb would still be in bed with a hangover, Lily's anxiety kept her alert nevertheless.

The cook was about her business of cooking breakfast for the family upstairs.

'Morning,' Lily said quietly, knowing the woman would be sporting the usual hangover.

'Hmm,' the cook answered, proving Lily to be right in her thinking.

A plate of greasy bacon and an egg fried to within an inch of its life was slapped on the table. Lily sat down to eat but her stomach roiled. She couldn't face food this morning.

'What's up with you?' the cook asked as Lily pushed her plate away.

'I'm not hungry,' the young girl answered, 'I'll just have a cup of tea.'

The cook nodded to the teapot, indicating Lily should help herself. 'Best stir your stumps, this will be ready in a minute,' the cook said, waving a fish slice in the direction of the frying pan.

Lily nodded and left the kitchen. Standing at the door of the dining room, she halted. She didn't want to go in, this was where . . . The feeling of fear and shame enveloped her as she stood looking at the closed door. Taking a deep breath, she rushed through the door and made straight for the dumb waiter. Opening the little doors set into the wall, she saw the shelf inside filled with dishes of food with lids on to keep it warm. Placing each dish on the sideboard, she closed the little doors and fled the room. Running back down to the kitchen, she was panting for breath on her arrival.

'Am they up yet?' the cook asked, rolling her eyes towards the ceiling.

'I have no idea and . . . no, I'm not going to wake them!' Lily said firmly.

'You'm getting above yourself, young lady,' Cook said as she poured them both more tea.

'You know what, Cook? I don't care!' Lily spat.

'Oooh hark at you!' The older woman laughed.

'I think it's time for me to leave this godforsaken place anyway,' Lily countered.

'Why? What's happened to make you say that?' Cook was surprised at the maid's outburst.

'*Him*!' Lily said with utter distaste.

'Who?'

'Seb Ryder!' Lily's temper was rising now.

'The master's son? What's he done now?' Cook asked, totally taken aback yet again.

'Cook, you wouldn't believe me if I told you!' Lily's voice held a note of desperation.

'Try me.'

Lily shook her head, tears of anger lining her lashes.

'Oh my God! He ain't gone and . . .?' Cook gasped as she looked at the stricken girl. Cook was at her side in an instant. 'That little bleeder!'

'Oh, Cook, I don't know what to do! I have to stay away from him! What if . . . he tries again? What if . . . I'm . . .?' Lily's despair was evident.

'Well now, staying out of his way is going to be difficult, I can see that. And as for whether you might be . . . you'll just have to wait and see I suppose.' Cook knew her words weren't helpful but she felt obliged to say something.

'I can't stay here, Cook, I'm open to danger whichever way I turn.' Lily wiped her tears on her apron.

'What about telling her upstairs?'

'What, that her precious son had done something like that?' Lily almost laughed.

'Ar, I see what you mean,' Cook said before screwing up her mouth around her toothless gums. 'So where will you go? What will you do if . . . you know . . .?'

'I have no idea!' Lily was distraught.

'Oh Lily, I ain't half sorry. That young bugger should be horsewhipped! He has no thought for any but hisself!' Cook sat in the rocking chair by the range and lit her clay pipe. Then she added, 'You got any money . . . any savings?'

'I have a little,' Lily said quietly.

'Well that won't last forever. You'll need to find work somewhere. You don't want to finish up in the workhouse.' Cook spoke as if to herself.

'I know, I've already thought about that.' Lily moved to sit next to the range herself.

'When you gonna go?'

With a loud sigh Lily said, 'No time like the present. I'm sorry to leave you in the lurch like this.'

'It don't make no mind to me, lovey, it's them upstairs as will suffer. Now the master will regret his decision not to hire more staff like the mistress wanted. Serves him right for not wanting to seem a show-off in the eyes of his peers,' Cook harrumphed.

'But who will dust and clean as well as set their meals out?' Lily was feeling more wretched by the minute.

'I have no idea what will happen, but I tell you this – I won't be doing it! My job is Cook and that's what I'll do – and no more!'

'Maybe I should stay then and hand in my notice so they can replace me,' Lily hated the idea but felt compelled to voice it.

'No you won't! It's too dangerous for you here now, Lily, you have to get away while you can,' Cook said with some urgency.

Lily nodded at the truth of it and giving Cook a quick hug, she ran up to her room to change her clothes. Folding her uniform, she placed it on the bed. Shoving her few belongings into her carpet bag, she took a last look around the room. It wasn't much, but it had been her home for the last few years until . . . With a shudder of relief, she turned and walked through the door, which she closed quietly behind her.

Unable to face the mistress to explain why she was leaving, and after a quick goodbye to Cook, she walked from the house by the front door and marched down the gravel driveway; away from the place in which she'd once been happy.

As she walked, Lily recalled a couple of joyful occasions and she smiled to herself. She remembered Cook one Christmas when she was so drunk she wrote a letter to Santa Claus asking him to bring her a man like King Edward VII. She even posted it up the chimney! Another memory sprang to mind when the family had gone to London for a weekend where they visited the theatre and dined out with its wealthy patrons. Lily and Cook had eaten in the family dining room and had drunk wine from the well-stocked cellar. But these memories had now been marred by the son of the household and Lily scowled.

Mrs Ryder had been kind to Lily over the years and she felt badly at leaving as she did, but she had no choice. She had to be away from the house as soon as possible.

She thought about her tiny box room, which had been her home, and sadness enveloped her at having to leave it. She had enjoyed her time at Ryder House – all except that one day.

Trudging on, Lily wondered if she would ever feel pleasure again, for the happiness she had known had been ruined by a spoilt young man. It was possible he may have ruined her whole life . . . only time would tell.

CHAPTER 2

Lily walked across the heath past Old Park railway sidings before reaching Holyhead Road.

Walking down this main thoroughfare, Lily looked at the houses. All identical and jammed one against the next, the line was broken only by side streets. Glancing down each street as she passed, she saw they too were lined with buildings. Everywhere, houses, shops and small warehouses stood covered in coal dust.

She nodded to the women leaning on their front windowsills canting as they watched their young children playing.

Coming to the crossroads, she turned left to follow the tramway a short distance before walking into Union Street. Here, the shops were located, selling all manner of things.

Following this road, she knew she would eventually reach the marketplace., She felt this would be the best place to ask about work. The women standing at the stalls knew everything that went on in the small industrial town. If anyone would know of a job going begging, they would. Being

14

in sight of her destination, the tiredness that she'd felt earlier left her aching limbs and she marched on full of renewed vigour.

Entering the market via Union Street, she heard the calls of the vendors.

'Vegetables, come and get 'em. Cheap and fresh, come and get your vegetables.'

'Second-hand boots, halfpenny a pair.'

'Fresh baked pies, still warm from the oven.'

Asking her question at the first stall, Lily received a negative response so, buying a meat and potato pie, she moved on.

Walking the length and breadth of the market, her high spirits began to melt away. There was no work to be had anywhere.

Lily had noticed, as she traversed between the stalls, the women standing at them. Their long skirts were patched and worn; blouses none too clean at the cuffs and shawls full of holes. The meagre takings clearly were only enough to help feed their families, with nothing left over for new clothes. The women's eyes showed a tiredness that sleep alone would not eradicate, this was bone-weariness at their plight of being poverty-stricken. Lily knew they would stand in all weathers just to earn a few coppers.

As afternoon turned to evening and the sun began its journey towards the horizon, Lily began to think about where she would spend the night. Sitting on her carpet bag with her back against a building wall, she munched on her pie.

Suddenly the wind picked up and the sky began to darken. *Oh no*, she thought, *please don't rain yet*.

Looking up, she saw a flock of birds flying past and the wind grew a little stronger. She needed to find shelter, there was a storm coming. She felt the temperature drop as she watched the stall-holders hurriedly pack away their wares. Soon the market would be empty and she'd be all alone. Glancing at the sky again, she thought, *Right, time to move*.

Lily trudged up Church Street as the drizzling rain was carried on the prevailing wind like smoke. By the time she reached St Bartholomew's Church it had begun to pour down and she was soaked to the skin. Cutting across the grass, she stopped at the lea side of the church building. Dropping her carpet bag onto the wet grass, she leaned against the wall. Not much of a sleeping place, but she considered it might afford her some shelter. The big church was locked up overnight so outside its walls would have to do. Upending her battered bag, she sat on it. Slowly the rain subsided and darkness fell. Alone in the churchyard, she felt tired, wet, cold and miserable. Then again, on a brighter note, she was no longer afraid of being found by Seb Ryder.

Thinking of her meagre savings, she wondered if it would have been better to rent a room for the night. No, for then she would have had no money left for food. Eating was more important than a bed.

Leaning her back against the church wall, Lily

closed her eyes. She was bone-weary and tomorrow she would have to walk the town again searching for work. Using her bag as a pillow, Lily pulled her coat tight around her and lay down on the wet grass.

Looking up, she saw the velvety black sky with its tiny twinkling stars. *Diamonds on velvet,* she thought as she felt her eyelids droop. It was not long before she was fast asleep.

The dawn chorus woke her and Lily sat up wondering where she was. Then she remembered, she was in the churchyard. She shivered in the early morning chill and her stomach rumbled. It would be a while yet before the market set up, so she would have to wait to find something to eat. Again her stomach groaned its displeasure at being empty. Standing, she stretched her arms and back to rid herself of the stiffness brought on by sleeping on the ground in wet clothes. Hitching up her long skirt and coat, she shot in amongst the trees to answer the call of nature. She hoped she'd be forgiven for peeing on Holy ground.

Sitting on her bag once more, Lily watched the sky brighten little by little until the sun peeped a cheery head over the horizon. As it ascended, it bathed everything in a golden glow. Tipping her face to the little warmth it provided, she closed her eyes and smiled.

Hearing the rattle of cart wheels on the cobble-stone road nearby, Lily stood. Picking up her bag, she walked from the churchyard. The town would soon be coming to life and she would be able to buy herself something for her breakfast.

Ambling down Church Street, she headed for the marketplace. She saw the stallholders setting up and wandered around looking for a food stall. There was a lot of noise as rickety tables were loaded with wares. Old boots and shoes on one, second-hand clothes on another. Tin pots and pans clattered as they were piled up, and fruit and vegetables laid out to tantalise shoppers.

Shouting and laughter filled her ears as she walked on and then the rich warm aroma reached her nose. The meat pie stall stood right in front of her. As she fished in her coat pocket for her money, her belly groaned loudly. The still warm meat and potato pie she bought didn't last long and she continued her journey feeling better for having eaten.

All day Lily roamed the streets searching for work. Her small carpet bag with her few possessions became heavier with each step, and she wondered about leaving it in a hiding place by the church. No, this was all she had left and she couldn't risk it being stolen. Shifting the bag to her other hand, she trudged wearily back to her sleeping place in the churchyard.

She was up early the following day again to watch the sunrise. Tiredness made her irritable as she walked once more into the town, hunger gnawing at her belly. Maybe today she would be lucky and find a job.

Unfortunately it was not to be and Lily found herself once more heading for the church that evening. Sitting on a bench to rest her legs, Lily picked up a newspaper someone had left behind. She began to read the contents hoping somebody was advertising for a maid.

Her attention was drawn to the article concerning the war. Britain had been fighting the Boers since 1899 when the Boers invaded Natal and lay siege to the British garrisons in Kimberley and Mafeking in South Africa. Now it seemed Lord Kitchener had turned that situation around and retaken those locations.

Although having no idea where South Africa and Swaziland were, and despite her circumstances being so bad, Lily felt far better off than the poor soldiers fighting that terrible war. *Please God let it end soon,* she thought.

As darkness made reading more difficult, Lily tucked the newspaper in her bag and went back to the churchyard.

Her rumbling tummy kept her awake most of the night and by morning Lily felt exhausted. She knew she wouldn't be able to go on like this much longer, and with a heavy heart she began her search yet again. Every bone in her body ached as she hobbled slowly into the town. She had to eat first, then she would drag herself around begging for a job. She'd do anything to earn a few pennies – enough to buy a decent meal. She was rationing what she spent in order to feed herself not knowing how long it would take to find work.

Lily realised she had lost a little weight for her skirt was looser around her middle already and she was constantly cold despite the sun shining.

Each night she cried into the darkness and prayed the following day would be lucky for her.

Lily roamed the town every day for a week looking for work, and each night she slept in the churchyard. Her money was only spent on a warm pie in the morning and an apple or carrot for her supper. Finding no work brought her to even lower depths of misery.

As Lily sat on her bag in the marketplace late one afternoon she saw the sky begin to darken yet again. Another storm was brewing, so now would be a good time to head back to the churchyard.

Standing up, Lily grabbed her bag and as she turned it swung out and caught the leg of a young woman rushing past.

'I'm so sorry! I didn't see you there,' Lily said as she saw the girl stop and rub her knee.

'It's all right,' the girl answered, 'I was going rather apace. I wanted to get back before the storm started.' As she spoke, the first raindrops began to fall. Looking at Lily, she said, 'Me and my big mouth!'

Despite her misery, Lily laughed along with the girl then she said, 'I am sorry, I hope you'll be all right.'

'I'm fine. Where are you off to?'

Lily shrugged and said, 'I need to find some-where out of this rain.'

'No home?'

'No,' Lily answered quietly.

'I live in a boarding house in Church Street, just up there . . .' the girl pointed in said direction, 'and I know there's an empty room there if you have any money.'

'I have a little,' Lily said. She knew it was dwin-dling fast and wondered if she should stay put in the churchyard until she found a job.

'Come on then before we get drenched,' the girl urged.

Hitching up their long skirts, the girls ran along the cobbled road towards Church Street. Just as they reached the boarding house the heavens opened and the rain pelted down.

'Phew! Just made it in time,' the girl said, closing the door on the inclement weather. 'I'm Rose Downey.'

'Lily Rae. Fancy us both having the names of flowers.' Again the girls shared a smile.

'Ah, Miss Downey, you're in I see.' The voice came from a middle-aged woman who stood ramrod straight. Dressed in a long black dress, her greying hair was pulled back into a tight bun at the nape of her neck. Wispy curls by her cheeks softened the look and her blue eyes held a smile.

'Yes Mrs Johnston, we just missed the storm,' Rose answered.

The woman turned her attention to Lily and raised an enquiring eyebrow. 'And you are?'

'Lily Rae. Rose said I might be able to rent a room from you.'

'Did she?' Mrs Johnston glanced at Rose before returning her eyes to Lily. 'Do you work Miss Rae?'

'Not as yet,' Lily answered, already feeling dejected by the woman's question. 'However, I will find something soon. I was in service but . . . I was no longer needed.' The little white lie might help her secure a bed here if only for one night.

'I see. Are you able to pay board and lodging, Miss Rae?' Mrs Johnston asked as she crossed her hands in front of her skirts.

'Yes, well that is – it depends on how much, but I have my savings,' Lily added quickly.

Mrs Johnston's mouth lifted at the corners. 'Savings – very sensible, Miss Rae. Now, I don't usually take boarders who are not in work, but I can see you're a determined girl . . .' Raising a forefinger, she went on, 'However, should you be unable to find work and your savings are used up, thus being unable to pay me, you will be out on your ear. Is that quite clear?'

Lily nodded. In her peripheral vision she saw Rose do the same and she stifled the smile rising to her lips. 'Perfectly, Mrs Johnston.'

'Good. Now, you can have the room next to Rose but we have house rules you must adhere to.'

Lily nodded again.

Beckoning Lily with her finger, Mrs Johnston turned and walked down the corridor talking as she went. 'There are to be no men brought to your room! Your money is to be paid on Friday evening before supper. If you are unable to pay, you will leave this house. The front door will be locked at 10 p.m. sharp every night, so if you are not in by then – you stay out until the following morning. I will provide, bed, breakfast and evening meal – lunch will cost extra.' Stopping outside a door, Mrs Johnston asked, 'Do you have any questions?' Lily shook her head. 'Good. This will be your room. Dinner is at 7 o'clock on the dot, at which time I will provide you with your room key.' Opening the door, Mrs Johnston finished with, 'Welcome to my boarding house, Miss Rae, I hope you'll be happy here with us. I'll see you both at dinner.' Turning on her heel, she strode back down the corridor.

Lily stepped into her room with Rose right behind her. 'This is lovely,' she said, 'thank you, Rose. I didn't know where I was going to spend the night. Probably back in the churchyard.'

'Oh Lily, how awful for you! It's nice to have you here. You settle in and I'll give you a knock at five minutes to seven and take you to the dining room.'

Lily began to unpack her bag and put her clothes away. She didn't have much, so there was plenty of space left in the dresser drawers and the tallboy. A jug and bowl sat on the dresser top with a mirror on the wall above it. A small chair stood in the corner and a tiny bedside cabinet held a small oil lamp. Drawing back the curtain, Lily looked out onto a patch of land which someone was using as an allotment to grow vegetables.

Sitting on the comfortable bed, she couldn't believe her luck although she was worried what it was going to cost. She considered herself fortunate indeed to have met Rose on the street. Now she just had to find work. Lily sent up a silent prayer that her luck would hold.

A knock to the door woke her with a jolt. Unaware she'd even been asleep, she rose and opened the door.

'Come on, or we'll be late for dinner!' Rose said as she grabbed Lily's arm.

They walked down the corridor and entered a large room on the left.

'Ah there you are, girls,' Mrs Johnston said, then clapped her hands twice. 'Everyone, this is Lily Rae, please make her feel welcome.'

Lily blushed at being stared at by all the girls sat at what looked like refectory tables.

'Come on, sit with me,' Rose said.

No sooner were they sat than a couple of maids began to bring in bowls of soup. The rich aroma of tomatoes wafted up to Lily's nose and she breathed it in. Large plates of freshly baked bread sat at intervals on the long table. It was the best food she'd had in days and she tucked in eagerly.

Quiet chatter ensued as the soup was consumed.

The maids removed the bowls and Lily stood to leave.

'Where are you going?' Rose asked. All eyes turned to Lily.

'Well, we've finished – haven't we?'

Rose smiled. 'No, that was only starters. We have our dinner now and then a pudding.'

'Oh,' was all Lily could manage and she retook her seat feeling very embarrassed. As a maid she was used to only having one course at dinner time.

The plate put before her now was filled to its edge with potatoes, vegetables, two slices of pork and a rich brown gravy.

Low voices resumed their conversations until the maids collected the empty plates. This time Lily stayed put. A few minutes later a dish of stewed apple and custard was placed before her.

Lily could barely breathe by the time she had finished. As she and Rose sauntered back to their rooms, Lily said, 'I'm so full I could burst! Is it always like this?'

'Yes,' Rose nodded, 'that's why she charges what she does, sixpence a week.'

'Sixpence a week is a bit expensive, but now I see why. If I'm to stay though I'll have to find work very soon.'

'Come into my room and we can chat,' Rose said.

'Miss Rae!' Mrs Johnston came bustling up to them. 'I'm so sorry, my dear, I almost forgot your key.'

'Thank you,' Lily said, taking the key from the woman. 'Mrs Johnston, that dinner was the best I have ever tasted, thank you so much.'

'Oh, how nice of you to say. I'm so glad you enjoyed it. Breakfast is at 7 a.m. Enjoy your evening, ladies.' With that she walked away.

Once inside Rose's room, they sat on her bed and Lily said, 'What a nice lady she is.'

'Mostly yes, but if you cross her she turns into a dragon!' Rose laughed. 'So, you lost your job in service then?'

Lily nodded, thinking it best to maintain her story. After all, no one would be any the wiser unless . . .

'What work do you do, Rose?' she asked as she pushed the awful thoughts away.

'I work in the milliners in Union Street. I serve in the shop, and I'm on my feet all day. It's hard on the legs, I can tell you, and the customers – you wouldn't believe!' Rose chatted on and Lily listened, stifling yawns here and there. 'Oh Lily, you look exhausted, you'd best get some sleep. We can talk any time.'

Saying goodnight, Lily went to her own room and no sooner she was in bed than she was asleep.

Breakfast was designed to set the girls up for the day. Bacon, egg, tomato, mushrooms, toast and jam and both tea and the 'new' drink – coffee.

'Good luck finding work,' Rose said as she parted company from Lily on the street.

'Thanks, see you this evening,' Lily replied, watching her new friend disappear round the corner.

Glancing around her, Lily couldn't decide which way to try first. Union Street held shops and houses. Church Street was mainly housing. Walsall Street had warehouses and businesses on either side.

Right, let's try the other end of the market, she thought and began to walk through the market-place which was already bustling. Reaching the end, she looked up Spring Head – posh houses, no good there. They would already be fully staffed. Ridding Lane consisted of small businesses and the other way was the tramway.

Lily heaved a big sigh before making her way back. She would start in Union Street and fan out into the smaller streets, that way she could cover as much ground as possible in one area.

All day Lily walked the streets of Wednesbury looking for work and by late afternoon she was exhausted – and still out of work.

Returning to the boarding house, she decided to rest a little before dinner. Sitting on her bed, Lily felt her spirits take a dip. She had been so sure she would find some sort of work. This was going to be more difficult than she thought.

Again, the knock to her door roused her from slumber.

'Any luck?' Rose asked as she opened Lily's door.

'No,' Lily answered, 'I walked my feet off today!'

Sitting at the dinner table, Lily watched as onion soup was served. This was followed by cottage pie and vegetables. Fresh fruit ended the meal and again Lily felt stuffed to the gills.

Rose said, 'Let's go to the sitting room and you can meet some of the others.'

The large room next to the dining room was filled with overstuffed chairs and small tables. Bookshelves filled with books of all sorts lined the one wall and gas lamps burned all around, casting a cheery glow.

Rose introduced Lily to the girls sitting conversing, then the two retired to a couple of chairs away from the others.

'Don't get downhearted, Lily, you'll find something I'm sure of it,' Rose consoled her new friend.

'I know, but it's hard not to,' Lily replied. 'My money won't last forever and when it runs out Mrs Johnston will throw me out.'

The girls talked all evening until it was time to retire to their beds. Lily slept well and by the morning she was again ready to trawl the town in search of work.

As the week wore on, Lily became more and more despondent. Every day she tried a different area and every evening came home feeling tired and demoralised.

Checking her savings, she worked out she would only be able to stay at the boarding house for a month before her money ran out. She *had* to find work – and soon. At least in that time she would be well fed, and although it was tiring trudging the streets, at least it was still summer. Then again she didn't want to be still looking for work when winter arrived. With no money or home, she would freeze to death on the streets.

Sitting on her bed, Lily's thoughts roamed. She could always go back to the Ryders and try for her old job back, but as a shudder took her she knew she would die a frozen death first.

She had seen the 'breadline' – out of work men gathered in certain areas hoping to be given a job – grow steadily longer. Another colliery had just closed down and the miners were now standing the line with many others.

Lily sighed as she wondered where to look next for employment. Life was hard for such as herself. Then a small smile crept over her face as she thought, 'I wonder if Queen Victoria needs a maid?'

The next evening in the sitting room Rose was rattling on about her day and Lily's mind wandered. She thought about what would happen if she found herself to be pregnant, but it was still too early to tell yet. Even if she found work, she would have to give it up when she gave birth. How would she take care of a baby when she couldn't look after herself? Would she want to take care of it? It wasn't as though she'd had any say in the making of it. Could she love a child born of rape?

Rose laughed loudly snapping Lily's attention back. 'Don't look so miserable, you'll find a job doing something or other before long,' her new friend said, thinking the worry on Lily's face related to her being unemployed.

Lily forced a smile and nodded. Looking around the room, she saw the others chatting and laughing. It was all right for them, they all had work to go to. Some were secretaries, others were shop assistants, but all had shaken their heads when asked if they knew of any work going.

Stretching out her aching legs, she rolled her feet in circles to ease the pain in her ankles. Then she wondered how much longer her boots would last if she had to stomp the cobbles every day. With each thought, her mood dipped ever lower.

Excusing herself saying she was tired, Lily returned to her room. The tears began to fall even before she reached her door.

Sebastian Ryder was surprised to learn that Lily, their maid, had upped and left the household. Moreover, he was disappointed that it had curtailed his plans for her. His mood was sombre as he sat with his cronies in the Castle Inn in Walsall Street. He had quietly boasted to them of his taking the maid on the dining room floor, and they had congratulated him on his conquest. Now they laughed at him for having driven her away.

'Back to having to pay for it again!' one had said.

'Same as the rest of us,' said another.

His mood blacker than ever, he stormed from the inn in a fit of temper. The calls and jeers from his friends following in his wake.

Climbing onto his horse in the stables behind the inn, he threw a coin to the stable boy. Walking the horse out onto the street, he muttered under his breath. 'Bloody girl! It's to be hoped we don't meet again, Lily Rae!'

Leading his horse through the streets, Seb looked around him. Dirty buildings lined the thorough-fare, blackened by coal dust. People were milling around, dodging the carts rumbling over the cobbled road. Rotting food, made worse by the summer heat, reached his nostrils and he screwed up his face in disgust. He thanked his lucky stars he lived on the edge of the town, away from the filth and stink.

On through the streets he kept the horse to a walk. Part way up Holyhead Road the horse halted and whinnied. Seb kicked his heels into the sides of his mount, urging it forward once more. Then he heard the whistle of the steam train.

'Bloody contraption!' he muttered. The London and North West Railway line, which ran parallel with the Holyhead Road, sliced the town in half. The one side held the built-up area of houses, factories and shops, whilst the other side was mostly heathland dotted with disused coal shafts. This area was criss-crossed by the canal system with its many wharfs and basins for loading and unloading cargo.

Reaching the heath at last, Seb kicked his horse to canter as he headed for home. Thinking again about Lily Rae and how she'd made him look a fool to his friends, his temper rose and he whipped his mount to a gallop until he reached Ryder House.

Sliding from the horse in the stable, Seb unsaddled it and saw to its welfare. Stamping into the house, he made straight for the parlour, knowing his mother would be there. Bursting through the door, he said loudly, 'Mother, this simply cannot go on! I need a stable lad. It's not fitting that I should have to see to my own horse!'

Looking up from her escritoire, Eleanor Ryder smiled indulgently. 'You're right of course, my darling. I will telephone the Servants' Registry as soon as I have finished my correspondence.'

Seb nodded as he dropped into an overstuffed chair and began to tap his fingers on its arm.

'Is something wrong, my son?' Eleanor asked.

Sighing loudly, Seb answered with, 'I'm so bored, Mother! There's nothing to do and nowhere to go in this godforsaken town!'

Moving to sit on the couch near him, she tapped his arm. 'I understand. Why don't you go and see your friends?'

Shaking his head, he was quick to answer. 'I'm bored with them too!'

'Oh dear,' his mother said, 'well why not take the train to Birmingham? You could visit your tailor and take in the theatre . . .'

'I suppose . . .' the boy said sulkily.

'Good,' she said before returning to her seat at the writing desk.

Pushing his dark hair out of his eyes, Seb blew through his teeth.

Without looking up from the letter she was writing, Eleanor said quietly, 'There's some money in the bureau, take it and get yourself on the train.'

Without so much as a thank you, the young man stood. Grasping the money, he stalked from the room leaving the door open behind him.

Eleanor smiled and shook her head as she gazed out of the window. 'Boys!' she muttered before turning back to her letter writing.

Seb purchased a ticket at the train station and strode onto the platform. The great iron train stood hissing steam as people boarded and alighted. A porter stood holding the door open, which would lead to the first-class carriages. Doffing his cap, the porter smiled. Seb ignored him and climbed aboard. Inside, he saw a woman with two noisy children being herded towards the door by another train worker, Seb's grin split his face.

'But . . .' the woman began.

'I'm sorry, madam, but this is first class. You need third class, which is the carriage at the end of the train,' the man said as he pushed her nearer the door.

Looking through the window, Seb's grin widened. He saw the woman running towards the back of the train as the engine picked up. Smoke puffed out as the iron beast inched forward and he heard the doors slam and a porter's whistle sound.

Sliding the window down, Seb leaned out and

saw an exasperated woman and her two mewling children watching the train pull away from them. Slamming the window shut again, Seb laughed. *What a shame she missed the train,* he thought spitefully. He chuckled, and settling down to his journey, he began to read the newspaper he had bought at the station.

CHAPTER 3

Lily entered the Servants' Registry office and walked up to the woman sat behind the huge desk.

'Can I help you?' the woman asked.

'I hope so, I'm looking for work,' Lily answered.

'Name?'

'Lily Rae.'

'What sort of work are you looking for?' The woman's words were clipped as she wrote down Lily's details.

'I was in service,' Lily said guardedly.

'Was?' The woman looked up at the girl standing before her.

Lily nodded.

'Where?'

'Ryder House,' Lily sucked in a breath, knowing what would come next.

'Why did you leave?' The woman's eyebrows almost reached her scalp.

'I . . . I . . . There was a disagreement,' Lily managed at last.

'Really? You left your employ with a well-to-do family because of a disagreement?' The woman's

35

voice rose an octave. Lily nodded again. 'So you are now *intentionally* unemployed?' Sarcasm dripped from the words.

'I'm afraid I didn't have a lot of choice,' Lily muttered, feeling wretched.

'Why so?' the woman probed.

Lily felt her anger begin to rise. Why should she answer these questions? After all, why she left that employment was nothing to do with this woman.

'Personal reasons,' Lily said a little more firmly.

Leaning back in her chair, the haughty woman said, 'I'm afraid that's not good enough. If you wish my help then I need to know the reason for your leaving your last post.'

'I do wish you to help me,' Lily responded heatedly, 'but I do *not* have to tell you anything! I was a maid . . . I left. I don't have to explain myself to you! Your job, which you are paid to do, is to find work for others. Now, look on your books and tell me what you have available.'

The woman blanched. 'I don't think we have anything for you.'

Lily placed her hands on the desk and leaned forward. 'I suggest you look again,' she whispered with quiet menace. 'I'm sure the people who employ you will not be at all happy if they are informed of your refusal to help. They will be looking for someone to replace you if they consider you incompetent and unable to carry out your duties properly. In fact, you could well find our roles reversed.' Lily straightened up and, with raised eyebrows, brought her lips into a tight line.

The woman's mouth hung open and Lily could not resist saying, 'Close your mouth, there's a tram coming!'

Clamping her teeth together, the woman pulled a large ledger from the drawer. Taking a small piece of paper, she noted down an address. Passing the paper to Lily, she smirked.

Lily knew instantly what the woman was thinking. She thought Lily couldn't read. Looking at the paper, Lily read it aloud, 'Waitress needed at Ann's Café, number two, High Street.' Looking at the shocked face of the woman, Lily gave a grin and left the office. She thanked God she'd had some schooling before going into service when her parents died.

As she walked towards the High Street, she thought, *who do these people think they are with their high and mighty ways?*

Quickening her step, she hoped the post had not already been filled. Checking the names above each shop, she hurried along, looking for the café. Finding it at last, she peeped through the window.

Walking into the café, she saw the place was packed and a line of people stood waiting to be served with cakes and sandwiches they could take away with them. She joined the queue and waited patiently. She watched as a young waitress rushed about serving pots of tea, plates of cakes and occasionally a hot meal. The girl was rushed off her feet, it seemed.

'Yes, what can I get you?' the harassed woman behind the counter asked.

Lily said, 'I've come about the job.'

'Thank God for that!' the woman said, beckoning her round the counter. 'I'm Ann, I need someone to help Jenny out with the waitressing. When can you start?'

'Now?' Lily said with a smile.

The woman grinned and took her to the back room. 'Put your bag over there, it will be quite safe.' Handing Lily an apron, she continued, 'Jenny will show you the ropes – just don't take any lip from them out there. We can do without the custom of cheeky buggers!'

Laughing along with her, Lily was dragged through a door into the kitchen.

'Everyone this is . . .?'

'Lily.'

'Lily is our new waitress, be kind to her.' Applause rang out from two women cooks and Jenny the waitress.

Standing Lily by the door, Jenny Pickard said, 'Tables are numbered.' She ran a finger round the room. 'Write the table number on the order chits so you don't get mixed up . . . easy. Come on, I'll show you.'

The two girls walked to a table and Jenny took out her order pad and pencil from her apron pocket.

'This is table four,' she said to Lily as she wrote the number on the small pad. Writing down the order for a pot of tea for two, she took Lily back into the kitchen.

A pulley string ran around the room at above head height which held all the orders with small clips and Jenny added hers to the end of the row.

'See? Easy. You should have a pad and pencil in your pinny.' Lily nodded, taking out said items, and the girl went on, 'Right, off you go!'

Lily was pushed forward into the café seating area and saw a lady wave her over. In her mind she counted the tables but then saw a little marker on the table denoting the number. What a relief. Taking the order, Lily gave her thanks and moved towards the kitchen. Her skirt was caught by another woman who quickly gave her order. Lily flipped the paper up and took the order. Hanging the chits on the line, she had a tray pushed at her and was told, 'Table 6.'

By the time the café closed for the evening, Lily was exhausted but happy. She was in work at last.

Ann, the owner, made tea for everyone in her living room upstairs as she did every night. She thanked Lily for her hard work.

'Now,' she said, 'do you still want the job?'

'Oh yes please!' Lily gasped. 'I'm not afraid of hard work.'

'Ar, we all saw that. Right then, you'll be on the same wages as Jenny and we start work at 8 a.m. on the dot. Any questions?' Lily shook her head. 'Get yourself off home then and we'll see you in the morning.'

'Thank you,' Lily said as she accompanied Jenny out of the door. Catching the girl by the arm, Lily whispered, 'How much are the wages?'

Jenny laughed and whispered, 'Ten bob a week.'

'Ten shillings a week! Goodness me!' Lily gasped, thinking it a fortune.

Parting company, Lily had a spring in her step as she walked back to the boarding house.

'Good evening, Miss Rae,' Mrs Johnston's voice met Lily at the door, 'how was your day?'

'Very good thank you, Mrs Johnston, I am now in work!'

'Excellent! Well done, Miss Rae.' Mrs Johnston gave Lily one of her rare smiles before heading for the kitchen.

Lily banged on Rose's door as she passed. Rose popped her head out and smiled.

'Guess who's got a job then?' Lily sang.

'Oh Lily, I'm so pleased for you!' Rose threw her arms around Lily and they danced a little jig in the corridor.

Lily worked hard over the next weeks and settled into her new position like she was born to it. She quickly became a favourite of the customers as she laughed and joked with them whilst taking their orders. She got on well with the other staff members and the owner, Ann. Her jovial nature drew in more custom and the little café was busier than ever.

In the evenings, she and Rose would sit in the

comfortable chairs in the sitting room at the boarding house and exchange news of their day's work. Life was sweet and Lily was happy. She would often chat with Mrs Johnston, and the other girls were good-naturedly jealous, laughing when she pretended to take umbrage at their cheeky remarks at being 'teacher's pet'.

All thoughts of her previous life at Ryder House were pushed far back in her mind until one night, readying herself for bed, a thought shocked her to her core. When had she last seen her monthlies? In pure panic she dropped onto the bed desperately trying to work out the weeks and dates. She realised then she had been working at the café for almost two months. During that time she'd seen no sign of them.

'Oh God help me!' she whispered.

Lying in bed, Lily sobbed her woes into the darkness. She was pregnant with Seb Ryder's child!

Thoughts swirled in her mind as to what she should do. Once it was known, Mrs Johnston would throw her out, thinking her a wanton hussy. Ann at the café might terminate her employment too; it would not do to have an unmarried mother-to-be serving her customers.

That would then leave one option open to her – she would have to go to Portland House. This was a place for young women who were unwed and pregnant. They were not treated well in there, gossip had it. Left pretty much to their own

41

devices, they were given little help during the birth, and asked to leave two days later.

Lily shivered at the mere thought of it. Then she would be out on the streets with a newborn to take care of. No home, work or money would see them both in the workhouse for sure. She thought briefly about giving the child away, but then how could she go about doing that?

Stifling her sobs, Lily thought about the alternative, one that revolted her. She could endeavour to get rid of it before it was too late. It might be 1900, but it was very much socially unacceptable to do such a thing. Women who helped in these matters were extremely discreet, for if they were discovered they were driven out.

Lily knew there was a need for such women due to the amount of poverty and those with big families already being unable to feed an extra mouth. Still, she was horrified at the thought. Could she be so callous as to go through with it? But then how could she keep a child when she could only just take care of herself?

All night she agonised and tossed the pros and cons over in her mind, until she was exhausted and could think no more on the predicament.

By the time morning came, Lily was tired from lack of sleep but she had finally made her decision. She had to be rid of it; she could not bear the thought of giving birth to Seb Ryder's bastard. A cruel word, but one she knew others would use should she go through with the birth. No, her mind was made up. She would never love it and she would not lose her home and job again because of that man!

Pushing her breakfast plate away untouched saying she felt unwell with a head cold, Lily left for work wondering how to go about finding someone to help her out of her predicament.

It was as the two waitresses took their lunch break that Jenny asked, 'What's up, Lily?'

'I'm not feeling too good,' was all she said.

'Oh, that time of the month is it?' Jenny enquired.

'I wish,' Lily said without realising.

'Oh . . .'

The girls eyed each other, then in a rush Lily whispered, 'Jenny, please don't say anything – please!'

'I won't, don't worry, but what will you do?'

'I can't have it!' Lily wailed, 'Jenny I was . . . raped.'

'Oh my God! Lily, I'm so sorry!' Jenny hugged her new-found friend. 'Listen, my mum knows somebody who can help. Why don't you come home with me after work and talk to her?'

'Jenny, I couldn't . . .' Lily protested, still feeling dreadful about having reached this decision.

'You can! Look, between you, me and the bedpost, my mum has been – twice!' Jenny said in a whisper.

'Blimey!' Lily gasped.

'We have six kids in our family, Lily, and mum can't afford to feed any more.' Jenny was matter-of-fact in her speech.

Lily nodded, 'All right – I have to do something,

and your mum might just be the one to help sort out this mess.'

So it was agreed, Lily would accompany Jenny home in the hope of finding a solution to her unwanted problem.

Once the younger members of the family were in bed, Jenny's mum, Vera, listened to a sobbing Lily explain about what Seb Ryder had done to her.

'That young man needs a thorough thrashing!' Vera Pickard said.

Lily sniffed. 'I can't have it! I won't love it! I have a good home and job now, how would I live if I lost them both? I'd have no money – I'd finish up in the workhouse for the rest of my life!'

'Now, now, you won't. I know someone who can help and she's good. It ain't nice mind you, but it works. You have to be very sure this is what you want though,' Vera said, giving Lily's hand a squeeze.

'It is! I have to do this . . . I don't care what it costs!' Lily sobbed.

'Right then. I'll see the lady concerned and send word with our Jenny. You want me to go with you?' Vera asked kindly.

'Would you do that for me? Oh Vera, that's so kind!'

'It's no bother. I'll mek the arrangements and let you know. It had better be soon an' all if you ain't had a show in a couple of months.'

Lily thanked the woman and set off for the

boarding house feeling slightly better for her visit. Now she just had to wait. She'd have to take at least one day off from work, but she could always tell them she was ill. Besides, she would probably be feeling poorly after . . .

Shaking her head free of the dreadful thoughts, she stepped smartly into the boarding house.

Seb Ryder, on yet another shopping jaunt and having been measured for more new clothes, felt no better. Something was on his mind which he couldn't shake off. He walked through the streets of Birmingham, which for all the world could have been his home town of Wednesbury. The same dirty buildings lined the cobblestone roads; people hanging around talking – didn't anyone work here?

Stepping over a pile of horse manure in the road, he wrinkled his nose in disgust that it had not be cleaned away. Filthy smoke poured from chimneys, leaving the smell of soot on the air. Further along he saw a woman throwing a bucket of dirty water out into the street and watched as it ran down the gulley set into the cobbles. That would stink before too long, he thought as he made sure it didn't touch his leather boots.

Walking into the nearest tavern, he ordered an ale and sat in the corner of the bar. He brooded as he watched men come and go, all dressed in working clothes. No doubt they had slipped away for a quick pint before returning to the daily grind.

At least someone was working, he corrected his earlier thought.

Glancing out of the window, he thought he saw . . . but no, it was not her. It was not Lily Rae, the girl who had barely left his thoughts these last months. Sipping his beer his thoughts swirled. What was it about that girl that would give him no peace? Why was she constantly on his mind? Inarguably he had enjoyed her that day; he had loved the fight in her. However, she was only a maid and those were two a penny.

Remembering his visits to the brothels in the town, he winced as he recalled his eventual lack of performance, so he had stopped the visits. It was Lily's fault he couldn't take pleasure in other women! It was the memory of her that left all others wanting, as far as he was concerned. Damn the girl!

Tipping the nod to the landlord for another beer, Seb continued to brood. He wondered, not for the first time, where she'd gone. Was she still in Wednesbury or had she moved on? Could he find her if he searched? What if he had left her pregnant?

Still, as he sat quietly in the beer house he could not rid his mind of her. Dark hair with wisps that escaped from the sides of her cap. Hazel eyes that had glared her defiance. Trim figure which, even beneath that awful uniform, showed its shape as womanly. The gentle sway of her hips as she walked from a room.

Good God man! Pull yourself together and stop mooning over that blasted girl! he thought as he emptied his glass. Leaving the public house, he strode out for New Street Station. It was time to meet up with his friends . . . a good night's drinking was called for.

Seb was welcomed into the fold once more and the drinking began in earnest. It was in the early hours of the morning when Seb fell off his horse in the stable at his home. Laughing fit to burst, he rolled over in the hay and was soon sound asleep.

The new stable boy, woken by the noise, shook his head and as he drifted back into slumber he thought, *That, I take it, is the master's son. Wonderful!'*

Eleanor Ryder eyed her son over the breakfast table. 'Seb,' she said quietly, 'you really should not come home in that state. Your father is not amused and has threatened to find you a job.'

Seb's head shot up from where his chin had rested on his chest. 'You can't be serious, Mother!' he yelled, instantly regretting it as his head felt like it would explode.

'I assure you he is serious, darling. Now, I have tried to dissuade him, but if you persist with this behaviour . . .' His mother shook her head.

'I know,' he cut across, 'I'm sorry, Mother, I know I should stop drinking, and I will.'

'You must!' Eleanor emphasised. 'Otherwise God only knows what your father will do. He might even cut off your allowance!'

The boy groaned as he leaned his elbows on the table, dropping his head into his hands. His promise to quit drinking was more in an effort to get his mother off his back than one he would adhere to.

'Look at yourself, Seb, you are a mess!' his mother stated, quite unnecessarily as far as he was concerned.

'Mother, please . . . my head hurts,' he moaned.

'It's no wonder,' his mother went on.

He could see she was not about to let this rest. 'All right!' he yelled then groaned again. In a hushed voice he went on, 'Mother, I will ensure I do not come home drunk again. Now, if you're satisfied I thought to ride into Wednesbury.'

'Fine,' Eleanor said, taken aback somewhat at his outburst. 'Your new stable boy arrived yesterday while you were . . . out. It took a while to find one, but he will do your bidding, just treat him well.'

Nodding, he rose slowly from his seat and, with another groan, walked from the room.

Eleanor stared out of the window. 'It's those friends of his I blame!' she muttered to herself.

Still holding his head in his hands, Seb spoke to the new stable boy. 'Horse . . . saddle . . . quietly.'

'Yes sir!' the boy replied rather loudly as he watched the young Mr Ryder wince. He smiled to himself as he saddled the horse and helped Seb climb up. The boy smacked the horse on the rump, then said even louder, 'There you go, sir.'

Seb winced again as his mount jumped at the boy's slap. He thought, *I can see you and I are not going to get along at all, young man!*

He nudged the horse sharply with his heels, and it walked forward and down the drive, its rider only just staying in the saddle.

Deciding to settle in the first pub he came to, he determined a hair of the dog was needed. Once he felt a little better he would begin his search. He'd made up his mind; he was going to find Lily Rae.

CHAPTER 4

Two weeks had passed since Lily had spoken to Vera Pickard regarding her 'little problem'. She had fretted constantly during that time. Unable to eat or sleep, she knew she was making herself ill, but the worry which hung over her was almost too much to bear. She cried every night when alone in her room and knowing Rose was concerned about her made her burden heavier. Over time she and Rose had become firm friends but still she could not share her terrible secret.

One evening as she retired to her bed there was a knock on her door. Opening it, she said in a rush, 'Rose, tell me tomorrow . . . Oh Mrs Johnston, I'm sorry I thought it was Rose.'

The owner of the boarding house asked, 'Miss Rae, may I come in for a moment?'

Lily stepped aside, allowing the woman entry, then closed the door behind her. Indicating the chair, Lily said, 'Please take a seat.'

Emily Johnston sat and Lily plonked herself on the edge of the bed.

'Forgive my intrusion, Miss Rae, but I'm most concerned about you. You are not eating and the weight has dropped off you. I guess you are not sleeping either and . . . I've heard you sobbing at night. Now, is it you are unhappy here with us?'

'No! Oh Mrs Johnston, please don't think that. I'm very happy here, you've been so kind to me since I came.' Lily's tears threatened.

'Then whatever is the matter, girl?' Emily wrung her hands which sat in her lap.

'I'm not well, that's all,' Lily answered and swallowed hard.

'Have you seen the doctor?'

Lily nodded. She was about to tell this kind woman a pack of lies and hated herself for it. 'He thinks I'm a bit anaemic.'

'I see, and did he give you a tonic?'

Shaking her head, Lily thought quickly. 'No, he said . . . the best thing was to drink stout.'

'Stout?'

'Yes,' Lily forged on, 'something to do with improving the iron level in the blood.'

Emily Johnston nodded. 'Well, if you need anything, be sure to let me know.' She rose to leave.

'Thank you Mrs Johnston, I'm sorry if I worried you. You really are very kind to me and I do appreciate it.'

Alone again, Lily muttered, 'Christ Vera, get your skates on, time's passing!'

'Jenny,' Lily whispered once they were on their break the following day, 'what's going on with your mother?'

51

'She's still waiting to hear from the woman,' the girl whispered back.

'If I wait any longer it will be too late!' Lily was beside herself.

'I'll see what's what when I get home tonight and let you know tomorrow. I ain't half sorry, Lily, but I can't tell you what I don't know.'

Ann trooped into the kitchen, shouting, 'Jenny, break's over, get your arse moving!' With a kind smile, she patted the girl's shoulder as they passed each other. 'Now Lily, I ain't one to bandy words so . . . what's up?' Ann asked as she sat next to the girl.

Here we go again, thought Lily. *God forgive me all these lies.*

Spinning the same yarn to Ann that she'd spun for Mrs Johnston, Lily hoped she would again be believed.

Ann nodded, 'Will you be needing time off if you ain't well?'

'No!' Lily shot back, then more gently, 'Thanks Ann, but no, I'll be fine. Besides, I need the money. My boarding house isn't cheap.'

Sharing a smile, Ann nodded. 'Fair enough, but you take it easy. I don't want you collapsing out there . . .' she tilted her head towards the café area, 'you'll put folks off their dinner!'

Lily rose as they laughed together. 'I'll get back to work then.'

Ann watched her go. Whatever it was that was wrong, and she suspected it was definitely not anaemia, it had Lily looking like a shadow of her former self. Shaking her head, Ann sprinted back into the café as Jenny shouted there were customers waiting.

Bad news awaited Lily the following morning. Jenny pulled her aside and whispered urgently. 'Mum couldn't get hold of that woman.'

'What! Why not?' Lily's heart sank.

'The woman has only gone and died!' Jenny said as she stole a quick look around them.

'Oh no!' Lily muttered.

'Sorry Lily. There might be someone else, but Mum doesn't know.' Jenny felt wretched to be the bearer of such news.

'Thanks anyway,' Lily patted her friend's arm, 'tell your mum thanks for trying.' She walked away, her heart heavy in her chest.

It was going dark when Lily set off for home and a cool wind blew, which forecasted a chilly autumn ahead. Her long woollen coat over her thick skirt shielded her legs from the wind, and knitted mittens covered her hands. She had draped a shawl over her head, crossed it beneath her chin and tied it at the nape of her neck. She wore men's woollen socks under her new leather side button boots. Walking a pace, she wondered how she would manage when winter arrived. Then her thoughts returned to the bad news Jenny had given her. Whatever was she going to do now?

She reached the end of the High Street where she would turn left into Church Street. *Almost there,* she thought as she rounded the corner.

It was just then she heard a familiar drunken laugh. The sound had her stop in her tracks, her heart beating loudly in her chest. Looking to her right, she saw him. Seb Ryder was coming down Walsall Street, straight towards her. Drunk as a lord, he was being held up by two of his cronies and laughing like a lunatic.

She had to cross the road and she was terrified he would see her! If she kept her head down and ran for it, he might not recognise her. He might be too drunk to see her anyway. Regardless, the longer she debated, the closer they came.

Dragging in a huge breath, Lily bolted forward. Then there was a shout and she felt excruciating pain as she seemed to fly through the air. Landing on the hard cobblestones, her senses reeled. Trying to get to her feet, she heard the commotion going on around her. She had double vision and all sound was muffled in her ears. Her leg and arm ached and the pain in her hip was agony.

'You all right lady?' A man's voice filtered through the fog in her brain. She attempted to focus on the man speaking to her, the one who was helping her to stand. 'Whatever were you doing running out in the road like that?'

'I . . . I . . .' Lily held her head in her hands. 'I'm sorry. What happened?' Lily looked around for Seb and his friends but could see no sign of them.

'You ran out into the hossroad and straight into my wagon, that's what happened!' The man was shaking from head to foot; was it shock or anger? 'I thought I'd bloody killed you!'

'My fault,' Lily whispered. 'I'm all right, I'm sorry.' Turning away, she ambled unsteadily up the street to the boarding house, leaving the traumatised man where he stood.

'Miss Rae,' Emily said as Lily walked through the door, 'good grief, are you all right?!'

Lily looked down at her coat covered in dirt. Nodding carefully, she muttered, 'I just got knocked down by a carter . . . it was my fault, I didn't look before crossing the road.'

'Go to your room, I'll bring you some sweet tea,' Emily instructed before marching to the kitchen.

A short while later she was handing the cup and saucer to Lily. Sitting on the bed, the girl's hands shook as she tried to drink the hot sweet liquid.

'Are you sure you're all right? Do you need to see the doctor?'

'No, thank you. I'm fine, I'm just shaken. I think I'll settle to bed now.'

Emily Johnston was worried but left the room, closing the door behind her with a quiet click.

Lying in the dark bedroom, Lily thought how easily she could have been killed by not paying attention to crossing the road. She always looked around before stepping out – why had she not done so this time? She had been in a blind panic, that's why! She had spotted Seb Ryder coming towards her and she'd ran, the result of which had seen her collide with the carter's wagon.

Easing herself into a more comfortable position, she felt the aches and pains of her accident begin to bite. Her leg ached and her elbow was sore. Her hip would be black come morning. Thinking herself very lucky to be alive, she closed her eyes in an attempt to prevent the tears escaping. It didn't work, the droplets squeezed between her lashes and ran down the side of her face. Lily was feeling very sorry for herself, and she sobbed out her misery as she lay in the darkness.

Without realising she had fallen asleep, Lily suddenly sat bolt upright in bed, a pain tearing through her stomach. Lighting the oil lamp on her bedside cabinet, she pulled back the bedclothes and gasped. Thinking she had wet herself, she was horrified to see blood in her bed.

'Oh God!' she gasped as another sharp pain gripped her belly. This was not her monthlies, it was far too severe. Then she realised . . . she was losing the baby!

Picking up her boot, she banged on the wall then staggered to the door.

'What? What's the matter?' Rose said, standing in the corridor in her nightgown, rubbing sleep out of her eyes.

'Fetch Mrs Johnston . . . now!' Lily gasped again and closed the door on her friend.

A couple of minutes passed before Emily Johnston was at Lily's side, having packed Rose off to her bed.

Taking one look at Lily and the bed, she said, 'Right! I'll ring for the doctor. You lay still!'

Going to the newly installed telephone in the hall, Emily explained the situation to the doctor who was not at all happy at being woken so early.

The doctor arrived in double quick time and sent Emily to make some tea while he administered to Lily.

Giving her a tonic to drink, the doctor said, 'All right young lady, prepare yourself, this is going to hurt.'

Lily's senses swirled as the laudanum began to take effect. She had little idea what was going on, only that it felt like her insides were being torn out. She screwed up her face as the pain rolled over her but made barely a sound. Gritting her teeth, she kept her hurt inside, she dared not wake the others in the house with wailing.

When it was all over, Emily paid the doctor, who left shaking his head. Lily's senses came back into focus and she guessed what he would be thinking: these young girls today are wanton!

Emily sat on the chair next to the bed and passed Lily a cup of tea. She watched silent tears slip from hazel eyes and her heart went out to the girl.

'I'm so sorry, Mrs Johnston,' Lily whispered at last.

'Don't think on it, Lily.' This was the first time she had used the girl's Christian name and Lily was surprised. 'If you need to talk I will listen.'

Lily nodded and bit by bit she related the story of being raped by Seb Ryder and of her search for someone to help her get rid of the unwanted child. 'I couldn't tell you, Mrs Johnston! I didn't want to leave here and I thought you would throw me out if you knew.'

'No, I wouldn't have. You see, Lily, the same thing happened to me many years ago.' Lily's intake of breath was sharp as her eyes widened. 'I was married at the time and working in service, just as you were. It was the master of the house in my case and he left me pregnant. I couldn't tell my husband and I could not have him raise another man's child, especially one born of rape. So, I sought help. Unfortunately for me, things went badly wrong and I almost died. However, over time I recovered, but I was told by the doctor I could never have any more children.'

'Oh Mrs Johnston, I'm so sorry!' Lily grabbed the woman's hand. 'What did your husband say?'

'He left me, Lily. He nursed me until I was well enough to take care of myself, then he walked out.'

'Oh my God! That's awful!' Lily was shocked to her core.

Emily went on, 'Some years later I heard he'd died of pneumonia. Eventually I married again and had a happy life.'

'Did you tell your new husband about . . .?'

Emily shook her head, 'There was no need, and I was pretty much past child-bearing years by that time anyway.'

'Surely that has been only recently?' Lily asked, surprise written all over her face.

'Fifteen years ago, Lily. My second husband passed on five years ago, leaving me this massive house. So, I turned it into a boarding house for young ladies.'

'Well,' Lily drew the word out, 'I don't know what to say other than I'm sorry.'

'Lily, no one will be any the wiser. I certainly won't utter a word of this. I propose we keep it to ourselves.' Seeing the girl nod gratefully, she resumed, 'I will send word to your work tomorrow of the carting accident, informing them you will be at home for the rest of the week.'

'I can't take time off, Mrs Johnston! I won't get paid!' Lily was aghast at the thought of losing her wages.

'You will stay home, rest, eat and get well. I will brook no argument. We will forgo you paying board this one week and that's an end to it.' Emily's stern words were tempered by a warm smile.

Lily leaned forward in her bed, wincing in pain, and gingerly placed her arms around the woman's neck. 'Thank you!' she breathed. She felt Emily's arms wrap gently around her and they stayed that way for a long while.

* * *

The rest of the week saw Lily rested, well fed and generally doted on by her landlady. She was visited by Rose frequently. She learned Mrs Johnston had told the others Lily had suffered a blockage in her tummy which the doctor had relieved. Not so very far from the truth.

Emily Johnston and Lily became closer than ever, much to the amusement of the others, but they would never know the secrets held fast between the two women. Secrets which would be taken to their graves.

Everyone at the café was concerned about Lily when she returned to work the following week. In a quiet moment, Jenny pulled her friend aside. 'Are you all right now?' she asked pointedly.

'Yes, Jenny, all is well now.'

'Oh, right,' Jenny muttered, not knowing quite what else to say.

Breaking the uncomfortable silence, Lily said, 'Come on or Ann will sack us both!' She tugged on the other girl's arm and they both smiled.

As Lily resumed her work at the café, Seb Ryder awoke in the guest room of a friend's house set at the top of Spring Head. The street bore testament to moneyed people as many fine houses sat in their own grounds away from the road.

Groaning, he carefully sat up in bed and took in his surroundings. 'I really must give up the drink,' he muttered to himself as he climbed out in order to dress. Bending to retrieve his clothes, which he'd hung on the floor the previous night, he raised a hand to his forehead. The pounding in his head increased and little lights danced before his eyes. His stomach rolled and threatened to spill its contents. Slowly dragging on his clothes, he moaned again.

Carefully negotiating the long sweeping staircase, he picked his way to the dining room. His friends were seated around a large table. With heads in hands, no one looked up at Seb when he entered.

The maid produced a fresh pot of tea and, shaking her head, she left them to their self-inflicted misery.

It was late in the afternoon when Seb felt in any sort of condition to mount his horse and ride home.

Sliding from the saddle in the stable when he arrived back at Ryder House, Seb raised a hand to the stable boy as a warning not to speak, then he turned and walked towards the house.

Taking a deep breath, he walked into the parlour and saw his mother sat by the fire.

'Good afternoon, Mater,' he said jovially.

'Hello my son, we missed you at dinner last evening.'

'Ah sorry . . . meant to say . . . the boys and I ate out . . . Apologies. It won't happen again,' Seb said in his usual clipped manner. His stomach roiled at the thought of food and he felt the colour drain from his face.

'Oh Seb! You haven't been drinking again, have you?' his mother asked.

'A couple only, Mother, I swear,' he answered, the lie slipped easily from his lips. Eleanor nodded as he went on in an effort to dissuade his mother from harping on about his drinking. 'Did you hear about the accident in town the other day?'

'No dear,' Eleanor said, turning her eyes to her son once more.

'Well,' Seb began as he took a seat opposite her. 'A young woman ran across the road at the end of the High Street and was knocked down by a carter.'

'Oh my goodness!' Eleanor breathed, her hand coming to her chest.

'Hmm, it was around 6 o'clock if I remember correctly and I was just leaving the tavern in Walsall Street. We saw the whole thing!' He had mentioned the time specifically knowing his mother would pick up the idea they had left their drinking early. It would not occur to her that Seb was blind drunk even at that early hour.

'Was she killed?'

'No, but she took a terrible tumble. She couldn't have been too badly hurt though as she walked away from it.' Seb raised his eyebrows.

His mother then launched into a tirade about how the town was becoming unsafe to walk; how carters didn't give a damn about people on foot . . . and so it went on.

Seb listened like a dutiful son, nodding gently in all the appropriate places.

A knock came to the door, then in came a new maid with a tea tray set for two.

'Ah Dilys, thank you. Seb, this is our new maid. Dilys, this is Sebastian, my son.'

Dilys bobbed a quick curtsey then left the room.

'Mother! Where did you get her from?' Seb laughed.

'Whatever do you mean?' Eleanor asked as she poured tea for the both.

'She's . . . she's . . . old!' Seb said in astonishment.

'Seb Ryder! You mind your tongue, young man! Dilys is younger than me!' Eleanor was most put out.

'Mother, I didn't mean . . . what I meant was . . .' Seb struggled, knowing he was digging himself into a big hole.

'What you mean is . . . she's not young and pretty!' His mother's anger was now clearly on show.

Seb clamped his teeth together, he felt it to be the wisest move under the circumstances.

Eleanor went on, 'It doesn't matter what her age, she's a perfectly good maid!' That closed the conversation between mother and son.

Sipping his hot tea, Seb's mind turned yet again to another maid. Lily Rae, with her dark hair and engaging smile. It was time he endeavoured to discover where that girl was hiding herself. Then, seeing his mother's face, he decided he would stay home tonight and be a model son. Tomorrow was a new day and he could start his search bright and early.

'I shall be dining with you and pater this evening,' he said with a grin.

Eleanor gave the boy a beaming smile. 'That's nice, dear.'

His mother placated, Seb settled to enjoy his tea by the roaring fire.

CHAPTER 5

During her time recovering from her accident, Lily had thought many times about the baby lost to her. She was sad the child had had no chance of being born and having a life, but she could not reconcile the fact that she would never have loved it. Mrs Johnston had said it was God's way of ridding her of something that was impure; something that was got from an evil doing.

She had wondered whether it would have been a boy or girl; whether it would have looked like her. Then she had considered her own circumstances – living in the boarding house and working at the café. She couldn't possibly have raised a child and gone out to work, they would have both ended up in the workhouse.

Rising early, Lily lit the small paraffin heater Mrs Johnston had put in her room. It would soon beat off the cold and she could dress in the warmth it threw out. Jumping back into her warm bed whilst the room warmed up, her thoughts strayed again to Seb Ryder.

It stood to reason with him living just outside

the town, their paths would cross eventually. What would happen then? Lily shivered, but not from the cold. Maybe she should move to another town; that way she could be sure of never meeting him again. Frowning, she thought, *Why should I have to move? Why should I allow that man to drive me out? I have a home, friends and a job here, why should I give that up because of him?*

The anger she felt rising in her suddenly disappeared as her thoughts countered with . . . *he could assault me again!* No, he couldn't – she would never allow anyone to abuse her again. She considered carrying a weapon of some sort, a knife maybe, but dismissed the idea. She could be arrested by the police. If she wanted to remain in Wednesbury, she just had to be sure of staying out of his way.

Dressing warmly, Lily set out for her work. The sky was heavy with snow and she knew by the end of the day it was possible the pretty snowflakes would be falling. As she walked down Church Street, she felt the cold bite her nose and she sniffed. Glancing at the cobbled roadway, she saw tiny sparkles of frost glisten in the dreary light. She wondered if Christmas, a few weeks away, would be a white one.

'Ah good, you're here Lily,' Ann said as the girl rushed in through the door closing it quickly behind her. The others were already assembled and Lily listened to Ann speaking as she took off her outdoor clothing.

'We're all having Christmas and Boxing Day off,

girls,' Ann watched glances being exchanged. 'No, it won't affect your wages!' Cheers sounded and Ann looked round at her staff. 'We've all worked bloody hard these last months and I thank you for that. As a reward, there will be a little extra in your pay packet Christmas week.' Applause rang out in the café. 'Right! Let's get to work, them buggers will be in for their breakfasts soon enough!'

Lily smiled to herself at the way 'Black Country' women swore so much. It was commonplace and used in their everyday language. No one took that much notice.

The café filled rapidly and Lily and Jenny were rushed off their feet. As the morning wore on there was no let-up in the amount of customers coming and going. Lily stood by the kitchen door and looked around the seating area. A thought struck and the idea lingered as she continued her work. She could voice it to Ann over tea at the end of the day and see what sort of reception it would receive.

So busy was she after a quick bite of lunch that she didn't notice the man sat by the window until he called her name.

'Lily!'

Stopping dead in her tracks, she felt her heart freeze. The voice she heard and had prayed she would never hear again belonged to Seb Ryder.

Panic seized her and held her stiff. She felt the blood pumping around her body and heard her own heartbeat quicken. Her breathing became laboured as terror enveloped her. He had found her! Lily's hands began to shake and sweat beaded her brow.

In her peripheral vision everything moved in slow motion. She saw Jenny look at her and then at the man. The conversations going on around her became a slow drawl in her ears.

She had to move, she needed to get away from the man who still petrified her.

'Lily!' The call came again.

Then suddenly as everything snapped back into real time, her fear turned to anger. She was furious at this man for abusing her, for causing her so much aggravation, for losing the child – albeit unwanted – and for now coming to her place of work!

Ignoring the call, she turned her attention back to the woman she was taking an order from with an apology for being momentarily distracted, although she was visibly shaken. The order taken, Lily rushed it to the kitchen and placed the chit on the end of the line. Drawing a deep breath, she leaned against the table. How had he found her? Was he even looking for her or was it a coincidence him coming into the café?

Jenny came bustling in and when she saw her friend looking ashen asked, 'Are you all right, Lily?'

'That man . . .' Lily mumbled.

'Oh ar, I saw him. He's a looker!' Jenny quipped.

Lily gripped the girl's arm tightly and rasped, 'You stay away from that one, Jenny . . . I mean it!'

'Is he . . .?'

'Yes,' Lily whispered, then put a finger to her lips, indicating Jenny should say no more. The girl nodded, but couldn't contain herself.

'What are you gonna do?' she whispered.

'Ignore him!' Lily straightened her apron and cap and marched into the café once more.

So this is where you've been hiding, Seb thought as he watched Lily bustling around. He saw her smile and joke with the customers, all the time deliberately ignoring him. He ordered more tea from Jenny and when she delivered it, he asked, 'How long has Lily worked here?'

'I'm sorry sir, I can't discuss the staff with you.' No smile accompanied her words, and she spun away to serve another customer who was tugging on her apron.

Seb sighed loudly. Did that girl know what had happened between Lily and himself? He doubted it, after all it was not something she would have discussed with anyone else. Her flat belly told him she was not pregnant with his child and he was momentarily saddened by the thought.

He sat all afternoon in his seat by the window and other than when he had called to her, Lily had not looked at him again. He was not angered by her ignoring him, it just made him more determined he would have her again.

Ann saw the last of the customers out and locked up the café. Upstairs now, she and the others sat with their feet up on little stools. All day she had been consumed with thoughts and fear at her unexpected run-in with Seb, but now in the safety of Ann's room she thought it a good time to voice her thoughts of earlier in the day.

'Ann, would you mind if I made a suggestion?'

The owner replied, 'Not at all, you go right ahead.'

'Well . . .' Lily drew out the word as all eyes turned to her. Being fairly new here, she chose her words carefully. 'The café works well . . .' she saw the others nod, '. . . but I think if it was rearranged, it could function even better.'

'How so?' Ann asked, all ears now.

'At the moment there are tables dotted around the room, and the space between them is wasted. If the rectangular tables were placed around the edge, and the circular ones put in the centre with just enough room to stand between them, then there would be room for more tables.'

Ann nodded as she considered the idea. Putting down her cup, she said, 'Come with me.'

Everyone followed Ann along the short corridor. Opening a door to a spare room, she lit the gas lamp on the wall with the matches from her apron pocket. The dim yellow light spilled out onto tables and chairs stacked in piles.

'Can you do anything with that lot?'

Lily nodded. 'It would have to be done overnight if you wanted to be open the following day though.'

Turning off the lamp, they retreated back to

Ann's living room. 'Tell you what,' Ann said, 'we'll sort it out the day after Boxing Day. I'll put a notice up saying we will be closed for one day due to refurbishment. You girls up for it?'

Everyone agreed it was an excellent idea and began to chat excitedly about how to go about the task before them.

Despite her excitement at the plans for the café, as Lily wrapped up against the cold temperature that evening, she was very concerned Seb Ryder could be waiting for her in the street. 'Jenny, I'll walk out with you.' The other girl nodded, knowing exactly what was meant.

Once outside Lily looked around; there was no sign of the man she hated with a vengeance.

'Will you be all right walking home on your own?' Jenny asked.

'Yes, thank you, Jenny. I appreciate you keeping my secret,' Lily answered with a smile. 'I'll see you tomorrow.'

Looking around her yet again as Jenny walked away, Lily hitched up her long coat and skirt and walked swiftly down the street. She reached the boarding house and dashed inside out of breath.

'Miss Rae?' Emily Johnston asked as Lily sighed with relief.

'It's so cold out there,' Lily answered before pulling her lips together in a tight line.

'I see. May I speak with you later – after dinner?'

'Of course, Mrs Johnston,' Lily answered. Her eyes smiled at the lady who had become like a mother to her in the short time she had been at the house.

Going to her room, she wondered what Mrs Johnston wanted to talk to her about.

Later, with Mrs Johnston sat in the chair and Lily on her bed, she related the events of the afternoon.

'I thought there was something, that's why I asked to speak with you,' Emily said. 'In my opinion, ignoring the man was the wisest thing to do, under the circumstances.'

'It's the coming and going – the walking to and from the café, when I get scared though,' Lily confided. 'It won't be as bad when the light nights come again, but that's a way off yet.'

'Don't you be worrying yourself about that, I'll sort it out for you.' Emily patted the girl's hand before walking out, leaving Lily wondering what she had planned.

In the sitting room later, the girls heard the front door slam. 'Where's Mrs Johnston off to, I wonder?' Rose asked. Heads shook and conversations resumed.

The following morning Lily discovered exactly where Emily Johnston had been the previous evening. Leaving the boarding house, she saw a horse-drawn cab standing outside.

'Miss Rae?' the cabbie called. Lily nodded. 'Climb in, courtesy of Mrs Johnston. I'll be here every morning for you and every night to fetch you home.'

Lily climbed into the cab with grateful tears glistening along her dark lashes.

Seb Ryder sat in the café by the window virtually all day, every day for weeks, watching Lily work.

Ann noticed him; it was impossible not to, he had become such a regular customer. One day just before closing, Ann said, 'Lily, I think that young man is quite taken with you.'

Lily just nodded and changed the subject. She was looking forward to having the next two days off to celebrate Yuletide, so turned the conversation to that fact.

Eventually the café was locked up for the night and Jenny bustled into the kitchen. 'Lily, I found this on that man's table, it's addressed to you.'

Lily took the prettily wrapped small box from the girl who held it out to her. Sure enough, her name was written on a small card attached to the top. Ignoring the jibes of the others, she pulled off the card and turned it over. She read the two words. *I'm sorry.* Opening the box, she saw a beautiful gold cross and chain nestled inside.

The others were eager to see, so she passed the box around, slipping the card into her skirt pocket.

'Good grief! He really does like you!' Ann gasped.

Shoving the returned box into her pocket with the card, Lily frowned in disgust. Did Seb think a present such as this would appease her after what he'd done? There was no way on God's green

73

earth she would forgive him – gift or no gift! All comments ceased as the others noted the look, and conversation turned swiftly to the café refurbishment.

Dinner at the boarding house was exciting that night as each of the boarders gave Mrs Johnston a small Christmas gift, Lily included. As a treat, wine was served with their food and afterwards Mrs Johnston organised some games in the sitting room. Later, she played the piano as everyone sang carols.

Slowly the girls drifted away to their rooms which left Lily and Mrs Johnston sitting together. Mrs Johnston lifted her head in question and Lily showed her the box and card. 'I knew something had happened as soon as you came home.'

'I don't know what to do!' Lily wailed. 'The cab was a wonderful idea, but I can't allow you to continue to pay for it. I will take over paying the cabbie.'

'You'll do no such thing!' Mrs Johnston snapped. 'Lily, this may sound strange to you, after all we've only known each other a relatively short time, but I've come to look on you as a daughter.' She saw Lily smile. 'You are a very special young lady and I care for you a great deal.'

'And I, you,' Lily replied, trying not to cry.

'So tell me what's worrying you,' the woman said gently.

'He sits in the café all day watching me. It makes me very uncomfortable. It's scary!' Lily gave an embarrassed little laugh.

'You do realise the day will come when you will need to confront him, don't you?'

Lily nodded. 'Ann and the others think he's carrying a candle for me.'

'So do I Lily.' Seeing Lily's eyes open in shock, she went on, 'It's my considered opinion you have stirred something in him that no one else could.' Watching Lily frown, she added, 'That man is in love! Don't misunderstand me, Lily, it's the idea of you he's in love with. It's my guess he's hankering over something he'll never get, namely you!'

Lily gagged at the thought. 'No! No!'

'Yes, yes,' Emily replied, 'he won't leave you alone until you confront him and show him you are no longer afraid of him.'

'But I am!' Lily protested.

'Then don't be. Arrange to meet with him. I could be your chaperone if it would help. He can't hurt you while I'm there. Once he knows how you feel, it may be then he will stop pestering you.'

'What if he doesn't?' Lily asked, feeling the fear rise in her.

'We will cross that bridge as and when. Now, it's late and tomorrow is Christmas Day. Santa won't come if you're not in bed asleep, you know.'

Laughing together, they shared a hug before retiring to their respective rooms.

Lying in his own dark bedroom, Seb wondered what Lily would think of the gift he'd left for her. He'd bought it on impulse and now he considered whether he should have wasted his money. Still, it was done.

Throwing his arm over his eyes, he sighed loudly. 'Oh Lily, I won't see you for three days, whatever will I do?'

CHAPTER 6

Christmas had passed and all in the boarding house had enjoyed a jolly time. Now Lily, wrapped warmly against the weather, walked carefully over the icy cobblestones towards the café. She looked in awe at how Mother Nature had turned the dirty town into a white wonderland. Hoar frost covered everything; windowpanes sported beautiful patterns as the ice had formed on them. Ice crystals sparkled in the dreary light giving the impression the road was made up of tiny diamonds.

Ann was waiting for her as she walked in the door, hot tea in hand. 'Thought you might need this,' Ann said, passing the cup to Lily.

'Thanks. Isn't it beautiful out there?' Lily sipped her tea gratefully.

'Ar, but it's bloody cold!' Ann laughed.

Jenny and the cooks bustled in and all sat in the living room upstairs forming a plan of how to rearrange the café to make the best use of it.

Lily suggested, 'If we stack the chairs first, we can move the rectangular tables to the sides then arrange the round ones afterwards.'

Ann and Gwen, one of the cooks, went to the spare room to bring down and dust off more furniture, while Jenny and Lily began work in the café area. Margy, the other cook, began to prepare their lunch in the kitchen.

The women worked hard all morning and by lunchtime they were tired and famished. Over their food they chatted excitedly about the new look of the premises.

'Ann,' Lily said tentatively, 'can I make another suggestion?'

'Yes, providing it don't mean putting that lot back the way it was before!' She tilted her head to the shop area as laughter sounded.

'Please don't take offence but . . . the bare tables . . . well I think they need some pretty tablecloths.'

Ann nodded, 'Good idea, it will brighten the place up a bit. Do you fancy a walk to the town to see what you can find?'

Lily nodded and grabbed her coat as Ann gave her some money. Wrapping her shawl over her head, she walked through to the front door, making a quick count of how many cloths would be needed.

Rounding the corner into Union Street, Lily made for the Home & Colonial Store; that, she decided, would be the first place to try. Finding white cotton tablecloths bordered with a fine lace, Lily worked the figures in her head. She was one shilling short. Feeling in her coat pocket, she found two sixpenny pieces in amongst the copper. Delighted, she paid for the cloths and made her way back to the café, sure all would be happy with her purchases.

Lily was right, everyone was pleased and the tables were now covered with the pristine white cotton cloths. 'There's something missing . . .' Lily said.

'What?' Ann asked, thinking the room looked fine as it was.

Lily pondered, saying, 'In the summer – flowers, but now, in the dreary light of winter . . .' She moved to the kitchen with the others in tow. Rummaging in a cupboard, she found what she sought. Taking cook's sharp knife and a chopping block, she placed a stubby candle down and cleaved it in half.

Margy gasped as she watched Lily with her precious knife. 'Don't worry, I'll get it sharpened for you,' Lily laughed as she searched the crockery cupboards. 'Aha! These will do nicely.' Pulling out some small thick glass ramekins, she then lit a candle. Dripping the hot wax into the glass bowl, she quickly shoved a half candle into it and held it in place while it set. Taking the candle glass to one of the tables, she sat it in the centre. She turned as the other women applauded her effort. Returning to the kitchen, candle work began in earnest.

By the end of the day, the room looked homely and comfortable. Ann had found some different curtains for the bow window and had beaten the chair cushions outside to rid them of the dust of her spare room.

In the living room once more, Lily said, 'Ann, you need to tell people what's on offer. Maybe some menu cards on the tables and . . . prices by the side.'

'Who's gonna do all that?' Ann asked, feeling exhausted.

'I'll do it,' Lily laughed. With a pencil and paper, she made a list of what was for sale and its corresponding price. 'I'll bring them in tomorrow,' she said, 'I'll get my friend Rose to help write them out. I'll drop into the printer's for some good paper on my way home.'

Ann again provided money for the menu cards, saying, 'Thanks, ladies. If this works, and I'm sure it will, you will all get a rise in your wages.'

Teacups chinked as they congratulated each other on a job well done.

The gas lamps in the street were lit when Lily left the shop to walk round to the printer's shop. The roadway glittered in the lamplight and the hoar frost still coated everything in a thick layer.

The printer advised Lily on some heavy but cheap paper when she explained they would be changing the menus when the springtime came. She headed home with her package under her arm.

Walking carefully on the icy surface, she recalled how she had thanked the cabbie for his service of taking and fetching her from her workplace. However, she was now freeing him up to go about his normal business. Mrs Johnston had railed somewhat when she was told, but Lily had insisted. With Seb Ryder spending his days in the café and gone before she left, Lily felt easier about walking home. Eventually Emily had relented.

That night, all the girls in the sitting room at the boarding house helped out with the writing of the new menu cards. The prices Ann had given, in Lily's opinion, were far too low, so she had changed them, hoping people wouldn't baulk at the small increases.

Showing Ann the cards the following morning, Lily waited with bated breath. 'I hope you'm right,' was all Ann said, regarding the increased prices, 'but these cards am lovely, Lily. Ta very much.'

With the cards on the tables, the door sign was turned to 'open', the cooks busy in the kitchen, Ann behind the counter, Lily and Jenny stood ready.

The door opened and in walked the first customer of the day – Seb Ryder. Over the Christmas break, Lily had hoped he would leave her alone now, but evidently that was not his reasoning.

Lily sighed audibly and turned to walk into the kitchen, leaving Jenny to serve him.

Seb ordered tea, asking, 'Did Lily like her gift?'

'I told you before, sir, I ain't at liberty to discuss the staff,' Jenny answered before leaving his table.

In the kitchen she relayed the conversation to

Lily. *Right!* she thought determinedly and fished in her bag for the box he had left for her. Marching into the seating area, she walked smartly to his table. Placing the box before him, she noted his surprise.

'You didn't like it then?' he asked, smiling up at her.

'Mr Ryder,' Lily began, 'despite thinking the gift beautiful, I cannot accept it.' Raising her hand to forestall his interruption, she went on, 'Now then, how you choose to spend your days is entirely your own affair. However, please be assured I will not speak to you again, neither will I serve you.' Lowering her voice considerably, she added, 'I will never forgive you, Seb Ryder, for what you have done to me! You have endeavoured to ruin my life, but you have failed. I'm strong, and I'm no longer afraid of you. So I suggest you stop pestering me at my place of work and make something of your life!' Turning on her heel, she walked back to the kitchen and the quiet stares of the women who had watched from the doorway. Unable to hear the conversation, they had presumed it concerned the returning of the gift.

Lily leaned against the table in the kitchen. She was shaking from head to foot. Then, taking a large breath, she let out a laugh. She had stood up to the man who had terrorised her for months. The heavy weight of fear lifted from her and she nodded her relief. The others continued to stare, wondering what was going on. Just then the little bell on the door tinkled and Jenny said, 'Hey up, here we go!'

As she and Lily walked into the café ready to begin their work with the surge of customers they presumed were trundling in, both were surprised to see that Seb Ryder had left, leaving the money for his tea on the table.

With another sigh of relief, Lily settled comfortably into her workday as the café began to fill with people coming in out of the cold, and Seb's table instantly being taken by someone else.

Seb Ryder walked down the street, kicking at the icy cobblestones as he went. Well, Lily had certainly told him what was what!

Damn you to hell Lily Rae! He thought as he felt the little box in his pocket.

Slamming open the door of the first pub he came to, he ordered a beer. Being told they weren't open yet, he scowled. However, the landlord, unwilling to lose a sale, poured a glass of ale and watched Seb take a seat.

He brooded. He was not surprised she would never forgive him, but it didn't really bother him either way. What did irk him was wanting something he couldn't have namely – Lily Rae.

He thought about what his friends had said. He would have to pay for his pleasures from now on, as did they. No, he couldn't. If he couldn't have Lily Rae, he didn't want anyone – at least for the moment. The pain he was feeling he knew was bruised ego, and he smiled as he remembered how badly he had treated the girl on that fateful day. How could he get her onside again? Would it even be possible? She had become a challenge to him now.

Walking his horse, which he'd stabled with the smithy, down the frosty streets then out onto the small heath later that evening, Seb's mood was sombre. He saw nothing of the beauty of winter around him. Reaching home, he slid from the saddle and with a nod to the stable boy, he slowly walked into the house.

Sauntering into the parlour, he dropped into a large armchair and tapped his fingers on its arm. A loud sigh escaped his lips as his mother walked in.

'Oh there you are, darling, I didn't hear you come in,' she gushed.

Seb grunted something unintelligible.

'Are you all right, sweetheart?' Eleanor asked.

Seb grunted again.

Eleanor shook her head as she watched her son. Something was eating at him, but she felt sure he would tell her what it was in his own good time.

CHAPTER 7

One bitterly cold morning in early January, Lily arrived at the café to see everyone stood outside.

'What's going on?' she asked.

'Ann ain't opened up yet,' Jenny said, stamping her feet in an effort to beat off the cold.

'Have you knocked the door?' Lily asked.

'Yes!' Margy snapped, feeling put out at being left to stand in the freezing wind.

Lily stepped back into the empty road and looked up at the windows of the upper building. 'Ann! Ann!' she yelled. Nothing. 'This isn't right,' she said, walking to the door. She rattled the handle but the door was locked. Walking down the entry leading to the back of the building, she tried the back door. This was locked too. Looking around, she saw the yard brush leaning against the privy wall. Grabbing the broom-stale, she swung the head around and it hit the small window, shattering the glass.

'Bloody hell!' Margy gasped as they all watched Lily push out the remaining glass with her elbow.

Lily squeezed herself through the window frame

and unlocked the back door, allowing the others entry. Dashing to the stairs, she took them two at a time.

Opening a door, she called out, 'Ann, are you in here?' The room was dark, the curtains still drawn across the window. Lily shivered, then moved to pull back the heavy drapes. The others, who had followed behind, gasped as Lily turned. Ann was lying in her bed, her face as white as the pillow her head rested on.

'Oh Christ!' the cook muttered.

'Jenny, fetch the doctor . . .' Lily said, looking at the staring girl. 'Jenny!'

'Right . . . yes . . .' The girl bolted from the room and down the stairs.

'You think her's dead?' Gwen whispered.

'I would think so looking like that,' Lily said as another cold shiver crept up her spine.

'So what do we do now?' Margy asked.

'We wait for the doctor,' Lily answered sadly.

'Then what?' the cook persisted.

Lily shook her head. 'I don't know.'

The doctor wrote out the death certificate and handed it to Lily. 'Heart attack, brought on by too many years of back-breaking work I shouldn't wonder. She wouldn't have known anything about it, most likely slipped away in no pain.'

Jenny was dispatched to inform the undertaker, who arrived minutes after her return. While they carefully placed Ann in a wooden coffin and carried her down the stairs to the waiting cart, Lily put a notice on the door. *Closed due to bereavement.*

Sitting now with hot tea in the kitchen of the café, Lily said she would make all the arrangements for the funeral. The cooks were drying their tears and Jenny asked, 'Lily, what do we do about the café?'

'I don't rightly know. Did it belong to Ann?' She watched the others shake their heads; obviously they had no knowledge of ownership. 'Right then, we need to go through her paperwork . . .'

'We can't do that!' Margy snapped.

'Look,' Lily went on, 'we need to know what to do about this place. We need to see if she made a will; did she have any children to pass the café on to? We need to ensure her bills are paid up to date.'

'Well, I'm not rummaging through her personal things . . . it ain't right,' Margy maintained.

'I'll do it,' Lily said with a sigh.

Going upstairs once more, Lily began methodically searching the drawers for anything pertaining to the running of the café. Quietly she spoke into the empty room, 'I'm sorry about this, Ann, but I know you'd want it sorted out.' Silent tears ran as she continued her search.

Returning to the kitchen, Lily placed a document on the table. 'Ann's will. Who's going to read it?'

The cooks backed away, both saying they didn't read too well. Jenny shook her head vigorously.

With another heavy sigh, Lily said, 'Looks like it's me then.'

Picking up the document, she opened it and began to read aloud. *'Ann Pryce, being of sound mind . . .'*

She read through the whole paper and when she'd finished she dropped it on the table. Looking around at the surprised faces, no one said a word.

The café remained closed for the following week, the curtains drawn across the windows as a mark of respect. The only mourners at the graveside were the staff. Snowflakes fell as the coffin was lowered into the ground and each mourner dropped a handful of dirt onto the box. Sobbing sounded across the quiet churchyard of St John's Church and the women walked away as the gravedigger stepped forward. They heard the shovelling of the earth and the clatter as it hit the coffin.

At the gate, Lily said, 'I'm taking the will to a solicitor to get it verified. Meet me at the café on Monday morning, usual time.' Nods and sniffs were given in answer as they parted company.

Lily crossed over into Lower High Street and entered Stockdales Solicitors. Explaining the circumstances, she handed over the document.

Mr Stockdale read it and handed it back.

'Miss Rae, firstly I'm sorry for your loss. The last will and testament of Ann Pryce is quite legal. I, myself, drew it up very recently. That is my signature and my clerk signed it as a witness. Again, my condolences.'

'Thank you Mr Stockdale,' Lily said, tucking the paper into her drawstring bag.

As she walked back to the boarding house, Lily's thoughts whirled. She was now the owner of the café! Ann had seen fit to leave it to the young woman in her will. Wiping away yet another tear, Lily muttered, 'Thank you, Ann, may the Lord protect you.'

Entering the boarding house, Lily asked Mrs Johnston for a moment of her time. Now sitting in the quiet of her room, Lily began.

'Ann's will was verified today by the solicitor who drew it up. She left the café to me,' Lily said with mixed emotions.

'That's wonderful!' Emily grinned then said more sombrely, 'Although it is still very sad . . . losing her like that.'

Lily nodded. 'My predicament is, do I move into Ann's accommodation or stay here? Do I try to run the café or sell it on? To be truthful, I have no answers.'

'You are still in shock, sweetheart,' Emily comforted. 'You could make use of Ann's living quarters but you may find it lonely after a while. I, and the other girls, would miss you terribly . . . you've become very popular with everyone. If you sell the café, would you be guaranteed a job there? Would the new owners run it or change its use?' She watched the emotions flit across Lily's face as she spoke. 'The place was closed for a week, rightly so I might add, but in that time it has made no money. Leave it closed much longer and you could lose your custom – they will go elsewhere.'

'I know nothing about running a business, Mrs Johnston!' Lily became agitated.

'Don't go thinking that. How would it be if I went over the books with you? I could help with advice regarding wages and the purchases you would need to make.'

'Oh Mrs Johnston, that would be marvellous! Thank you,' Lily brightened.

'Good. Firstly, you really need to start calling me Emily. Tomorrow I'll come with you and take a look. Let's see what, if any, improvements and savings can be made. Then you can decide later whether you intend to live there or not.' Emily smiled.

The following morning saw the two women in the kitchen of the café, the accounting ledgers spread out on the table. Lily made tea while Emily scoured the pages, totting up the numbers in her head.

'It looks like Ann was an astute businesswoman,' Emily said, 'all the books are in order and the invoices all paid up as they should be.'

'So, are the wages fair, do you think?' Lily asked, casting an eye over the books.

'For the cooks, yes, but for the waitresses – a little more would need to be paid, I think. They are the ones doing all the running around, are they not?' Seeing Lily nod, she went on, 'I also think the cooks are not being used to their full potential.'

'How do you mean?' Lily asked, feeling confused.

'At the boarding house I also have two cooks and they do a lot more than making pots of tea!' She continued, 'You have to decide whether this is to be a tea house or café. A tea house would serve tea, naturally, and cakes. A café would provide good wholesome home-cooked meals for breakfast and lunch.'

'I see your point,' Lily said, 'that would be more lucrative, I suppose, but how the cooks would take to the idea . . .'

'They at least would still be in work. You are the boss now, Lily. You make the decisions and make sure your staff carry out your orders. Yes, by all means consider their feelings, but you are in business and that means making money. The more you make, the more the staff can be paid – in time.'

Lily gave a great sigh as her head rocked slowly up and down.

'You will need more staff, another waitress at least – maybe two,' Emily recommended.

'I'll go to the Servants' Registry tomorrow,' Lily said.

'Oh and you will have to change the name too,' Emily added.

'Why?' Lily enquired.

'Because, my dear girl, this is Lily's café now!'

'Thank you, Emily, I don't know what I'd do without you,' Lily beamed, feeling a whole lot better.

★ ★ ★

Early the next morning Lily stepped into the Registry office once more and walked up to the haughty woman she'd met before.

'Oh it's you,' the woman said snidely, 'lost your job again have you?'

Ignoring the jibe, Lily asked, 'Do you have any waitresses on your books?'

'I have no one who would be willing to take you on!' The woman's words were caustic.

'Excuse me, but I don't remember saying I was looking for a job as a waitress. I asked if you had any waitresses on your books.' Lily kept her temper in check.

The woman frowned as if not understanding the question.

With an exasperated sigh, Lily said, 'I am looking to employ two waitresses in my café.'

'*Your* café?' the woman gasped.

'You know I've never met anyone quite as nosy as you. Look, never mind, I'll go elsewhere.' Lily turned to walk away.

'No, no . . . I have a couple of girls who may be interested. Should I send them round?' the woman said as she scrabbled for the details of the girls.

'Right away,' Lily said, holding up her head. 'You know the address, tell them to look for "Lily's Café".' Giving the woman a satisfied smile, she walked from the office.

Across the town, Seb Ryder walked from room to room in a perpetual state of ennui. His mind constantly returning to Lily Rae. She had sent him off with a flea in his ear the last time he saw her. It was all he could do to stay away from the café; even watching her working gave him pleasure.

Wandering out of the house, he walked towards the stable and leaning in the doorway he watched the stable boy grooming his horse. If he took a ride into town, he might catch a glimpse of her as he passed by the café. The cold made him shiver and he returned to the house for his winter coat.

'Ah there you are, dear. Will you be dining with us this evening?' his mother called.

'Erm . . . not sure, Mother . . . going out . . . will let you know.' Grabbing his coat, he left the house.

Eleanor shook her head. Now what was her son up to?

Seb waited for the lad to tack up his horse, then took off along the gravel driveway, the horse's hooves kicking up tiny stones behind them. Nudging his mount to a gallop as he reached the heath, he felt the icy wind bite.

Reaching the town, he brought the horse to a walk. As he neared the café he pulled sharply on the reins to halt his steed.

'Lily's Café'. The new sign hung over the door. How had she managed that? Where did she find the money to buy the place? He stared at the sign for a long time until a carter yelled for him to move aside. Nudging the horse again, he found a tavern with stabling and left his mount there to rest a while.

Walking back the way he'd come, he debated whether to go in and take tea. Making up his mind, he boldly walked in and sat down. Instantly he noticed what Lily had done with the place during the time it had been closed. The large counter had been removed, being replaced by more tables and chairs. Pretty cloths and candles adorned each table. Three waitresses dressed in long black skirts, white blouses and black cardigans buzzed between the tables. Their caps and full aprons spotlessly clean. He watched as plates of hot food were served to hungry customers.

Jenny broke his thoughts with, 'What can I get you, sir?'

'Tea please,' Seb answered.

'Sir, this is a café not a tea house,' Jenny said curtly.

'Ah right. Well, what's good to eat?' Seb felt suitably rebuked.

'Everything . . . sir.' Jenny tapped her pencil on her small pad impatiently.

'Excuse me, waitress,' someone called out.

Jenny turned saying, 'I'll be right with you, ma'am.' Then to Seb. 'So what will it be?'

'Cottage pie and vegetables please.' Seb smiled at the girl serving him. She scowled back and walked to the woman who had called her, the scowl replaced by a smile.

A moment later Seb's breath caught in his throat. Lily walked out of the kitchen in a black suit. The jacket tucked in at the waist highlighted her hourglass figure. The long skirt with half apron ended beautifully at the top of black leather side button boots. His gaze travelled back up to her white high-necked blouse and he saw her dark hair swept up neatly. She was a vision to behold.

Seb watched her chat easily with customers, ensuring all were happy with their food and the service. So, Lily was indeed the boss. She had confidence in abundance. Did she know he was there? Had she seen him? Should he call out to her? Remembering the last time, he decided to err on the side of caution and keep his mouth shut.

Jenny arrived with his food and as he ate he watched Lily float from table to table. Would she come to his? Would she speak to him? His throat constricted, making him cough. Eyes from the nearest tables turned to him and a woman close by stood and banged him on the back. 'You're supposed to eat it, not breathe it!' She laughed. Nodding his thanks, he waved his hand, indicating he was all right. The woman returned to her seat.

Lily, he noted, had ignored the situation. She didn't even look up, which told him she was aware of his presence. Pushing his plate away, his eyes never left the woman, and even as she returned to the kitchen, he watched the door for her return. For the next hour he waited, but of Lily there was no sign. Feeling thoroughly annoyed, he paid his bill and left.

Walking along the icy street, he ducked into the nearest alehouse. Ordering his drink, he heard the rowdy behaviour of his friends from the corner of the bar. Picking up his beer, he walked over to join them. He had no intentions of leaving this place until he was carried out. Settling himself amid the noise, he began to drink in earnest.

By early evening Seb Ryder found himself in the street, having been ejected by the landlord. Barely able to stand, he muttered as he turned in a full circle on the cobblestones of the road.

Staggering forward, he yelled, 'Lily Rae! Where are you, my little flower? Lily!' Coming to the café once more, he fell in through the door. Few customers remained and they soon left as Ryder began to yell again. 'Lily! My Lily of the Valley! Lily!' He watched, from his sitting position on the floor, the dark skirt as a figure approached him. Following the form up, his gaze rested on a beautiful but angry face. 'Ah Lily, there you are.'

'What is the meaning of this?' Lily rasped, her fury evident by her stance. With hands on hips she leaned forward as she hissed, 'Get up and get out!'

'Aw Lily, don't be like that,' Seb slurred.

'Seb Ryder, I'm warning you! Leave this instant or I'll send for the constable!'

Scrambling to a kneeling position, he clasped his hands as if in prayer. 'Pleashe Lily, don't shend me away.' He giggled like an errant child then went on, 'Lily, my Lily . . .'

'I am not your Lily!' The young woman's voice held exasperation as well as fury. 'Get up, you ridiculous man!'

96

Tipping forward, Seb grabbed Lily's long skirt to prevent him falling face down on the floor.

'Get off me!' Lily shouted as she backed away from him, snatching her skirt from his hands. Suddenly the old feelings of fear enveloped her and she shuddered. Her yell brought the waitresses to her aid. 'Get him to his feet and throw him out please,' she said, gathering her confidence again, 'then lock the door. We're closing early.'

She watched as the three girls dragged the crapulous man to his feet and manoeuvred him through the door. Letting go of him in the street, they watched as his legs folded beneath him and he lay on the cold surface still calling Lily's name.

Seb heard the café door close and the bolt shoot into place. Then he heard his friends laughing as they picked him up and carried him away.

CHAPTER 8

'He's not going to give up!' Lily wailed as she sat in the living room with Emily that evening. The other girls had retired to bed and Lily had related the incident at the café regarding Seb Ryder.

'What will you do now?' Emily asked.

Shaking her head, Lily said, 'Nothing. I will continue to ignore him. However, if he should try getting physical, I will inform the police.'

Emily Johnston nodded. 'You just be careful, keep the girls around you.'

Lily gave one nod and stifled a yawn. Sharing a hug goodnight, the women retired to their bedrooms.

It was the following morning, as the winter wind whipped around her, that Lily had the shock of her life. Approaching the café, thinking of a hot drink and getting herself warmed through, she stopped dead in her tracks.

People were running around; men shouted to her to get off the street. Women were screaming and children were crying. Lily felt the ground beneath her feet begin to move. Was this what folk called an earthquake?

'What's going on?' she called to a man running towards her.

'Get off the street! The bloody road is collapsing!'

'What!' Lily looked ahead of her. Creaking wood sounded, brickwork grated and then there was a crash of glass. Her café windows blew out, littering the cobbled road with glass. People scattered in an effort to avoid the sharp shards intent on causing injury.

Again the ground rumbled loudly and Lily watched, as if in slow motion, a massive sinkhole open up in the street. She stared, her eyes on the café. She heard a resounding crash and saw the café implode and sink into the hole beneath it.

Lily drew in a breath and held it as she saw a plume of dust rise high into the air. Slowly the air left her lungs as she continued to watch the dust mushroom which then began to dissipate and fall back to the ground.

'Oh! Oh . . .!' she muttered, hearing bricks settle into place. Lily gasped for breath, feeling like she'd run a mile. Shock was settling over her as she was unable to drag her eyes away from the devastation. Then she realised there was an eerie silence. There was no more screaming and shouting; the people were standing staring, as she was herself.

Lily's hands had flown to her mouth as she had watched her livelihood disappear into the ground. She stared at the pile of rubble and broken glass and the large crack that split the cobblestone road. What on earth had happened?

'Bloody hellfire!' Jenny gasped as she ran to her shocked employer. Lily looked at the girl she had not heard approach. 'What the hell happened?'

Lily shook her head as she looked back at the devastation before her. Slowly the shock began to take its toll and she began to shake from head to foot. Silent tears ran down her cold cheeks. She felt Jenny's arms wrap around her and she gave in to her emotions. The two girls sobbed in the freezing cold street.

A large crowd had gathered to see what all the noise had been about and quiet shocked mutterings ran around freely.

Lily heard a woman comment, 'I bloody knew this would happen one day! Ain't I been saying it for years? Bloody council! That's what happens when you build over old coal workings! Them houses in Earp Street will be next, you mark my words!' Heads nodded in agreement then the woman spoke again. 'Damn shame, that girl worked hard – made it into a lovely place. Hey Lily, you want to get your arse down the council and give 'em hell over this!'

Jenny said quietly, 'Come on, let's get you home. You need a hot cup of tea with plenty of sugar.'

Lily allowed herself to be led back to her lodging house.

Emily Johnston came to meet the girls at the doorway as they stepped inside. 'Oh my dear girl! Are you all right?' Helping an ashen-faced Lily into the sitting room as she yelled to the cook for tea she asked, 'Whatever has happened?'

Jenny answered, 'The café has fallen down! It disappeared into a bloody big hole as we watched!'

'Oh my God!' Emily said her hand to her chest. 'It's lucky you weren't inside at the time!'

'Ar,' Jenny muttered as she watched Lily begin to shake once more. 'I'm Jenny, the waitress, by the way.'

Emily nodded. 'Pour the tea, Jenny, I'll fetch a blanket.'

The cook stood staring at the sobbing girl, wondering what the matter was. 'Thank you,' Jenny said pointedly to the cook who, seeing it as a dismissal, returned to the kitchen to gossip. 'Lily, drink this, it will help.'

Lily took the cup which rattled on its saucer. In a daze she sipped the hot, sweet liquid.

Emily wrapped a thick woollen blanket around the girl, who was shaking and sobbing. She waited quietly as Lily managed to finish her tea.

Slowly, as the warmth of the blanket seeped into her body, Lily began to calm. She tried to smile her thanks but was overcome by emotion once more and burst into tears. She cried her woes into the quiet of the sitting room.

'Let it go, Lily, cry it out.' Emily held the sobbing girl, whilst Jenny looked on.

Eventually, the tears stopped and as she listened to Jenny explaining the event, a dry sob escaped her throat.

'We couldn't believe it, we heard a bloody great rumble when we got there. Then all of a sudden a sinkhole opened up and swallowed the café! A woman said it was built over the old coal workings!' Jenny said, still shocked herself.

'Most of Wednesbury is, Jenny. It's a wonder to me that it doesn't happen more often. I wondered what the noise was, I heard it from here!' Emily shook her head.

'Well, I've only lost my job, Lily's lost everything!'

Another dry sob brought their attention to the girl who was grieving the loss of her livelihood. 'I'm sorry, Jenny,' she whispered.

'It ain't your fault!' Jenny retorted.

'I should get down to the council and see what they have to say about it.'

'Ain't you got any insurance?' Jenny asked tentatively.

Shaking her head, Lily answered, 'No, I was going to sort it out but . . .'

'Never mind that now,' Emily intervened, 'your first port of call is the council, but not until we've had more tea and you've recovered from the shock.'

Wrapped in their outdoor clothing, the three women trudged through the frosty streets to the local council office.

The council officer had heard about the collapse of the building and had instantly dispatched a worker to assess the situation. The worker swiftly returned with his report.

'It falls under an "Act of God",' the officer said.

'What!' Lily was aghast. 'God didn't put that building over the coal pits . . . your council did!'

'Be that as it may,' the officer said, 'I'm afraid I am unable to help you. It clearly states . . .'

'I don't care what it clearly states,' Lily was exasperated, 'everything I've worked for has gone! I have nothing left . . . no business, no money!'

Raising his eyebrows, the officer said, 'I'm very sorry, Miss Rae, but there is nothing I can do. You should have insured the place.' He spread his arms, then dropped his hands flat on his desk.

'That would not have helped,' Emily stated. 'As it is considered an "Act of God", they would not have paid out!'

'True,' the officer said, 'now if you ladies will excuse me, I have work to do.'

As they left the office, Lily heard the officer mutter, 'Women shouldn't be in business anyway.'

Turning, she marched back to face him. 'I hope, sir, you never find yourself in my position. As for women being in business – get used to it, for it's happening more and more!'

The officer was surprised the girl had heard his comment and scowled. The scowl turned to shock as he heard the words from Jenny, who stood in the doorway.

'If twaddle was music you'd have your own jazz band!'

Despite her misery, Lily burst out laughing.

Emily tried desperately to hide her amusement but lost the battle and joined in the laughter.

Jenny's comment had broken the tension and the three women howled all the way back to the boarding house.

Jenny returned home, promising to keep in touch whilst she searched for another job, and Lily and her landlady sat with tea in the sitting room.

'I have savings,' Lily said, 'so at least I can stay here with you, but I must find work.'

'Don't fret about that just now,' Emily comforted, 'you need to recover from the shock of it all first.'

'Oh Emily! I can't go back to the Servants' Registry! I can't face the woman who will only enjoy gloating.'

'I know, I can understand that. So what were you thinking to do?'

Lily shook her head.

'Well, it's the Registry or trawl the streets again.' Mrs Johnston tried to comfort the distraught girl, but was doubtful Lily would find work anytime soon.

They both knew that people were fighting for jobs all over the town. They were surrounded by unbelievable poverty and the breadline stretched further every day.

'I'll go tomorrow, I can't face any more disappointment today,' Lily sighed loudly.

'Good idea,' Emily agreed as she gave a tight

little smile. 'Can you believe what Jenny said to that council officer?'

Lily burst out laughing again, saying, 'So typical of her, she has a saying for most occasions. There are six kids in that house, can you imagine what it must be like?'

'Oh my God!' Emily feigned a faint on her chair, causing Lily to laugh again.

'Thank you, Emily, you've been so kind to me,' the young girl said, serious once more.

'You are like the daughter I never had, Lily, I love you like you are my blood.'

'I love you too, like a good daughter should.' Lily returned with a smile.

News of the building's collapse spread like wild fire. People stood in groups gawking at the rubble and discussing the café's demise, oblivious to the cold weather. The council was bombarded with questions about the safety of the other premises in and around the High Street, as well as other areas. It was front page news in the newspapers and the well-to-do mulled it over across their breakfast plates. As it didn't affect them directly, they moved on to discuss what the next theatre production would be, or an upcoming ball to be attended.

Seb Ryder read the article in the paper before rushing out to the stables. Waiting impatiently while his horse was saddled, he paced the hay strewn floor. Swinging into the saddle at last, he took off down the driveway. Knowing from the newspaper no one was hurt, he wanted to see for himself.

Halting the horse in the High Street, he gasped at the remains of what was once the café. *Dear God! It was lucky no one was inside!*

Looking around, he wondered where the young woman was. He had hoped he would see her as he scanned the gathered crowd, but she was nowhere to be seen.

Returning his eyes to the ruined building, he shook his head in disbelief. Turning his horse, Seb made for the Golden Cross Inn in the marketplace. If ever he needed a drink it was now. Leaving the horse in the stable at the back of the Inn, he walked inside and ordered a beer. Looking around, he was pleased his friends were not in evidence. He wanted to be alone, to think about what he'd just seen as well as the girl who would not leave his mind.

Settling in a dark quiet corner, he took a quaff of his ale then standing the tankard on the table he leaned back and closed his eyes. Exhaling slowly, his eyes opened.

Had she been close enough to have seen it happen? Or had she come upon it after the event? Either way, she would be feeling bereft for sure.

Rubbing his hands through his dark hair, he sighed heavily. Why was it he always wanted the things he couldn't have? He knew Lily Rae would never forgive him for what he'd done to her, but somehow that made the prize even more worth having.

Seb was convinced Lily would never accept him as a suitor but the challenge of it had become like a drug to him.

Biting his bottom lip, he wondered when he had set himself this task of wooing Lily Rae. He knew she saw him as a sybarite and to a degree he agreed with that. He *was* very fond of luxury and pleasure, and he *was* used to getting his own way.

Women, to Seb, were like cheap toys to be played with and then thrown aside when boredom set in. For a while he had thought this about Lily, but now the situation had become like a contest to him. Would he win her over to at least liking him, or would he fail? Either way, to Seb the hunt was always better than the kill.

Resting in her room in the boarding house, Lily's mind relived again everything that had happened to her. She scowled as she thought of Seb Ryder and what she'd endured at his hands. Remembering leaving the house in which she'd worked as a maid and trying to find work. Of meeting Rose and Mrs Johnston which had been so lucky, perhaps an intervention from the Fates. She felt again the shock of realising his abuse of her had left her pregnant. The bad luck of dashing across the road and being knocked down by a carter but, for the best, had resulted in a miscarriage. Eventually finding work in the café, but then the loss of Ann, its owner and her friend.

She shook her head in the semi-darkness of her room. Ann had left the café to her in her will, but now that was gone too. Her young life had been a series of ups and downs; the only constant being Emily and her friends. Closing her eyes, she sent up a silent prayer. *Please God, take care of Mrs Johnston and the others. Please don't let me lose them too.*

A tear escaped the corner of her eye as she dragged the brush through her thick dark hair. Then, climbing into bed, Lily's emotions burst their banks yet again. She must still be in shock to find herself bawling her eyes out so often. It must be because of the devastating occurrence of earlier in the day that had her feeling so low. Tomorrow she would rally her spirits, she had to, she needed to find work – and soon.

Lily chatted quietly with her friend Rose over breakfast and watched sadly as the others left for their work. Once Rose left too, Lily helped clear the tables before going to the sitting room. Dropping into a chair, she felt unable to find it in her to go out searching for work. Her spirits had dipped to an all-time low and, try as she might, she couldn't raise them.

Emily came to sit next to her. 'Well?'

Lily looked at the older woman. 'Well what?'

'Are you going to stir your stumps?' Emily asked.

Shaking her head, Lily answered feeling drained, 'Not today, I'll go tomorrow.'

'You will go today, young lady!' Emily snapped. Lily's head swung round at the harshness of the words. 'Look at yourself! Sitting there feeling so sorry for yourself! Work won't come to you, you have to go out there and find it!'

'I can't, not today,' Lily on a heavy sigh.

'Why not?'

'I just can't!' Lily's eyes met those of her friend. 'With everything that's happened to me, I can't face any more disappointment . . . a rejection would floor me right now.'

'Oh for God's sake!' Emily was exasperated. 'What would have happened to me if I'd given up all those years ago? You've had your fair share of misery you think? Well let me tell you, Lily Rae, you'll experience a lot more if you don't sort yourself out! Your savings will run out, you'll have to leave here . . .'

Lily's head shot up, her eyes brimming with tears.

'Yes,' Emily continued, 'then where will you go? What will you do? How will you live? I'm telling you this for your own good, Lily! I can't bear to see you so low, so get your bottom off that chair and bugger off out to find yourself a job!'

Lily's eyes widened. She'd never heard Mrs Johnston speak in such a manner and certainly not swear, she was always such a lady. Swiping the tears from her cheeks, Lily threw her arms around the woman who had become her rock. Without a word, the girl left the sitting room.

A couple of minutes later Emily heard the front door slam, and with a nod of her head she released a relieved breath. Her ploy had worked. She had roused Lily from her depressed stupor, now she prayed the girl would have some good luck.

Lily braced herself as she walked into the Servants' Registry and saw the woman look up at her.

'Miss Rae!' the woman said in surprise.

At least she remembers my name, Lily thought.

'I was so sorry to hear of your misfortune.' Lily saw the truth in the woman's eyes. 'Let's have a look and see if I can help you in any way.'

Lily nodded her thanks, not trusting herself not to cry. The change in the woman's attitude had taken her by surprise and she wondered what had caused it.

As she searched her listings, the woman said, 'That road has been on the sink for years and what has the council done about it? Nothing, that's what! You worked so hard to build up that business . . . .' She looked up at Lily then went on, '. . . I ain't half sorry, but I don't have anything for you, but if anything comes in, you'll be the first to know.'

'Thank you,' Lily said sadly as she turned and left the office.

The woman watched her go. It was a damn shame the young girl had lost everything through no fault of her own. She had watched and heard about the hard work Lily had done with the café; something she'd admired greatly. She sighed. The town was going to the dogs.

Lily walked down the street, the cold wind cutting through her clothes making her feel even more miserable. Looking at the sky, she thought there would be snow before nightfall. Increasing her pace in an effort to keep warm, she walked swiftly towards the market. She looked at each shop window to see if there was a card displayed offering employment. There was none. Pulling her shawl tighter around her head, she walked on. Someone, somewhere would need a worker surely? However, as she trudged on Lily was not so certain.

CHAPTER 9

Seb arrived at his house in Darlaston Road and the stable boy came running. 'Thank God you're home!' the boy gasped, for the moment forgetting his station. 'There's been an accident . . . it's your father!'

Turning on his heel and without a word, Seb ran into the house calling out for his mother. He rushed into the parlour but it was empty. Taking the stairs two at a time, he sped towards his parents' bedroom. With a quick knock, he threw the door open to see his father lying on the bed, the doctor at his side. Stepping to the other side where his sobbing mother stood, he asked breathlessly, 'Mother, what's happened?'

Eleanor dabbed her eyes on her lacy handkerchief. 'Your father . . . he fell off his horse!'

Seb frowned. He knew his father was an excellent horseman. How was it then that he'd fallen? He heard a groan and his eyes shot to the man on the bed. Sitting his mother in the chair near the dresser, Seb moved to the doctor.

'How is my father doing, Dr Dingle?' he asked, his eyes resting on his pater.

The doctor shook his head. 'I won't lie to you, lad, he's not good.'

Seb gritted his teeth as his father groaned again. Then he heard the whisper, 'Eleanor?'

Rushing to her husband, she said, 'I'm here, darling.' She picked up his hand and squeezed it gently.

Seb and the doctor moved back a few steps.

Dr Dingle spoke quietly, 'His horse's hoof found a deep hole on the heath – at a gallop – and went down. Your father's head hit the ground hard. The horse broke its leg and has had to be put down. Your father has a bruised brain, which is causing it to swell. It's touch and go, I'm afraid.'

'However did he get home?' Seb asked.

'Carried back by a couple of men out of work, apparently. It seems their kids were playing out on the heath and saw what happened. They ran home to fetch their dads.'

Seb's head rocked up and down in a slow nod. 'So what happens now?' He tilted his chin up as his eyes went to his father.

'We pray the swelling goes down,' Dr Dingle said resignedly, 'there's nothing more I can do for him. Moving him to the hospital in Wolverhampton could kill him, so I suggest keeping him still. Sorry I can't stay lad, but I have my rounds to do and they take a while.'

After seeing the doctor out, Seb returned to sit by his father's bedside.

'Seb?' his father whispered.

'Yes, Father, I'm here.'

'Seb my boy, look after your mother.'

'Father . . .' Seb choked on the word and could say no more.

'Eleanor . . . I know . . . I never showed it . . . but I've always . . . loved you.' With that, Seb's father's breath gave out and his head lolled to the side.

'Noooo!' Eleanor screamed.

Seb stared at his father's sightless eyes before placing his hand over them to close the lids. Steering his sobbing mother from the room, he yelled for the maid.

'Bring tea for Mother in the parlour. Then send the stable boy for the doctor to come back when he can, and also the undertaker,' Seb instructed.

The maid bobbed a quick curtsey before giving her condolences.

Seb held his mother as she cried for her dead husband, his mind numb. Slowly the questions seeped between the cracks of the numbness. How had this happened? And so quickly? What was his father doing on the heath at this time of the afternoon? Why was the horse galloping? His father knew the dangers of the holes on that scrubland. All riders were careful crossing towards the town and kept to the well-worn pathways.

Realising his mother's tears had abated, he poured the tea brought in by the maid. Handing Eleanor a china cup and saucer, he said, 'Drink your tea, Mother, it will help.'

Eleanor nodded and sipped the hot sweet liquid. 'We will have to organise . . .'

'I'll do it, Mother,' Seb said as he poured his own tea. 'I'll see to everything.'

Eleanor sighed again and silence fell in the grand parlour, mother and son contemplating their own thoughts.

A little while later Seb heard voices in the hall. The doctor and the undertaker had arrived. Leaving his grieving mother in the parlour, he asked the maid to stay with her whilst he instructed the man who'd come to take his father away. Watching as two burly men carried a wooden box to his parents' bedroom, he followed behind.

The doctor passed over the death certificate and left shaking his head. Seb watched the men place the box on the floor by the side of the bed and gently lift his father, placing him inside. Replacing the lid, they hoisted up the box and carefully carried it down the stairs and out onto the waiting cart.

'I'm sorry for your loss, lad,' the undertaker said as he shook Seb's hand.

The young man nodded once and watched the cart rumble away down the drive. Closing the front door, Seb stared at it for long moments. His father was gone, never to return. Suddenly the immensity of the situation hit him and, drawing in a deep breath, he howled his grief into the quiet hallway.

Eleanor came rushing to her son and wrapped her arms around him. The maid stood in the doorway and watched as mother and son wept bitterly for the man they had both loved dearly.

After what seemed like hours, their tears abated, replaced by dry sobs as they returned to the parlour. The maid scurried away to make more tea.

Eventually Seb said, 'Mother, I don't understand what father was doing on the heath at that time.'

Eleanor dabbed her nose with her handkerchief and looked at her son with watery eyes. 'It's our wedding anniversary, Seb, and we were going to the theatre this evening to celebrate. I told him this morning not to be late home!' Once more the tears flowed. 'I wish I hadn't . . . I wish . . .'

'Mother, don't. You can't blame yourself, it was an accident,' Seb comforted and saw his mother nod her acceptance at his words.

'Seb, you will have to sort out his business affairs.'

'Me! Mother, I don't know anything about business!' Seb was aghast at the thought.

'My son, you will have to learn – and quickly!'

Seb sighed loudly as he thought about what lay ahead. He had no idea about his father's business or how to go about sorting it out. He guessed he would have to read through any paperwork in the study and then go from there. Hearing his mother sobbing again, he thought all that could wait until after the funeral.

Moving to sit next to his mother, Seb held her

as she wept, his own tears rolling down his cheeks unchecked.

A week had passed in mourning and Seb stood waiting in the hall for his mother. The carriage containing the coffin, drawn by two black horses adorned with funeral apparel, turned into the driveway.

Eleanor came down the stairs dressed all in black. Her long woollen coat reached to her leather side button boots. Her hat held a black net veil, which fell over her milky-white skin. Black kid gloves covered her hands and a drawstring bag hung from her wrist.

'Ready, Mother?' Seb asked.

A nod confirmed she was as ready as she would ever be – it was time to bury her husband.

The wind was bitterly cold as they walked behind the funeral carriage down Darlaston Road. Turning into Wellcroft Street, Eleanor saw people stop and watch the cortège pass by. Men removed their caps and laid them on their chests as a mark of respect. Women crossed themselves and children gazed at the beautiful horses.

Slowly the carriage moved along Ethelfleda Terrace and on to Church Hill. The vicar was waiting at the graveside, along with other mourners. Friends of the couple were in attendance as well as business associates. As the service began, Seb looked around at the sad faces. He was surprised at the number of people who were there to give his father a good send-off.

As the coffin was lowered into the grave, Seb caught his mother as she began to collapse. He heard her sobs and he held her tightly. The vicar's words were faint in his ears and suddenly he realised all had become quiet.

Looking at the vicar, he saw the man tilt his head towards the grave. Leading his mother towards the gravedigger, Seb grabbed a handful of earth from the box the man held out to him. Sprinkling it onto the coffin, he watched his mother do the same. Then the mourners followed suit.

Thanking the vicar, Seb led his mother out of the cemetery and onto the street. Hailing a waiting cab, he helped the sobbing woman alight. The cab moved off, followed by others which carried the mourners. Now would come the wake back at Ryder House.

Lily Rae had read about the death of Mr Ryder senior in the local newspaper. She felt sad for Eleanor, her one-time employer who had always treated her with kindness. She could not, however, find it in her heart to feel sorry for Seb.

Sitting in the living room, Lily's thoughts roamed. Seb Ryder would receive no more hand-outs from his father; now he would have to find work to keep himself and his mother. *Good luck with that!* she thought. She considered whether they would be able to stay on in that big house or whether they would have to sell it. There would be no more drunken outings with his friends either, and that would not go down well at all. Seb would have to take on the responsibilities of his father now and work for a living.

Lily chastised herself for wasting time thinking about that awful man. She had her own problems to brood on. She was out of work and her savings were dwindling. How much longer they would last she had no idea, but one thing was for certain, when her money had gone – she would be out of a home too. As fond as Emily was of her, Lily knew she couldn't rely on the woman's charity so she either had to pay her way at the boarding house or move out.

Walking up the High Street, Lily saw the council labourers beginning their work of clearing the café site. Stopping close by, she watched as bricks were shovelled into hessian bags and stacked on a cart. Feeling tears sting her eyes, she tried to hold them in check.

One of the men working the site walked over to her, saying, 'This was your place, weren't it?'

Lily nodded and choked back a sob.

The man held up all that was left of the sign, *Lily's Ca—* 'Will you be wanting this?' he asked.

'What for? I don't have a building to hang it on now, do I?' Lily snapped.

Shrugging his shoulders, the man walked away, throwing the sign on the cart as he did so.

Lily felt wretched and yelled after the man, 'I'm sorry I was rude to you!'

The man turned and called back, 'It don't matter,

I'm sorry you lost your café.' He doffed his cap and Lily nodded; she could not manage a smile.

Feeling the bite of the winter wind, she walked on past the working men. Time to continue her search for work.

As she went she thought about all the furniture, crockery and pretty tablecloths that had disappeared into the hole. All her hard work gone in a matter of minutes. She was glad she had always carried the takings home with her in the evenings. She had worried that she could have been robbed had anyone known what she'd carried in her shopping bag, but at least the money had been saved. That and her meagre savings was what she was living on now and she knew it wouldn't last forever. She felt sorry for Jenny and the cooks, they were now out of work too.

She trudged on up the High Street towards the High Bullen, stopping at every shop along the way. Having asked at each if there was any work going, she was met with the same answer – no, there was nothing.

Lily passed the Theatre Royal and eventually turned into the High Bullen. She asked her question at each of the small factories and workshops as she traversed the street. With each rejection her spirits fell a little lower, and at the corner she turned into Union Street. No work was to be had there either and at the end of the street she had walked three sides of a triangle, finding herself in the marketplace once more.

With her head down against the cold wind, she pulled her shawl tighter around the shoulders of her coat. The men's socks beneath her boots were keeping her feet warm, but her fingers felt frozen albeit wrapped in woollen gloves.

She walked along the tramway heading for Lower High Street and frowned as the noisy tram rumbled past her on its iron rails, screeching to a halt at the end of the market.

Lily walked the town all day and as darkness descended she made her way home. She was exhausted, hungry, still out of work and thoroughly depressed.

Stepping into the living room, she was met by Emily. 'Any luck today, Lily?'

Lily shook her head as she shoved her gloves into her coat pockets. 'No, there's nothing. I've been all over the town pretty much. No one is hiring.' She blew warm air on her cold hands and rubbed them together.

'Go and get a warm by the fire, dinner won't be long.'

Lily took off her shawl and coat and draped them over an easy chair. Standing in front of the fire, she stretched out her hands to its warmth, feeling her fingers tingle as the life came back into them. She was weary to the bone and her spirits were again at an all-time low.

After dinner Lily chatted quietly with Rose in the living room. Slowly the others drifted off to bed, Rose included, and Lily sat alone by the fire.

Her thoughts were broken as Emily bustled in and joined her.

'That's that done,' Emily said as she sat by the fire. 'Everything is ready for the breakfasts. Now, Lily Rae, tell me about your day.'

'Well,' Lily said, 'firstly I had morning tea with Queen Victoria, then I popped in to see the Prime Minister before. . . .'

Emily burst out laughing. 'At least you still have your sense of humour.'

Suddenly the enormity of it all hit Lily like a thunderbolt. 'Oh Emily,' she sobbed, 'I can't find a job anywhere! I don't know what else to do!'

Emily shot from her chair and wrapped her arms around the crying girl. 'I know, it's not easy, but you have to keep looking.'

Drying her eyes, Lily said 'I've looked everywhere! There's nowhere left to look!'

'Something will turn up, you'll see,' Emily tried to comfort Lily as best she could. 'Come on, get yourself to bed, things will look brighter in the morning.'

Lily nodded and did as she was bid, taking the newspaper with her.

Looking at the front page as she lay in bed, Lily was shocked. Queen Victoria had died that day and the whole nation was in mourning. She had wondered why people looked so gloomy as she'd travelled across the town but had put it down to the inclement weather.

Emily had not mentioned it either; was that

because of Lily's circumstances and not wanting to add to her unhappiness?

Reading the article, she realised they now had a new King. Edward VII had acceded the throne and would soon be crowned. There would be a state funeral for the late Queen and Lily knew people would line the streets to pay their last respects and watch the cortège pass by.

The people of Wednesbury would not see it of course, as it would most likely take place in London. However, that would not prevent them mourning with the rest of the country.

Lily laid the newspaper on the bed and whispered, 'God keep you, Queen Victoria. Time to be with your beloved Albert once more.'

It was some while before Lily finally succumbed to sleep.

CHAPTER 10

Walking through the door of the funeral parlour after another fruitless search for work the next morning, Lily was greeted by a tall thin man. 'Good morning, my dear, please come in and take a seat.' When he saw she was seated, he went on, 'What can I do for you?'

Lily burst into tears.

'Bereavement is very difficult, I know,' the man said. Lily shook her head as she dried her tears. 'Please take your time, my dear,' the man leaned back in his chair and waited for her to compose herself. 'Now then, I am Stan Webb. What is it I can help you with? Is it funerary arrangements?'

Again Lily shook her head. 'No, Mr Webb, I'm looking for work and hoped . . .' Tears again lined her lashes.

'Oh,' Mr Webb said surprised. 'Well, I'm afraid . . .'

'Please!' Lily said in desperation, 'I'll do anything!'

Stan Webb studied the young woman sat opposite him. It was then that he recognised her.

'Didn't you run the café in the High Street – the one that collapsed?'

With a nod, Lily's tears again rolled down her cheeks.

'Oh, my dear girl!' Stan said. 'I'm so sorry. That was a terrible thing to happen.' Shaking his head, he went on, 'What's your name?'

'Lily Rae.'

'Well, Lily, this is not really the place for a woman to work. I'm not sure you would be able to cope,' Stan said, trying not to upset her any more than she was already.

'Mr Webb, I've asked at every shop and factory in Wednesbury! You are my last hope!' Lily felt utterly miserable.

'Miss Rae . . . Lily . . . this is an undertakers, we deal with the dead. I'm sorry to be so blunt, but that's our trade. Do you have any idea what that entails?' Stan asked.

'No,' Lily answered, 'but I had no idea how to run a café at one time either!'

Stan gave a little smile at the girl's forthright manner. 'Let me explain. We have to deal with distraught people here in the shop. Help them to choose a package they can afford at what is an already distressing time. However, we have to make a profit too, otherwise we'd go out of business. We collect the deceased and make them presentable.' He saw Lily shudder before continuing. 'We lead the procession to the graveyard where the coffins are interred. Now there are times, a lot of times, where we have to conduct pauper burials, which are paid for by the Parish. Some people have to be laid outside of the lych-gate also, such as suicides, as they're not allowed burial on consecrated ground.'

Lily nodded, she knew this to be true.

'Besides which, we have to be kind and considerate to the bereaved families.' Stan laid his hands on the arms of his chair.

'I understand Mr Webb, and it's a wonderful service you provide. I remember from when we buried Ann, the previous café owner.' Lily wiped her nose on her handkerchief.

'Ah yes, I recall now, but, Lily, this work can be very distressing, and I see you now in tears; do you think you could cope?'

'I'm only upset because I have no work, Mr Webb! My savings are fast running out and I can't . . . no, I *won't* end up in the workhouse!' Lily felt her last reserve of strength come to the fore. 'Please, Mr Webb, find me a job, I promise I won't let you down.'

Stan Webb again studied the girl as he rubbed a forefinger below his lower lip.

'Look,' he said at last, 'how would it be if I set you on in the shop? We could do with an assistant, that's for sure. I'll see how you get on with the folk that come in. I'll give you a month's trial at ten shillings a week. How does that sound?'

Lily beamed. 'It sounds grand to me, Mr Webb, just grand! Thank you, thank you so much!'

'Right, you can start tomorrow. Come in at 8 a.m. sharp and I'll show you the ropes. Welcome to Webb's Funeral Directors, Lily.'

'Thank you, Mr Webb, you won't regret this, I promise you!' After shaking hands, Lily left the shop, her high spirits restored once more.

Stan Webb watched her go, a little smile playing on his face. 'I think, Lily Rae, you could be an asset to this little business,' he muttered.

Lily didn't feel the cold as she rushed back to the boarding house to share her good news with Emily.

'Mrs Johnston!' she called out as she entered and closed the door behind her.

Emily came bustling from the kitchen and saw the grin on Lily's face. 'Good news?'

'Yes!' Lily threw her arms around her friend. 'I start tomorrow – at Webb's Funeral Directors!'

'Oh,' Emily gasped, 'the undertakers?'

'Yes, I'll be working in the shop – not in the back where . . . well you know.' Lily laughed.

'Ah, I see. Oh Lily, I'm so pleased for you, I really am.' Emily hugged the girl again. 'Come on, let's have tea and you can tell me all about it.'

It was after dinner in the living room that Lily shared her news with the others. Rose was horrified. 'Lily! The undertakers!'

Lily laughed at the disgusted face Rose pulled. 'It's a job, Rose! You know how desperate I've been to find work, and Mr Webb was good enough to take me on.'

'I know but – the undertakers!' Rose wrinkled her nose again.

'Rose, it's an important trade, one that won't die out!'

Both girls fell about laughing at Lily's unintended pun. Then the conversation returned to the dearly departed Queen and the new King.

The following morning Lily walked through the door at Webb's at five minutes to eight. Stan was there to greet her. Flipping out his fob watch on its gold Albert chain from his waistcoat pocket, he checked the time. 'Early, that's a good sign, Lily. Come on in and we'll begin.'

Taking off her coat, she hung it on the coat stand in the corner and followed Stan to the desk by the window.

'Now,' he began as he motioned for her to sit behind the desk, 'in those drawers is everything you need. Forms to fill in, a catalogue of our services with the prices, and a catalogue showing the coffins with their prices. The diary is there,' he pointed to a large book on the top of the desk. 'Just be sure you don't double-book. We can only be in one place at a time.'

Lily smiled up at him.

'Oh by the way, I hope you can make a good cup of tea!' He laughed.

'Tell you what, Mr Webb, I can sort that one out right away.' Lily grinned.

'Kitchen is through there,' Stan pointed to a door then whispered, 'and the lavvy is out the back. I'll be in the back room when tea's ready, just give me a yell.'

'Will do,' Lily said as she walked towards the kitchen.

Lily read through the forms and catalogues as she sipped her hot tea. There was a lot to remember but she knew she'd get the hang of it. Just then the little bell over the door tinkled and a large woman walked in. Lily's nerves jangled; this was her first customer.

Stan had heard the bell and walked through into the shop He wanted to see how his new employee dealt with the first client of the day.

Lily stood up saying, 'Good morning. Please take a seat.'

The woman plonked herself down on the wooden chair, which groaned under her weight.

Lily cast a quick glance at the woman's clothes. *Not very well off*, she thought.

'How may I help you?' Lily asked quietly.

'I need to get my old man under the sod,' the woman said in a matter-of-fact voice. 'He don't deserve me spending my money on him, but what can a woman do? I ain't got a lot of money, so don't be showing me any of them fancy caskets. A wooden box is all he's worth!'

Lily clenched her teeth in an effort not to smile. 'I'm very sorry for your loss,' she said.

'Well I ain't!' the woman said loudly. 'He were a bloody waster! Good riddance I say. So, what you got on offer then?'

'I'll show you, Mrs . . .?' Lily drew out the catalogues.

'Brown . . . Edna Brown.' The woman gave a single nod as Lily opened the catalogue and pushed it over the desk.

Lily could feel Stan's eyes on her as she wrote down the woman's name on the form. 'Can I take your address, Mrs Brown?'

Looking up, the woman said, 'I ain't decided yet!'

'It's just a formality, Mrs Brown, please take your time.' Lily pointed to the catalogue the woman was browsing.

'Oh right. I live at number two Brick Kiln Croft.' The woman returned her eyes to the booklet. 'Bloody hell! This lot's dear, ain't it?'

Lily clamped her mouth tight as she stole a glance at Stan who stood with a smirk on his face.

'The cheaper ones are at the back, Mrs Brown,' Lily said, giving the woman her attention once more. Then pointing a finger at a picture, she went on, 'That one is good value for your money, it's in our Regal range, as you can see. I know it's a little more expensive than the others there, but on an open carriage with flowers on the top it looks beautiful.'

'Ar, I'll bet it does at that price!' the woman harrumphed.

'Mrs Brown, I think your neighbours and friends would be most impressed were you to choose that one.' Lily was determined to make a good sale.

'Well . . .' the woman debated, 'I suppose you'm right. All right then, I'll have that one – on an open carriage. If I'm to spend my hard-earned cash on that old bugger, then I want all and sundry to see it!'

'A very wise choice, Mrs Brown,' Lily nodded. 'Now, I have to take a few more details and then we can consult the diary for an interment date.'

Having completed her task, taken the money and given Mrs Brown her copy of the form, Lily showed the woman out of the shop, assuring her that her husband would be collected that day and placed in the Chapel of Rest.

Stan Webb applauded as she walked back to the desk. 'Well done, gel. That was very well done.'

Lily nodded her thanks with a smile and sat down as Stan disappeared into the back rooms.

This isn't so bad, Lily thought as she again perused the catalogues in an effort to learn and remember the names and prices.

At 1 p.m. Stan came through and turned the door notice to 'closed for lunch' and beckoned Lily to the kitchen. As the two sat around the tiny table, he unwrapped a cheese sandwich and stared at it.

Lily watched as he threw it back onto its grease-proof wrapper and stood to the put the kettle on the pot-bellied stove.

'No appetite, Mr Webb?' Lily asked.

'What?' he said as he put the cups on a tray. 'Oh no, it ain't that. It's just that I'm sick of cheese.'

'Why don't you tell your wife you'd like a change?'

'I make my own.' They laughed together, then he added, 'I've been doing my own since I lost my Maggie.'

'I'm sorry, I didn't know,' Lily said quietly.

'It's all right, gel, it were some years ago now.' Stan shook his head.

'Mr Webb . . .' Lily began.

'Stan. Call me Stan,' he interrupted.

'Stan, have you only had cheese sandwiches since then?' Lily was aghast.

Looking at her, he nodded and they both burst out laughing.

'I'm just popping out for a minute, I'll be back before the tea is mashed.' Lily sprang from her seat. Grabbing her coat, she left the shop.

Rushing down through the street known as the 'Shambles' and past all the old market stalls, she entered a little shop on the corner. Delicious aromas reached her nose of baking pies.

The assistant asked, 'What can I get you, lovey?'

'Two large meat and potato pies please.'

With her hot purchases in her hand, she hurried back to Webb's. Placing the pie bags on the table, she pushed one over to Stan. 'Lunch.'

His eyes widened as he took out the pie.

Just then two men walked into the kitchen the

older one saying, 'Cut that in half, Stan, and give us a bit.'

Stan introduced the men to Lily. The older was Fred Wilkinson, the coffin maker, and the younger, with an awful smell surrounding him, was Albert Blenkinsop, the mortician.

Stan and Lily cut their pies in half and shared them with the others. When all had finished they thanked her for her kindness.

'That's the best lunch I've had in years!' Stan said, licking the crumbs from his lips.

Everyone burst out laughing.

It was mid-afternoon when the shop bell tinkled again and Lily saw a man standing in the doorway.

'Please come in,' Lily said as she walked towards him. She closed the door, shutting out the cold. 'Won't you take a seat?'

The man looked to be in his fifties and stepped forward as if in a daze.

Lily retook her seat. She saw the man was in shock and said gently. 'What's your name, sir?'

'Joe Pincher,' the man muttered, his eyes down.

Stan had again come to watch and stood to one side eyeing the situation carefully.

Lily wrote down the name, then said, 'Mr Pincher, are you all right, sir?' The man's head rocked up and down on his neck. 'What can we help you with, Mr Pincher?'

'I have to . . . I need . . .' Suddenly he drew in a breath and his chin dropped to his chest. His shoulders heaved as he sobbed silently until his lungs

133

were empty. Drawing in another huge breath, the man cried out his anguish into the quiet shop.

Lily shot Stan a shocked look, then moved round the desk to the man crying his heart out. She passed him her clean handkerchief and laid a hand on his shoulder. She stood there for a long time until Joe Pincher's tears abated.

'Thank you . . . thanks,' he managed between sobs.

'I take it, Mr Pincher, you need our assistance with a loved one?' Lily asked gently. The man nodded. 'All right, I need some details from you firstly.' Lily kept her voice low and compassionate.

Taking down the details, her shock registered again as she realised he was about to bury his grandson. Lily's heart went out to the man as he said, 'It ain't right! It should be me as goes first! That's the nature of things!'

'I'm so sorry for your loss, Mr Pincher. We'll do all we can for you.' Lily took out a small booklet and passed it to him.

As he looked at it, his tears ran free again. He pushed the booklet aside. 'I can't . . . you choose – please!'

Lily picked up the booklet showing an array of small white coffins – children's coffins. 'Mr Pincher, I'm sorry to ask but I have to know how much you have to spend . . .'

Getting quickly to his feet, Joe Pincher shoved his hand in his pocket and threw a handful of money on the desk. 'Please, just sort it out for me.

Just tell me when.' The man's eyes had stayed on the handkerchief in his hands the whole time.

Consulting the diary, Lily said as gently as she could manage, 'We will be with you at 2 o'clock next Wednesday. I will arrange for your grandson to be brought to the Chapel of Rest straight away.'

Nodding his thanks, Joe Pincher shoved the form into his pocket and left the shop.

Lily sat back in her chair and heaved a great sigh.

Stan walked over to her and asked, 'Which one did you choose?'

She pointed. The white casket, lined with white silk in a cushion effect, with two small gold handles on each side. She said she would contact the florist for a teardrop shaped bouquet to be laid on top.

Stan nodded. 'Good choice.' As she looked up at him, he added, 'I know it's so hard sometimes, but just so you know, you handled that exceptionally well.'

Leaving her to her thoughts, Stan retired again to the back rooms to organise the collection of the child.

Lily felt like bawling her eyes out. Joe Pincher's distress had been heart-rending to witness. She wondered how she'd managed to remain calm as she'd watched him breaking his heart. She also wondered if she was, indeed, cut out for this work.

At the end of the day Lily was putting on her

coat to leave when Stan came through. 'Lily, I'd like you to lead the procession for Joe Pincher's family,' he said.

'Me? Stan, I can't! I don't know how . . . what to do!'

'You will, I'll show you. Tomorrow you're coming with me, so wear your best black clothes.' He clapped her on the shoulder as she walked from the shop.

Lily was all set the following morning and ignored the looks from the others as she sat for breakfast all dressed in black.

She donned her long black coat and walked to work. Stan awaited her and presented her with a black felt ladies' riding hat. Around the crown was wrapped a length of black chiffon which fell down her back as she put it on her head. It was a little big and taking it off she saw inside a drawstring in the lining. Pulling the string a little tighter, she tried the hat again. Fitting well now, she tied a knot in the string to hold it in place.

Stan nodded and handed her a beautiful pair of black kid gloves.

Following behind, she was led through to the back yard. There, on an open carriage, lay a coffin adorned with flowers. Two black horses were harnessed to the carriage, their feathered plumes bobbing as they waited patiently.

Stan climbed up into the driving seat and helped Lily up to sit beside him. Neither had spoken a word; Lily's nerves jangled as she thought about the role she faced.

Clucking the horses to walk on, they passed through the massive gates which Fred waited to close behind them.

As they pulled out onto the street, Stan spoke. 'Some people have the closed carriage, others prefer the open one. Whichever they choose, the mourners follow behind. Sometimes they want someone to walk in front of the carriage. I suspect Joe Pincher and his son, or son-in-law, will want to carry the coffin themselves. So, that being the case, you will lead them and I'll bring the carriage behind them. The rest of the family and friends will follow me.'

Suddenly Lily gasped. 'How will people take to a woman leading the funeral procession?'

'We'll soon find out, won't we? As for the family – I think they'll be too upset to care that much . . . no disrespect to you.'

Lily nodded, saying worriedly, 'Oh Stan, I won't know where to go!'

'You will, I'll show you on our little map back at the shop. Don't fret, you'll be fine. All you have to do is hold up your head and walk slowly.' He gave her knee a little pat.

Halting the horses outside a small house, Lily watched as he climbed down and knocked at the door. He removed his top hat, holding it along his left arm as the mourners poured out and took up their places behind the carriage.

Replacing his hat, he climbed aboard again and set the horses to a slow walk along the streets to the graveyard.

Lily took careful note of the whole proceedings so she would know what to do at the Pincher funeral.

As she and Stan returned to the parlour, she felt more confident about her role as conductor and leading the cortège.

CHAPTER 11

Seb Ryder had ignored his father's study and the business papers held within. He had concentrated his efforts on consoling his grieving mother. Two weeks had passed since his father's funeral and he knew his mother would wear her widow's weeds for some time yet.

He watched his mother over the top of the newspaper he was pretending to read. Sitting on the couch, she stared into space. At least she was no longer crying, but her blank look unnerved him. Was she losing her mind? Had her grief at the loss of her husband sent her slightly mad?

Eleanor gave out a great sigh and Seb quickly moved his eyes back to the newsprint. After a moment he peeped again over the top of the paper; his mother sat still and quiet, hardly blinking.

Shaking the paper, he refolded it and slapped it on the table, watching his mother closely. Nothing. No reaction whatsoever. Drawing in a breath, he said, 'Mother, what say we take the carriage out? The fresh air will do us both good.'

Eleanor ignored him. Had she heard him speak to her? 'Mother,' he tried again. 'Mother!' Still nothing.

Getting to his feet, he walked out to the stable. 'Saddle one up, lad,' he said to the stable boy. Seb paced as he waited. Once the horse was saddled, he climbed up and took off down the drive.

It was some time later when the doctor arrived at Ryder House. Seb had gone to ask he attend his mother, but the doctor had not been at home. Seb had left a message with the housekeeper.

The maid led the doctor to the parlour, where Seb and his mother sat in silence.

'Dr Dingle, thank you for coming,' Seb said, shaking the man's hand.

'What seems to be the trouble?' the doctor asked.

Seb lowered his voice, 'It's mother. She doesn't speak, she eats like a bird and I doubt she's sleeping. It's like she's in a trance. I'm not sure whether she even hears me when I talk to her.'

'Right. I'll take a look at her.' Placing his bag on the table, Dr Dingle sat beside Eleanor on the couch. Lifting her wrist, he found her pulse and took out his pocket watch. Letting go of her arm, he watched it fall back to her lap. Eleanor never moved, her eyes still blank as she stared ahead.

'Mrs Ryder,' the doctor called out, then again louder, 'Mrs Ryder!' Seeing no reaction, he looked at Seb, who raised his eyebrows. 'I see what you mean,' the doctor said.

Taking a pin from the lapel of his jacket, he stabbed it into the back of Eleanor's hand. Seb winced but his mother never moved.

The doctor checked her eyes and said sadly,

'Well, it looks very much like she's gone over the edge.'

'Oh God!' Seb railed. 'Dr Dingle, what am I to do?'

'There's only one thing you can do, I'm afraid. You must have her committed.'

'Dr Dingle! I couldn't possibly . . . she's my mother!' Seb couldn't believe his ears.

'Look,' the doctor said quietly, 'who will look after her? You? Will you feed and bath her? Will you take her to the lavatory? No of course not. There are people who will do this, Mr Ryder, people who can take care of her for you.'

Seb sighed loudly, 'I suppose you're right. What must I do now?'

Dr Dingle picked up his bag. 'Nothing. I'll contact the people concerned and they will come and collect her. Now, don't you worry about a thing.'

Seb thanked the doctor, who said he was on his way now to see to a woman who was about to give birth to her thirteenth child. He heard the doctor mutter as he left, 'You'd think the woman could manage by herself after having had twelve kids already!'

Seb sat looking at his mother and wondered if the people coming for her would be from the lunatic asylum. Dragging his hands through his hair, he said quietly, 'I'm sorry, Mother, but I didn't know what else to do!'

★ ★ ★

It was the following day when two men in grey uniforms arrived to collect his mother. Seb had to sign a committal form and the men lifted Eleanor to her feet. Holding her arms, they led her out to the waiting wagon which had bars on its windows.

Seb watched from the doorway as his mother meekly climbed into the wagon; the door was shut and a bolt was pushed into place. The wagon rolled away. Seb wondered if that would be the last he would ever see of his mother.

Seb dropped into an easy chair and watched the flames dance in the fire. The house was quiet, not that it had ever been noisy, but this was an eerie silence. It made him feel uncomfortable and lonely as it appeared to close in around him. He wished Lily was here with him.

Suddenly he realised he had barely thought of her these last few weeks, what with his father's death and now his mother's committal.

'Where are you now, Lily Rae?' he muttered into the quiet of the room. He felt sad there was no one there to answer him.

Jumping to his feet, he searched the bureau for money he knew his mother always kept there. Pocketing the coins, he walked out to the stable. He was going to seek out his friends. He felt in desperate need of a drink; actually he felt he needed to get very drunk. Maybe then he would be able to get his head around everything that had happened recently.

★ ★ ★

Waking with a headache that threatened to burst his skull open, Seb opened his eyes. Standing over him was the stable boy. Seb lifted a hand to prevent the boy from speaking and attempted to sit up. Groaning he realised he had slept in the hay scattered on the stable floor – again.

'Oh God!' he whispered as he got to his knees. Warily, he managed to stand and scowled at the stable lad who was grinning. 'You say one word and I'll bloody sack you!'

The stable boy stepped back and watched Seb stagger outside. His grin remained on his face as he saw the master of the house doing a drunken lurch towards the kitchen door.

'Any minute now,' the boy whispered, 'and thar she blows!' He laughed before going for a pail of water and the yard brush to clean away the vomit his employer had left on the cobbles.

Seb dragged himself up the stairs slowly, holding tight to the banister rail. In his bedroom at last, he lay down carefully on the bed.

'Never again . . . never . . . again!' His eyes closed and he was soon in a deep sleep.

The day arrived for Lily to lead the Pincher funeral cortège. She paced the shop floor, her nerves taut.

Stan came through and said, 'Right, gel, if you're ready.'

'Oh Stan!' Lily wailed. 'I'm not sure I can do this! Can't someone else do it?'

'There is no one else to do it, Lily. Fred is busy

143

out back with his coffin making and Albert is putting the finishing touches to the bloke who was hit by the tram,' Stan answered.

Lily shivered at the thought. Taking one more look at the map of Wednesbury hung on the wall, she tapped the top of her hat with a gloved hand. 'I'm ready.'

The small white coffin lay on the open carriage topped with a teardrop of white and cream flowers interspersed with greenery.

Climbing up to sit beside Stan, she took a few deep breaths to calm her nerves. She felt the comforting tap on her knee and nodded to Stan.

The two black horses walked slowly and steadily to Russell Street and were brought to a halt outside a shabby-looking house.

Stan nodded to Lily, who climbed down and knocked on the front door. Taking off her hat, she laid it across her left forearm.

The door opened and a throng of sobbing people poured out. No one noticed Lily except Joe Pincher. He nodded to her and she nodded back. She watched as Joe and another younger man gently lifted the coffin and hoisted it up. Joe rested the coffin on his left shoulder at the back, the other man on his right shoulder at the front.

Lily replaced her hat and walked to the front of the carriage. She heard the coffin bearers take their place behind her. Holding up her head, she walked forward slowly, then heard the carriage wheels crunch on the cobblestones.

From the corner of her eye she saw people stop and watch the procession pass by. Keeping her eyes looking ahead, she led them down Russell Street and out along the tramway. Slowly they made their way to the graveyard at St John's Church.

As they reached the graveside, Lily stepped back to allow room for the coffin to be placed on the two straps by the grave. She felt Stan appear at her side and the two moved back behind the mourners.

They stood quietly as the service was conducted and watched the small white coffin lifted on the straps and lowered gently into the hole.

Lily heard a scream which rent the air of the quiet churchyard and saw a young woman lurch towards the grave. The woman fell beside the grave and her cries broke the heart of every person there. Lily saw Joe Pincher gather the young woman into his arms and lead her away. It must have been his daughter, Lily surmised, and she had just buried her young son.

The mourners trickled away and Stan touched Lily's elbow. As she looked at him, he tilted his head towards the carriage. They too quietly walked away.

The journey back to the shop was spent in silence. Stan knew Lily would have a lot to think about so he didn't disturb her.

Once more inside, Stan made strong sweet tea in the small kitchen. 'You did really well today, Lily,' he said at last.

'Thanks, Stan,' Lily gave a weak smile, 'but my God, that poor woman!'

'I know, it's always worse when it's a kiddie. I have to agree with Joe Pincher, no parent should ever have to bury their child, it ain't right.'

Lily sipped her tea, thinking over the day's events. When she had started work at Webb's Funeral Directors she thought she'd only be working in the shop. Never in her wild imaginings did she see herself leading a funeral procession. It was not the sort of job one could say they enjoyed, but Lily knew now she could do it. She wondered if she would become hardened to it; she hoped not. As she had stood at that child's graveside, she had felt grateful for the life she had.

Her thoughts were interrupted by Stan's voice. 'I'm thinking to get a girl in to watch the shop while you and me work together on the carriages.'

'Oh Stan! Really . . . do you think I could?' Lily was pleased with the idea.

'Well you did it today!' Stan gave a little laugh which lightened the mood. 'Besides, I could manage a few coppers more in your pay packet.'

Lily smiled. 'Thank you, Stan, I do appreciate your faith in me.'

'Look, there's things you need to understand though.' Stan sat at the table opposite her.

'Like what?' Lily asked, her brow furrowing into a frown.

'Like when we get back here, you have to let it go. You can't carry everyone's sorrow, Lily, so you have to see this as a job. Oh I ain't saying you have to be hard as nails, I'm saying . . . today for instance, that job is done and now we have to look to the next. Do you see what I'm trying to tell you?'

Lily nodded. 'Yes, I understand. I see the sense of that, otherwise we'd go mad with other peoples' grief.'

'Exactly!' Stan said. 'And another thing, we have to have a laugh and lark about. You may think Fred and Albert are a little irreverent at times, but they're not. They have to have something to lighten their load too. So if you hear something you think is in bad taste, stop and put yourself in their shoes. Fred makes coffins for a living and Albert – well he's in the mortuary every day. Imagine that!'

Lily sighed heavily. 'I hadn't considered that.'

Stan resumed. 'Just because we bury the dead, it don't mean we can't be happy and share a laugh.'

Lily cut through his sentence, 'Only at appropriate times though.'

'That's my gel!' Stan smiled.

Just then Fred and Albert entered the kitchen for their tea break.

Lily's nose wrinkled involuntarily at the pervading smell which seemed to surround Albert at all times. He noticed and said, 'Sorry, Lily, it's not exactly "La France Rose", I know.'

'It's me who should apologise, Albert. I'm sure I'll get used to it.' She returned his smile.

Fred dropped into a chair, saying, 'Stan, have you told her about casket crawlers yet?'

Lily's frown told the older man she had no idea what he was talking about.

Stan began, 'Sometimes when the coffin is in the Chapel of Rest, say a husband, then his widow might come to visit. On occasions these poor women become so overwrought at losing their husband they try to crawl onto the casket.'

'Oh my God!' Lily was shocked.

The three men howled with laughter at her reaction, but before long she had joined them.

This was what Stan meant about letting go of the sorrow, relieving the tension and moving on with life.

CHAPTER 12

March had finally arrived and the weak sun peeped its head over the horizon. The cold winds of winter had abated and spring came in like a lamb. The breezes which wafted around began to hold a little warmth and everywhere the land which was not built upon sprouted new growth. Tiny seedlings pushed their heads through the soil, seeking the sun's rays to strengthen them. Trees awakened from their long winter slumber, stretching out their branches in readiness for an abundance of leaves to grow.

Queen Victoria had been laid to rest the previous month and life in Wednesbury went on as usual.

Watching the sun as it climbed into the sky, Seb Ryder felt the energy flow through his veins. He had decided it was time to sort out his father's study.

Up until now he had lived on the money he knew his father had kept in the family safe. However, those funds were running out quickly and he realised he needed to see to his father's business.

Seb had prevaricated regarding this task, his excuse being he was still in mourning, but he was now being pestered by his father's business associates. Never having had to worry about it, Seb had no clue about the business side of making money. His father had bought and sold. Exactly what he had bought and sold, Seb had no idea, and he thought it time to find out.

Standing in the study, he gazed around him. Where to start? Moving to the huge mahogany desk, he considered this to be the best place. Pulling out drawers, he piled the papers onto the desk and began to read through them.

Page after page held business transactions that meant absolutely nothing to Seb. Walking around the study to stretch his aching legs, he felt his frustration mounting. Clearly he could not take over his father's occupation, so he would have to close down all commercial activity.

He determined each time an associate called in to Ryder House, he would explain, face to face, the business being conducted was no longer viable. Happy with his decision, he gazed around the study once more. A smile crossed his face as he thought it would make an excellent drinking den for him and his cronies.

Striding from the room, he yelled out for the maid. The house was his now he felt, as his mother was still incarcerated in the mental asylum, and he intended to make changes, starting with the study.

The maid bustled into the parlour and Seb said, 'Now then . . . erm . . . sorry, what's your name again?'

The maid sighed audibly, 'Dilys, sir.'

'Right yes, Dilys. I have decided to clear out the study, so I'll need all that furniture moved out.' Seb sat on the sofa with outstretched legs and ankles crossed, his arms spread out along its back.

'Moved to where?' the maid asked.

'Erm . . . anywhere. The pater's bedroom maybe?' Seb had not expected questions and thought quickly for the answers.

'Beggin' your pardon, sir, but you ain't expecting me to shift it, are you?' the maid said indignantly.

'No, no. Hire a couple of out of work men to do it.' Seb gave her a little smile.

Dilys ignored it, saying, 'Right, and just what am I supposed to pay 'em with?'

'Ah yes, I will provide you with some funds.' This was something he hadn't considered either.

'Ar, and while you're about it, will you provide some funds for my wages? I ain't been paid since the missus was took off!' Dilys stood her ground, her hands clasped in front of her apron.

'Oh yes, I can see how that might be a problem for you. I'll sort that out later.' He began to realise there was more to running a household than he had first thought.

'What about the master's papers and suchlike?' Dilys asked.

'Erm . . . papers yes . . . maybe we could . . . erm . . .' Seb searched his mind for an answer.

Dilys provided it sarcastically, 'I'll shove 'em all in a box, shall I? Put 'em in the pater's bedroom with all the furniture?'

'Good thinking. Well done, Dilys! Right then I'll leave you to it. Must dash – have an appointment.' Seb rose and walked swiftly from the room.

Dilys watched him go muttering, 'That lad has no idea! He can't even put a sentence together properly! Bloody kids today.'

The maid chuntered all the way back to the kitchen where she made herself a cup of tea. Sitting by the range, she picked up her book. She loved reading a good 'penny dreadful'.

Seb kept his horse to a walk down Darlaston Road and on into Trouse Lane. He noticed there were some fine houses along this stretch, and thought it a pity the tramway had been built the length of it. Keeping his horse to the side, he heard the rumble of a tram on its rails. The horse jerked its head in fear of the noise and tried to flee as the tram came to a screeching halt quite close. Calming his mount, Seb urged it on down into the High Street away from the din.

A steam whistle sounded from the railway station and again the horse jumped at the shrillness.

Eventually coming to the marketplace, Seb guided the horse to the stables at the rear of the Golden Cross Inn. It was as he walked around to the front door of the establishment that he saw a funeral procession coming through the market. He stopped to watch and then he realised with great surprise it was being led by a woman!

A quiet descended in the street as men took off

their caps and women hushed their screaming children.

Seb caught his breath as the woman walked slowly past him, the entourage following behind.

The woman was Lily Rae! Seb stared after her, his mouth hanging open. He couldn't believe his eyes. Lily was working for the undertaker!

Stepping into the alehouse, he ordered a beer which he took to a quiet table in a dark corner. Seeing Lily leading the mourners had shocked him. He had wondered where she was, but with all that had happened to him, he had not had time to search for her.

His attention now squarely on Lily, he smiled at seeing her lead the funeral cortège. She was a survivor and no mistake. Losing everything when the café fell, she had picked herself up and gone out there to find another job. He couldn't help but admire her for that. Her confidence had grown since leaving Ryder House, and that upped the stakes in the challenge he had set himself. It would make it more difficult for him to win her round, but he relished it presenting a good test of his abilities.

Yes, he was looking forward to pursuing Lily Rae, he intended to make this conquest his finest yet. Sipping his ale, Seb began to think of ways to go about it.

Lily had seen him in her peripheral vision as she had walked slowly past; that brute, Seb Ryder! Her heartbeat had quickened but she maintained the dignity which her position called for. Her hammering heart had not slowed until she had reached the graveside. She heard nothing of the service being conducted, her mind on that chance sighting of the man who had abused her so badly.

It was after dinner that evening when she told Emily Johnston of the encounter.

'It was bound to happen sooner or later, Lily,' Emily said.

'I know, but it took me by surprise, I just never expected it. However I maintained my dignity and strode forward and ignored him.' the young woman answered pushing her nose in the air. Emily laughed then Lily went on. 'Anyway, Stan wants me to work with him from now on and he's looking to employ someone else to work the shop and . . . I'll get a raise!'

Emily grinned, 'Oh Lily, that's wonderful! I am so pleased for you.'

Lily returned the grin. 'I wondered if Jenny might be interested.'

'Jenny?' Emily asked momentarily at a loss as to who they were speaking of.

'Yes, the waitress from the café – you remember, a saying for every occasion.' Lily smiled.

'Oh of course, yes!' Emily laughed, recalling the girl.

'I think I might take a walk over and see her now,' Lily said as she stood up.

'Good idea. Lily, just be careful – you know what I mean.'

'I will. I won't be long. I'll be back before you lock up for the night,' Lily called over her shoulder.

Grabbing a shawl from her room, she left the boarding house and headed for Camp Street. It had been a long time since she'd seen Jenny and her family, and Lily chided herself. They had been good to her and she had been too busy to visit since the collapse of the café. How would they feel about her just turning up on their doorstep now? Would she be told to 'sling her hook'? There was only one way to find out, she thought as she quickened her pace.

Lily knocked on the back door of the shabby house in Camp Street. She heard the noise of the children inside as they laughed and argued; it brought a smile to her face. She knocked again, louder this time.

Vera's voice boomed out, 'Will one of you lot answer the bloody door?'

The door opened and Jenny squealed her delight at seeing Lily standing before her. Throwing her arms around the girl, she called out, 'Mum, it's Lily!'

Dragging her friend indoors, Jenny led her into the kitchen. 'Oh, it ain't half nice to see you!' she said. 'Come on in and have a cuppa.' Then to her younger siblings she yelled, 'Will you lot clear off upstairs to play!'

Lily saw the mad scramble as the children fell over each other as they made for the bare staircase. She heard the rattle of boots on the wooden treads as they thundered up into the rooms above her.

'Sit down, Lily, how are you? I have to say you look well,' Jenny rambled on as she made fresh tea.

Lily smiled and let her talk. Just then Vera walked in. Lily could not hide the shock showing on her face. Vera was pregnant again.

'Hello Lily, nice to see you.' Placing a hand on her swollen belly, she sighed wearily, 'I know, it was a surprise to me an' all.'

'Oh Vera! Is there no one who could have . . .?' Lily snapped her mouth shut, fearing she'd spoken out of turn.

Vera shook her head. 'I searched everywhere. There ain't anyone able to help, so I'm stuck with it.' Lowering herself onto a kitchen chair, she went on, 'I'll be bloody glad when I'm too old for all this.' Her smile betrayed her words as she patted her belly.

Lily didn't know what to say to that, so she immediately came to the point of her visit. 'Jenny, are you in work yet?

The girl shook her head resignedly, 'No, there ain't nuthin' going anywhere.'

'Well, I know where there's a job if you've a mind to apply for it,' Lily became excited.

'Where?' Jenny asked. 'I'll go anywhere, do anything!'

'Webb's Funeral Directors,' Lily answered, waiting for the reaction she knew would come.

'What! The undertakers?' Jenny was aghast. 'Oh Lily, I ain't sure . . .'

'Jenny, they're looking for someone to mind the shop!' Lily explained.

'Well, that ain't so bad, but – them dead bodies.' Jenny shivered.

'The men deal with all that, you would have to work the diary and sell people the best package . . . coffins and the like.' Lily saw Jenny wrinkle her nose. 'It pays ten shillings a week.'

Vera chimed in, 'You get yourself up there tomorrow morning, our Jenny, and get that job! God knows we need the money more than ever now.' Her eyes fell to her stomach once more.

'But, Mum, you'll need me when the babby comes.' Jenny was almost pleading.

'I managed you six on me own, so I can see to this one,' Vera snapped. Then more gently she said, 'You have to try, love. The others bissent old enough to work yet, you know that, and with what little your dad brings in – it ain't nearly enough to go round.'

Jenny plonked herself on a chair with a loud sigh. 'All right. I can't deny I'm dying to get back to work,' Jenny said in all innocence.

Lily and Vera burst out laughing, then realising her faux pas Jenny joined in.

Walking home later, Lily thought Jenny would be perfect for the job and crossed her fingers in the hope they would be working together again soon.

CHAPTER 13

Jenny Pickard walked into the funeral director's not at all sure she was doing the right thing. The watery spring sunshine had done nothing to alleviate the chill she had felt as she had walked briskly through the network of streets. She shivered, knowing the coldness she was feeling was from fear. She had never seen a dead person before and she dreaded the thought of seeing one now.

Lily greeted her with a smile. 'I'm so glad you came, Jenny,' she said. 'I've told Stan all about you and he'll want to have a chat with you.'

'What about?' Jenny asked, casting her eyes around the room.

'The job,' Lily answered, sensing her friend's discomfort.

'Oh right,' Jenny sat in the chair by the desk and watched Lily disappear through a door. She looked around her again. This was a nice place. It was clean but she detected a faint smell she couldn't quite place.

Stan bustled through, 'Ah Jenny,' he said, shaking the girl's hand, 'it's nice to meet you.'

Jenny tried to force a smile, but she was feeling immensely uncomfortable.

'Lily has told me a lot about you,' Stan went on.

'None of it good, I'll bet,' Jenny muttered. Surprise showed on her face as Stan's laughter boomed out.

'On the contrary, gel, it's all good.' Stan's voice lowered, 'You don't have to be scared, it's a shop girl I'm looking for not a mortuary attendant.'

'Thank the Lord for that!' Jenny said on a sigh.

Stan laughed again and the young woman began to feel her fears drain away.

The two talked for some time, occasional laughter breaking their conversation. Eventually Stan stood and, opening the door to the kitchen, he yelled for Lily.

'Lily,' he said as she joined them, 'Jenny is to be our new shop assistant. I wonder if you would show her around and then instruct her on her duties.'

Lily nodded and as Stan left the room, she hugged her friend. 'See, I told you you'd get the job!'

'Thanks, Lily, I think! I was worried when I first came in, but Mr Webb was so nice to me.' Jenny smiled.

'Stan is a lovely man. You'll meet the others at tea break. Come on, I'll show you the kitchen first, then we'll look over the paperwork.' Lily hooked her arm through her friend's and they went to the small kitchen chatting happily.

Jenny sat at the desk with a cup of tea and pored

over the forms and catalogues, while Lily took a tray of tea to the others in the back rooms.

'How are you getting on?' she asked as she returned.

'Fine. This don't look so bad, but ain't it expensive to die these days?' Jenny said in all innocence.

Lily nodded then asked, 'So you can manage this then?'

'Oh yes,' Jenny answered confidently.

'Jenny, the people who come into the shop are upset, naturally. They are grieving so . . .' Lily wasn't sure whether the girl would understand what she was trying to say without feeling affronted.

It was then that the bell tinkled and a thin woman walked in.

'Good morning,' Jenny said quietly.

Lily stood by and watched, listening keenly.

'I need . . . I have to . . . it's me mother,' the woman faltered.

Jenny nodded, saying, 'I'm sorry to hear it.'

Eyes brimming with tears looked back at her. 'Ta, I gotta arrange . . .' The woman's tears fell as she tried to find the words.

'It's all right, you take your time. What's your name?' Jenny asked gently.

'Rowbottom,' the woman said, wiping her nose on the frayed cuff of her blouse.

'There's no rush, Mrs Rowbottom. Would you like a cup of tea to help you get yourself together?'

'Tea? I ain't had tea in an age!' The thin features gazed at the kind young girl.

'Right then. You just hang on there, I won't be but a minute.' Jenny winked at Lily as she shot from the room.

Lily smiled. She'd just had an idea and wondered if Stan would go for it.

Jenny returned with a pottery mug full to the brim with strong sweet tea. Placing the mug before the woman, she said, 'Careful, it's boiling hot.'

Mrs Rowbottom nodded her thanks, her eyes never leaving the mug for fear of it disappearing. Unable to contain herself a moment longer, she picked it up and slurped noisily.

Jenny and Lily exchanged a brief smile at seeing the woman's eyes close in pure pleasure.

'Now, Mrs Rowbottom, we'll have a little chat over our tea if it's alright with you?' Jenny asked.

'That would be nice,' the woman answered.

'Right then. Where is it you live?' Jenny noted down the address given. 'I need to know your mum's address an' all.' The quiet questions and answers impressed Lily as she looked on.

Jenny took out the catalogues and turned to the cheaper coffin selection at the back. Seeing the woman's face change to sorrow once more, she said, 'It sounds like your mum was a special lady, so it's fitting she has a special send-off, don't you think?'

Mrs Rowbottom forced a tiny smile.

Lily listened in awe as Jenny turned the whole sad affair into an almost bearable shopping experience for the bereaved woman.

At last the deal was done and Jenny assured Mrs Rowbottom that her mother would be lying comfortably in her new 'bed' very soon.

The woman left gushing her thanks, not only for the kindness shown to her but also for the tea, something she'd not tasted in a very long time.

Lily congratulated Jenny on a job well done then gasped at the girl's next words.

'I know that lady's mother, and I tell you now – she won't fit into a normal coffin! Her's the size of a whale!'

Lily rushed into the back room yelling for Stan.

Fred and Stan came hurrying into the shop.

After being introduced to Jenny, Fred asked, 'How big is she?'

Jenny looked around and pulling the coat stand out of the corner, she stood Lily to one side of it and Stan the other. She stood in front of it holding out her hands.

'Oh bloody hell!' Fred said as he took in the measurements with an expert eye.

Stan and the girls burst out laughing.

Fred went off muttering, 'I got a big one out the back but – I just hope her ain't swelled, otherwise we'm stuffed!'

An hour later Stan and Fred loaded the extra-wide coffin onto the cart and set off for the address given.

Lily and Jenny were having lunch in the kitchen when Albert Blenkinsop strolled through. Lily introduced the young man to Jenny.

The girl wrinkled her nose, saying, 'My God! What's that awful smell?'

Albert gave an embarrassed smile, 'I'm afraid it's me.'

'Oh sorry,' Jenny said awkwardly.

'It's all right,' Albert gave her a grin. 'You'll get used to it.

'If I live to be a hundred I don't think I will!' Jenny muttered.

Albert and Lily howled as the girl looked at each of them wondering what was funny.

A little while later Fred and Stan arrived back.

'How did it go?' Lily asked, making them each a cup of tea.

'It was an absolute farce!' Fred said. Suddenly everyone's attention was on him. Fred sat at the table, his flat cap wedged firmly on his head hiding his thinning hair. His unshaven chin was resting on a large calloused hand. Brown eyes twinkled at those sat around him.

Thanking Lily for the tea, he then began to tell them the tale of Mrs Rowbottom's mother.

'It's a good job it was to be a closed casket cos we had the devil's own job fitting her in. Fortunately she was in the parlour.' Seeing puzzled looks he went on. 'She couldn't get up the stairs, they weren't wide enough, and so the family put her bed in the parlour.'

Smirks were hidden behind hands as Fred continued. 'Well, we gets her into the box but her arms were hanging out. It was lucky rigor hadn't set in.'

'Rigor?' Lily asked.

Albert explained, 'Rigor mortis. It's a stiffening of the muscles a few hours after death. About twelve to eighteen hours later the whole body becomes stiff, that's why people call it a "stiff". After about twenty-four or forty-eight hours the body then begins to relax again.'

Lily shivered but Jenny was all ears. She asked, 'What about putting coins on the eyes, what's that all about?'

'Rigor starts with the eyes, Jenny, then moves across the body. People close the eyes as soon as possible after death as it's thought to be a threat to any kin looking on the body. The coins keep the eyelids closed and it's also thought the spirit may need money in the afterlife.'

'Blimey! You learn something new every day!' Jenny said.

Fred said, 'Well, coming back to Mrs Rowbottom's mother, Stan came to the rescue with a bit of string he found in his pocket.'

Lily gasped, 'Fred, you didn't!'

'We had to,' Fred answered.

'What? Had to what?' Jenny was desperate to know.

'We had to bend her arms and tie her hands round her neck! We've never nailed a lid on so fast, have we, Stan?'

Stan nodded. 'We sent Mrs Rowbottom out of the room while we got it done.'

Lily gasped; Jenny grinned.

'Then,' Fred went on, 'Mrs Rowbottom wanted her mother's coffin to lie on the kitchen table so folks could pay their respects!'

More gasps and titters ran round the room.

'Well I had to tell her. *It can't happen*, sez I. *She'll break the bloody table*, I said.' Fred shook his head as everyone fell about, their titters now full-blown laughter.

Stan took up, 'Luckily Mrs Rowbottom saw the funny side of it. She said the whole thing had been made more bearable for her because we weren't straight-faced and miserable.'

'We didn't, however, tell her about the string,' Fred muttered, setting them all laughing again.

Stan added, 'Mrs Rowbottom said the young girl in the shop was very kind to her,' he eyed a blushing Jenny. 'You took the time needed to help her come to terms with having to deal with it all.'

A round of applause sounded in the small kitchen. As Jenny's face flushed with pleasure, she missed the look of admiration that crossed Albert Blenkinsop's face.

She had no idea that Albert was already beginning to fall for her. The moment he'd first looked at her, he felt like he'd been poleaxed.

Lily, however, had caught the look and realised immediately that Albert had experienced what people called 'love at first sight'. She smiled to herself and then decided to bring up her idea, 'Jenny made Mrs Rowbottom a cup of tea, something she'd not had for a long time. So, I was wondering if we could do that for all our clients. It would give a homely touch to what is a dreadful time for them, don't you think?'

Stan clapped his hands together. 'Damn good idea! You two gels are a real asset to this firm!'

CHAPTER 14

As the weeks passed, the spring sunshine grew stronger. The trees filled with leaves, spreading their canopy high overhead, providing shade for anyone who sat beneath. Birds twittered loudly as they went about their nest building and wild flowers bloomed in every available space. For those fortunate enough to have gardens, the lawns grew full and green, their flower borders blossoming with a myriad of colours.

Lily was in the kitchen making tea for everyone when the shop doorbell tinkled. *That will be Jenny*, she thought as she walked through the kitchen doorway. Without looking up, she placed a pottery mug on the table, saying, 'There you go, a nice cup of tea.'

'Thank you.' Turning at the voice, Lily was shocked to see Seb Ryder standing in the shop.

Taking a deep breath, she smoothed the skirt of her long black dress. 'Mr Ryder.'

'Hello Lily,' he said quietly, 'how are you?'

Answering his question with one of her own, Lily moved a step back. 'What can I do for you?'

Picking up the cup meant for Jenny, he took a

sip. 'I have come to arrange a funeral – for my mother.' He replaced the cup on the desk.

Lily sucked in a breath. 'I'm sorry to hear that; Mrs Ryder was a nice lady.'

Seb nodded and sat in the chair Lily indicated.

Pulling out the forms and catalogues from the drawer, she passed them to the young man sat opposite her.

He completed the form and pushed it back to her, then opened the booklet displaying the range of caskets.

Lily read through the form and again shock shook her to the core. 'The lunatic asylum?'

'Yes,' Seb replied sadly. 'She was taken there after my father died. She refused to speak, then she would hardly eat anything. She couldn't sleep, so the doctor suggested she be looked after in there. They tried to force-feed her but she just made herself sick. In the end she starved herself to death. Apparently she spoke at the end, saying she just wanted to be with her husband again.'

'Oh my God!' Lily was astonished. 'I'm so very sorry.'

'Thank you. So, now I have to arrange all this – again.' He tapped the catalogue.

'Well we can bring her to the Chapel of Rest until . . . if you'd like that.' Lily spoke quietly.

'I would, thank you. I don't want the funeral led from that dreadful place.' Seb's tears lined his lashes and Lily felt his sorrow.

'Of course, I'll arrange that right now while you

drink your tea.' Taking the form into the back room to Stan, she returned quickly to see the young man sobbing.

Jenny came bustling in and frowned when she saw who it was sat crying.

Lily shook her head and then tilted it towards the kitchen.

Waiting for his tears to subside, she then asked, 'I know how difficult this is, Mr Ryder, but have you decided?'

Nodding, he stabbed a finger on the booklet.

Lily picked it up and completed yet another form. He had chosen from the 'Coronet' range. A beautiful mahogany coffin, highly polished, with four gold coloured handles – two on each side. A tiny gold coronet was inlaid on its lid.

'I'm sorry to have to ask, but payment is required today I'm afraid.' Lily always hated this part. The asking for money seemed callous at such a time, but it was necessary. The client was, after all, paying for a service.

Seb pulled out a pigskin wallet and, checking the price again in the booklet, he counted out the money, which he pushed across the desk.

Lily consulted the diary, saying, 'Thank you. We can arrange for Friday next week if that would suit you?'

The young man nodded.

Lily filled in the date in the diary and said, 'You can visit the Chapel of Rest on Friday morning if you wish.'

Another nod.

'Would you like someone to lead the procession?' she asked tentatively.

Looking at her with tear-filled eyes, he answered, 'Yes, you. She always liked you, and she would have liked you to . . .' His tears fell and he choked back a sob.

'Certainly, Mr Ryder. I'll see you again on Friday morning.' Lily rose from her chair as did Seb.

Walking to the door, he looked back once then left the shop.

Lily sat down with a huge sigh. It seemed no matter what she did, or where she went, she was destined to keep meeting this man.

Jenny came through to the shop. 'Blimey!' she said as she dropped onto a chair. 'He was the last person I expected to see when I come in this morning!'

'Me too,' Lily replied.

'Shame about his mother though, I was earwigging at the door.'

'Hmm,' Lily's thoughts were swirling in her brain. She would have to face him again on the day of the funeral, and she didn't much care for the idea. However, she would carry out her duties in a professional manner, and when the service was over she would return with Stan as she always did.

She realised Jenny was still chattering as she snapped her attention back. 'Sorry, love, what were you saying?'

'I said as how I think me mum ain't far off from

having the babby.' Jenny grimaced at the thought. 'I don't know how she does it, I ain't having that many kids, I'll tell you that much!'

Lily smiled as she remembered the way Albert had looked at Jenny, and how he always seemed to find an excuse to see her.

'You should ask Albert how many children he would like,' Lily teased.

'Albert? Why would I ask him a question like that?' Jenny was horrified at discussing such a thing with a work colleague.

'Oh Jenny! Haven't you seen how he looks at you? Have you not noticed how often he comes to talk to you?' Lily laughed at her friend's shocked expression.

'Who, Albert? Albert and me? Bloody hell, Lily, you'm joking ain't you?' Jenny saw her friend was very definitely not jesting with her. Then she said after a moment's thought, 'Well, I could do worse, I suppose.'

Lily howled with laughter and as Jenny joined in, Albert walked through the door. The girls laughed harder still as the young man looked down at himself then all around him. He obviously was not going to be privy to the girls' private joke.

Seb sat alone in the parlour thinking about the past few weeks. The maid, Dilys, had found herself another job and had walked out after demanding her wages. His father's business had gone down the drain after associates had confirmed by letter they were now dealing elsewhere. His friends had deserted him when they discovered his money was running out. Now, to top it all, his mother had died in the lunatic asylum.

His life was a mess and if he didn't get his hands on some money soon he would find himself destitute. Jumping up, he looked around the room. There had to be some money hidden in this house somewhere. If not, then he would have to start selling off the paintings and furniture.

Seb groaned as he thought again about needing to find work of some sort. He had no training in any trade, so finding a job in a poverty-stricken town would be nigh on impossible.

Firstly though he needed to search the whole house for any funds his mother may have secreted away. He opened drawers carefully, aware the furniture would fetch a higher price if undamaged. Finding nothing in the parlour, he took his search to the kitchen. The bedrooms revealed nothing either, so that just left the study.

Checking the desk, bookshelves and cupboards, Seb sighed in frustration. Opening the safe, he took out the papers and sat to read them. Maybe his father's money was in the bank; he hoped he would find a bank book as he leafed through the pile of papers.

Coming upon a letter from the London City & Midland Bank, he read it avidly. His mouth dropped open as the letter fell from his hands to land silently on the desk.

The house was mortgaged to the hilt. Checking again the date on the letter, he sighed loudly. It was dated a week before his father had died. The mortgage had not been paid and the bank were repossessing the house! Again he checked the letter, maybe he could speak with the bank manager, explain his position of having to pay for his mother's funeral now too. It was then he realised the bank's date for taking back the house was Friday of next week – the same day as the funeral!

Seb kicked the wastepaper basket in temper, sending it crashing across the room. Raking his hands through his hair, he forced himself to think. Even if he managed to find some work, he could never find the money owed to the bank in time to prevent being turned out of his home. Sucking in a breath, he yelled, 'Christ, Father! You've left me in a right mess!'

Stomping outside to the stables, he shouted for the stable boy. 'Sorry, lad, but I'm no longer in need of your services.'

The boy looked aghast. 'Why? Are you not happy with my work?'

'I can't afford to pay you. Just get your things and go!' Seb snapped.

The lad rushed off to collect his meagre belongings and Seb watched him walk down the drive, his head low on his chest.

Walking back to the parlour, he thought about what he would do after the funeral. He had nowhere to go, and no money to go with. He did have his clothes and his horse however, and there was an old carriage in the stable.

Seb Ryder made up his mind. If the bank was about to take his house, they would find it empty. He would sell the lot, paintings, furniture, figurines, porcelain, crockery – everything. At least then he'd have some money in his pocket.

A smile crossed his face as he began to take the pictures from the walls of the parlour. He would have to work quickly, but at least he'd made a start.

CHAPTER 15

It was a couple of days later when Lily walked down Church Street on her way to Webb's. The sun was already up and it promised to be a lovely day. She looked at the grime-laden buildings as she passed them and shook her head at the filth lying on the road. Sprinting forward at a yell from above, she narrowly escaped the water cascading down from an upstairs window to land with a splash behind her.

Waving to the market stallholders dragging handcarts, she knew they would be set up in the 'Shambles' in no time. As she entered the market-place proper she heard the shrill sound of the train's steam whistle.

She waved as she saw Jenny coming towards her along the tramway. Then she noticed the girl was limping. Frowning, she wondered what had happened to cause her friend to walk with a strange gait.

Waiting outside the shop for Jenny to join her, she saw her pallid complexion. The girl was unwell, that much was clear.

'Jenny, what's happened? Why are you limping?' she asked as they entered their workplace.

175

'My leg don't half ache. I scratched it on a nail in the privy a couple of days ago, and I didn't think anything more about it, but blimey it hurts now and it's a bit swollen,' Jenny said as she sat carefully behind the desk.

'Have you seen the doctor?' Lily asked.

Jenny shook her head. 'I can't afford it,' she whispered. 'Anyway, I'll be all right in a couple of days.'

The doorbell tinkled and another day's work began.

By lunchtime Jenny was looking pale and said she was feeling terrible. Lily spoke quietly to Stan after dragging him from the kitchen. 'Stan, I think Jenny should see Dr Dingle and I need to go with her. She can't afford his fee, but I can. Besides, I know she won't go on her own.'

'I agree, get her up there now, and see what the doctor makes of it,' Stan whispered back.

Jenny began to make a fuss when Lily told her they had to go to the doctor's surgery, but Stan insisted and eventually the girl relented.

Walking slowly, they made their way to Dr Dingle's house which also served as his surgery.

Lily sat in the little waiting room while Jenny went in to see the doctor. There was no one else there.

Suddenly an ear-splitting scream rent the air and she heard Jenny sobbing. The door opened and the doctor hooked a finger for Lily to join them.

Lily rushed to her friend who was crying uncontrollably. Wrapping her arms around Jenny, she looked at Dr Dingle, questions written all over her face.

'Lily, is it?' the doctor asked. A nod confirmed it was. 'Jenny here has septicaemia in her leg.'

'Oh my God!' Lily blurted out. Then she added, 'Jenny said she'd only scratched it on a nail!'

'Yes, but that scratch has turned septic and is badly infected,' the doctor stressed.

'Lily, he wants to cut my leg off!' Jenny yelled amid sobs. 'Please, Lily, don't let him! Don't let him cut off my leg! Pleease!'

Lily held on tightly to her friend and her frightened eyes turned back to Dr Dingle. She saw him nod, and she sucked in a shocked breath.

'Why?' she managed at last.

'Because if we don't remove that leg below the knee, she could die.' The doctor shook his head; his heart went out to the two women now both sobbing their hearts out.

'Isn't there something else that can be done?' Lily asked. 'Medicine or something?'

The doctor again shook his head. 'This is the only course of action to be taken, I'm afraid, and, Jenny, it needs to be soon.'

'Thank you,' Lily whispered as she helped Jenny to her feet.

Dr Dingle nodded as he watched the girls go. He shook his head yet again. *What a shame,* he thought. *If only people would come to me sooner!*

Lily hailed a cab and helped Jenny inside. The girl was sobbing her heart out. 'Oh Lily! Please don't let them cut off me leg! Please!'

'Jenny!' Lily said sharply, then more gently she said, 'You're my friend and I don't want you to die! I'd rather have you with half a leg and alive!'

Jenny snuffled. 'I s'pose,' she said eventually. 'Oh me poor mum, she'll be beside herself with worry over all this.'

'Your mum is strong, Jenny, just like you. We'll all get through this together. Now, dry your tears and try to be brave.'

An hour later Lily was sitting in the small living room at Jenny's house in Camp Street. She was explaining to Vera Pickard what the doctor had said.

Vera held her daughter as she cried. 'Mum, you can't let them do it! Please don't let them!'

Vera snapped, 'Now you listen to me, my girl, and you listen good. If losing half your leg means saving your life, then it has to be done.'

'Noooo!' Jenny wailed.

'Yes!' Vera was adamant. 'Now, you get your things together cos we'm gooin' up the 'ospital!'

Jenny limped her way upstairs terribly upset and very afraid.

'Thanks, Lily, you most likely saved my girl's life.' Vera wiped away her tears.

'Oh Vera! I was very worried about her, that's why I took her to see Dr Dingle.' Lily was distraught.

'I'm glad you did, gel, and that's the truth.' Vera

groaned. 'This babby ain't far off either. I 'ave to admit I could do without it, what with our Jenny an' all.'

'You need to rest, Vera.' Lily heard the other children shouting and screaming upstairs and realised the stupidity of her remark. 'Sorry,' she said, 'I can see how that's impossible for you.'

Vera nodded, 'I'm going next door to fetch Mrs Jackson to mind the kids while I take our Jenny up the 'ospital.'

A moment later Jenny appeared with a battered old brown box suitcase held together with a belt. She placed it on the floor and dropped into a chair in a daze.

'Right!' Vera's voice made Lily jump. 'Lily, get back to work and tell Mr Webb what you told me. I just have summat to do, then, our Jenny, you can get your arse off that chair, we'll be off to see Dr Dingle again afore we goes up the 'ospital.'

Vera dashed into the kitchen and grabbed her husband's hammer from the toolbox kept beneath the sink and shot out to the privy. Locating the offending nail, she hit it squarely on the head with all her strength. With each strike she cursed the nail as well as the person who had made it. Once she was satisfied it would harm no one else, she strode indoors and threw the hammer on the table.

Sitting in the doctor's office half an hour later, he patiently explained to Vera what he'd told her daughter a few hours before.

'Septicaemia is more commonly known as blood

poisoning and if we don't treat this straight away, it will travel through her body and . . .' Dr Dingle left the sentence hanging mid-air to add emphasis. Silently he prayed it was not already too late.

'Bloody hell! Beggin' your pardon, Dr Dingle. So if I take her up to the 'ospital now, when will they . . .' Vera snatched up Jenny's hand and squeezed it tightly as the girl began to cry once more.

'I will give you a letter to take with you. I will stress I think this must be done straight away.' Then to Jenny he added, 'I am sorry, Jenny, but in time you'll see the sense of it.'

Quiet descended, except for the occasional dry sob from Jenny as the doctor wrote out the letter and handed it to Vera.

Jenny and her mother boarded the train and settled on the wooden seats in the third-class carriage. Any other time a train ride would have been exciting, but not today. Fear gripped mother and daughter as the train moved off. They were heading for the Wolverhampton & Staffordshire General Hospital.

Vera's thoughts roamed around how she could find the money for the train fare to visit Jenny once her operation had been carried out. She would manage, she just hoped the new baby wouldn't come too soon.

In the meantime, Fred, Albert and Stan sat in the small kitchen listening intently as Lily filled them in on Jenny's condition.

'Oh dear God! That poor girl!' Albert said, his eyes filling with tears. 'I'll have to go and see her!'

Stan raised his eyebrows and looked from the young man to Lily.

'You must give her time, Albert,' she said. 'I know how you feel about her but she will have a lot of healing to do. She will have to learn to live with the loss of a limb, both physically and mentally.'

Stan and Fred exchanged a surprised look. They had no idea Albert had been carrying a candle for young Jenny.

'I suppose you're right,' Albert said sadly. Then he added, 'Lily, do you suppose . . . in time . . . she might marry me if I asked her?'

Fred spluttered his tea and coughed. Stan banged him on the back a couple of times.

Lily smiled, 'I think she'd love to be asked, although I couldn't say whether she would accept.'

'Blimey, what a day!' Stan said as he stood to make more tea.

The rest of the day for Lily passed in a daze, her mind unable to think about anything but Jenny. She wondered what it must be like to be in hospital. Poor Jenny would be scared witless. She knew Vera wouldn't be able to stay once the operation was over, she had her other children to see to.

That evening in the living room of the boarding house, Lily voiced her thoughts to Emily Johnston. It was long after the other girls had retired to bed and Lily had explained about Jenny's misfortune.

Lily sobbed, 'I feel so sorry for her, she's a lovely

girl, as you know yourself. I can't imagine how she'll cope with this.'

'Well, she will either cope or she won't. Worrying for her won't help. You have the Ryder funeral coming up you said, so you need to have your mind on that.' Emily tried to snap Lily out of her misery but she could see it wasn't happening. On a softer note, she added, 'Why don't you pay Jenny's mum a visit after work tomorrow? At least then you'll know what's what.'

Lily dried her eyes and hugged the woman who had become such a good friend to her. 'Thank you, Emily, you always know just what to do in any given situation.'

Going to her room, Lily thought about the circumstances surrounding the Pickard family. Jenny was to have a horrendous operation which, if she survived, would most likely see her in a wheelchair for the rest of her life. The two-up, two-down house they lived in would have to be rearranged to accommodate a disabled person. That would mean Jenny would have to sleep in the living room. Lily knew there was no room for a bed in there, so the sofa would have to do.

She sighed, her heart ached for her young friend. Her thoughts then turned to Vera. With a husband, the rowdy children and Jenny as an invalid, she also would have a new baby to care for very soon.

Lily shook her head in the darkness as she wondered how Vera would cope. Then another thought struck her. There would be only one wage going into the household now! Whatever would happen if Jenny's dad lost his job as a miner? The collieries were closing down fast and Lily knew it was only a matter of time before Mr Pickard would be standing in the breadline.

Lily closed her eyes as her tears rolled onto her pillow. She had to find a way to help, but how?

The following evening, Lily sat in the small living room listening to Vera.

'I only got back from Wolver'ampton a few hours ago,' she said. 'They did the operation this morning. The matron was a diamond, she let me sit with our Jenny all night. They ain't supposed to do that, but with me being almost to term,' she patted her belly, 'she med an exception.'

'How is Jenny?' Lily asked.

'Her seemed all right when I left. The doctor said her would sleep a lot over the next few days, so there'd be no point in visiting, with it being such a long way to travel.'

'Oh Vera! What if she wakes and there's no one there? She'll need you to be with her!' Lily was becoming agitated.

'I know that, but what to do?' She spread her arms out, 'I have this lot to sort out. God knows where I'm going to put Jenny when her comes 'ome! I have to see to the kids and rearrange the bedrooms. The new babby will come in with us at first, so the others will have to bunk up as they do now.'

'So will Jenny sleep on the sofa?' Lily asked.

'Yes, her'll 'ave to. Oh God! My poor little wench!' Vera burst into tears.

Lily rushed to the sobbing woman, her own tears running freely. Holding Vera while she wept, Lily had been surprised at the show of emotion. Jenny's mother was such a strong character, always dealing with difficulties and problems in a matter-of-fact manner. However, this latest upset with Jenny had devastated her.

'Shall I make a cuppa?' Lily asked. Vera nodded as she dried her eyes.

Bustling into the tiny kitchen, Lily looked around for cups.

My God! How do they all manage in this little house? she thought as she began to make the tea.

CHAPTER 16

It was the day of his mother's funeral and Seb Ryder sat in the quiet of the Chapel of Rest staring at the coffin.

Shaking his head, he muttered, 'It's just as well you're not here, Mother; the mess I'm in would really have upset you. Father had mortgaged the house and now the bank are taking it back. I've had to sell everything in order to survive. I'm so sorry.'

A gentle knock to the door told him it was time. Stroking the coffin, Seb walked from the room.

Holding the reins of his horse out on the road, he saw the great wooden gates open and Lily walk out, followed by the horses pulling the open carriage. He nodded to Lily before taking his place behind the carriage.

Slowly the cortège made its way through the streets where people stopped to pay their respects.

At the churchyard the casket was placed gently down on the ropes lying on the ground as the service began. Carefully the box was lowered into the ground and each mourner threw in their handful of earth.

Stan and Lily walked back to the carriage. They had been instrumental in ensuring Eleanor Ryder lay next to her husband.

Seb watched Lily climb onto the driving seat and he turned away. He walked to his horse tethered nearby and swung up into the saddle. Riding away from the church, he thought how things could have been so different. If only his parents hadn't died; if only his father hadn't mortgaged the house; if only he was rich.

A huge sigh escaped his lips as he considered what he should do now. The house was gone, so he had to find somewhere to live. That would have to be his first priority. Once settled in a room somewhere he would have to get himself a job. Easier said than done in a small town being strangled by poverty. The coal mines were closing one after another and the breadline grew longer each day. He could stand the line with other men, but having no trade or experience of any sort it was very unlikely he would be taken on.

He continued to walk the horse back into town when a thought struck. He was well known in the taverns, albeit for drinking himself into oblivion, but maybe he could find work as a barman. Cheered by the possibility, he wondered which hostelry to approach first. If he could find work it would mean he could stay in Wednesbury, which in turn would mean he could still see Lily on the odd occasion. After all he had made up his mind to have her again – one way or another.

Coming upon the Golden Cross Inn, Seb thought it a good place to try his luck at finding a job.

On their journey back to Webb's, Lily asked, 'Stan, would there be any possibility of holding Jenny's job open for her to come back to?'

Stan eyed the girl sat next to him. 'Well, that might be a bit awkward, who would see to the shop in the meantime? I mean, it could take a long time for Jenny to get better, and even then she might not want to come back.'

Lily sighed. 'I could mind the shop when I'm not leading a funeral, but as you say, she might not decide to return. It will be hard for her being in a wheelchair.'

'The chair wouldn't be a problem in the shop, but she might not want folks to know about it,' Stan explained.

Lily sighed again and nodded. 'Oh Stan! You should see how the family are living and only one wage coming in! If Mr Pickard should be laid off from the colliery, they'll all end up in the workhouse!'

'Now then, Lily, don't get all het up about something you can't do anything about,' Stan patted her knee like an affectionate father.

'I have to do something, Stan! I don't know as yet what that might be, but I have to help somehow.' Lily looked at the man she had become very fond of.

'Look,' Stan went on, 'how about we keep Jenny's

job open for . . . a couple of months say, and see how she's getting on. Then, if she wants to come back to work, she can. If not, we can look for someone else.'

'Oh Stan, thank you! You're such a kind man.' Lily beamed.

'Ar well,' Stan felt embarrassed at the compliment, 'let's see how young Jenny goes on. It's early days yet. By the way, will you be going up to Wolverhampton to see her?'

'Visiting time would be over by the time I got there, but it would be nice, I must admit.'

As the horses halted outside the shop, Stan said, 'We've nothing on tomorrow, so why don't you take the day and go and visit her?'

Lily threw her arms around the man as they stood waiting for the gates to open. 'Thank you! I really appreciate it.'

Stan patted her back, then stepped forward as the huge gates swung open.

Bright and early the next morning, Lily boarded the steam train for Wolverhampton. She had bought a posy of flowers from the market for Jenny. She had mixed feelings as the train pulled away. On one hand she was glad to be going to see her friend, but on the other she was afraid of what she would find. How poorly would she be? Would she be in dreadful pain? How would she be feeling about her missing limb?

Lily's eyes were not focussed on the streets or

188

the countryside as the train trundled along on its rails, all she could think about was Jenny. She had been in the hospital for a few weeks now and Lily felt bad that she hadn't visited before this.

The train pulled into Monmore Green Station and steam hissed loudly as it ground to a halt. Stepping down onto the platform, Lily looked around her. Following the throng of people, she found herself in the street.

Stopping a lady passing by, she asked directions to the hospital. Pointing a finger, the woman said, 'It's that way, but it's quite a step. You can catch the tram over there and it will drop you right outside the hospital.' Thanking the woman, Lily walked to the tram stop and waited.

Boarding the tram and buying a ticket from the conductor, she was relieved to hear him calling out the stops, at least now she'd know where to get off.

Eventually she alighted from the tram and stood staring at the massive building in front of her. How would she find Jenny in such a huge place?

Swallowing her fear and grabbing her courage with both hands, she strode in through the double doors. A woman sat behind a desk with a Reception sign hanging over her head.

'May I help you?' the woman asked.

'I've come to visit my friend,' Lily said.

'Name?'

'Lily Rae.'

Scanning a list in front of her, the woman said, 'We don't have a Lily Rae, I'm afraid.'

'Oh I'm sorry, that's my name,' Lily felt like an idiot, but the woman smiled warmly.

'I take it you've not been here before?' she asked kindly and as Lily shook her head she went on. 'What is your friend's name?'

'Jenny Pickard, she's had an operation on her leg.'

Checking the list again, the woman said, 'She's in Queen Victoria Ward on the second floor. The stairs are over there.' A finger pointed and another smile accompanied it.

'Thank you, you've been most kind,' Lily said before turning towards the stairs.

On the second floor a long corridor stretched out before her. It seemed to go on forever and, swallowing hard, Lily began to walk. As she scanned the names of the different wards either side of the green and cream painted corridor, she wrinkled her nose. There was a distinct smell that was none too pleasant. Lily ignored it and walked on.

Then to her left she found the name she was looking for. Walking through the door, she saw a nurse coming towards her.

'Can I help you?' the nurse asked as she smoothed her pristine white apron.

'I've come to see Jenny Pickard,' Lily answered.

'Well it's not visiting time yet,' the nurse said sharply when she was stopped short by a commanding voice.

'Nurse Pitt, back to your station please!' the

190

Matron eyed Lily standing with her posy of flowers. 'You are here to see young Jenny I hear?'

'Yes, ma'am. I've come all the way from Wednesbury. Please don't tell me I can't see her.' Lily became agitated.

'Hush now,' the matron whispered, 'come with me.'

Lily followed the large woman whose back was ramrod straight. Nurses scattered as they spied the dark blue uniform approach. At the end of the ward Lily saw Jenny sitting up in her bed. She felt elated, she'd been afraid her friend would be at death's door.

Turning abruptly, the Matron said quietly, 'You have my permission to visit and stay as long as you wish.' The wink she gave took Lily quite by surprise and she whispered her grateful thanks.

'Lily!' Jenny beamed. 'It's so lovely to see you! Fancy you coming all this way to see me!'

'I brought you these,' Lily said, placing the posy on the bed, then she threw her arms around Jenny. 'How are you? You look so well!' It was all Lily could do not to stare at the place where Jenny's lower leg should have been.

'Well, considering what they've done to me, I ain't doing all that badly. They give me some medicine when the pain gets too bad, and it makes me all woozy . . . it's quite a nice feeling actually. I would imagine that's how a drunk feels when he's had a skinful!' Jenny grinned as she rambled on.

Lily listened as Jenny told her how kind everyone was and that she would be able to get out of bed in the next couple of days. 'They said I can have a wooden leg if I want, but I ain't having no jokes about it. The first one to shout "Ar Jim lad" gets it wrapped round their neck!'

Lily laughed. 'Jenny, I can't believe how well you've taken all this . . .' She halted her words as Jenny piped up.

'Well, the matron told me what's what. I have to say, Lily, I was feeling right sorry for meself after they chopped off the leg,' she patted the bed where the empty space was, 'but the matron said I could be a miserable devil for the rest of me life, or I could get on and live it!'

'Oh, Jenny, good for you! I'm so proud of you.' Lily grinned.

She stayed until mid-afternoon and told her friend about Stan keeping the job open for her. Jenny whooped with delight, which drew a smile from everyone in the ward.

'Hey Matron,' Jenny yelled, 'how soon can I have my peg leg? I have a job to get back to!'

The girls saw the matron beam, then, coming over to them, she said, 'Jenny Pickard, although you are an inspiration to us all, I do wish you'd keep your voice down. People in here are poorly, you know. As for that leg, how about we try for next week?'

'Yes!' Jenny said enthusiastically.

'It won't be easy, Jenny. You'll have to learn to walk all over again and it will be painful to begin with.'

'I ain't bothered, just give me the leg. You've all

been very kind to me, Matron, and I'm sure you'll miss me when I'm gone, but I need to get back to work.'

Eventually the time came for Lily to return home and it was a tearful goodbye the girls shared. Leaving the ward, Lily presented the matron with a flower she had plucked from Jenny's posy. 'Thank you . . . for everything,' she whispered.

'You're most welcome, my dear,' the Matron said with a smile. 'Visitors cheer our patients up no end, and I'm a firm believer in allowing an out of hours visit for a special patient.' With that she tucked the flower under the strap of her pinafore.

Lily returned the smile and left. She decided to drop in on Vera on her way home to update her on how well Jenny was doing.

Stopping off at the grocer's shop in Union Street, Lily bought a quarter pound of tea which was wrapped in brown paper and tied with string. She also bought the same weight of sugar, similarly wrapped but in blue paper, a loaf of bread, a pat of butter and a bottle of milk. She hoped Vera would not take offence at her little offering towards the household.

Vera was delighted at Lily's gift, especially the sugar and butter. It was something the household budget could not stretch to very often.

As they sat at the table, Lily told Vera about how well her daughter was doing.

'She was born with one leg a little shorter than the other. Did you never notice her built up shoe?'

Lily shook her head. 'Well anyway, other than that our Jenny was always pretty healthy. When she has new shoes, the cobbler builds up the sole and it seems to have worked cos she never walked funny until the other day.'

'I can't believe I never noticed her shoe,' Lily was surprised, 'and she was on her feet all day when she worked at the café.'

'Our Jenny bissent one for letting things get her down for long; she won't let anything get the better of her.' Vera smiled thinly.

'I saw that today,' Lily grinned.

'There won't be need of the cobbler now though,' Vera choked back a sob.

In a desperate bid to forestall the tears she saw threatening, Lily said, 'But think of the money you'll save not having that shoe cobbled.'

Lily thought she'd made the biggest mistake of her life as she saw Vera's shocked expression at her words, then she sighed with relief when the woman burst out laughing.

'Oh Lily, our Jenny is so lucky to have such a good friend in you. I bless the day you two met.'

At last it was time to leave and Lily gave Vera a hug. 'If you need anything, let me know,' she said over her shoulder as she waved goodbye.

CHAPTER 17

The weeks had rolled past with Lily barely noticing the summer coming and going. She had been busy in the shop and had visited Jenny in the hospital again as well as keeping an eye on Vera and her brood.

Then one morning came the fog. The grey dampness hung in the air which held a distinct chill. The already drab town seemed even drearier as people walked with heads down against the bleak weather.

As Lily walked down Church Street, she felt the chilly wind and saw it swirl the fog around her. It was an eerie feeling being unable to see the buildings she knew so well. With a shiver she walked a little faster. She could hear cart wheels on the cobblestones but couldn't see through the pervading fog which wrapped everything in a dirty grey blanket. Voices echoed the length of the streets as people grumbled about the sudden change in weather. Carters yelled for folk to get out of the 'hossroad' lest they be knocked over.

Lily had a most welcome day off from her work. Wrapped up warmly, she was making her way to Camp Street. She was visiting Vera and her brood.

Stopping on her way, she bought half a pound of boiled sweets from Teddy Grey's stall. Vera's children would share them out and it would help keep them quiet and give their mother some much-needed peace.

Arriving at the house, Lily knocked the back door and stepped inside, calling out, 'Hello Vera, it's Lily.' The five youngsters came thundering down the stairs to greet her. Passing the sweets to the eldest, she said, 'Share them out fairly then get ready for school. Where's your mum?'

Thanking her for the confectionary, she nodded to the living room. The children shot back upstairs and Lily greeted Vera with a smile. Then she realised her friend didn't look at all well. 'Are you all right?' she asked, a sudden fear enveloping her.

Vera gasped, 'The babby's coming. It's way overdue, it's bin trying this past week and now . . .' Another pain stole her words.

'Oh Vera, what can I do?' Lily was looking around the room as if it would provide an answer.

'Fetch . . . Mrs Jackson . . . from next door,' Vera managed. 'This . . . ain't right!'

Lily fled from the house and banged loudly on the front door of the next house.

'All right, all right!' She heard from within. 'What's all the racket about?'

The door opened and Lily said shakily, 'Mrs Jackson, please come – it's Vera!'

The woman nodded, saying, 'Get her to bed, I'll be there in a minute.'

'Please hurry,' Lily said over her shoulder as she ran back to Vera.

Helping her friend upstairs, Lily yelled for the children to go and play in the living room. She helped Vera out of her clothes and into a voluminous cotton nightdress. The woman groaned again as more pain rolled over her and Lily saw beads of sweat forming on her brow.

'Bloody hell!' Vera whispered.

Just then Mrs Jackson came bustling into the small room. 'It's about time,' she said to Vera as she pushed Lily out of the way. Vera nodded as she panted. 'Right then, we'll need some hot water, towels and a swaddling cloth,' Mrs Jackson said to Lily.

Lily bounded down the stairs to put the kettle to boil. Searching the room, she found a good-sized bowl which would do for the hot water. Carefully she carried it upstairs and laid it on a small dresser.

'In the drawer,' Vera gasped from her prone position on the bed.

Lily dragged the drawer open and found the towels and a length of clean white cloth.

Mrs Jackson knelt at the foot of the bed and looked at Lily, saying, 'Put them on the bed then fetch another bowl and a damp cloth to wipe her down.'

Lily ran from the room again. From the kitchen she heard the children laughing and playing totally oblivious to the goings-on upstairs. Clearly they had decided against going to school and Lily had no time to berate them. Unable to find another bowl, Lily grabbed a large jam pan from its nail in the wall. Snatching up the teacloth, she plunged it into the pail of water that always stood by the brownstone sink.

Back in the bedroom she placed the jam pan on the floor as indicated by Mrs Jackson. Lily gently wiped the sweat from Vera's brow with the wet teacloth.

'Not long now,' Mrs Jackson said as she peeped between Vera's bent knees.

With another agonising contraction, Vera lifted her head and held her breath as she pushed down hard.

Lily watched in frightened fascination as Vera continued to try to push her child into the world. She made no sound save for the breath escaping between clenched teeth before she took another huge breath to push again.

Lily saw Mrs Jackson shake her head. Lily thought, *something must be wrong! Why is it taking so long?*

Mopping Vera's brow again, Lily began to feel fear and panic. Surely the child should have come by now.

'Right, this time, Vera, and if it don't come I'll drag it out by its ears,' Mrs Jackson said.

Lily shot her a horrified look but then realised Mrs Jackson was smiling up at Vera who was becoming exhausted. She watched as Vera sucked in a huge breath and lifted her head, the strain showing on her face and her hands holding on to the iron bedstead.

There was a squelching sound as Vera relaxed and Lily gasped in awe as she saw the baby emerge. Her eyes then moved to Mrs Jackson. She watched the woman tying off the cord with a bit of string from her pocket. Producing scissors she snipped the cord that had joined the baby to its mother. Then, resting the child over her arm, she gave it a sharp slap on the bottom.

Lily's hand flew to her mouth. What was this woman doing to the newborn infant? Suddenly the baby let out a lusty cry.

Mrs Jackson smiled as she turned the child over, bringing it to lay in the crook of her arm. 'It's a boy!' she said to Vera, who nodded weakly. Holding out the baby to Lily, she went on, 'Come on, wash him down in that bowl, then dry him off and wrap him in the swaddling cloth.'

Lily moved as if in a daze. As she took the baby carefully, she gazed down at his tiny wrinkled face. Very gently she bathed him in the bowl of water and patted him dry. Her nerves jangled in fear that she might drop him, but he lay still as she wrapped him in the cotton cloth. Turning back to the bed, she made to pass the baby boy to his mother. 'Not yet, gel, we have to shift the afterbirth first,' Mrs Jackson said.

Lily had no idea what she meant. Watching, the baby snuffling in her arms, she saw a towel laid on the bed beneath Vera's legs. Mrs Jackson then moved to the side and laid her hands on Vera's naked belly.

'Ready, Vera?' she asked.

Vera sucked in a breath and nodded. Mrs Jackson leaned her quite considerable weight onto Vera who pushed down hard. Another squelch sounded in the quiet room and Lily gagged as she saw the blood and mess slop onto the towel. Mrs Jackson swiftly rolled it up and dropped it into the jam pan beside her.

Nodding to Lily, she carried the pan out of the room. 'I'll just go and burn this in the yard; you can make us all a nice cup of tea.'

Lily only then realised, as she gently laid the baby in Vera's arms, that tears were rolling down her face. She had been overwhelmed by the miracle she had witnessed and whispered, 'He's so lovely, Vera.' She sobbed as the exhausted woman kissed the tiny head of her new son.

Descending the stairs to the kitchen, she called out to the other children, 'You have a new baby brother!'

They clapped and cheered as Lily went to make the tea.

Walking home later in the fog which had not lifted all day, Lily thought about all she had seen. The miracle of childbirth, the other children's delight at having a new brother, the neighbour who dropped everything to help. Even in the midst of poverty and misery, beauty and happiness could be found. Vera's family had one small wage coming in, yet they would manage to feed another mouth. Her daughter had suffered losing a limb to septicaemia, but a healthy boy had been born.

Lily felt very privileged to have been part of aiding Vera in her time of need and she wondered what name the new baby would be given.

Jenny had been in the hospital for six weeks and was due to come home. Vera, with her new baby, was unable to fetch her daughter and had asked Lily if she would oblige. Naturally Lily had agreed to collect her friend and bring her home, although she had no idea how she would accomplish it. As she sat in the kitchen at Webb's, she voiced her worries.

'What about the open carriage?' Albert asked.

'What!' Lily said, horrified at the suggestion.

'Good idea, we won't need it tomorrow anyway, so she could come back on that,' Stan said.

'Stan, it's a hearse!' Lily was shocked.

'Only when it's decked out with flowers, otherwise it's just a cart. The horses won't have their plumes on, so nobody will be any the wiser,' Stan laughed.

Thinking for a moment, Lily said, 'I suppose it makes sense. Jenny might have a new leg, but I suspect she'll have a wheelchair as well. I couldn't manage that and her on the train by myself.'

'I'd be happy to drive you,' Albert put in before Stan could make the same offer.

201

And so it was agreed, Lily and Albert would collect Jenny and her chair the following day.

Albert Blenkinsop had bought a posy of flowers for Jenny which Lily carried as they journeyed to Wolverhampton. They chatted amiably as they travelled and eventually Albert said, 'Lily, I – I'm going to ask Jenny to marry me.'

'Oh Albert, I'm so pleased for you and – I hope she accepts.'

'Why – do you think she might refuse me?' he said, panic lacing his words.

'It's not that, Albert, it's just – have you considered she might think you are asking because you feel sorry for her?'

'But I don't!' Albert snapped as agitation overcame him. 'I love her, Lily. I love that girl with all my heart and soul!'

Smiling, Lily said gently, 'Then that's what you must tell her.'

Albert nodded.

Halting the horse outside the hospital, he gasped in awe at its size. With a nosebag each, the horses would stand and wait patiently.

Following Lily, Albert was excited and couldn't wait to see Jenny. Walking into the ward, the posy hidden behind his back, he saw the love of his life sitting in her wheelchair by the bed. Rushing forward, he held out the posy, a beaming smile spread across his face.

Lily had stopped to chat with the nurse as the matron walked in. Lily explained they had come to take Jenny home. The matron tipped her head towards Albert who was chatting excitedly, question in her eyes.

Lily whispered, 'He's besotted with her.' Together they walked over to the couple.

'Now then, you take care, Jenny; we're going to miss you around here,' the Matron said with a smile.

'At least it will be quieter when I'm gone!' Jenny grinned.

'Sadly yes, but at least the other patients will be safe from you careening around in that chair!' the Matron said.

'Right then, let's be off! Albert, give us a push cos my arms are tired!' Jenny winked at the matron as Albert got into position and began to push. 'Oh wait . . .! My leg, I can't go without my new leg!'

Handing her the wooden leg, the matron let out a loud belly laugh. She thought how Fate had dealt the girl a cruel blow, but her positive attitude would see her through.

'Ready when you are, Albert!' Jenny called out as she placed her wooden leg across her lap. Waving goodbye, Jenny was pushed from the ward and down the long corridor. Albert halted the chair at the stairs.

'Oh bugger,' Jenny cursed.

Taking the false leg, he passed it to Lily. Lifting Jenny easily with muscular arms, he asked, 'Can you manage the chair as well, Lily?'

Nodding, she put the leg on the chair and began

to bump it down the steps. Albert carried Jenny like she was made of glass.

'I could get used to this,' Jenny whispered with a smile.

'Marry me, Jenny, and I could let you,' Albert whispered back.

At the bottom of the stairs, he placed her back in her chair then knelt before her. He saw the shock of his words still on her face. Taking a small box from his pocket, he said quietly, 'Jenny Pickard, I have loved you from the moment I first saw you. I love you with my heart and soul and will until the day I die. Please say you will be my wife.'

Jenny's mouth hung open and she didn't see the small crowd gather to see what was going on. Lily was surprised too as she stood holding onto the false leg.

'Good grief!' Jenny managed at last. 'Well, if that don't take the biscuit!' A small titter ran around the people standing watching. 'Albert – I'm a cripple!'

'No! You are not! You are a kind, loving person. You are beautiful, Jenny, and I will always see you as that. I don't see your disability, I see only you and I want to spend the rest of my life with you.' Albert shuffled his weight on his knee.

Jenny saw the tears forming in his eyes as she said, 'Well in that case I'd better say yes!'

Albert took the ring and placed it on her finger, his grin spread from ear to ear. Applause echoed around from the people as they extended their congratulations and wiped away escaping tears at the scene before them.

Lily hugged them both before they left the building.

'What the hell . . .!' Jenny gasped when she saw the cart.

'It was this or walk,' Albert said, his eyes twinkling in mischief. 'Lily couldn't get your leg and your chair on the train so . . . your carriage awaits, ma'am.'

Lifting her onto the driving seat, he secured the wheelchair on the cart along with the wooden leg. Relieving the horses of their nosebags, he threw them next to the chair.

Lily squashed up beside her friend and Albert climbed up onto the other side.

'Home, Albert, and don't spare the hosses!' Jenny yelled, pushing her nose in the air.

All three burst out laughing as Albert flicked the reins and the horses walked on.

CHAPTER 18

Albert took the wheelchair from the open carriage and laughed as the Pickard children fought and scrambled to try it out. Lily picked up the false leg and, knocking the back door, announced their arrival. Jenny inched across the driving seat and with Albert's hands on her tiny waist was lifted down. She balanced precariously on her good leg for a moment before Albert lifted her into his arms and carried her indoors. Sitting her on the sofa, he went to fetch her chair which was being mobbed by her siblings.

Vera hugged her brave young daughter, tears coursing down her cheeks. 'It's so lovely to have you 'ome, our Jenny,' Vera sobbed. Then, spotting the ring on Jenny's finger, gasped, 'what the . . .?

Albert walked in just at that moment, pushing the wheelchair which he parked in the corner.

Jenny grinned, 'Mum, this is Albert Blenkinsop, he's the mortician at work and – my fiancé.'

Vera, mouth open, looked at the young man and back to her daughter.

Albert stood next to Jenny protectively. 'I'm very pleased to meet you, Mrs Pickard, please forgive my impetuosity in asking Jenny to marry me without first gaining your permission, but I'm afraid I couldn't wait any longer!'

'Is that so? Well I don't know what her father will make of all this, I'm sure.' Vera said, having found her voice again.

'Mrs Pickard, I would have gladly followed protocol and asked his permission first, however I didn't know where you lived until today. Please accept my apologies.' Albert placed a hand on Jenny's shoulder and she beamed up at him.

By the way he spoke, Vera could see he was a well-educated young man. 'So, how long has this been going on?'

'I have had feelings for your daughter from the first day I met her, Mrs Pickard, feelings which will remain until the day Lily heads my funeral.'

Jenny smiled. 'Lily told me how Albert felt about me ages ago, Mum. Since then, I've thought about it a lot, especially while I was in the hospital. I care for him, Mum . . .'

'Ar, but do you love him?' Vera interrupted.

Jenny nodded. 'Yes, I think I do.' She smiled up at the man who was to be her husband.

'Right then, that's good enough for me,' Vera said, then turning to Lily added, 'Put that leg down, lovey, and fetch the babby from upstairs, he'll be wanting a feed.'

The children all stared at the leg placed across the wheelchair before dashing outside to resume their play.

Lily found the baby asleep in a drawer which was lying on the floor next to Vera's bed. Lifting him gently, she wondered where he'd sleep once he'd outgrown his makeshift cot.

Once downstairs she placed him in Jenny's arms and watched as she cuddled her new brother.

Vera brought in cups of tea for everyone and chatter began around how well Jenny was doing after such a major operation and Lily's help with the birth of baby Bertie.

'So, when's the wedding then?' Vera asked.

'Blimey, Mother! We've only just got engaged!' Jenny blustered.

Laughter filled the room, then Albert spoke up. 'Mrs Pickard, if Jenny agrees, I'd like it to be as soon as possible.'

Vera glanced at her daughter.

'No, Mum, before you even ask, I'm not pregnant! Besides, they wouldn't have done my operation if I had been now, would they?'

Vera looked suitably chastised. 'So what's the 'urry, Albert?'

'Please don't be offended, Mrs Pickard, but there is little enough room for your children here and I suspect Jenny will have to sleep on here.' He patted the sofa as Vera nodded. 'I have my own house in Loxdale Street. It has two bedrooms, living room, kitchen, scullery, and now has an indoor lavatory downstairs. This is not a boast, Mrs Pickard, but you see how much easier it would be for Jenny. There is also the fact that we

208

could travel to and from work together. I can buy a pony and trap which would enable Jenny to visit you any time she wished.'

Vera was impressed. Turning to her daughter, she asked, 'Are we to start planning the wedding then?'

Jenny beamed. 'I think so, Mum.'

Lily walked home, thinking about the day's events. She'd had no idea Jenny had been considering marriage to Albert all this time. Smiling to herself, she wondered what Stan would make of it all. As she strode up Church Street she thought she had a lot to tell Emily Johnston this evening.

Emily and Lily talked long into the night, way past the time the other girls had gone to their beds.

'How is it you came to be alone, Lily?' Mrs Johnston asked out of the blue.

Drawing in a huge breath, Lily let it out slowly.

'When I was little we lived in Bilston. My mother died in childbirth when I was five and my father worked away a lot and couldn't take care of me, so I ended up in the workhouse in Wolverhampton.'

Emily gasped in horror. 'Did your father send you there?'

'No, Dad went off to work one day and the school inspector came round to see why I hadn't started school. Finding me all alone, he reported it and I was collected that same day and carted off to Wolverhampton.' Lily shook her head sadly.

'Why did your father never come to find you?'

'I don't suppose he'd know where to look. He may have searched the town, but he wouldn't have known to look in Wolverhampton. I could have been anywhere. Besides, he had to work to survive – I know that now, but I didn't understand at the time.'

'But he could have asked – at the Council or the Magistrates . . .' Emily pursued.

'Maybe he did, but anyway I was in the Wolverhampton Union Workhouse until I was thirteen. God, it was awful in there! I lived in with the other girls and worked in the kitchen and sometimes in the laundry. It was hard and we had no pay. I remember being hungry all the time. It gave me the shivers that day I visited Jenny in the hospital because the tram passed right by it.' Lily gave an involuntary shudder. 'Then I discovered I could sign myself out of that dreadful place – so I did!'

'What did you do then?' Emily was hanging on Lily's every word.

'I searched for my father but I couldn't find him. No one had seen him in a very long time so I hitched a ride on a cart to Wednesbury. I lived on the streets for a couple of years doing any work I could find to earn a few pennies. Then I dropped lucky. Someone told me Ryder House was looking for a maid, so I applied. I couldn't believe my luck when Mrs Ryder took me on. I was happy there until . . .' Lily's eyes clouded over as she recalled the reason for having left Ryder House.

'My God! You've been through so much in your short life, I had no idea!' Emily was shocked.

'What doesn't kill you makes you stronger,' Lily said in a matter-of-fact tone. 'I promised myself when I walked out of the workhouse gates I would never go back there, no matter what.'

'Well, look how far you've come since then,' Emily said with a comforting smile, 'you have a good job, a nice place to live, even though I say so myself, and lovely friends.'

Lily nodded, then said, 'I'm glad Jenny accepted Albert's proposal, it will be easier for all concerned, and I think he'll dote on her.'

'I wonder if he knows what he's taken on,' Emily grinned.

'I'm sure he'll find out before too long,' Lily returned the grin.

'What about you, Lily, have you any plans to settle down and marry?' Emily thought she knew the answer but asked anyway.

'Good grief no!' Lily shot back. 'Not after . . . no, I'm not sure I'll ever get married. I like my life the way it is. I'm not having a man telling me what I should and shouldn't do.'

The two women continued to chat for a while longer before retiring to their respective beds.

It was Job Newton, who ran the Market Tavern in Russell Street, who had finally given Seb Ryder a job as barman. He also rented him a room above the bar. Laying down the rules, Job insisted Seb be punctual for work and under no circumstances would he be allowed to drink whilst on duty otherwise he would be out on his ear. Wages were agreed between them and Seb stabled his horse at the back of the public house.

Once his belongings were stowed in his room, Seb began learning the trade of barkeep. He was shown the cellar where huge barrels of beer were stored. How to tap and vent a barrel once they were delivered by the dray cart. How to clean and connect the lines. He learned how to wash glasses properly as well as sweeping the bar room clean of its sawdust every night after closing time. He was to lay fresh sawdust each morning before opening, at least until they could find a cleaner.

It was late that first night when Seb fell into bed completely exhausted, but at least he was sober. Too tired to eat the meal provided for him by Job's wife, he had thanked her and wearily climbed the stairs to bed.

Aching from head to foot, he lay on his bed thinking how hard it was to work for a living. He also realised how fortunate he was to have a job and room. Watching through his window the clouds passing over the moon, he hoped the work would become easier. His feet throbbed from standing all day and his arm muscles screamed at pulling pints and shifting barrels.

He thanked his lucky stars as sleep overcame him and the pain receded into blackness.

Seb woke with a start; it was early but he rose

from his bed and washed in the bowl on the dresser. Once dressed, he made his way downstairs to the kitchen. Lighting the range, he set the kettle to boil. He badly needed a drink and saw his hands shake as he put a cup ready on the table. How had he become so dependent upon alcohol? He knew the answer. He had been spoiled rotten by his mother who had provided the money for his indulgence. He also knew if he wanted to keep his job he would have to fight his need for alcohol. Easier said than done when he worked the bar.

Making a pot of tea, Seb sat at the table and pondered. It was imperative he didn't let Job or himself down. He was sure he could do it, he just had to take things one day at a time.

Hearing footsteps, Seb grabbed another cup and poured the tea. Mrs Newton wandered into the kitchen, surprised to see him. Accepting the tea offered gratefully, she joined him at the table. It was not long before he realised he was pouring out his life story to the kindly woman sat opposite him. All, that was, except his abuse of Lily Rae.

The work in the tavern did become easier for Seb, as did his abstinence from alcohol. He settled in well and laughed and joked with the customers who came in for a well-earned pint of best ale. He learned a lot about the townsfolk in the short time he had worked there; far more than he'd known before.

These were hardworking people, with very little money. However, what they had, they shared.

There was the odd punch-up outside on occasion, one that was forgotten the following day when the men were the best of friends once more. Life was hard, but they made the best of their lot. Seb admired them greatly. Suddenly he realised – he was now one of them.

CHAPTER 19

The trees were a kaleidoscope of colours as Mother Nature finally lay her autumnal cloak over the landscape. Crows cawed and fought among the brown and yellow leaves, some of which fluttered lazily to the ground. Sparrows chirped as if telling the noisy crows to settle down peacefully. The wind held a dampness which added to its cold embrace. The sun dragged its head up wearily, casting its watery aura over the buildings and people. Flowers struggled to raise their heads towards the weak glow and even the weeds began to die back. The squirrels in the park scampered around in an effort to collect as much food as they could to see them over the long winter months. Jays collected single acorns which they stashed under small piles of fallen leaves.

Lily saw fine cotton summer dresses replaced by serge skirts and thick blouses lying beneath woollen cardigans. Side button boots were worn as opposed to dainty shoes in readiness for the impending rains. Mufflers were brought out to be tied around necks in place of large cotton handkerchiefs. Flat caps were pulled low over eyes that had lost their sparkle.

She knew once the bad weather really set in, they would be busy at Webb's Funeral Directors. The winter took young and old alike to meet their maker; the bitter cold would not be discriminatory.

Jenny, in her wheelchair, had returned to work and Lily admired her friend's tenacity at how she was dealing with her disability. The wooden leg caused Jenny a lot of pain, Lily knew, when visiting the privy out the back, but for the most part the girl remained in her chair.

Having settled so well at Webb's, Lily was happy enough but often wondered what life held in store for her as time passed. One morning she was pondering this thought yet again when the doorbell tinkled and in walked a very handsome young man.

Nodding to her as he took off his flat cap, he took the seat indicated by Jenny. Lily listened as he explained he was to arrange the funeral of his uncle. Davy Hurst's gentle voice held Lily transfixed. The deceased had been the owner of Hurst's Grocers in Ladbury's Lane, which had now been passed down to Davy, it seemed. His black hair shone in the dim light and his brown eyes held a sadness that belied the laughter lines that surrounded them.

'Would you like Miss Rae to lead the party to St Bart's?' Jenny asked, tipping her head towards Lily.

Davy Hurst's eyes met Lily's and he nodded.

'That would be nice, I think.' He gave her a small smile which Lily returned as she tried to control the heat rising to her cheeks. Her heart hammered in her chest as his gaze lingered on her. She swallowed hard as his attention was drawn back to Jenny.

Then, getting to his feet, his cap held to his chest, Davy nodded his thanks to Jenny. Turning to Lily, he said, 'I will see you next week, Miss Rae.' Nodding, she watched him leave.

Dropping into the chair he had vacated, she blew through her teeth and Jenny roared with laughter.

'He is a bit of a looker, ain't he?' Jenny said at last.

'A bit? A lot if you ask me,' Lily answered dreamily.

'You could be in there, girl, I saw how he looked at you.' Jenny laughed again.

Lily shook her head, saying, 'Oh no, I'm not ready for a courtship.'

'Oh ar, we'll see. It's my thinking that young fella will be wanting just that.'

Lily rolled her eyes as she walked to the kitchen.

Despite her conviction never to marry, Lily's thoughts over the following days were consumed by Davy Hurst. Eventually she confided in her friend Emily Johnston.

'I can't stop thinking about him, it's ridiculous!' Lily said testily.

'Lily, maybe it's because you are in love.' Emily smiled.

'What! No, oh no! I don't think so. I don't want to be in love!' Lily wrung her hands in angst.

'My dear girl, wanting has nothing to do with it. When love strikes, that's it.'

Lily cut across her friend's words. 'I've only met him once for goodness' sake!'

'Once is all it takes, Lily. Why are you so desperate to deny your feelings?' Seeing the look on the girl's face, she added, 'Oh, Seb Ryder.'

Lily nodded. 'Even if Davy Hurst felt the same, how could I tell him about . . .?'

'If it turns out he does feel the same, why tell him anything? He doesn't need to know, so why spoil something that could be beautiful?' Emily said gently.

'But it would be like living a lie!' Lily returned.

'No, it would be an omission – not a lie. He wouldn't need to know every detail of your life prior to meeting him. Besides, do you intend to rob yourself of a happy life because of that one incident?'

'But . . .' Lily began.

'But nothing! I felt as you do now. What would have happened to me had I not married Mr Johnston? I would have been a miserable old maid by now. Lily, don't shut yourself off from the world and all it has to offer. You could be so happy for the rest of your days; you just need to let go of the past. It's baggage you no longer need to carry.'

'Maybe you're right,' Lily acquiesced.

'I am, you'll see.'

'Anyway, it's early days yet. I'll be leading the funeral on Friday and that's hardly the time or place for a romantic tryst.'

'I agree, but I have a feeling that won't be the last you see of Davy Hurst.'

The funeral on the Friday was a sombre affair. Lily led the entourage to St Bart's, all the time thinking how dashing Davy Hurst looked in his black suit.

Standing back from the graveside with Stan, she heard the service but her eyes never left the handsome young Davy. She saw him smile his thanks as he shook hands with other mourners. Then he looked directly at her and her heartbeat increased. He smiled and nodded to her, which she returned.

Stan's elbow dug her in the ribs; it was time to leave. Walking back to the open carriage, Lily's heart threatened to burst from her chest. Despite the chilly wind, she felt the heat rise within her and her cheeks burned. She shivered and at Stan's glance she murmured, 'It's rather cold today.' She knew Stan had witnessed the look that had passed between Davy and herself, and his knowing smile confirmed it. However, he said nothing as the carriage rumbled over the cobblestones back to the shop.

Lily slept fitfully that night. Her dreams were full of Davy Hurst and their wedding, only to be ruined by the appearance of Seb Ryder who shouted to all of the incident in the dining room of Ryder House. She woke in a sweat despite the coldness of her room. Slowly she calmed as she realised it had all been a dream. She rose, washed and dressed knowing the uneasy feeling from the dream would hang over her all day.

It was mid-morning when Davy Hurst came into the shop with a big box of fresh vegetables. Placing it on the desk in front of Jenny, he said, 'By way of thanks.' Picking up the posy laying on the top of the box, he glanced around. 'Is Miss Rae not here?'

Jenny thanked him for the gift and yelled out, 'Lily!'

The door opened and her friend glided into the room.

'Mr Hurst!' Lily said, quite taken aback.

'These are for you with my thanks,' he said, stepping towards her and holding out the posy.

'Oh! Thank you, but there was no need,' Lily began as she blushed.

'Yes there was, I wanted to say you all did a sterling job yesterday.' His cap now in his hand, Davy shuffled from foot to foot. 'I was wondering, should the weather permit, if you would take a walk out with me tomorrow. I presume you don't work on Sundays?'

'Oh erm . . .' Lily glanced at a grinning Jenny and then returned her eyes to Davy's. 'That would be very nice, if you're sure you feel up to it.'

Grinning like a Cheshire cat, Davy said, 'The funeral is over now, Miss Rae, and life goes on. Where should I come to collect you?'

'Let's meet in the park by the bandstand.'

'Righto, say around ten in the morning?' Davy asked.

'Ten will be fine,' Lily nodded.

Saying his goodbyes, Davy Hurst left the shop.

A moment later Jenny burst out laughing. 'I never thought to see the day you would be stepping out.'

'Nor did I!' Lily laughed back.

Lily woke early the following morning and excitedly searched her wardrobe for just the right outfit. Something warm but smart – she settled for a cream high-neck blouse and brown serge suit. A drawstring bag and an umbrella lay on the bed as she looked for a hat. The brown felt one she chose sported a flower and small feather. Pleased with her efforts, she made her way to breakfast.

Sitting with Rose at the table, the two chatted quietly. 'Shouldn't you have a chaperone?' Rose asked.

'In this day and age? It's not the Middle Ages, Rose,' Lily laughed.

'I suppose – just be careful,' Rose warned.

'What could possibly happen in the park?' Lily smiled but took her friend's warning to heart as she stood to leave.

Walking towards the bandstand, Lily saw Davy Hurst pacing back and forth. She smiled inwardly; he was obviously eager to meet her again. She saw him wave to her as he spotted her and he ran to greet her.

'I thought you weren't coming,' he laughed.

Lily grinned back as the church clock began to strike the hour.

They strolled the pathway that ran through the park, greeting other people doing the same. The rain held off and the wind held a cold dampness which made Lily shiver.

Seeing this, Davy said, 'Let's go to the tea shop, it will be warmer there.'

Lily agreed and they hurried from the park. Over tea and cakes the young couple chatted the hours away, until eventually Lily stood to leave.

'I'll walk you home,' Davy said as they walked back through the park.

'There's no need, really.'

'I insist! It's not safe for a woman to walk alone. You could be whisked away by – pirates – never to be seen again!' Davy said, dramatically drawing an imaginary sword.

'Pirates? In Wednesbury?' Lily laughed loudly as they walked back to the boarding house in Church Street.

At the front door Davy took Lily's gloved hand. 'May I see you again, Miss Rae? Please say yes, for if you refuse I will die of grief!' His other hand covered his heart and he dropped his head.

'I agree, Mr Hurst. I can't have you dropping dead on the doorstep now, can I?' Lily laughed at the melodrama.

They agreed to meet the following Sunday. Davy said they would take a carriage ride around the town and lunch out at a nice hotel. Seeing her safely indoors, Davy walked away with a smile stretching across his face.

Later, over tea with Emily Johnston, Lily was brimming with happiness at having had such a lovely day.

'He's such a nice man,' she gushed.

'I'm so glad. This could be the start of a whole new chapter of your life. Live it well, Lily, and enjoy every moment,' Emily said.

'I will,' Lily grinned, 'I will indeed.'

CHAPTER 20

As he stepped out of the tavern Seb Ryder had seen Lily walking briskly towards the park and had followed discreetly behind her. He watched a man run to meet her before they strolled away laughing together. His eyes passed the information to his brain, which reeled in surprise – Lily had found herself a man.

He had dragged himself around all day as he followed at a safe enough distance not to be noticed, until at last they had stopped in Church Street. So this was where Lily was living, not that the knowledge would do him any good now.

Seb walked back to his lodgings, which was also his place of work. He stepped over the horse manure in the road absent-mindedly, his thoughts swirling around Lily and her male friend. His hands in his trouser pockets, he dragged his feet along the tramway. He automatically stepped to the side as his mind registered the sound of the tram headed towards him. He didn't see it stop, or the people alighting; his eyes were fixed firmly on the ground as he trudged along.

He was very surprised to see Lily walking out

with a man, but then what did he expect? Had he thought she would never have a beau? Had he expected her to live a life alone? Shaking his head at his own stupidity, he lumbered on into Russell Street. He kicked a stone in frustration, which flew across the road. Why did Lily Rae still haunt him after all this time? What was it about her that trapped his heart in a web of desire?

Sighing loudly, he stomped into the Market Tavern, letting the door bang shut behind him. It was his day off from his work as barman so he went straight to his room.

Sitting alone on his bed, he wondered if he should call on Lily now he knew where she lived. No, she would most likely call in the Bobbies. He didn't want to be hauled off to jail for harassment.

He had to face facts, he was losing any hope of having her. Lily would not give him the dirt from under her fingernails, let alone anything else.

Lying back on the bed, he threw his arm over his eyes. Lily was playing a dangerous game in allowing herself to be courted. She was no longer pure – he had seen to that. He smiled to himself. What would happen when her relationship developed and this man discovered her secret? Lily would find herself alone again and possibly disgraced if that secret were shared. Poor Lily, life really was being wicked to her. He smiled again and he eventually fell asleep with Lily on his mind.

★   ★   ★

Time marched on and winter began to push autumn aside. The trees stood bare of their leaves and the migratory birds had already set off on their long journey to warmer climes. Animals settled to their hibernation and only the odd robin put in an appearance. People shivered as the temperature began to fall lower with each passing day. Cab drivers pulled out their knee blankets and overcoats were donned by those lucky enough to possess one. Others, less fortunate, scurried through the streets in an effort to keep warm. The price of coal shot up and more and more women took to scavenging the slag heaps looking for tiny coal nuggets to burn. The winter would see coal prized higher than gold.

Lily, wrapped in her long woollen coat and shawl draped over her head and tied at the nape of her neck, strolled along with Davy Hurst. Her boots tapped out a steady rhythm on the cobblestones as they walked towards the park once more. She shivered as a cold wind blew and Davy said, 'It's becoming too cold to walk out, Lily.'

'Well we can't sit in the tea rooms all day,' she answered.

'We need to do something if we intend to go on seeing each other,' Davy sighed.

'I agree, but exactly what escapes me,' Lily said as they strode through the gates and she steered him towards the bandstand.

'We could just get married,' Davy said simply.

Lily stopped in her tracks, shock rooting her to

the spot. Turning to face him, she said, 'Davy, we have only known each other for a very short time . . .'

'I know, but I love you, Lily! I love you with all my heart. Please say you will marry me – or at least consider it.' Davy's face held an anguish which melted her heart.

'I need time to think about it,' she said, a blush rising to her cheeks. She still hadn't told him about Seb and the thought continued to worry her.

Over time, Lily had fallen deeply in love with Davy, something she thought would never happen to her. She counted her blessings that he felt the same way about her and knew if she agreed to his proposal, they would have a very happy life together.

Davy suddenly danced around, his delight blatantly evident. As Lily took a seat in the bandstand he stood at its heart. Raising his arms high, he yelled at the top of his voice, 'Please God let Lily say yes! I want her to agree to become my wife!'

Lily heard the laughter coming from people walking in the park, before she dragged Davy away. 'Come on, Davy, it's too cold to be here today.'

That evening as she sat in the warm sitting room with Rose and Emily Johnston, Lily shared her news. Rose immediately began to discuss plans.

'I haven't said yes yet!' Lily announced.

'I realise that, but you will – won't you?' Rose laughed.

'Maybe. It's a lot to think about, Rose. I need

time to make my mind up, after all it's a major decision.'

Rose gave her a hug and sauntered off to her bed, leaving Lily alone with Emily. 'Do you think it would be the right thing to accept Davy's proposal?' she asked at last.

'More to the point, do you think it would be?' Emily raised her eyebrows, waiting for the answer.

'I do love him, I think I did from the first time we met. I am worried though.' Lily sighed heavily.

'I understand, but as I said before there are things he doesn't need to know.' Emily patted Lily's hand comfortingly.

'It would also mean leaving you.' Lily felt the sadness creep over her.

'True, but you could always visit. You know you would always be welcome here.' Emily felt the tug of her heartstrings.

'Thank you, Emily, you've been like a mother to me.'

'I will always be here for you no matter what,' Emily responded as a tear formed.

'Oh just look at us! Thinking about a wedding is supposed to be a happy time and here we are both crying!' Lily sniffed.

'Tears of joy if you accept the proposal. Jenny and her family will be so excited for you if you do.'

'I know just what she'll say,' Lily said rolling her eyes.

'What?' Emily asked.

'She'll say, *I bloody knew it!*' Both women fell

about laughing at Lily's impersonation of Jenny's speech.

Emotions once more under control, Emily asked in all earnest. 'So will you accept Davy's proposal?'

'Yes. I like the idea of spending the rest of my life with him.' Lily smiled and pushed the thoughts of intimacy out of her mind.

The following day Lily made an early morning visit to Hurst's Grocery store.

'This is a lovely surprise,' Davy said as he caught sight of her.

'I've come to say yes!' Lily breathed.

Davy's grin threatened to split his face. 'I love you,' he whispered.

Lily grinned and saying 'I love you' back to him shyly she swirled in a turn and left the store.

Everyone at Webb's was delighted at Lily's news and Jenny, true to form, said exactly what Lily knew she would.

When the shop closed for the evening, Albert brought the trap round and lifted Jenny up onto the driving seat. He stowed her wheelchair on the back and climbed aboard. Lily squashed herself in beside Jenny; she was going to visit the Pickard family before going home.

Vera made her welcome as usual with hot tea and plenty of gossip. 'Two weddings then,' she said, 'our Jenny plumped for the warmer weather – what about you?'

'Sometime in the summer, I expect,' Lily answered.

'Who's gonna give you away then?' Vera asked.

'Oh Vera, I've only just decided there will be a wedding, there's plenty of time to decide.' In truth Lily had not thought yet of the details. Then added, 'Maybe Stan would do me the honour.'

'Good idea, ask him tomorrow when you go into work,' Vera agreed.

Lily laughed as all the family began to list all the things she needed to organise.

As she walked home later she pondered the list again. There was indeed a lot to think about, maybe Emily Johnston could help out.

Lily smiled to herself as she braved the oncoming cold on her way home.

The weather turned colder and the first snow flurries fell silently overnight. People woke to see a cold whiteness that coated the streets.

Lily was correct in her assumption that Webb's would be busy at this time of year, but she had not foreseen the influenza breakout that would ravage the town. The elderly succumbed as did the new-borns as the terrible illness took its toll.

Stan had had a new telephone installed and an advertisement placed in the newspaper informing people of their number. The town crier also included this snippet of news, for those unable to read, as he trudged the snowy streets.

Lily's sadness grew as more tiny white coffins were ordered. It was a shame that young babies were dying even before they'd had a chance of life. She headed cortèges for the old and yet others for the young; their wailing mothers following behind, held up by their husbands and older children. The doctors were run ragged and were dropping with exhaustion as the flu ran its course. Few families had escaped unscathed and in a matter of weeks the population appeared to have been culled drastically.

Lily had received a tiny diamond engagement ring from Davy as her Christmas gift and she had presented him with a pocket watch. However, with Webb's working overtime she had little time to enjoy it.

The New Year of 1902 brought with it yet another cold snap which, it was felt, was what had finally killed off the influenza germs. At last work began to slow and Lily managed to find time to spend with Davy. She had agreed to marry him and now it was time to get to know the man she loved to distraction.

One bitterly cold Sunday morning Lily decided it was an opportune moment to see Davy's house in Trouse Lane, after all she would be living there in a few months' time.

Climbing into a cab, Davy wrapped a blanket over her knees, saying, 'The house belonged to my uncle and I thought it would be nice to move in together after the wedding.'

'Oh, I thought you already lived there . . .' Lily began.

'I have remained in my little two-up two-down

in Earps Lane. I thought you may want to change things around or redecorate. You decide when you see it, my love.' Davy smiled and his chocolate drop eyes twinkled.

'You are so thoughtful, but I'm sure the house will be fine the way it is.' Lily returned his smile.

The cab stopped outside a big house on the corner of where Trouse Lane met Church Steps. Davy paid the cabbie before leading his wife-to-be inside. A large hall led to a kitchen and scullery at the end. A sitting room lay on the right and a parlour on the left. The stairs to three bedrooms branched off the sitting room; Lily thought it a strange design. Also the upstairs sported a bathroom which had been newly installed. Lily was ecstatic at the prospect of not having to go out into the yard to use the lavatory. The furniture was old but well maintained and perfectly serviceable.

'Change anything you want,' Davy said as he slipped an arm around her waist.

'No, Davy, it's perfect as it is,' Lily said as she moved out of his embrace.

'Lily, may I kiss you – properly I mean?' His eyes held a longing which touched her heart and she felt she could not deny him. She hesitated and he said, 'If you'd rather I didn't . . .'

Swallowing hard, she stepped towards him. Davy gently enfolded her in his arms and placed his lips on hers. The thrill that ran through her was like fire in her veins. Without realising, her arms reached up and snaked around his shoulders as her body leaned against his. With her eyes closed, she savoured the feel of his muscular torso as he held her close to him. She had no idea it could be like this; the gentleness rather than force with which he held her made her shiver.

Davy slowly withdrew his lips and saw Lily standing with her eyes still closed. She had enjoyed that kiss every bit as much as he had.

'Lily Rae,' he whispered, 'I love you so much.'

Opening her eyes slowly, she smiled, 'I love you too, Davy Hurst.'

His wide grin showed even white teeth as he picked her up and swung her around. 'Come, let's go to the tea house, we have plans to make.'

They spent the afternoon chatting excitedly about their forthcoming wedding.

Later that evening Lily asked Emily Johnston for a moment of her time. Ensconced in Lily's bedroom, she said, 'I'm afraid, Emily, what if I can't . . . you know, when I'm married!'

'Oh, my dear girl, you don't need to worry. Tell Davy to be gentle with you, tell him you are scared, he will understand,' the older woman said.

'But what if it's like . . .' Lily's tears formed as she spoke.

'It won't be. From what you tell me, Davy is kind and caring. It's my guess he won't force you to do anything you don't want to. When the time comes you have to relax and enjoy your new husband. All thoughts of the past must be pushed aside – forgotten. You cannot carry Seb Ryder with you into your life with Davy, it will only hold you back and spoil everything. This relationship is between you and Davy – there is no room for Seb Ryder. You have banished him from your life, now you must banish him from your mind.' Emily gave Lily a hug and added, 'Do that and you will have a happy life with Davy.'

'I know you're right and I know it will be hard, but I will do it. I want to make Davy happy. Thank you, Emily, once again you came to the rescue.' Lily dried her tears and managed a smile.

'That's my girl,' Emily said. 'Now, what about a wedding gown, have you decided yet?'

Lily shook her head, 'Will you come with me to choose one?'

Emily clasped her hands together and laughed, 'I'd be delighted!'

CHAPTER 21

As February rolled by, Vera Pickard had sewed her eldest daughter's wedding dress. She had saved every penny she could to buy the material, and by the dim yellow light of the gas lamp had painstakingly sewed it together when everyone else was in bed.

With the last stitch in place she hung it on a hanger hooked over the top of the living room door. Sitting in her chair by the fire, she gazed at her handiwork. Silent tears rolled down her face as she visualised Jenny wearing the pretty white dress.

Vera whispered into the silence, 'Oh my girl, I hope you know how lucky you are to have Albert. I never thought to see the day you'd be wed.'

Looking over to the sofa where Jenny was sleeping peacefully, Vera smiled. Then she glanced at the wheelchair pushed into the corner of the room. *Poor little bugger, having to go down the aisle in that contraption!*

Vera had no way of knowing at that moment that Jenny had no intentions of wheeling herself down the aisle, nor having anyone push her in the cumbersome chair. She had made up her mind to walk holding her father's arm and had spent every available minute practising with her wooden leg.

Drying her tears, Vera covered the dress with a big cotton bag she had fashioned from an old sheet then wearily climbed the stairs to bed.

In the meantime Albert Blenkinsop had hired some builders to widen the doorways in his house in Loxdale Street to accommodate Jenny's wheelchair. The stairs he could do nothing about; he would have to carry her up and down those. However, the kitchen, scullery and downstairs indoor bathroom would all now be accessible to her.

St John's Church had been booked for the ceremony and all would enjoy a knees-up afterwards at Vera's cramped house. The wedding was to take place in April.

Every morning Albert collected Jenny from home in the trap to journey to work together, and every evening he returned her in the same manner. With every day that passed, Albert was becoming more excited at the prospect of being married to Jenny Pickard.

Nothing was too much trouble for Albert where his wife-to-be was concerned, and everyone thought they fit together like hand in glove.

Jenny's spirits were high despite the cold weather and she never allowed her disability to get her down.

March arrived and with it came a weak sunshine. Cold winds still blew but gently and people welcomed the spring coming in like a lamb. As the days passed, new growth sprang up. Buds appeared and new leaves adorned the bare trees. Birds sang with gusto as the slush puddles dried up. People still wore their warm clothing but walked with heads held up as if searching for the warmth of the sun. Dirty-faced children spilled out onto the streets to play their games of 'tag' and 'hopscotch'. The noise from their laughter and squeals echoed through the streets and around the tightly packed houses. The sound of out-of-work fathers banging old pram wheels onto makeshift go-carts for their offspring rang out loudly. Mother's voices could be heard yelling for their kids to go and play outside; there was spring-cleaning to be done. The better weather had brought a new energy to the small industrial town and everyone was making the most of it.

All preparations were in place for Jenny's wedding and at last the day had arrived. Her father, John, had taken the day off from his work at the last working colliery and had scrubbed himself clean in the tin bath in the kitchen. Dressed in his best clothes, he tied the wheelchair to the back of the waiting cab.

Vera was helping Jenny into her wedding gown of white damask, her veil held on by a small coronet of white roses. Giving her daughter a hug,

Vera rallied the rest of the family and set off for St John's Church.

Jenny was struggling with her wooden leg when her father came in to collect her.

'What you doin', girl?' he asked.

'Dad, I'm going to walk down the aisle with you, if I can ever get this bloody leg on!'

John Pickard looked at his brave young daughter as she tried to fasten the leather straps on the leg. With tears in his eyes he knelt to help.

'I'm so very proud of you, my little love, and I pray you and Albert have a happy life together like your mum and me,' he whispered.

'Thanks, Dad, but we won't if I don't get this sodding leg on!'

Father and daughter burst out laughing as together they finally managed to strap the false leg in place. Helping her to stand, John then whisked her into his arms and carried her out to the cab.

Slowly the cab trundled over the cobblestone roads dragging the wheelchair behind it. The horse's mane and tail had been plaited with white ribbon and people waved as the cab passed by.

When they arrived at the church, everyone was inside waiting. John unfastened the wheelchair and ran with it up the gravel path where he parked it just inside the church door. Then he ran back to Jenny who was waiting patiently. Lifting her down and as she held onto him, he puffed, 'I'm getting too old for all this!'

Jenny laughed as he picked her up. Nodding to the cabbie, John carried his daughter to the church door and set her on her feet.

'You sure you can do this?' he asked.

'Yes, but I'll have to lean on you quite a bit,' she returned.

'Right then, let's do it,' John said as the organ struck up with the wedding march.

Jenny limped her way down the aisle to the gasps of the guests standing in the pews. Spontaneous applause broke out as she made it to Albert who stood open-mouthed.

John gave Albert a tear-filled smile before he stepped back. Jenny leaned against her intended for support. Vera's sobbing could be heard as the applause died down and the service began.

Throughout the ceremony Jenny pushed away the pain of her stump resting in the cup of the wooden leg, but by the time she became Mrs Blenkinsop her face had paled and she felt exhausted.

'I now pronounce you man and wife,' the vicar droned on and it was then that Albert caught Jenny as she finally collapsed.

Carrying her down the aisle to the waiting cab, they drove back to Vera's house.

With her leg stowed in the corner, Jenny sat in her wheelchair with a cup of hot sweet tea. Lily sat on the sofa next to her as Davy helped Vera with setting out the food in the kitchen.

'Jenny, you were so brave today, you took everyone by surprise!' Lily gushed.

'That was the idea, but Hell's teeth it d'ain't half hurt!'

'How does it feel being a married woman?' Lily asked with a smile.

'It don't feel no different yet, but when we go to our own house later I expect it will. Anyway, you'll know yourself before too long.' Jenny nodded to Davy who brought them both plates of food.

'Lily, for you,' he said, handing her a plate, 'Mrs Blenkinsop, for you,' giving the other plate to Jenny.

'Oooh that sound nice although it will take some getting used to,' Jenny laughed.

The day wore on with guests eating their fill. The beer flowed and singing and dancing spilled out into the back yard. Eventually everyone stood in the street to wave off the happy couple on the trap, the wheelchair tied securely to the back.

Lily and Davy sauntered back to Mrs Johnston's boarding house discussing the day's events and how well everything had gone.

Kissing Lily goodnight on the doorstep, Davy stuck his hands in his trouser pockets and wandered off home, whistling as he went, his thoughts centred around the next wedding being theirs.

CHAPTER 22

Reading the newspaper, Seb Ryder felt his smile return. He read of the forthcoming marriage of the eminent Mr David Hurst of Hurst's Grocery to Miss Lily Rae who worked at Webb's Funeral Directors.

All he knew was, he would not concede.

With a smile he whispered, 'Oh Lily, are you sure you want to do this?'

Knowing his question into the quiet of his lonely room would do no good, Seb wondered what to do next. In truth there was nothing to be done. Lily was set to marry and that was all there was to it. No, he would not give up so easily.

Snatching up the newspaper, he read it again. The wedding was set for 2 p.m. on 1st May at St Bartholomew's Church. Should he go? He could sneak in and hide at the back of the church. No, he wouldn't lower himself, he was better than that.

The newspaper slipped from his fingers as he conjured a picture of a smiling Lily in his mind. Drawing a breath, Seb nodded silently. There would be time enough to carry out his task, even if she was married.

With a grin he washed and changed his clothes, then went downstairs to the bar to begin work.

The young girl taken on as the new cleaner in the Market Tavern had taken quite a fancy to the dark-eyed barman and strove constantly to catch his eye. Tilley Green pushed the wisps of sandy-coloured hair off her face in what she thought was a provocative manner. Her ice blue eyes cast a glance at Seb Ryder as he cleaned the glasses behind the bar. Leaning on her sweeping besom, she stared at the handsome young man who always appeared to have an air of sadness surrounding him.

Feeling eyes burning into him, Seb looked up at the pale complexion of the girl watching him. 'What?' he asked.

'Why am you always so sad?' Tilley asked, strolling towards him.

'None of your business!' Seb snapped.

'I was only asking,' Tilley said dejectedly.

'Well don't!' Seb said as he went back to his task.

Undeterred, Tilley went on, 'What you need is a good woman to look after you.'

'And that would be you would it?' he asked with a sneer.

'You could do worse,' Tilley smiled.

'I doubt it!' Seb whispered under his breath.

'Well I'm here if you change your mind,' Tilley grinned before continuing to sweep the sawdust into a pile.

Seb watched her for a moment. Tilley was a nice enough girl, always ready to lend a helping hand in the kitchen after her cleaning was done. She was nothing to look at but beneath her raggy clothes she had a fairly decent figure. She had little education but she was honest, forthright and loyal to her employer.

Shaking his head, Seb resumed his work. Suddenly he heard the most beautiful singing and as he turned he saw it was Tilley. He listened in amazement until she had finished.

'You have a lovely voice, Tilley, you should be on the stage,' he said.

'Ar, sweeping it probably,' she laughed.

'No, really you should try at the music hall, they're always looking for new talent,' Seb encouraged.

'Mebbes, but I'm happy enough here,' Tilley cast a glance around the bar room.

'You ever been to the music hall, the one just off Dudley Street?'

'No,' Tilley sidled up to the bar. She was thrilled to be having a conversation with this young man at last that didn't involve insults and snapped comments.

'You should go,' Seb said as he polished a glass with a teacloth.

'Oh ar, and who would I go with? I live with me old mother who can't get out no more. Besides, it costs and I can't afford it.'

'It's a shame, I'm sure if they heard you sing they'd give you a job.' Seb shook his head.

'I got a job, a good one!' Tilley said proudly.

'Cleaning a Tavern? You could be a famous singer one day if you applied yourself.' Seb snatched up another glass to polish.

Picking up the besom, Tilley waltzed around the room singing, *'Hello, hello, who's your lady friend?'*

Seb was stunned at the beauty of the sound coming from such a plain-looking girl. He jumped at the screech that came from the back room.

'Tilley Green! Shut that caterwauling and get your arse into the kitchen!'

With eyebrows raised Tilley whispered, 'His master's voice.' With a girlie giggle she ran lightly from the room.

Continuing his glass cleaning, Seb's mind worked on the idea that had come to him while he listened to Tilley sing. If he could get her to the little hall, she might be taken on and he could be her manager. Maybe, if it all worked out, they could travel the country and he would be making more money than he was at present. However, that was thinking ahead, firstly he had to get her to sing on the stage of the makeshift music hall.

Wednesbury sported a small theatre, the larger one was in Birmingham but an enterprising man, known by the name of Honest John, had bought the run-down building just off Dudley Street. He'd had the wooden benches and the cheap stage renovated, the back wall of which had been painted with a woodland scene. An old piano stood in front of the stage and he hired a young pianist who knew all the popular songs of the day.

Honest John scoured the surrounding towns for any likely acts that he could use to draw in custom. There were singers, dancers, comedians, jugglers and comedy songsters, and he was always on the lookout for more.

The Theatre Royal drew in people from all over and, at a penny, entrance fee was affordable for a lot of folk. Every night it was packed to capacity, with some standing at the back.

Seb mulled this over and decided to ask Tilley to accompany him on his next day off.

The following morning, with trust in the Lord and one foot forward, Seb asked Tilley to join him at the music hall on Saturday night. Tilley accepted gladly, thrilled to have been asked out by this handsome man, and so the date was set.

Tilley had slept with her hair tied in rags. She was excited it was the day she would be out on the town with Seb Ryder. Leaving the hair rags in place, she cleaned the bar before she returned home to see to her aging mother. As the day wore on she became more and more excited. Not only did she have a date, but she was going to the music hall for the first time in her life.

She packed her small basket with chunks of fresh bread and wedges of cheese. Two bottles of pale ale she stood in the basket too, covering all with a clean tea towel.

Pulling out her Sunday best clothes, she smiled. She was going to have the best time of her life and wanted to look the part. Once dressed, she stared into the cracked mirror in her bedroom. She had no money for make-up so she pinched her cheeks in an effort to show a rosy glow. Taking out the rags she carefully styled the long sandy ringlets. She was ready.

Picking up her basket, she set off to meet Seb at the Market Tavern.

As they strolled along, Tilley's excitement grew.

'I have the tickets,' Seb said, patting his jacket pocket, 'we're on the front row.'

Tilley beamed and in the dim light of the street gas lamp Seb thought she almost looked pretty.

Settling themselves on the bench, Tilley gazed around her. The place was filling up quickly and the noise of chatting and laughing was deafening.

Suddenly the piano struck up and silence descended. The show was about to start.

Honest John strode out onto the stage to rapturous applause. 'Good evening one and all,' he yelled.

As one the audience replied, 'Good evening!'

'For your delectation this evening . . .'

The audience let out an 'oooh!'

'Let me present our own, our very own, Bertie Pickles!' Honest John left the stage as applause and whistles echoed around the room.

Tilley screamed laughing at Bertie Pickles' ribald jokes as did the rest of the people there. She watched in awe as the high-kicking dancers ended their spot with the splits. She enjoyed the jugglers, amazed at their skill, and when a woman came on to sing, Tilley was transported to another world.

They had consumed their picnic, but Tilley couldn't remember eating it. She was totally transfixed on the stage and its occupants.

All evening Seb had watched her out of the corner of his eye; she had taken the bait. Tilley Green had fallen in love with the music hall.

The piano began to play the last song of the evening and the whole crowd joined in, but it was Tilley's voice that was heard above them all. Without her realising, the audience slowly quietened to listen to her. Tilley was lost in her own little world as she sang out, *'If you were the only girl in the world . . .'*

At the finish the audience, silent up to that point, erupted. Clapping, whistling and foot stomping showed their appreciation as Honest John stepped forward to Tilley. Bidding her stand, he led her up onto the stage.

Looking at all the smiling faces, she grinned from ear to ear. Honest John spoke into her ear and she nodded and spoke back. Then he spoke to the pianist who also nodded.

Holding up his hands, he called for quiet. 'This young lady is Tilley Green, and she has kindly consented to sing one last song for us all.'

The audience went wild with enthusiasm at the unexpected addition to the programme.

The piano tinkled the introduction and Tilley

began her rendition of 'I don't want to play in your yard'.

There was absolute silence as Tilley strolled the boards playing to the crowd; she was a natural born entertainer. Handkerchiefs were pulled out and sniffs were heard. Tilley finished with a curtsy, her hand on her chest.

The audience were on their feet shouting for more and Tilley basked in their appreciation.

Honest John led her back to her seat as the folk continued to applaud. Seb patted her arm as she sat down beside him.

Seb and Honest John exchanged a few words as people began to leave the hall. Tilley stood to leave but Seb motioned for her to wait.

When at last the place was empty, Honest John joined them on the bench and conversation began.

He wanted Tilley as his main attraction and was willing to pay well for her. She listened as Seb explained he was her manager and all discussions should go through him. He said he would discuss the offer made with Tilley and let the man know their decision the following day. Shaking hands, they parted company.

Tilley floated along, oblivious to anything around her, she was happier than she'd ever been.

'Are you listening to me?' Seb asked.

Tilley nodded.

'Right, how much do you earn at the Tavern?'

'Sixpence a week,' Tilley said in a sing-song voice.

'Sixpence! Tilley, Honest John was offering three

shillings a week for you to sing there every night!' Seb grabbed her arm to stop her dancing around in the street. 'He might even go a bit higher if I push him!'

'Look, I've got a good job at the Tavern, they've been good to me there. Besides, I got me mother at home to see to.'

'Just think how much better you can look after her with an extra shilling a week in your pocket!' Seb was becoming exasperated. He only earned a shilling a week himself and the extra would come in useful. He pressed her further. 'You haven't been in the job that long, you don't owe them anything other than a thank you and goodbye!'

Tilley was shocked. 'They took me on when nobody else would!'

Seeing he'd upset her, he spoke more gently. 'All right, well look at it this way. Which do you enjoy the most – cleaning or singing?'

'Singing,' she said thoughtfully.

Seb saw his chance. 'Well then, you could be doing something you love, being paid well for it and – I'll be with you to sort it all out money-wise.'

'You'd come with me?' she said, her eyes lighting up.

'Yes! You'll need my management skills when you're rich and famous!' Seb now knew he had her.

'Well,' Tilley drew the word out, 'if you think it's a good idea . . .'

'I do!' Seb said as he picked her up and swung her round.

'Oooer . . . put me down!' Tilley said, all the time hoping he'd ignore her.

Placing her on her feet, Seb said, 'I'll go tomorrow and arrange with Honest John. Once that's done, we can both quit the Tavern.'

'All right, but where you gonna live?' Tilley asked all innocently.

'Oh I didn't think of that!' Seb rubbed his chin. 'I don't suppose your mother would take in a lodger?' he joked.

'I can ask,' Tilley said.

Seb couldn't believe the girl's naivety but then again he would need somewhere to stay, and surely the old woman wouldn't be long for this world.

The two walked along chatting about the bright new future that lay ahead for them both.

CHAPTER 23

Emily helped an excited Lily into her wedding outfit. She had chosen a cream silk suit, the fitted jacked topped a long skirt which held pleats at the back. Small cream shoes peeped from beneath the hemline. A cartwheel hat held a large cream rose at the front. Her teardrop bouquet was made up of fresh cream roses.

'Oh Lily, you look gorgeous!' Emily gushed.

With a wide grin Lily nodded her satisfaction and together the women went outside to the waiting cabs. Emily, dressed in pale blue, climbed into one cab which set off for the church.

Stan opened the door of the other cab, holding out his hand to Lily. He had kindly agreed to give her away as she had no father to perform this important duty.

Arriving at the church, she heard the organ music begin and with her arm hooked through Stan's they walked down the aisle.

The service started and a door slammed in the quiet of the church. A latecomer.

The vicar droned on as Lily and Davy only had eyes for each other. 'Should any man here know of any reason why these two should not be joined in matrimony . . .'

There was complete silence whilst the vicar's eyes searched the congregation. As the clergyman looked back at the couple standing before him a voice sounded out, 'I do!'

Lily's head shot round and the colour drained from her face. Footsteps echoed as Seb Ryder strode forward. Her dream of this man disrupting her wedding came flooding back to her and she gasped for air. She felt the colour drain from her face and her heart hammered in her chest. *Please God don't let him do this!*

Her eyes bore into Seb as he stood boldly in front of her and she heard the gasps and mutters from the people filling the pews.

The vicar blustered, 'What is the meaning of this, young man?'

'You can't marry this couple vicar because – she has a secret . . .'

'I'm afraid that is not a good enough reason to stop this wedding! Whatever are you thinking?' the vicar admonished as he cut across Seb's words.

Davy was aghast as he looked from Lily to the young man and back again.

Lily's breath was held tight in her throat as she stared at Seb Ryder. Then she rasped, 'I've warned you before to leave me alone!'

'Lily, you shouldn't do this! You know you shouldn't and you know why.' Ryder's eyebrow shot up.

Lily's breath came out in a contemptible rush. 'How dare you! Get out of this church right now!' She was shaking from head to foot as the congregation's mutterings increased in volume.

Davy muttered, 'Lily, what's going on? Who is this man?'

Seb yelled, 'Does he know, Lily?'

Panic hit the young woman like a sledge hammer. Was Seb going to reveal the terrible secret she'd held fast for so long? Her breath came in gasps as she tried to find a solution. *Oh God! Please don't let him do this! Please don't let this man steal my happiness again!*

From the corner of her eye she saw Emily turn in her pew to speak to Stan.

Lily's hands clenched at her sides in anger and fear and she felt Davy's eyes glaring at her. All eyes turned to Emily as she stepped into the aisle followed by Stan and Albert.

'Get him out of here!' Emily commanded.

'Lily! Have you told him?' Seb asked, a nasty grin spreading across his face. Stan and Albert caught his arms in order to escort him from the church.

'Why can't you leave me alone?' Lily said in hardly more than a whisper.

'You know why!' Seb whispered back.

Lily became aware of the stirrings in the congregation as the mutterings began once more.

Seb struggled against the two men holding him back. 'Get off me! Lily, hear me out. Please just listen to what I have to say! Lily . . . Lily!'

Seb Ryder was dragged to the back of the church and thrown unceremoniously through the doors. The bolts were slid into place before Stan and Albert resumed their places in the pews, to the accompaniment of congregation applause.

Turning away, Lily could feel Davy's eyes on her as the fear in her built. Would he call the wedding off there and then? Tears pricked the back of her eyes as she looked at him.

Davy's eyes held questions and, she thought, hurt. How on earth was she going to explain this? Would she be forced now to reveal the truth of her past? Lily trembled, knowing whatever happened, she didn't want Davy to ever know of the incident which took place at Ryder House.

She bit her lower lip as she watched Davy turn back towards the vicar and she held her breath.

'Please proceed,' he said quietly.

Lily heaved a great sigh of relief.

'Erm . . . yes well . . .' The vicar did as he was bid. Mutterings ran round the congregation again and the vicar called for quiet before he continued.

Lily's heart pounded and she was feeling a little faint. Her wedding day had been ruined by that despicable man. Now she would have to find an explanation.

At the close of the service, she looked up into Davy's eyes. Was that mistrust and question she could see still written all over his face? The warm kiss she had expected became a quick peck on her lips. Close to tears, she walked back down the aisle with her new husband, trying her best to force a smile.

The doors were unlocked and opened for the newly-wed couple to walk outside. Lily's eyes searched the grounds for Seb Ryder, but he was nowhere to be seen.

Inside the carriage taking them to the hotel booked for the reception, Davy whispered, 'Well Lily . . .?'

With a deep breath and a prayer of forgiveness, Lily told her half-lie. 'He was the master's son when I worked in service. I left there because he was constantly pestering me. I thought he'd given up, but evidently he has not!'

The only part of her explanation to be untrue was that he was constantly pestering her whilst she was at Ryder House.

'I see.' Davy turned away from her to look out onto the landscape as the cab trundled along.

Lily was crestfallen. Was it that Davy did not believe her explanation? Did he think that she had previously had a liaison with Seb Ryder? Davy gave her no clues as they neared the hotel for their wedding reception. Obviously he was mulling it over in his mind. Not wanting to make the situation any worse, Lily chose to keep quiet and wait for him to speak first.

Then suddenly he turned to her and said, 'I'm so sorry that dreadful man spoiled your day.'

Looking into his eyes, she saw the mistrust had disappeared and the love shone forth once more.

Davy kissed her lovingly and she relaxed in his arms. He had accepted her explanation after all. She thanked God that Ryder had not spoken the reason she feared he might.

After a couple of days, Lily visited her friend.

'Thank you, Emily, for what you did in the church. I was petrified Ryder would divulge . . .'

'I know, sweetheart, that's why I had Stan and Albert throw him out as quickly as possible. It was a close thing though.' Emily smiled kindly.

'It certainly was. I told Davy he had pestered me at work when I was their maid and I took it upon myself to leave.' Lily's face was sad at having to lie to her new husband.

'And how did he take it?' Emily asked.

'He believed me.'

'Good. Now you can settle down to being Mrs Lily Hurst,' Emily said.

The two women shared a loving hug as Lily stood to leave.

'Lily, I love you like you are my own and I'll not let anyone hurt you if it's in my power to prevent it.' Emily's eyes held glistening tears.

'I would have loved having you as my mum,' Lily returned as a tear escaped the corner of her eye.

'Be off with you now and say hello to Davy for me.' Emily smiled.

After Lily had gone, Emily sat thinking. It was time someone had a word in Seb Ryder's ear.

★　　★　　★

Lily settled down to being a good wife. She continued to work at Webb's although Davy had at first tried to dissuade her from working at all. She was determined she could work and see to the house without one having a detrimental effect on the other.

Time slipped by and the summer heat was heavy and cloying. Wearing black all day did nothing to alleviate Lily's discomfort but she continued to maintain the professionalism called for by her role as conductor at funerals.

Then one morning Lily felt queasy as she rose for work. Suddenly realising her monthlies had stopped, she decided to visit the doctor before going into work.

Sure enough, the doctor confirmed she was pregnant. Lily was beside herself with joy and couldn't wait to tell Davy that evening. All day she tried to suppress her excitement. Although bursting to tell Jenny and the others, she wanted Davy to be the first to know, after all it was his child.

Davy was just as excited about the addition to the family and instantly began turning the spare bedroom into a nursery.

'You'll have to give up work now, Lily,' he said one evening as they sat in the living room.

'No, not yet. Besides, I can always return after the baby is born.'

'Who will look after the baby then?' Davy was horrified by the idea.

'We could hire a nanny,' Lily answered in a no-nonsense way.

Albeit not happy with the idea, Davy kept his counsel.

As time wore on, Lily suffered and as her belly grew she had constant backache. Morning sickness prevailed throughout the day and she struggled to keep her food down. On the outside she looked radiant, her complexion was smooth and her hair shone. On the inside she felt dreadful. She was tired all the time and eventually she had to concede and quit her work. Sadness suffused with happiness had everyone in tears as Lily left Webb's on that last day.

Early one morning Lily visited Emily Johnston. Over tea in the living room Lily grumbled. 'I'm so fed up! I miss working so much, and I feel rotten all the time. I shall be glad when this little one is born.' She patted her belly affectionately.

'I'm sure,' said Emily distractedly.

'Is something wrong?'

Emily shook her head, 'Not wrong exactly.'

Lily frowned. Emily Johnston was being very mysterious. Seeing the question in Lily's eyes, Emily began to explain.

'After your wedding, I sought out Seb Ryder.'

'You did what!' Lily was aghast.

'I thought it about time for some straight talking. He's working as a barman at the Market Tavern. It seems his father left him penniless which was what drove his mother mad. He had to sell Ryder

House.' Emily halted and waited for Lily's barrage which she felt was imminent.

'Good! Serves him right! But, Emily, whatever made you do it? You should have left well alone!' Lily was irritable and felt, as much as she loved Emily, it was not her place to interfere.

'Yes well, we had a long talk and I told him straight. You are a married woman now and he must leave you alone. I said if he bothered you again I would have him hauled off to jail.'

'No more than he deserves,' Lily muttered.

'The poor boy is a complete mess . . .'

'*Poor boy!* That *poor boy*, as you call him, abused me against my will; he left me pregnant!' Lily yelled.

'Lily, calm down, it's not good for the baby you getting all excited like this.' Emily had never seen Lily so het up.

'I'm sorry, but the way that man behaved, then had the gall to spoil my wedding day!' Lily finally burst into tears.

'Oh dear, pregnancy doesn't suit you at all, does it?' Emily said, trying to placate the sobbing girl.

'So what did that *poor boy* have to say for himself?' Lily asked sarcastically as she sniffed into her handkerchief.

'He agreed, albeit reluctantly, to stay away from you. He realised his behaviour had been aberrant, and now he knows for certain you would never entertain the idea of even being in the same room as him. It has destroyed him, Lily, and I don't think he will ever recover.' Emily sighed as she shook her head.

'You know what, Emily? I don't care!' Lily said spitefully.

'Lily!' Emily was shocked.

'No, Emily, after what he did to me, I don't care what happens to him. I live in constant fear Davy will find out. What if Ryder gets drunk and seeks Davy out and tells him? What if he tells someone else and it gets back? Davy would never forgive me!' Lily's tears flowed again.

'I can understand your worry, Lily, but I really don't think that will happen. He's not drinking anymore and keeps himself to himself.' Emily tried to soothe her distressed friend.

'I hope you're right, Emily, because if he ruins my marriage to Davy, I will not be responsible for my actions!' Lily said vehemently.

As she walked home later, Lily's thoughts revolved around her conversation with Emily. The threat of her secret being revealed hung over her like a lead weight. She had to find a way of being certain it would never be divulged. Even as she thought it, she knew it to be impossible.

Lily was struggling her way through the summer heat and looked forward to autumn when she could finally enjoy the cooler weather. She visited Emily often and they chatted for hours. She also kept in touch with Vera, as well as seeing everyone at Webb's at least once a week. She missed her work dreadfully but she knew the baby and family life must come first.

Most days she walked in the park. She would be having her baby in the New Year and she knew it would be too cold to take walks then, so she revelled in nature's beauty while she could.

On the 9th of August, the newspapers were full of the coronation of King Edward VII and Lily realised some people had taken a day off work to celebrate. Most, however, were unable to afford such a luxury. They would have to work every day of their lives just to feed their families.

As she strolled back through the streets, she smiled at the bunting flapping in the wind. Long tables were set out and laden with food; music was being played and women were kicking up their heels in time with the beat. The people of Wednesbury were rejoicing in officially having a new king.

Life went on much the same for Lily throughout the autumn and she watched the birds and animals begin to prepare for the winter months. The people also were beginning to don warmer clothing.

When winter finally began its approach, Lily opted to stay by a roaring fire rather than walk out in the cold. She spent many hours knitting matinee coats and leggings, bonnets, mittens and booties for the baby. She began preparing for Christmas which would be on her in no time.

Lily was happier than she'd ever been in her

life as she stayed home more and more while the weather turned. She felt she was pretty much prepared as her birthing time drew ever nearer.

CHAPTER 24

As they moved into February Lily's pains began and panic gripped her. Davy was still at work in the grocery store and she didn't know what to do. She lay herself on the bed and tried to relax. There was nothing to be done until Davy came home. As she lay there she thought it was similar to the pain that came with her monthlies; it wasn't so bad.

Rising she began to undress and slip into her nightgown. Lying down again under the covers to keep warm, she ran over the preparations she'd made. Everything was ready. All she had to do now was wait for her husband who would fetch the doctor. Closing her eyes and keeping her breathing even, Lily began to doze. As another pain came she wondered why women made such a fuss. Closing her eyes again, she fell into a light sleep.

Davy woke her, asking why she was in bed.

'My pains started this afternoon but they seem to have gone now.' Lily smiled.

'I'll fetch the doctor!' Davy yelled as he dashed to the door.

'No, darling, it's not necessary, but if Emily can

spare some time I'd love to see her.' Lily grinned sheepishly.

'Right. Emily. I'll go now. Are you sure you'll be all right while I'm gone?' Davy fussed.

'Go, I'll be fine,' Lily said.

She heard the front door slam as a much sharper pain caught her. Holding her breath for a few seconds, she released it as she lay back on the pillows. Blowing through her teeth, she wondered how much worse it would get. Maybe she'd been a little hasty thinking childbirth would be a doddle.

Leaving the cooks in charge at the boarding house and the girls within, Emily climbed into the carriage with Davy.

'How often are her pains coming?' she asked.

'I don't know. I never asked, I just came straight to you!' Davy answered, panic lacing his words.

'Right well, when we get there, you fetch the doctor and I'll see to Lily.'

Davy called to the cab driver to hurry, his wife was having a baby. The horse's hooves clattered over the cobblestones and the occupants of the carriage were thrown around as it veered round a corner, seemingly on two wheels.

As they arrived, Emily dashed into the house and up the stairs, calling out to Lily. She heard a groan and found her young friend writhing about in bed.

'Oh Emily, thank goodness!' Lily gasped.

'It's all right, Davy's gone for the doctor. Now,

let's have a look at you,' Emily said as she took a quick look beneath the bedclothes. 'It will be a while yet, I'm afraid.'

Lily clenched her teeth as another contraction held her in its grip. As it subsided she panted, 'Please God let it be soon!'

'You may have a few more hours yet, Lily, so save your strength, you'll need it.' Emily fetched a bowl of water and a cloth to mop the girl's sweating brow.

'How do you know so much about all this?' Lily breathed, already feeling exhausted.

'There's a lot you don't know about me, Lily. I was once a midwife.' Emily smiled.

'Oh, I didn't know that,' Lily whispered.

'Yes, when my first husband left me, I went to nursing school to become a midwife. Unable to have children of my own, I wanted to help women to have theirs.'

Holding Lily's hand as more pains came and went, she continued, 'When Mr Johnston died, I gave up the midwifery to run the boarding house.'

'You've led such a varied life,' Lily said in hardly more than a whisper.

'So have you. Working in service, then the owner of the café, and to top all that you worked in a funeral parlour! You can't get more varied than that.'

Footsteps on the stairs told them Davy was back with the doctor in tow. Davy was sent to make tea as old Dr Pryce dropped his bag on the bed.

'Right, let the dog see the rabbit,' he said pushing Emily aside.

Lily let out a titter as Emily pulled a face.

After a quick examination the doctor said, 'It will be hours yet, why was I brought this early?'

Lily's cry heralded another contraction. Turning to the young woman in such pain, he snapped, 'Stop that noise! You're having a baby, not dying!'

Lily burst into tears; it was all too much for her.

Emily fronted up to Dr Pryce, saying, 'She's in pain! Have you experienced childbirth? No, of course not! So how on earth can you possibly know what it's like? Your bedside manner is appalling!'

Davy walked in with a tray just at that moment. Laying it on a table, he rushed to his sobbing wife.

'I don't have to listen to this! I'm leaving! You know where I am . . . nearer her time!' With that the doctor stormed out.

'Emily, what's going on?' Davy demanded.

'Don't worry, Davy, we don't need the likes of him. I can help Lily do this. You just keep the kettle boiling.' Emily soothed.

It was the early hours of the following morning when Lily screamed out in agony and brought her daughter into the world.

Eventually Davy was allowed into the bedroom. He had paced the landing hearing his wife scream and cry all night and he was almost as exhausted as she was.

Emily passed the baby to him, all swaddled and

quiet now, and he gazed down at her tiny face. Tears rolled down his cheeks as he gently touched the fine layer of dark hair. She snuffled and he smiled.

'She's perfect – just like her mother,' he whispered. 'What shall we name her?'

'Clara, after my mother,' Lily said as the baby was passed back to her.

Davy nodded his agreement. Turning to Emily, he said, 'Thank you, you have been wonderful.'

Emily just smiled. 'I'm going home, so I'll leave you both to enjoy Clara.'

She gave Lily a quick hug, kissed the baby's head and shook hands with Davy, then with a wave she was gone.

'Would mother like a cup of tea?' Davy asked with a grin as he placed the baby in Lily's arms.

'Yes please, Father,' Lily laughed.

Kissing her fondly, he swept from the room humming a little tune.

The following day Emily arrived bright and early with a large bottle of stout to build up Lily's strength. She packed Davy off to work, saying she would stay until he got home.

Lily's 'lying in' period was a week and she was told the baby's confinement should be a fortnight. The weather wasn't conducive for Clara to be out and about before that. Lily would be allowed to potter about after a couple of days, but to rest immediately she felt tired. Emily said she would come every day for the first week to ensure her instructions were carried out, after that Lily was on her own.

Clara was a golden child. She fed well, slept well and cried little. Lily felt blessed indeed.

The house was alive with visitors coming and going, Jenny and Albert being the first.

At last Lily was able to take Clara out for some fresh air, snuggled up in her new perambulator. Her first port of call was Webb's. As she pushed the pram along the street she revelled in the feeling it gave her at being a new mother. She also wondered if she would be able to resume work at an appropriate time. For now though, she was happy being a wife and mother.

It was a couple of weeks later when Emily arrived on an unannounced visit. Welcomed in, she was thrilled to be handed Clara for a cuddle.

'I was wondering if you two might want to have an evening out. I'd be more than happy to look after Clara,' she said, smiling down at the sleeping baby.

'That would be lovely,' Davy said, wrapping an arm around his wife's waist.

'I'm not sure . . .' Lily wavered, 'Clara is so young yet . . .' Seeing Emily's face fall, she added, 'But, Emily, you are perfectly capable of taking care of our daughter. Thank you so much.'

'Good, that's settled then. Davy, why don't you take Lily to the music hall? I hear they have a wonderful new singer there.'

'Good idea. How do you fancy that, Lily?' Davy squeezed her waist.

'I'd love that! I've never been, but I've heard a lot about it.' Lily clapped her hands quietly.

'You'd best get tickets, Davy, I hear it gets packed solid every night.'

The evening was spent discussing the baby's progress and what they might enjoy at Honest John's music hall.

CHAPTER 25

Job Newton had wished both Seb and Tilley Green all the best when they informed him they would be leaving his employ at the Market Tavern.

Tilley's mother had agreed to taking in a lodger saying the extra few coppers would be welcome. So, Seb had moved his few belongings into the spare bedroom. He had sold his horse which meant he no longer had to pay stabling fees.

He had negotiated for more money for Tilley, but three shillings was all Honest John would offer. Having accepted, Tilley's singing career had begun.

She was drawing in the crowds; many being turned away for lack of space. Tickets to the music hall were like gold dust.

Honest John provided a couple of costumes for Tilley to wear onstage and Seb had a permanent front row, end of aisle seat. The audiences raised the roof at each of Tilley's performances, yelling for her to 'sing another'.

Young Tilley for her part was in her element, singing all the favourites. Occasionally she would entertain the people with an extra rendition of 'I'm shy Mary Ellen, I'm shy'. She was an instant success and her talent was talked about all over the town.

Seb split the money equally between them, which he was happy to do for the moment. However, once Tilley was performing at larger and high-profile places, he would negotiate the money in secret. He fully intended to take the larger share of whatever Tilley earned from her singing.

Watching from the sidelines, Seb saw the seats quickly begin to fill; he caught his breath however, as his eyes alighted on Lily and her husband who sat front and centre. His heartbeat increased as he heard her laugh; he saw her eyes twinkle in the light of the gas lamps. Her dark hair shone and he noticed she was a little thinner. Had she been ill? However, the loss of weight did not detract from her beauty.

Seb sidled into his seat at the end of the row as the piano tinkled into life. Ignoring the performances he'd seen so many times before, his eyes stayed on Lily.

The all too familiar feeling of lust ran through him as he watched her laugh at the risqué jokes of the comedian. All evening he could not tear his gaze from her and as Tilley took her place on stage and started to sing, Seb saw Lily accept a handkerchief from the man beside her. Watching her dab away her tears as the beautiful voice of Tilley

Green floated around the room, Seb had an over-whelming desire to hold Lily in his arms and more – much more.

He watched her hand being kissed by her husband and the loving exchange in their eyes. If only her husband knew that he had not been the first to enjoy Lily.

It was at that moment, as Tilley ended her song, that Lily's eyes roamed the audience who were on their feet yelling for an encore. Seb slipped from his seat and moved to the back of the room. He had assured Lily's friend Emily that he would stay away, but living in the same town, this was proving extremely difficult. He had hoped for a better outcome but Lily was now married and nothing could come from that now. Seb knew in his heart, however, it was time to move on and Lily's marriage was another reason for him to do so. He had to take Tilley Green to another place which had a bigger theatre.

As the crowds pushed their way out of the hall, Seb made up his mind. Tomorrow he would travel to Birmingham. Maybe he could get Tilley a singing spot at the Grand Theatre. He could possibly negotiate a higher fee there too.

Standing in the shadows, he watched Lily laughing as she walked through the door. His mind captured the image holding it fast. He wondered if it would be the last time he would ever see her.

★   ★   ★

Seb boarded the train for Birmingham the next day, telling Tilley he would be back before she went on stage that evening.

Alighting the train at New Street Station, Seb pushed through the throngs of people and headed for Lower Temple Street. He felt trepidation as he walked along. Shoving his hands into the pockets of his newly acquired overcoat, his pace quickened.

Rounding the corner into New Street, he saw the place he was looking for – the Grand Theatre. Pushing open the door, Seb stepped inside. Looking around, he gasped at the grandeur – and this was only the foyer.

The walls were painted in cream and burgundy. The ceiling was cream with the embossing etched out in gold. Wooden easels stood displaying large posters advertising the delights in store for theatre-goers, such as Marie Lloyd, a famous singer and comedienne.

Speaking with the girl at the ticket desk, Seb followed where her finger pointed. Pushing open the double doors, he walked through into the theatre proper. His breath caught as his eyes roamed the massive room with its decorated ceiling.

He slowly walked down the aisle between the wooden benches situated at the back. As he neared the front, he saw seats had replaced the benches. *Obviously for the wealthier clientele!*

All was quiet as he reached the front. Turning around he looked back. From this different perspective the room looked even grander. High up on either side sat the boxes for the extremely wealthy to sit and enjoy the performances. Here they could take wine and a light meal as they looked down on the acts on stage. Gas lamps adorned the walls and a small orchestra pit sat in front of the raised stage.

Seb blew through his teeth as he gazed around in awe. This was it! This was where Tilley Green needed to be! It was here, as her manager, he could earn good money!

'Can I help you, sir?' a voice spoke quietly in the silence of the massive theatre.

Seb turned to the man who had spoken to him. 'I hope so, I'm here to see the manager of this magnificent place!'

Extending his hand, the man said, 'I am he. Thomas Sutton at your service.'

'Sebastian Ryder,' came the reply as they shook hands.

'What can I do for you, Mr Ryder?' Sutton asked.

Seb took in the man's appearance. His features were sharp, akin to a fox, with bright beady eyes. The smile he gave lifted only the corners of his mouth as he spoke. He wore a white shirt sporting a black dicky-bow, black trousers and a tailcoat. *Strange daytime attire, clearly a uniform of sorts.*

Seb explained the reason for his visit and waited for the man's reaction.

'I see. Of course, Miss Green would have to come and sing for us, an audition if you like, before we could make any decision as to her being employed by the theatre,' Sutton answered, looking down his beaky nose.

Seb nodded his understanding.

'If it should be that Miss Green is taken into our employ, she would have to be lower billing,' Sutton continued. Seeing Seb's frown, he explained further, 'She would be listed at the bottom of the programme. Please understand, Mr Ryder, we have top performers here; Marie Lloyd and Dan Leno to name but two. So, naturally, Miss Green would be listed last on the billing to "warm up" the audience, if you take my meaning.'

'Of course. When would it be convenient to bring Miss Green along to see you?' Seb asked.

'In one month's time at three o'clock. That is usually the time we give over for interviews and auditions, but you must be aware, Mr Ryder, we see a lot of people and securing employment cannot be guaranteed,' Sutton sniffed audibly.

'Thank you, Mr Sutton. We will see you then.' Seb shook the hand of the man standing with his nose in the air.

He was excited as he returned to New Street Station. Tilley would be delighted when he told her the news. Finally he felt he was on his way to better things. Now he could envisage becoming a well-known manager and, who knows, maybe he could open his own theatre business one day.

Riding the train back to Wednesbury, Seb thought about his future and the sort of acts his prospective business could take on. He was lost in a world of music, dance and comedy as the train trundled along its rails.

Once more at the house where he lodged with Tilley and her mother, Seb was explaining to the girl where he'd been.

Tilley listened as she prepared a lunch of bread, cheese and home-made chutney.

'This could be your big chance, Tilley! You could be as famous as Marie Lloyd!' Seb was bubbling over with excitement.

Placing the plate of food on the table in front of him, Tilley said, 'I like it here. I like singing at Honest John's.'

'I know you do, but just think of the money and the prestige. You could be world famous one day!' Seb tried again to coax Tilley to his way of thinking.

'I don't care, I don't want to go!' Tilley banged a cup of tea on the table, its contents spilling over the rim.

'Tilley . . .' Seb said, mopping up the spillage with his handkerchief, 'you and I earn three shillings a week at Honest John's, but think what you *could* earn at the Grand Theatre!'

Tilley sat down at the table and shook her head. 'What about me mother? What will I do about her, eh? Have you thought about that?'

Seb nodded slowly as he thought rapidly. Tilley's mother had not even entered his head. Then he said, 'Yes, I have considered your mother. With the money we'll be earning, we could hire a woman to come and look after her.'

'I don't want just anybody in our house or looking after me mother!' Tilley was horrified at the suggestion.

'Of course not,' Seb said, patting her hand, 'you would have to interview people and choose the most suitable. Someone honest who would be kind to your mother. A woman who would look after her well and who your mum liked.'

He watched as Tilley considered his words. 'I ain't sure, what if they don't like my singing up in Birmingham?'

'How could they not? You are a beautiful singer. Believe me, Tilley, they will love you. Remember, nothing ventured – nothing gained. Besides, if you don't like it you don't have to do it. You can always stay at Honest John's.'

'What about you?' Tilley asked at last.

'Me? I'll be with you wherever you sing, Tilley, I thought you understood that.' Seb gave her a smile. He felt no remorse at wilfully playing with her affections and manipulating her into his way of thinking.

With a heavy sigh, Tilley relented. 'All right, I'll go but if I don't like it I'm coming straight home!'

'Fair enough,' Seb said, then tucked into his lunch.

Pleased he had persuaded her to visit Birmingham the following month with him, his thoughts centred on negotiating a decent wage with Mr Sutton. It would have to be enough for them both and Seb needed to conduct these discussions out of earshot of Tilley Green. After all, he was her manager and felt entitled to the lion's share of any monies earned. He just hoped now that Mr Sutton would take Tilley on as a performer.

CHAPTER 26

Life in the drab little town of Wednesbury went on as usual. New lives came into the world as old ones slipped peacefully away. Seasons came and went in all their individual glory and more men stood the breadline in the hope of being given work.

Davy Hurst's grocery store kept him busy and Lily was constantly tired looking after Clara who was now eighteen months old.

In an effort to keep her out of mischief one Sunday morning Lily decided they should all go to the park. Wrapping up warmly, they walked over to Brunswick Park, Davy carrying his daughter.

Clara wriggled to be on her feet as they arrived and Davy set her down on the grass. She instantly bent over and plucked at the stubby growth, fully intending to see how it tasted.

Lily laughed as she said, 'Oh no you don't, you little madam.'

Clara giggled and with tiny stomping steps she ran across the grass when Davy chased her clapping his hands.

Lily watched them with a smile. She felt

supremely happy as Clara squealed with delight at being caught and swung round by her daddy.

During the morning they walked the pathway that surrounded the lawns. It was still chilly and after a while Lily suggested they have a hot drink in the tea rooms.

Clara tucked into a sponge cake and glass of milk as her parents chatted over their tea. A little later Davy persuaded Lily into a walk to town. There was a rag doll in the toy shop he wanted to buy for his little girl.

'You spoil her,' Lily said with an indulgent smile.

'I know but I don't care, she's worth it,' Davy grinned.

Lily knew the shop would be open even on a Sunday; for some it was the only day they had time to shop. Shopkeepers opened every day in the hope of sales they couldn't afford to miss.

Clara was thrilled with her new dolly and clutched it to her chest, occasionally kissing it tenderly.

Lily was overcome with love for her small daughter as she watched.

Slowly they made their way home and Lily prepared their meal. Clara insisted on sharing her dinner with her new 'baba', much to Lily's amusement.

Even before she had finished eating, Clara's eyelids began to droop.

'I'll take her up, she's worn out,' Lily said. Davy kissed his baby girl and watched them go.

Lily returned to the living room shortly afterwards. 'She's sound asleep. She has her new dolly and her rag rabbit in bed with her.'

Davy smiled and Lily saw the tiredness cross his face. She yawned, suddenly feeling bone-weary herself.

'It's been a hectic day, let's have an early night. We both need to sleep.'

'Good idea,' Davy said on a sigh.

Damping down the fire and putting the guard in place, Davy turned off the gas lamps and followed his wife to bed.

That night as they both fell into a deep sleep, neither of them heard little Clara wake and climb out of her bed. She had only just begun to totter around and was still unsteady on her little feet.

The howl the following morning resonated through the house as Lily found her young daughter hanging from the bedrail, strangled by her own nightgown.

Davy rushed to find his wife on her knees in the child's room; her hands grasping her hair. She was screaming and crying. Seeing his daughter hanging limply between the bedrails, shock robbed him of his breath. He stepped towards Clara, his hand outstretched, when suddenly common sense snapped his attention back. He must not touch her. Unable to help himself, he gently touched the little one's cheek. Snatching back his hand, he realised her face was ice cold.

Lily's screams sounded again as she rocked back

and forth on her knees. Her husband's actions had confirmed it – her baby girl was dead.

Davy tried to lift his wife to her feet, but her knees gave way and he caught her before she hit the floor. Carrying her downstairs, he sat her on the sofa.

'Lily . . . Lily, I must fetch a constable. Stay there, sweetheart, don't move.' Then he added, 'I have to fetch the police and the doctor, Lily, do you understand?' Seeing her nod, he turned and dashed out into the street.

There he yelled like his lungs would burst. 'Help me! I need the police! Help me please!'

In but a moment he heard a police whistle blow and he yelled again, 'Constable, over here – quickly!'

A young policeman came running towards him.

'Quick! Upstairs – my daughter!' Davy yelled, pointing to the open front door of the house.

The young officer took the stairs two at a time and ran into the bedroom. 'Oh my God! Dear Lord Almighty!' he whispered.

Turning, he ran back into the street and blew his whistle for all he was worth. He kept whistling until another answered his call. An older constable came rushing to join him.

'What's up, lad?' the out-of-breath constable asked.

The lad just pointed to the house, his face was ashen. The two went into the house where they saw Davy and Lily sitting together in a daze.

Lily's face was wan and she began to shake uncontrollably.

The older policeman then followed the younger up the stairs and into the bedroom.

'Bloody hell!' he gasped. Turning to the other, he said, 'Fetch the doctor, lad, and hurry up about it! I'll wait downstairs with the parents as it's my guess the little lass is a goner.'

Shortly afterwards Dr Pryce arrived and followed the young constable upstairs. Making an examination, he said brusquely, 'Death by strangulation.' Taking a sharp knife from his bag, he cut the child's nightdress to release her, then laid her on the bed. 'Someone should send for the undertaker.'

The young constable nodded and proceeded down the stairs, thinking the doctor was an unfeeling swine!

Dr Pryce wrote out the death certificate and handed it to Davy. 'I'm sorry for your loss,' he said before turning and walking out.

'Miserable bugger, he's got no feelings that one!' the older policeman muttered. Turning to Davy, he said, 'Sir, we need to inform the undertaker.'

Davy looked up and nodded. 'I need to fetch Emily first – she's our friend.'

'Tell the young constable the address and he will escort her, you need to stay with your wife.'

Hailing a cab, the young bobby set off on his errand whilst the other found the kitchen and made hot, sweet tea.

It was not long before a rap came to the door.

The policeman answered it and in rushed Emily Johnston.

'Lily! Oh God, Lily!'

The sight of her friend opened the floodgates once again and Lily wept tears of utter despair. Emily held her tightly as her own tears rolled down her face.

Davy stared into space, ignoring the teacup in his hand.

'Lad,' the older policeman said to his colleague, 'do me another favour and fetch someone from Webb's.'

Nodding, the young constable set off on yet another errand.

A little while later Stan and the constable arrived at the house.

Stan walked into the living room and, folding the sobbing woman in his arms, he said, 'Oh Lily, I'm so very sorry.' He saw Davy rocking back and forth on the sofa. *Poor bugger! He's in shock.*

Sitting Lily down, Stan scooched down to face her. 'Lily, I'm going to take Clara with me now, do you understand?'

'Noooo!' Lily wailed.

'I have to, wench, you know that. She'll be all right with me. I'll look after her like she's my own.' Stan's words were gentle and quiet. Seeing Lily nod, he stood up. Moving to Davy, he placed a hand on his shoulder. 'Davy lad, I'm going upstairs now.'

In an instant Davy was on his feet fighting mad.

'Don't you touch my daughter! Don't you bloody dare!' he yelled.

Stan jumped back as the two constables fought to restrain Davy. 'Do it quick!' the older one said.

Stan fled from the room. Snatching the small wooden box from the cart, he ran upstairs. Gently he lifted Clara Hurst from the bed and laid her inside; all the time he could hear Davy yelling and Lily sobbing.

Kissing his fingers, he touched them to the child's head, 'Sleep well, young Clara.' He placed the lid on the box and carefully carried it downstairs. Laying it on the cart, he climbed into the driving seat. Clucking the horses to move on, he thought, *Lily will know where to find her daughter when she's ready.*

CHAPTER 27

Mr and Mrs Blenkinsop stood on the Hurst's doorstep awaiting entry. Davy opened the door and shook hands with Albert. Jenny nodded and limped past him into the living room.

'Oh Lily!' she said, making her way over to her friend for a hug. 'I won't ask how you are, I can see for myself. Good grief, girl, you're a mess!'

Lily desperately sought out a tiny smile as she patted her uncombed hair. She had worn the same clothes for two days now; she had not washed or eaten a single thing.

'Lily, I know it's hard, but you have to come down to Webb's, there's arrangements . . .' Jenny said gently.

'I can't! Oh, Jenny, I just can't!' Lily cut across her friend's words.

'It has to be done, Lily,' Jenny tried again.

'Jenny – you choose . . . sort it out for me please. I . . . I can't face it.' Lily shook her head.

'All right,' Jenny said, looking to Davy who nodded his agreement.

Jenny was shocked also at the appearance of

Davy; he had aged overnight. His brown eyes had lost their sparkle and flecks of grey showed at his temples which she'd not noticed before. The lines around his dull eyes had deepened and his complexion was wan.

Lily looked no better. Her hair was lank and dry, her tired hazel eyes looked out from an ashen face.

Albert went with Davy to make tea and Jenny watched Lily stare into space. Trying to shield herself from the heartbreak she was feeling, Lily constantly drifted off into her own little world.

Jenny couldn't imagine what it must be like to lose a child at any age, let alone one so young and in such tragic circumstances. Her heart went out to her friend who was suffering in silence.

'Lily, do you want to talk about it? I can understand if you don't, but sometimes it helps.'

Lily just shook her head without taking her eyes from the blank space she looked into.

The men returned with a tray of tea. Davy placed a cup on the tiny table beside his wife, who ignored it.

Jenny looked at Davy, who shook his head. 'She won't eat, and she's had no sleep.'

'Neither have you, by the looks of it,' Jenny replied.

Davy shrugged his shoulders. 'It's so quiet now,' he said as tears formed and fell. 'I don't understand how it happened. We didn't hear Clara get up in the night. I don't know why she did that. Normally she would cry out and one of us would go to her. Maybe she had called and we'd not heard her . . . Oh God! If only I'd woken!'

'It ain't your fault, Davy, it was an accident,' Jenny tried to comfort the distraught man.

Blowing his nose on his handkerchief, he nodded. 'Lily found her the following morning. Her nightie had caught on the bedpost and she'd slipped between the rails. Her own nightie had strangled her! Oh my poor baby!'

Albert laid a hand on Davy's shoulder as he sobbed.

Jenny looked back to Lily who was oblivious to it all.

'Davy, Lily's not grieving. We have to get the funeral sorted out quickly otherwise we could lose her too,' Jenny said quietly.

Davy nodded. 'As soon as possible, Jenny. It has to be done, so let's get it over with.'

Two days later Lily, dressed in her black coat and hat, climbed into the cab that would take them to Webb's. She spoke no words; shed no tears. Davy was worried out of his mind, but no amount of coaxing would get his wife to speak to him. Even the Coroner's letter recording death by misadventure did nothing to break Lily's trance.

The open carriage with its two black plumed horses stood waiting. The small white coffin lay in the centre completely surrounded by fresh flowers. Stan was in the driving seat ready to go.

Davy and Lily fell in behind the carriage. Emily

Johnston stood behind them. Jenny, in her wheelchair pushed by Albert, followed along with Vera, her mother, at their side.

Slowly the entourage moved forward toward St John's Church. People lined the streets paying their respects, as the woman who normally led the carriage was now walking behind.

Travelling slowly down the tramway, all traffic stopped. The tram drew to a halt so the entourage could pass by, and carters pulled in to the side of the street.

Lily saw nothing of the sad faces of the people who lined the roadway, her eyes were firmly fixed on the small white coffin preceding her.

The vicar was waiting at the graveside as they arrived and Stan and Albert lifted the little coffin from the carriage. Laying it across the straps on the ground, they stood back.

The coffin was lifted carefully on the straps and as it was lowered towards the grave, a shriek rent the air.

'Nooooo! Clara . . . Clara . . . my baby! Don't put her in there, please . . . Clara!' Lily fought to free herself from Davy's strong arms as she wailed.

Quiet sobs from mourners became audible sniffs as they watched Lily struggling to get to her daughter. As the coffin disappeared from sight, Lily collapsed to her knees. Her howls of despair ringing out across the quiet churchyard as she banged her fists on the ground.

Davy lifted his wife into his arms and with a

nod to the vicar, then to Stan, he carried her away to a waiting cab. Lily's grieving had begun and Davy felt the best place for her now was at home.

Lily kept the curtains closed for the whole week and all mirrors were turned to the wall. The superstitions surrounding looking into a mirror in a house so soon after a death were well-known. It was feared another death would soon follow. The other superstition was if the mirror was not turned, it would trap the soul, which would be taken by the devil. So strong were these beliefs that virtually everyone carried out the rituals.

Having slept from pure exhaustion, Lily had eaten sparsely. She sat in the living room in a trance-like state, her mind reliving over and over what had happened to Clara. Questions filled her head; could she have prevented the death of her small daughter? If so, how? She blamed Davy for insisting Clara get used to sleeping in her own room. She blamed herself for not arguing against that idea. If she hadn't been so tired, she would have heard the child call out. If – if – but now it was too late, Clara was gone.

Silent tears streamed down her face as she stared into the gloom of the darkened room. She thought about Emily Johnston, her friend and confidante, whom she had sent away, and of Jenny who she refused to open the door to. Stan and Albert too had tried to see her, but she had refused to see or speak with anyone. She knew it was unkind, but Lily just wanted to be alone with her grief and memories. She knew also that she was shutting Davy out, but she couldn't help herself.

Rising from her seat, she walked wearily upstairs and into Clara's room. Sitting on the little bed, she grasped the old rag rabbit to her chest. It had been Clara's favourite toy, one she would not be parted from and wouldn't settle without.

A sob caught in her throat as she looked around. Everything had been left as it was, except Clara was no longer there to enjoy it. Toys littered the floor, the doll's house stood in the corner with its doors open. The bedclothes were still pushed back where Clara had climbed out.

Lily moaned into the silence as she saw again her beloved daughter hanging from the bedrails. Floods of tears poured down her face as she rocked back and forth on the small bed.

'Oh, Clara, I'm so very sorry, sweetheart,' she whispered.

Davy found her sitting quietly clutching the rag rabbit to her chest.

'Lily, come away, darling,' he said gently. Helping her to her feet, he led her downstairs. Trying to prise the rabbit from her fingers, he whispered, 'Let me put this back in Clara's room, my love.'

Lily held onto the precious toy, refusing to let go.

Davy relented, saying, 'All right, you hold it for a while, then we can take it back together.'

Lily shook her head and with a venom he'd never seen in his wife before she said, 'You stay out of Clara's room!'

'Sweetheart . . .' Davy began.

'No! I told you she was too young to have her own room – I told you!' Lily snapped. Her eyes blazed fire as she glared at him.

'Lily, for God's sake, it was an accident!' Davy was exasperated. Lily turned away from him as he spoke again. 'You have to let go, Lily, this is not healthy!'

'Leave me alone! Go away! Just leave me in peace!' Lily spat.

Davy shook his head and turned towards the kitchen.

Sitting at the kitchen table, Davy looked at the bottle he'd found in the cupboard. Pouring the brandy, he downed it in one, before pouring another. He couldn't believe the change in his wife. The once bright and cheerful girl had been replaced almost overnight. Now she was sullen; scathing in her words. He knew she was grieving, but so was he. Couldn't she understand that? No, Lily was so wrapped up in herself she could not see his sorrow.

Swallowing the alcohol, he refilled his glass once more. How could he get through to her? How could he make her see he too was bereft without their little girl? Lily was pushing him further away with each day that passed and he was afraid he was losing her love.

Marching back to the parlour, he looked at his wife nursing the rag rabbit like a child. His heart was breaking and Lily couldn't care less. Suddenly fury filled him and he yelled, 'Lily! You have to come to terms with this! Clara is gone and, as much as I want to, we can't bring her back!'

Lily's head snapped round and the hate-filled eyes which looked at him shocked him to the core. 'Do you think I don't know that? I know my baby lies in the earth – I know, Davy!' she rasped. Tears welled in her eyes as her anger and frustration mounted. 'I know I can't bring her home ever again! It's your fault! If you hadn't insisted she sleep in that bed . . .'

Davy's shocked intake of breath stalled her words. 'Lily, it was an accident – no one was to blame!'

'I don't see it that way!' Lily yelled.

'Dear God, woman!' Davy yelled back.

Lily turned away from him once more and Davy finally realised – she blamed him for the death of their daughter.

Backing away from her in complete and utter shock, he turned and left the room. In the kitchen Davy drank down the rest of the brandy before laying his arms and head on the table. He slipped into a welcome drunken sleep with tears of pure misery still wet on his cheeks.

A little while later Lily stood transfixed in the doorway to the kitchen, her hand to her mouth. She stared at her husband, his head and arms draped across the kitchen table. Was he dead? Had she caused him to take his own life with her harsh words? Panic filled her as she rushed across to him. Laying her hand on his head, she heard him moan quietly and relief flooded through her.

Lifting his head carefully, he muttered, 'Lily?'

'Oh Davy – I thought . . .' Lily said with tears in her eyes.

'What, my love?' Davy said, holding his head, trying to relieve the thumping inside.

'Oh Davy, I'm so very sorry . . . I shouldn't have . . .' Lily's tears fell as her husband got gingerly to his feet.

'Don't, I understand.' Davy wrapped her in his arms and pulled her close. Kissing her hair, he whispered, 'I love you, Lily Hurst.'

'I love you too, Davy Hurst, and I'm so sorry for the terrible things I said to you.' She leaned against him, her head on his chest.

He had forgiven her, and now Lily knew she had to seek forgiveness from her friends for the way she had treated them. In her misery she had shut them out of her life and now it was time to make amends. She prayed silently they would under-stand and welcome her back into their lives.

CHAPTER 28

Seb sat in his room and thought about the recent past which had been a whirlwind of activity for Tilley and himself.

Seb had learned from Honest John that audiences could be fickle. A favourite act could be forgotten quickly if an exciting new one took its place.

He relived in his mind how he and Tilley had arrived at Wednesbury railway station for their sojourn into Birmingham. Tilley had gasped as she saw the train standing belching out great puffs of steam. People were pushing and shoving along the platform in an effort to board the train or leave the station. As they had neared the train, Tilley stopped in her tracks and looked at him.

'What's the matter?' he'd asked.

'I ain't getting on that thing!'

'Why not?' Seb had asked, feeling confused.

'It's bloody dangerous and I ain't doing it! I'll walk!' Tilley had turned to leave the station.

Catching her arm, he said, 'Tilley it's twenty or thirty miles! You can't possibly walk that far. Come on, the train isn't dangerous, you'll be safe, I promise.'

He smiled as he saw the porter standing by the open door of the third-class carriage.

'May I help, sir?' he'd asked.

'Miss Green is not confident regarding rail travel as yet,' Seb explained.

'Princess, may I escort you to your carriage?' the porter said as he held out his hand.

Tilley had grinned shyly as she took his hand.

Leading her to the open door, he had whispered, 'I've worked here for years and never yet had a ride on her.' He patted the carriage tenderly as he would have petted a horse. 'Mind the step, Princess.'

Tilley had climbed aboard, giving her thanks. The porter had indeed made her feel like royalty. Seb gave his thanks along with a threepenny bit as a tip. The porter doffed his cap as he'd closed the carriage door.

Tilley had held onto Seb's arm tightly as the steam whistle blew and the carriage jolted forward. She watched through the window in fascination as the engine chugged along. She saw houses and streets pass, people bustling around and fields appear to whizz by. She'd heard the clackety-clack of the wheels on the iron rails and the rhythm helped her to relax.

Before she'd realised they were alighting from the train at New Street station. Seb led her through the streets to the Grand Theatre, smiling at her disbelief that so many people could live in one place. Stepping inside, he had heard Tilley draw in a breath.

'Bloody hell, it's posh here!'

He smiled as he heard her words again.

As they had moved into the theatre, he had heard her gasp. Tilley had gazed around her as they had walked down the centre aisle where the manager was waiting for them.

'Tilley, this is Mr Sutton, the manager,' Seb said, which had snapped her attention back to him. 'Mr Sutton, meet Miss Tilley Green.'

Sutton had given a quick smile as he took in her appearance. Seb had noted that Tilley obviously was dressed in her Sunday best but Sutton had attempted to hide the look of distaste he had felt rising.

Tilley was dressed in a battered hat, one cherry only remained of the bunch which had adorned it. Her sandy hair did its best to escape the confines of the hat and fell in an unruly mess over her pale blue eyes. Her skin was alabaster white and she was as thin as a rail. An old green dress fell short of brown boots which had seen better days. Her coat hung open, the cuffs of which were frayed and grubby.

Seb knew Sutton was wondering what he'd let himself in for as he led the pair towards the pianist who sat waiting patiently.

Sutton and Seb had sat on the front row chairs while Tilley and the pianist exchanged a few words, then watched the young girl ascend the steps and stand centre stage.

The pianist tinkled the introduction, then waited.

Tilley was staring around the room with her mouth open.

Seb remembered seeing Sutton shake his head as the introduction was played through again. Tilley appeared not to hear it, however.

Standing up, Seb had yelled, 'Tilley! Sing!'

Tilley had given an embarrassed giggle and nodded to the waiting pianist who had smiled kindly. He started to play yet again and then Tilley began to sing her favourite song. *'I don't want to play in your yard, I don't love you any more . . .'* The sound floated out across the room holding Sutton spellbound.

It was the pianist who applauded when she'd finished; Sutton sat with an open mouth. Seb had nudged the man who then called out, 'Very nice, Miss Green. Do you know any more songs?'

Tilley had nodded and leaned down to speak with her accompanist once more. Whilst she had given her rendition of 'A bird in a gilded cage', Seb had endeavoured to negotiate terms with Mr Sutton. The manager told him to be quiet, he needed to listen to the girl singing her heart out. Seb had settled sulkily into his chair.

Tilley proceeded to sing a few more songs, then came off stage to the applause of all three men.

Sutton had rushed up to her. 'Wonderful! Miss Green, you are a breath of fresh air! I think the Grand Theatre would benefit greatly from your talent. I'm sure we can come to some arrangement regarding your fee and performance times!'

Tilley had grinned widely.

Seb had intervened. 'As her manager, Mr Sutton, I feel it my duty and responsibility to conduct these negotiations and arrangements.'

He settled more comfortably on his bed as he recalled Tilley nodding her approval before wandering off to chat with the pianist.

Sutton had tutted loudly, then led Seb to his office just off the main auditorium. Sutton had sat behind his desk with Seb being offered the chair opposite him. 'Mr Ryder, there is no doubt Miss Green possesses a raw, natural talent and I would like her to join us here at the theatre. Now, as to her fee – I'm willing to pay, per performance of course, two shillings.'

Seb had pulled the corners of his mouth down whilst he considered the offer he had no intentions of accepting. 'Mr Sutton, Miss Green earns more than that now, so I'm afraid your offer is quite unacceptable. I'm sure you understand.'

Sutton had stared at him and Seb could see the worry begin to build. He could, if he was not careful, lose the opportunity of bringing a bright new talent to his theatre. This worry had turned to panic as Seb stood to leave.

Seb had leaned down and said, 'Mr Sutton, I feel I should point out to you that Miss Green lives in Wednesbury with her aged, infirm mother. As you are no doubt aware, this would mean a train ride twice a day which costs money. Also, should Miss Green take up your offer of performing at *your* theatre, she would have to employ someone to take care of her mother – more expense. Then, of course, you can't guarantee how often Miss Green would perform each week.' Seb had straightened his stance and looked down at the manager.

He knew inwardly Sutton had fumed and had hoped to discuss finance with the girl herself. The man had immediately seen Tilley had little or no schooling

Seb smiled as he saw in his mind Sutton's discomfort. 'I see. I was unaware of those facts, Mr Ryder, and let me assure you I completely understand.' He had given a deprecating smile before continuing, 'I could, at a push, go to four shillings, but my budget will stretch no further, I'm afraid.' He had held out his hands in supplication, but the sly smile belied his actions.

Seb grinned now as he remembered the man's face at his next words. 'Then, Mr Sutton, I cannot accept your offer, *I'm afraid.* Miss Green would be welcomed into any theatre in London for a fee far in excess of what you are offering.'

Sutton thought he had Seb by the throat when he had asked, 'What about her aged mother?'

'We shall take her with us,' Seb said simply.

Sutton was mortified at being outwitted. 'Please, Mr Ryder, sit down. Maybe we can negotiate further – maybe I could manage a better fee for Miss Green.'

Seb felt again the pleasure of getting the better of the snobbish man. He'd watched Sutton pull a ledger from the desk drawer, open it and pretend to scan the contents. He had waited patiently, knowing exactly what Sutton was up to. The man had huge sums at his fingertips to pay the performers, but here he was quibbling over a few shillings.

'Mr Sutton, I really must get Miss Green home to see to her mother before her evening performance . . .' Seb had pushed, feeling rather annoyed at being kept waiting for so long.

'Yes, right. Well, I will pay five shillings and not a penny more!' Sutton had snapped the ledger closed and threw it into the open drawer, which he slammed shut.

Seb had stood and looked down at the man, whose face changed from triumphant to panic-stricken in an instant.

'I accept,' Seb had said and watched Sutton sigh with relief. They had agreed Tilley's debut performance would be in two days' time when she would sing two songs.

On the train home Tilley had gushed her excitement of the journey, the theatre, and how nice the pianist had been to her. Seb had explained Sutton had agreed to pay three shillings on the nights she sang and would pay Seb, who would then pay Tilley her share. Tilley had been delighted.

Seb closed his eyes with a smile on his face. He had duped Tilley Green and she was none the wiser.

CHAPTER 29

Lily and Davy talked long into the night, she apologising over and over for her bad behaviour towards the man she loved, and he saying he'd forgiven her. They were both grieving the loss of their little girl and neither thought they would ever get over her death. Davy said they could have more children in the future, but Lily dismissed the idea. She felt she would never love another child as much as she had loved Clara. She asked Davy how she could approach her friends after the way she had treated them.

'Go and knock on their doors, Lily, you might be surprised at their reaction,' he said as he cuddled close to his wife in the darkness of their bedroom.

'I will, I'll go tomorrow.'

The following morning Lily set out for the boarding house in Church Street. Full of trepidation as to how she would be received, she marched on. Knocking at the door, Lily waited, still feeling wretched. The door opened and Emily stood facing her caller.

'Lily! Oh my goodness!' Emily pulled the young

woman inside by her arm then embraced her warmly. 'Oh, my dear girl, it's so nice to see you! Come in, we'll have some tea.'

Lily's fear of being rejected melted away as she followed her friend into the living room. The house was quiet, all the girls being out at work, and so the two were able to talk without interruption.

Emily bustled to the kitchen, asking the cook that tea for two be brought into the living room, then she went back to sit with Lily.

'How are you, sweetheart?' Emily asked tentatively.

'I'm all right – no actually I'm not,' Lily said as tears sprang to her eyes. 'Oh, Emily, it's all gone wrong! It wasn't supposed to be like this! I shut you and Jenny out of my life and – I blamed Davy for Clara's accident!' Threatened tears poured down her cheeks and dripped onto her lap.

Emily enfolded the weeping girl in her arms and held her tightly.

'It was grief that made you do those things, Lily, and everyone knows that. No one will hold you responsible for those actions. Oh, my poor Lily, my poor darling girl.'

Slowly the tears subsided and Lily and Emily talked the morning away, mostly about Clara.

'I should be going, Emily, I want to go and see Jenny. She'll be at Webb's, so I can see the others too while I'm there,' Lily said at last.

'Well, don't be a stranger, come and visit anytime you want.' Emily kissed Lily's cheek as they parted company on the doorstep.

Lily walked down Church Street, heading for the marketplace. She saw the tight smiles given from women passing by and she knew they were feeling sad for her. Men doffed their flat caps and nodded. Standing outside Webb's, she took a deep breath then walked inside.

'Lily!' Jenny let out a squeal of delight at seeing her friend.

Walking to the desk where her friend sat, Lily gave her a hug. 'I've come to apologise for being so horrible to you. I'm so sorry, Jenny.'

'Don't worry about that, it's just so lovely to see you,' Jenny said with a beaming smile.

Lily knew her actions had been unforgivable but Jenny, like Emily, had dismissed them. Whilst they chatted tearfully the door opened and Stan walked into the room.

'Hello, Lily, it's nice to see you out and about again.' He wrapped his arms around her and hugged her tightly. 'I was just about to make tea, you will stay and have a cup?'

Lily nodded.

'Right. Jenny put the sign on the door telling folk it's dinner time and we'll all have a bite and a cuppa.'

'I'll do it,' Lily said quickly, wondering how Jenny would manage with her wheelchair.

'I can do it,' Jenny said with a grin. Grabbing her crutches which Fred had fashioned from wood left over from the coffin making, she stood and hobbled to the door. Flipping the sign from 'open' to 'closed for lunch', she ambled back towards the kitchen.

Lily was amazed at how well Jenny was walking on her wooden leg. Then she felt ashamed, thinking if she'd kept in touch over the last weeks, she would have known that fact.

Following her into the kitchen, Stan quipped, 'As you're here, you can brew up. I'll fetch the others.'

Lily smiled as she set the kettle to boil and sorted out cups for everyone.

Hugs were given as Fred and Albert joined them and Lily's heart warmed. These wonderful people had welcomed her back into the fold without question or recrimination.

'Have you made any extra-large coffins lately, Fred?' Lily asked.

'Always got one out the back,' he laughed as they remembered the large woman they had buried previously. 'You told her about the one last week, Stan?'

Stan shook his head, not at all sure Lily was ready to hear about the business so soon after burying her own child.

Lily frowned and said, 'Stan, it's all right. You can tell me, I have to get back to normality sooner or later.' Saying it was one thing, but doing it was quite another.

Fred could hold his tongue no longer and launched into the tale of the recent burial. 'Well, they've employed a young lad to help with grave-digging down at St John's Church. Lazy little bugger he is an' all.'

Lily could not help but grin. She had missed being here with her friends and, truth be told, she'd missed the work also.

'Any road up, the lad digs the grave and Stan turns up with the casket. The family am all standing around while the vicar does his bit. The wife is crying her eyes out and then comes the time for the sprinkling.'

Lily's mind cast back to seeing family members drop a handful of earth onto the coffin which had been lowered into the grave at the funerals she had presided over.

'Well . . .' Fred drew the word out, enjoying telling his story. 'The wife, with her handful of dirt, steps to the side of the grave and leans over. Then it happened!'

'What did?' Lily asked.

'The side of the bloody grave caved in and her went sprawling onto the coffin!'

Lily gasped, her hand covering her mouth.

Fred took up again. 'Her hat skewed sideways, her legs went up in the air, showing her bloomers to all and sundry, and her was screeching like a banshee!'

Lily's mouth dropped open as she listened.

'The poor woman couldn't get out, so Stan had to help her. Blimey, it was a farce!'

'Why did she fall in?' Lily asked. 'Did she lean too far forward?'

Fred shook his head. 'No. That lazy lad hadn't shored up the sides of the hole with planks!'

'Oh no!' Lily was aghast.

'Oh yes!' Fred countered. 'I don't know how Stan kept his face straight.'

'I very nearly didn't,' Stan said, 'that poor woman.'

The way he said it caused Lily to burst out laughing.

'I'm sorry to laugh,' she said eventually as they all settled down again, 'but it must have been such a sight.'

'You have no idea,' Stan said, 'one I don't want to see again. That woman's bloomers were bright red!' This sent them all into fits of laughter once more.

After tea and sharing Stan's pie, Lily felt so much better. Knowing they had to open for afternoon business, she said she should be leaving.

Fred and Albert disappeared into the back and Jenny retook her seat behind the desk. Stan walked Lily to the door, then said quietly, 'Your job is always here . . . when you're ready. That's if you want to come back of course.'

Lily hugged him tightly. 'Oh Stan, thank you! I've missed you all so much. I know it will be terribly hard, but I think it might help me come to terms with losing Clara.' Tears welled in her eyes at the thought of her little girl.

'How will Davy feel about it?' Stan asked.

'I'm sure he'll agree with me,' Lily said with a sniff.

'Right then, you come back whenever you like. Talk it over with Davy first though, eh?' Lily nodded. 'I can't deny we could certainly use your help.'

Bolstering herself, Lily said, 'Expect me next week.' Turning the sign, she called out to Jenny, 'I'll see you on Monday.'

Jenny frowned and called back, 'Monday?'

'Yes, I'm coming back to work.'

Jenny let out a whoop of delight and with a little wave Lily left the shop.

That evening Lily and Davy discussed her returning to work so soon.

'Lily sweetheart, you're still grieving as am I. Do you think you should give it more time before going back to Webb's?' Davy was concerned. His wife appeared to be recovering well but he still worried for her.

'Davy, you've gone back to work,' Lily said.

'Darling, I work in a grocery store – it's not quite the same thing.'

'Well, I sit around here all day moping. I can't bring Clara back, I know that.' Again her tears formed as she spoke. 'I don't think it's doing either of us any good me dwelling on Clara's death. I'm trying to remember her as she was when she laughed and giggled. When she tried to form her words; when she enjoyed her daddy playing with her.'

Davy let out a sob and she saw his tears roll down his cheeks. Her own tears fell and they held each other as she went on. 'I need to be occupied, Davy, I want to – no, I have to – feel needed again.'

Davy nodded his understanding. 'All right, my love, but you must promise me, if it all becomes too much you will come home.'

'I will, I promise.'

The couple climbed the stairs to bed hand in hand. Lily stopped by Clara's door and said softly, as she did every night, 'Goodnight Clara, sleep well sweetheart.'

Davy's arm around her waist felt comforting as he led her to their own room. Once in bed they snuggled close, each quietly thinking their own thoughts of the beautiful young daughter so cruelly taken from them.

CHAPTER 30

Tilley Green's debut performance evening finally arrived and Seb Ryder was more nervous than she was. He knew she would be a success but he didn't want her finding out about the money situation. He had told her not to discuss her pay with anyone else but him, saying the other performers might be upset to know she was earning more than them. Tilley had accepted his explanation, telling him he was a kind and thoughtful man.

They stood in the wings at the side of the stage waiting for the mime artist to finish his set. Seb had heard the audience, they were restless. Clearly they did not rate the mime very highly, however they clapped politely as he left the stage. True to his word Mr Sutton had placed Tilley low down on the billing.

'Bloody hell it's hard work out there tonight!' the artist said to Tilley as he walked past her.

Tilley shrugged her shoulders and listened to the compere introducing a wonderful new singer. Tilley wondered who that was and looked around her. Then she heard her name being called.

The compere walked off stage as she walked on to gentle applause. Standing centre stage, she gazed around. The gas lamps on the walls spilled out a warm glow over the audience. Looking up to each side, she saw all the boxes were filled with grand ladies and gentlemen.

Suddenly the small orchestra began to play the introduction and Tilley brought her attention back to the task in hand. Taking a deep breath, she began to sing. 'My Wild Irish Rose'.

Her eyes roamed over the people sat before her in silence as she sang loud and clear until at last her song ended. To her surprise and delight everyone stood and the applause was deafening.

Tilley laughed out loud as she took a bow. When the clapping and cheering faded out, the orchestra struck up again. Launching into 'Pretty Polly Perkins of Paddington Green', Tilley skipped across the boards playing to her audience.

She curtseyed as the song drew to a close to rapturous applause yet again. Waving to the people, Tilley left the stage feeling an excitement she had never quite felt before.

Seb gave her a hug when she returned to him. 'Well done, you were marvellous,' he whispered.

Tilley was elated. It was then that they heard the audience in an uproar.

'What's going on?' she asked.

Seb shook his head and placed a finger to his lips.

The compere had introduced the next act but

the audience were catcalling and heckling. They didn't want to see a ventriloquist they yelled, they wanted to hear more from Tilley Green!

Mr Sutton, the manager, rushed from his office to see what all the noise was about.

The compere rushed off stage as pieces of food began to pelt him. As he picked bits of sandwich from his clothes, he said to Sutton, 'I ain't going out there again unless it's to introduce her!' He jabbed a finger in Tilley's direction.

'She's done her turn already!' Sutton shouted over the noise of the audience who were now slow handclapping and stamping their feet.

'I know that! You can go out and tell them because I ain't going to!' the compere yelled back.

Sutton groaned, dragging his hands through his hair. His theatre was losing its air of sophistication and he was fuming. The ventriloquist was yelling at him about it being his turn on stage and how he'd never been treated so badly.

'You! Get out there and sing another couple of songs!' Sutton shouted at Tilley.

Tilley took a step forward, but Seb caught her arm. 'Sorry, Mr Sutton, but renegotiation will be needed for that.'

Sutton glared at the man who held Tilley back from the stage. Then to the compere, he said, 'You get out there and calm them down before we have any violence. Tilley, tell him what you'll sing, so the orchestra will know when he announces it.'

The ventriloquist stormed away, shouting he was going to quit.

Turning to Seb, Sutton said menacingly, 'You, my office now.'

Seb followed Sutton into his office, closing the door quietly behind him. Taking the chair indicated, he watched the other man fighting to control his anger.

'Mr Ryder! I am not at liberty to pay you more than I am at present . . .'

Seb held up a hand, saying, 'In that case I'll collect Miss Green now and leave this theatre.'

'No! You can't do that! I'll have a riot on my hands!' Sutton was gasping and running a finger around the inside of his starched collar.

'Mr Sutton, it would seem we have reached an impasse,' Seb said confidently.

'What can I do?' Sutton wailed, holding out his hands.

Seb lifted a finger and they both listened as Tilley finished her song. The audience were clapping and whistling fit to lift the roof.

'I'll tell you what,' Seb said as Tilley's voice floated out again, 'how would it be that when you don't have a famous artiste performing, you list Tilley Green as top billing?'

Sutton thought he would have a heart attack as he blustered, 'Have you any idea what you are asking? What about the others on the billing? How do you think they will react to that news?'

Seb hooked a finger behind his ear as the angelic

voice of Tilley Green faded and the applause began again. Then he said, 'That, Mr Sutton, is your problem.'

On the train back to Wednesbury, Seb explained to Tilley what had been said in Sutton's office.

'You d'ain't never say that!' Tilley's surprise showed clearly.

'I most certainly did!' Seb said with a smile. 'Tilley, your singing will ensure that theatre is filled to capacity every night. Now, when Sutton sees how much more money the theatre is making he's going to be very happy. That's when I will step in and demand a higher pay for you.'

'I don't need no more money, I got enough,' Tilley said.

'My dear girl, one can never have too much money.' Seb smiled and patted her arm.

'I s'pose,' Tilley muttered.

'You wait, Tilley Green, you and I are going places.' He laughed.

'Where we going?' Tilley asked innocently.

'We're going to the top. You are destined to become famous, and I'm going to make sure that happens.'

'You know what,' Tilley said, 'you am such a kind and honest man.'

Seb felt a tinge of guilt knowing he was giving her the lesser share of the money, but then dismissed the feeling. He was entitled, he was her manager after all.

★　★　★

By the end of that first week Tilley Green was at the top of the bill and tickets were selling like hot cakes.

Biding his time, Seb decided to wait for just the right moment to approach Sutton for a raise in earnings. He felt another week should do it.

Night after night he stood in the wings watching Tilley delight her audience. They couldn't get enough of her and the groaning was loud when she finished. She made them howl with her rendition of 'I'm shy Mary Ellen, I'm shy' as she acted out the part. She brought them to tears with 'I don't want to play in your yard'.

Tilley Green was a roaring success at the Grand Theatre in Birmingham and she was talked about everywhere.

Sitting in his room one night, Seb pulled out the box which lay beneath his bed. Taking out the newspaper clipping, he read it again. Shaking his head, he replaced it in the box which he shoved back in its place.

The article had reported Lily and Davy Hurst had lost their young daughter in a tragic accident. Seb couldn't imagine how she had felt, or indeed was still feeling. He only knew how his feelings still tormented him. He had hoped that spending so much time in Birmingham away from Lily would rid his mind of her but he couldn't stop wanting her. Lily was a married woman now and he knew she hated him with a vengeance, which made the idea of claiming her all the more sweet.

If he could entice her away from her husband, so much the better.

Seb stifled a laugh so as not to disturb Tilley or her mother. Turning his face into his pillow he sniggered. He would see this through no matter how long it took.

Seb then slipped quietly from his room to make a cup of tea. He sat for a few hours until the morning dawned and realised that all night his thoughts had centred on the woman who had become an obsession to him. Lily. He smiled as he thought of her name before she married Davy Hurst. To him she was, and always would be, Lily Rae.

It was a scream that brought him out of his daydream. Tilley was calling out for him.

Dashing back up the stairs, he saw the girl standing on the landing in her voluminous white nightgown. She was sobbing her heart out.

'What's wrong?' Seb yelled over her loud cries.

Tilley pointed to the bedroom she shared with her mother, and Seb knew instantly what had brought her tears.

Walking into the room, he saw the old lady in bed, looking as white as the sheet pulled up to her chin. Going to her, he saw her eyes staring lifelessly. Closing her eyes gently, he felt in his pocket. Drawing out two pennies, he laid them on her eyelids. He dismissed the old wives' tale of being threatened by death by being 'looked at' by a corpse, but he shivered nonetheless.

Leading a sobbing Tilley to the kitchen, he

poured her some tea, saying, 'I'm so sorry, Tilley.' Seeing her nod, he went on, 'I'll fetch the doctor then go to Webb's. You just stay there and drink your tea, I won't be long.' Seb thought how convenient it was that he would now have an excuse to go to the funeral directors and find out more about Lily.

Grabbing his jacket, he ran from the house. After speaking to a disgruntled doctor at having been woken so early, Seb walked round to Webb's Funeral Directors. It was still closed so he would have to come back later.

Returning to Tilley's house, he was told the doctor had been and given a death certificate recording the death to be of natural causes.

After making more tea and trying to comfort the distressed girl, Seb said he would try Webb's again.

The Funeral Directors was open he saw as he approached and stepping inside he was greeted by Jenny. He arranged everything and was just about to leave when Lily walked in from another room. He saw the shock on her face but she quickly recovered. He was surprised also, he hadn't expected to see her there, but felt even luckier at how this had all come together for him.

'Mrs Hurst,' he said. 'I was sorry to hear of your loss. You have my deepest sympathies.'

'Mr Ryder, thank you,' Lily said before turning and disappearing into the room she had come from.

Nodding to Jenny, he left the office and walked

back to take care of Tilley. Trudging through the streets, Seb's obsession with Lily had been stirred once more at seeing her again after such a long time. The passion rose within him and he felt he couldn't wait to see her again.

CHAPTER 31

Davy sat reading the newspaper and Lily was thinking about her meeting with Seb Ryder yet again. Having spoken to Jenny after he had left Webb's, she learned he had been arranging a funeral for a Mrs Green. It transpired it was Tilley Green's mother, the young girl she had heard sing so beautifully at the music hall. Why was Seb Ryder organising the funeral? What had he to do with the Greens?

Hearing a knock on the front door, Lily brought her eyes to Davy. Lowering the newspaper, he looked back at her. 'Are we expecting callers?'

Lily shook her head.

Folding the newspaper, Davy rose and dropped it on the chair going to answer the knock which rapped again. Opening the door, the breath caught in his throat.

'Hello Davy boy,' the woman said.

The colour drained from his face and he felt dizzy. Leaning against the door jamb, Davy sucked in a large lungful of air.

'Not glad to see me then?' the woman smirked.

'How . . .? I thought . . . you were dead!' Davy managed at last.

'So that's what he told you was it?' the woman, dressed from head to toe in black, pushed past him and walked into the house.

Davy, in complete shock, closed the door. He watched the woman as Lily called out, 'Davy? Who is it, sweetheart?'

The woman followed the voice into the living room, walking straight past Lily, who was now standing by the door. Sitting herself in the chair Lily had just vacated, the woman warmed her hands by the fire.

Lily stared at the stranger who had walked in off the street and made herself comfortable by their fireside. The woman was overweight and her dark hair streaked with grey was pulled into a bun at the back. Eyes that were so dark they looked black stared back at Lily. There were lines around her mouth and eyes which revealed years of frowning and pinched lips. The face was hard and made Lily shudder.

Lily turned as Davy walked into the room and instantly noted his ashen face and his nervous eyes.

'Davy, what's going on?' Lily asked incredulously.

Wrapping an arm around her waist, he led her to his chair and bade her sit. 'Lily, this is my Aunt Maud.'

'What? I thought . . .' Lily began as she looked at the woman sitting in her seat.

'So did he it seems,' Maud Hurst put in with a laugh. 'Davy boy, put the kettle to boil, there's a good lad. I'm fair parched.'

Davy turned to walk away and Lily stared open-mouthed at his compliance.

Davy shut his eyes tight, praying when he opened them this would be a figment of his imagination. His aunt's words shattered his fervent hope.

'Go on, Davy boy, shift yourself to the kitchen while I get to know your little wife here.'

Davy gulped and walked out of the room.

Lily was aghast. Turning back to the woman, she said, 'I'm surprised to see you, to say the least, Davy and I were led to believe you had passed away some years ago.'

'Well I'm here, large as life and twice as ugly,' Maud cackled at her quip.

Lily stared, trying to take it all in. Why was she here? Where had she been all this time?

'Close your mouth, dearie, you look like a trout,' Maud said as she settled herself more comfortably.

'Why have you come here?' Lily asked, ignoring the insult.

'I'm Davy's aunt as he told you, and I thought it about time to visit,' Maud answered with a sniff.

Davy brought in the tea tray and placed it on the small table by Lily.

Maud reached out and dragged the table towards her. Pouring the tea, she ignored Lily's astonished gasp at her forthrightness. Leaning back with her tea, she eyed the pair sitting opposite her.

321

Lily dragged the table back to pour tea for Davy and herself. She saw Maud grin at her actions.

'Ain't this all nice and cosy, I can see I'm going to be happy here.'

'What!' Davy and Lily spoke in unison. Then Davy said, 'Aunt Maud – you turn up here out of the blue when everyone thought you dead! The shock of that alone almost gave me a heart attack, and now you think to move yourself in with us?'

'Well it is my house, boy,' Maud said with a triumphant look on her face.

Lily looked from one to the other, her mouth opening and closing in disbelief. 'Your house!' she gasped eventually.

'Yes – my house. Davy's uncle left it to me in his will, but I couldn't come to claim it before now. All that don't matter though, we can talk about that after supper. What *is* for supper by the way?' Maud looked pointedly at Lily.

'We don't eat supper, and I think we should discuss it right now,' Lily snapped.

'What, no supper? Bloody hell, girl, you ain't looking after my nephew very well, are you? Never mind, I'll have a look in the kitchen and see what there is.' Maud made to stand up, dismissing Lily's words.

'Sit down!' Lily barked, making Davy jump.

'That's no way to speak to your elders and betters!' Maud snapped back. 'Davy boy, you d'ain't pick a wife very wisely, did you? Look at how she spoke to me. Are you going to allow it?'

'Aunt Maud, where have you been all these years?' Davy asked, ignoring her questions.

'That ain't none of your business, lad, suffice to say I've been – indisposed,' Maud huffed indignantly.

'Why didn't you come back here before this?' Davy pushed.

'Look, how many times do I 'ave to tell you? I am not discussing my business with you and that's an end to it!' Maud snapped.

'In that case, when you have finished your cup of tea, you can remove yourself from this house!' Davy said, showing a courage he wasn't feeling.

'Well said, Davy!' Lily turned to him. 'This is our home! I know she's your aunt, but I will not share this house with her or anyone else!'

'I ain't got nowhere else to go, so you'll have to take me in,' Maud intervened. 'Besides, it should be me saying that. I should be turning you out of *my* home!'

'It is not *your* home! This house was left to me – not you! It is clearly stated in Uncle Bertie's will.' Davy was exasperated.

'Well I've got a will an' all. So the question is, which one is legal?' Maud grinned.

Lily and Davy exchanged a worried look.

'So, *Lilian*, I suggest you show me to my room because I'm fair worn out,' Maud said.

'We don't have a spare room, and my name is Lily not Lilian!'

Maud sighed audibly. 'Well, *Lily*, you seem to

forget I used to live here. There are three bedrooms up there. You two in one and I can have one of the other two.'

'You cannot have Clara's room!' Lily was on her feet, her hands clenched by her sides.

'Clara? That your kiddie?' Maud asked.

'Our daughter yes!' Lily's anger mounted. Davy placed a hand on her arm and Lily sat once more, but her anger remained.

'Clara died a little while ago, Aunt Maud, and Lily has kept her room as it was.'

'Ar right, a bit morbid if you ask me, but no matter, I'll take the other room,' Maud said insensitively.

Lily was shocked to the core at the callousness of the woman. She looked to her husband, who shook his head.

'Aunt Maud, you can use the room until you find yourself alternative accommodation,' Davy said firmly.

'Oh, I won't be looking for anywhere else, at least not until we get these wills sorted out.' Maud's mouth twisted into an evil grin as she stood up. 'Don't disturb yourself, I know the way.' With that she walked from the room, leaving Davy and Lily staring at each other at her audacity.

Each sitting in their chairs beside the roaring fire, Lily said at last, 'Davy, I think it's time you told me what's going on.'

'I don't know what's going on, Lily, as far as I knew Aunt Maud died years ago. It was a shock to see her standing on our doorstep this evening.' Davy shook his head.

Lily nodded and waited patiently as her husband collected his thoughts.

'When I was a little boy, my parents and Aunt Maud and Uncle Bertie took me to the seaside for a holiday. We were supposed to go out on a boat trip but I was not feeling well, so my parents went and left me with my aunt and uncle.' Seeing Lily's face wrinkle into a frown, he quickly added, 'Mum and Dad didn't want to, but Aunt Maud insisted she was capable of looking after me for a couple of hours. You saw for yourself how persuasive she can be.'

'Persuasive . . . bullying you mean!' Lily interjected.

Davy nodded. 'Anyway, there was an accident – I believe a bad storm took up and capsized their boat. My parents both drowned.'

'Oh Davy! I'm so sorry, I didn't know.' Lily felt the tears prickle as she watched her husband relive painful old memories.

'It was a long time ago, sweetheart. Then I had to go and live with Aunt Maud and Uncle Bertie. They raised me and Uncle Bertie bought my parents' house in Earps Lane where I lived before we married. He kept it in good order until I was of an age to take up residence.'

'What a lovely thing to do, your uncle sounds like he was a good man,' Lily said quietly.

'He was, Lily, the best. Aunt Maud, however,

was a bossy woman right from the start. She made my life a misery as I grew up. It was a good thing I was at school all day. When I was home she often beat me. I spent a lot of time locked in my bedroom. I remember coming home from school one day and Aunt Maud wasn't there. Uncle Bertie told me she had died. Life was so much better for me then. Uncle Bertie said he would take me into the business at the grocery store when I was old enough. Now, oh Lily, she's back and all those memories are here with her!'

'Don't get upset, darling, we'll sort it all out. I wonder why your uncle told you she'd died. Very clearly she hadn't.' Lily cast her eyes to the ceiling as she imagined the woman making herself at home upstairs.

'I don't know, but I'm sure before too long we'll find out.' His eyes followed Lily's to where his aunt was no doubt poking around the rooms.

'Davy, we have to do something about her – I know she's your aunt but . . .' Lily tried to be diplomatic.

'What can we do? What if she has a legal claim to this house?' Davy spread his arms to encompass the room.

'We'll take your uncle's will to a solicitor and get it verified first of all. Then if it turns out it *does* belong to her, we'll just have to move out,' Lily said, endeavouring to be brave.

'But where would we go?' Davy asked, a look of sadness crossing his face.

'What about the house in Earps Lane you spoke of? We could go there.'

'I sold it when we married, Lily, I didn't think it worthwhile hanging onto.'

'Never mind that for the moment, first things first. We need to see a solicitor. Didn't your aunt say she had a will also?' Lily asked. Davy nodded. 'Good, then she can bring that and come with us.'

Davy hung his head. 'Oh God! I can't bear the thought of that woman being in my life again, Lily!'

Jumping up, Lily planted herself on Davy's knee. Her arms wound round his neck and she kissed him. 'Everything will come out right in the end, you'll see.'

Hearing a noise from upstairs, Davy groaned. 'Sounds like Aunt Maud is making herself right at home.'

If that woman thought to take over Lily and Davy's house, she had another think coming. There was no way on this earth Lily would allow that to happen.

CHAPTER 32

Tilley Green sobbed quietly as the men from Webb's carried the box containing her mother's body from the house. It was a lovely casket, she thought, but in the end it was still just a box.

Seb placed his arm around her shoulder and led her from the tiny two-up two-down house in Russell Street. Falling in behind the cart which held the coffin, Seb and Tilley walked sedately as the small procession began to move. They and a few neighbours were the only mourners.

As he walked beside the weeping girl, Seb cast his eyes around for Lily. His mouth twisted into a quick lopsided grin at there being no sign of her. Clearly she had chosen not to head this funeral in an attempt to avoid him.

Only now it registered with him why they were moving so slowly. The weather had turned and a mist had descended. The dampness hung in the air trapping the chill and he shivered beneath his overcoat.

Arriving at the church, the coffin was lifted down by Stan Webb, Seb and two gravediggers who were called over to help. The neighbours attending were all women, their men either out at work or standing the breadline in the hope of being given a job.

Linking arms with a gravedigger at the other back corner, they carried Tilley's mother to the graveside. As the casket was lowered awkwardly to the ground, Seb heard Tilley's sniffs.

The vicar said a prayer and Tilley cried the whole time. 'Ashes to ashes, dust to dust . . .'

An hour later they were back at the little house in Russell Street and Seb said quietly, 'Tilley, you know I'll have to move out now, don't you?'

'Why?' Tearful eyes turned to him over the rim of a teacup.

'Now that your mother is . . .' He struggled to find the words which would not upset her further, 'is in Heaven, it is not fitting that we remain under the same roof.'

'Why not?' Tilly couldn't understand why Seb was deserting her, and now of all times.

'Because we are neither married nor related. People will talk and cast aspersions on your good reputation.'

'Cast what?' Tilley had no idea what he was talking about.

'Tilley, talk will be rife. They will say we are living in sin,' Seb sighed at the inconvenience all this had caused him. After everything he'd done for Tilly it was he who was now losing his home.

'Oh, I never thought of that. But where will you go? I don't want you to go, Seb! I don't want to live here on my own!' Tilley burst into tears yet again.

A thought seeped into his mind. Seb wondered if it might work. Was he prepared for it? He considered as he watched the sandy-haired girl mop tears from her ice blue eyes. He could not afford to rent a property on his meagre earnings and a boarding house would probably prove expensive in the long term. He had only recently secured Tilley's place at the Grand Theatre in Birmingham and the train fares were eating into their coffers. So what was left open to him? He could suggest Tilley sell the house and they could try to find a small property for her in Birmingham. However, that didn't help him. He would still be in the same position – homeless.

There was another option, but Seb was not at all sure about it. Pouring more tea, he gazed at the girl sat opposite him at the kitchen table. For all her eyes were red and puffy, she wasn't a bad-looking girl. She was no beauty like Lily Rae that was for sure, but she didn't make you sick to look at her. She wasn't the sharpest knife in the drawer either; her academic learning was sadly lacking. In her favour though, she was an excellent cook and didn't mind hard work. Her best asset was her voice. Tilley Green had the loveliest singing voice he had ever heard, and anyone who heard her sing formed the same opinion very quickly.

If Seb was ever to get anywhere in this world it would all be down to Tilley. It was she who would eventually take him into the higher echelon of society once more. It was Tilley who would command better pay, albeit unknowingly, and take them to the finer theatres – maybe one day even to London.

Watching her blow her nose on her handkerchief, Seb frowned. Could he do what he was thinking? Would it be worth it for a possible rise to fame? Thinking again about the London theatres and the money he could make there, he considered it might just be.

Grasping his courage in both hands, he said quietly, 'Tilley, I know you wouldn't want to sell your mother's house . . .'

'No I wouldn't!' Tilley was shocked at the suggestion.

Holding up his hands as if in surrender, he went on, 'I know that, but I was thinking – we could always get married.'

Tilley was so shocked she dropped her cup on the table and the now cold tea spilled on the tablecloth.

'Get married! You and me?' she gasped.

Seb nodded with a grin knowing full well she'd jump at the idea. 'Yes, why not? Is the idea not appealing to you?'

'Not appealing – not . . .' Tilley was lost for words.

'Well what do you think? Could you take me for your husband, Tilley?' Seb's emotions were in an upheaval. On one hand he hoped she would say yes, if only to find him a home and better his finances. On the other hand he hoped she would refuse him for he wasn't at all sure he could live as man and wife with her. He liked Tilley Green well enough as a friend, but as a wife . . .? He gulped as he awaited her answer.

'Yes, I could take you as my husband!' Tilley said at last, her eyes lowered shyly to her hands twisting her handkerchief in her lap. She did not see the disappointed look that crossed Seb's face but was gone again in a split second.

'That's settled then, we'd best plan the wedding for as soon as possible lest the neighbours talk. Also, I will move to a lodging house until that time. I don't have much money, so the sooner we're married, the sooner I can move back in.'

Tilley smiled and nodded. It had not been the most romantic of proposals, but the question had been asked nevertheless.

'Now I think you should pop next door and tell the neighbours your good news while I pack up my stuff.' Seb forced a smile to his lips.

Tilley jumped up from her chair and fled the room, her excitement carrying her on winged feet.

Seb sighed into the quiet kitchen. Everyone would know soon enough Tilley was marrying Seb Ryder and he, as her lodger, would be moving out until that time. Tilley's unsullied reputation would remain intact and he would be seen as the gentleman he considered himself to be. That would certainly add to his kudos with the townsfolk of Wednesbury.

Seb made a big show of leaving the house that very afternoon. He saw the grubby curtains twitch behind the dirty windows of the neighbours' houses as he stood on the cobblestones. He knew everyone up and down the street would be watching and by this time they would all know of the forthcoming wedding. He would be held in high esteem by all at leaving, albeit on the day of Mrs Green's funeral. They would not even think about the few days Tilley and Seb had already spent together under the same roof without being chaperoned. They would only see him as a gallant young man offering a poor girl a chance of a better life in marriage.

Dropping his bag on the cobbles, Seb took Tilley's hand and kissed the back, knowing eyes were watching. Retrieving his bag, he walked away into the descending fog. He turned around to wave before the mist enveloped him.

Having told Tilley he would collect her later for their trip to Birmingham, Seb strode forward in search of cheap lodgings. The dirty yellowing fog wrapped around him as he walked. It was not the cold that caused him to shiver, but the realisation of what he'd committed himself to. He was to be married. Moreover, he was marrying a girl he did not love.

As he walked along the tramway towards the marketplace, Seb's doubts swirled like the fog that surrounded him. Why had he proposed marriage to Tilley Green? He could so easily have walked away, but then the girl was his meal ticket to a better life. Would he come to regret the decision he had made? Only time would tell. For now, he had to find somewhere to live temporarily – and fast.

Turning into Addison Terrace just short of the marketplace, Seb knocked on the door of a house where a sign stood in the window. *Rooms for rent.*

Explaining his need to rent a room to the woman who opened the door, Seb was led inside. Briefly outlining the circumstances he found himself in, he was pleased the woman agreed to take him in. The house rules were laid out in a no-nonsense manner and he was shown to his room on the third floor.

Passing over the key, the woman held out her hand, saying, 'Money up front if you don't mind.'

Seb handed over his rent for the week to the woman, who nodded her thanks. He let himself into the room as the woman walked away.

Looking around him, Seb was surprised. Everything was clean and tidy. Placing his bag on the floor, he tested the bed with his hand. It was a good mattress, again he was surprised. Sitting on the bed, his eyes gazed around. A small tallboy stood in one corner by the window, the curtains of which were pulled back to let in the light. A dresser with a jug and bowl stood against the wall and a bedside locker held a Bible and an oil lamp.

Walking to the window, he looked out. Being on

the third floor meant he could see out over the rooftops of the smaller houses that surrounded the one in which he now stood.

Unpacking his bag and hanging up his clothes, Seb felt very lucky to have secured such a pleasant room. Taking out his pocket watch, he checked the time. His landlady, Mrs Harris, had said she would provide his meal early due to his need to catch the train to Birmingham.

After a quick wash and change of clothes, Seb locked the door behind him and ran lightly down the two sets of stairs. Finding the dining room, he was delighted Mrs Harris was there to greet him.

'Sit yourself down, Mr Ryder, your dinner is on its way.'

Seb thanked her as a plate piled high with hot stew and dumplings with mashed potatoes was placed before him by a young girl. Nodding his thanks, Seb tucked in with gusto.

Pushing his empty plate away, he dabbed his mouth with his napkin, as Mrs Harris came towards him.

'Had enough, Mr Ryder? There's more if you'd like it.'

'No, no, Mrs Harris, I'm full to bursting. That was delicious, thank you. I'm afraid I'll have to run if I'm to get Miss Green to the station in time for the train.'

'She's that lovely young singer from Honest John's, isn't she?' Mrs Harris asked.

'Yes, but she performs in Birmingham now at

the Grand Theatre. Being her manager it's up to me to see she gets there in plenty of time.' Seb smiled.

'Best be on your way then,' Mrs Harris said as she picked up his empty plate. 'Breakfast is from six to eight o'clock in the mornings. Enjoy your evening, Mr Ryder.'

Seb couldn't believe his luck at finding Mrs Harris's boarding house and she was such a nice lady too.

As he strode through the dark streets towards Russell Street he felt the cold fog around him. It had not lifted completely all day and he felt sure it would remain for a while yet.

Suddenly he stopped as a thought pounded in his brain. If he had left Mrs Green's house and found this lodgings first, he need not have asked Tilley to marry him after all!

You blasted idiot, Ryder! What had he done? He'd committed himself to marrying Tilley Green when he need not have done so.

Seb continued to walk in the murky darkness, and his spirits began to sink. Could he get out of this promise somehow? How could he tell Tilley he didn't want to marry her after all? He knew he couldn't do that to her. She had, just that day, buried her mother. Her sadness had been tangible. Then after his proposal her misery had turned to joy. If he tried to explain he'd made a mistake regarding their marriage now, she would be heart-broken again. Seb realised, through his own greed for money and a better life, he had trapped himself. He had hoisted himself on his own petard.

As he reached Tilley's house, his spirits were at an all-time low. He had promised this girl a wedding and he knew he could not break that promise, no matter how much he wanted to.

Putting on a brave face, he knocked the door and waited in the lonely fogbound street.

CHAPTER 33

The following day Lily had risen early and dashed to Webb's. Explaining what had taken place the previous evening with Maud Hurst, she apologised to Stan saying, 'I *must* get to a solicitor, Stan! I'm so sorry to leave you in a mess regarding the funerals, but this is terribly important. I could lose my home!'

Jenny had listened in horror at her friend's plight. 'Just tell her to sling her hook, I would!' Jenny interrupted.

'I wish it were that simple, Jenny, but it might turn out she has a legitimate claim to the property.' Lily was clearly in a state about the whole thing.

'Well, if her don't, you just send her packing, else I'll be taking my wooden leg to her!' Jenny rapped her knuckles on her leg beneath the desk.

Despite herself, Lily laughed at the picture forming in her mind of Jenny hopping around trying to wave her prosthetic leg in the air.

'Don't worry about the work, Lily, we'll manage. You get yourself sorted out at home first,' Stan said, walking her to the door.

'Thank you, Stan,' Lily said before leaving the office.

Running back towards Trouse Lane in the fog, Lily knew her friends would be discussing her predicament. Changing her direction at the top of the market, she ran up Church Street. Emily Johnston would know what to do.

Lily banged on the boarding house door impatiently. The door opened and a cross-looking Emily stood there. 'Oh Lily, it's you! I was all set to give someone a dressing-down for making such a noise.' Then looking at the girl who stepped inside, she asked, 'Lily, whatever is the matter?'

In the sitting room Lily again explained the events of the previous evening ending with, 'Emily, I don't know what to do!'

'Well, as you've said, the first thing is to get Davy and his aunt, along with the wills, to a solicitor. He will be able to sort out this mess, I'm sure.' Emily tried to calm her young friend.

'What if he can't?' Lily asked, her nerves jangling.

'My dear girl, if he can't, then he's not worth his salt, and you find another solicitor. Lily, I know an excellent solicitor, would you like me to come with you?' Emily smiled kindly.

'Oh yes please!' Lily visibly relaxed a little.

'How will Davy feel about my poking my nose into his family business though?' Emily asked, feeling a little worried.

'I'm sure he'd welcome the support. However, how his aunt would feel is quite another matter.'

'Don't you worry about that, I can handle her.' Emily raised her eyebrows knowingly.

Grabbing her coat and hat, Emily set off with Lily towards Trouse Lane.

'My God, this fog is awful, you can barely see your hand in front of you!' Lily said as they hurried along.

'It's a real pea-souper and no mistake,' Emily agreed.

Once at home, Lily made tea while Emily settled herself in the living room with Davy, who assured her he was glad of the moral support.

As the three talked quietly over their tea, the door suddenly flew open. So hard was it pushed back, it slammed into the wall. Maud Hurst strode confidently into the room and using her fingers motioned Davy to give up his seat by the fire.

Davy obliged but said scathingly, 'There are other chairs, Maud.'

Lily felt Emily's eyes on her as she said, 'Good morning, Maud, I trust you slept well.'

The woman, settling her ample body in Davy's chair, responded sharply, 'I'm Mrs Hurst to you, girl and yes, I didn't sleep too badly. Who is this then?' Maud tilted her head to a shocked Emily.

'This is Emily Johnston, our friend,' Lily answered then to Emily said, 'This is Maud Hurst, Davy's aunt.'

The two women glared at each other for a moment, then Maud spoke again. 'Where's my breakfast then? I'm fair famished. Davy boy, make us a cuppa, there's a good lad.'

Davy said, 'We have eaten already, Maud, so if you want breakfast you will have to make it yourself.'

Emily tapped Davy's arm in a 'well said' gesture.

The movement did not escape Maud's beady eyes. She harrumphed, then looked at Davy again. 'Don't just stand there gawping, make the tea!' The boom of her voice reverberated around the room.

'Davy is your nephew not your slave!' Lily said, her temper rising rapidly.

'I wasn't talking to you, girl, so shut your yap!' Maud shot back.

Emily drew breath to challenge Maud but Davy quickly intervened, saying, 'As you are a *temporary guest* I will make the tea.' Then collecting the cups on the tray, he walked from the room.

Lily was fuming. Not only was this woman speaking to her like she was something she'd scraped off her shoe, but Davy was doing her bidding. What was wrong with him? Was he really still that afraid of this woman after all this time?

Maud smirked as Lily and Emily watched her by the flickering flames of the fire.

'Always was an insolent child was Davy. He led me a dog's life growing up,' Maud said, then peering at Emily as if trying to recognise her, she asked, 'So what do you do, or am you too old to work?'

'I run a boarding house for young ladies,' Emily answered very calmly.

Lily was reaching boiling point.

'Young ladies, eh? You sure it's a boarding house and not a bawdy house?' Maud burst out laughing at her own quip.

'How dare you speak to my friend in that manner!' Lily rasped.

Emily patted Lily's hand, saying, 'I think Mrs Hurst meant it as a joke – not a very good one, I'll grant you – but I think that was her aim.'

Maud glared at the woman who now sat smiling at her. She felt sure she knew Emily from somewhere but she couldn't quite remember who she was. However, it would come to her sooner or later.

Davy came through with a tray of fresh brewed tea and his spine tingled at the atmosphere he could have cut with a knife.

'About time an' all. I thought you must be picking the tea leaves yourself!' Maud said nastily as she helped herself.

Emily quietly watched Davy take a seat and shrivel under his aunt's watchful eye. Whatever had gone on between this woman and her nephew in the past had left its mark on the young man. He appeared to be terrified of her; robbed of all backbone when she spoke to him.

'When we've had tea, *Maud*,' Lily emphasised the name, 'we are all going to visit a solicitor with both wills. He will be able to determine and authenticate which of the two wills is the true one.'

Maud spluttered as she choked on her tea, coughing as she attempted to speak. 'You what! I ain't doing no such thing, girl, so you can forget that idea!' she managed eventually.

'Maud, we're going and you are coming too, like it or not!' Davy dragged his hands through his hair then down his face in utter frustration.

'Mrs Hurst, I believe you are laying claim to this property. Now, if that is the case then you will have to have written proof of that fact.' Emily spoke with calm confidence.

'I've got written proof! My Bertie's will, God rest his soul. Anyway, this ain't got nothing to do with you, so keep your nose out of my business!' Maud snapped nastily.

'It does have something to do with me as Davy and Lily have requested my presence at the forth-coming meeting with *my* solicitor.' Emily gave a tight-lipped smile.

'Well I don't want you there!' Maud snapped, hoping that would be an end to it.

Tiny alarm bells tinkled in Emily's head. This woman was either lying about having a will or she was doing something unlawful. Sooner or later all would be revealed.

'Oh for God's sake! Aunt Maud, get your coat on and let's be off to sort out this whole bloody mess!' The three women stared at Davy in surprise at his outburst.

'I ain't going!' Maud protested.

'Fine! Then we'll go to see the solicitor and if

you don't want to know what's said you can stay here!' Lily countered.

The strong-arm approach worked and Maud rushed to get her coat on.

Outside, Davy whistled to a passing cabbie, who pulled his horse to a halt. With his four passengers inside, the cabbie clucked gently and the horse walked on slowly through the murky fog.

Robert Halstead welcomed them all into his office in Holyhead Road. 'Please take a seat. Emily, nice to see you again.'

Emily nodded. 'Robert.'

'Now, what is it I can do for you all?' He looked at each person in turn.

'I got a claim on the house these two am living in. My husband, Bertie Hurst, left that house to me in his will and I want them out!' Maud spoke even before Robert Halstead had sat down.

'I see. Well, Mrs Hurst, do you have your late husband's will with you?' Robert asked.

Maud rummaged in her bag and pulling out a paper she slapped it on the desk.

Robert Halstead picked it up and began to read. Then to Davy he said, 'May I ask why you are living in the house Mrs Hurst alleges belongs to her?'

'Alleges! It is mine and that paper says so!' Maud snapped as she banged her fist on the desk.

'Mrs Hurst, please, you will have your time to speak, but for now I need to speak with Mr . . .?' The solicitor looked at Davy.

'Davy Hurst. Bertie Hurst was my uncle by

blood and Maud Hurst is my aunt *by marriage.*' Seeing the solicitor nod and hold up a finger to prevent Maud interrupting again, Davy went on. 'Uncle Bertie left the house to me, sir, as stated in his will, which I have here.' Davy reached into his pocket and pulled out the paper, which he passed into Halstead's hand.

All waited as the solicitor read. Placing the wills side by side on his desk, he asked Davy, 'May I ask when your uncle died?'

Davy gave the solicitor another paper.

Maud leaned forward in an effort to see what Robert Halstead was writing down on his pad. Turning his attention to her, he said, 'Mrs Hurst, how did you come by this will?'

'It come to me through the post, I was living in London at the time, why?' Maud was not quite so confident now.

'It appears from this death certificate that your husband, one Mr Bertram Hurst, died of a heart attack in October three years ago.' Robert Halstead looked at the woman over his spectacles perched on the end of his nose.

'Yes, and . . .?' Maud asked.

The solicitor went on, 'The will Davy Hurst has produced was dated exactly a week before his uncle's demise.'

'I ain't quite seeing your point,' Maud was feeling distinctly uncomfortable.

'The will you claim came to you by post, Mrs Hurst, was dated some years ago. Twenty years, to be exact.' Halstead looked at the woman frowning back at him. 'This means the will in Davy Hurst's possession supersedes the one you have.'

'No! That can't be right!' Maud began to yell as she stabbed a forefinger on the desk. 'Look at the bottom, my Bertie signed it and everything!'

'He did indeed, as he did this one.' Robert Halstead held up both wills. 'However, it is the dating of the wills which is of concern to us today. Basically, Mrs Hurst, the will you hold is out of date, being replaced by this new one drawn up by your husband. The property in question does unequivocally now belong to Davy Hurst and is his to do with as he wishes.'

Unable to contain herself any longer, Lily clapped her hands together silently. 'Thank you, Mr Halstead,' she said. Turning to Maud, she snapped, 'So when we get back to *our* house you can get your things together and clear out!'

Maud grabbed the will she had been sent, shouting, 'You ain't heard the last of this, Davy boy! You mark my words!' Then she stormed from the office, slamming the door behind her.

Lily and Davy shook hands with Robert Halstead and, as they left, Lily heard Emily say, 'Thank you, Bobby, let's get together soon.'

'Definitely, anything for my big sister.'

Outside the office, Maud Hurst was nowhere to be seen. 'Looks like Aunt Maud has disappeared yet again!' Davy laughed in pure relief.

'What about her things?' Lily asked.

'She didn't have anything with her except her handbag,' Davy answered.

Lily turned to Emily and gave her friend a hug. 'Thank you, you always have the answer to any problem.'

'It was no trouble. Besides, having a good solicitor in the family always helps. It was Robert who paid for me to attend midwifery school.' Emily grinned.

Hailing a cabbie they returned to the house which they were now certain belonged to Davy. Over tea in the living room, Davy said, 'It was strange how Aunt Maud just disappeared into the fog like that.'

'Do you think we'll see her again?' Lily asked.

'Quite possibly, she will see this as being done out of what she thought to be her inheritance. Knowing her as I do, I don't think for a minute she will let it rest at that.'

Lily sighed heavily.

'Don't worry, Lily, if we stick together we can outwit Maud Hurst easily,' Emily proffered.

Lily nodded but she felt uneasy. What, if anything, would the woman try next?

CHAPTER 34

Tilley Green's emotions were all over the place, Seb thought as they sat on the train clacking along the rails.

'What will you sing tonight?' he asked her.

'I dunno, I ain't in the mood really.'

'I understand, but your mother wouldn't want you to mope about. Why don't you dedicate your performance to her this evening?' Seb tried to bolster the girl's spirits, but he saw her shrug her shoulders.

It was then that a young boy sitting opposite said, 'Am you Tilley Green?'

Surprised at the question, Tilley nodded.

'Mum, that's Tilley Green!' the young boy excitedly said to his mother.

'Yes son, I know,' the woman smiled indulgently.

'Miss Green, will you sign my programme? Please?'

Tilley grinned and nodded.

Pulling out a stubby pencil and the programme, he passed them to Tilley.

Seb pulled out a fountain pen and offered it to Tilley, saying, 'The pencil will rub off in time . . . the ink will stay longer on the paper.'

'Oooh ta, mister,' the boy thanked him.

Tilley wrote her name on the bottom of the programme and, along with the pencil, gave it back to the boy.

'Thanks ever so,' the boy beamed.

'You're welcome,' Tilley replied, her face smiling to match the boy's. Giving the fountain pen back to Seb, she watched the boy following the letters of her name with his finger.

Satisfied it was correct, the lad gushed, 'Mum! Look what I've got!'

'You're lucky to have it, so take great care of it,' his mother replied. She nodded her hands to Tilley who smiled back.

Tilley's smile turned to a grin when she heard the boy's next words. 'Oh I will, Mum, this will be worth a lot of money one day!'

Once in the theatre, Tilley prepared herself as she stood in the wings. She heard her name and the loud applause then she walked onto the stage. The music began and Tilley held up her hands. The band instruments ground to a halt one by one until silence prevailed. She saw the audience looking at each other wondering what was happening.

In a strong voice, Tilley called out, 'Very recently I buried my mother.' She heard the oohs and ahhs from the audience.

Then a man yelled, 'Sorry to hear that, Miss Green.'

'Thank you,' Tilley replied, her voice still strong. 'Therefore, this evening's songs will be dedicated to her. Thank you.'

The audience were on their feet and the clapping and whistling was deafening.

The music began again and her voice rang out true and clear. On she sang, '*She was only a bird in a gilded cage.*' Tears streamed down her face as she sang as if it was only for her mother, but Tilley maintained her dignity until the end. Finally, she wiped away the tears and took a bow.

In the meantime Mr Sutton had rushed from his office to see what the hold-up was. He heard Tilley tell of her mother's death and frowned at Seb, who stood as usual in the wings.

'I don't pay her to talk, I pay her to sing!' Sutton's voice was low but harsh.

Seb rounded on the man. 'You listen to me! Tilley is in mourning for her mother but she still came to sing at your theatre! She didn't want to let you or the audience down, despite her own pain and misery. So, Mr Sutton, I suggest you think before you say anything that might upset my fiancée more than she already is!'

'Your *fiancée*?' Sutton gasped.

Seb nodded as the applause almost shook the rafters.

Sutton harrumphed and remained at Seb's side. He tutted loudly when Tilley called for silence.

'Thank you, now I will tell you that today I have become engaged to Mr Seb Ryder.' The audience went wild as Tilley hooked a finger and Seb strode boldly to her side. She wanted to show him off but was shocked at what he did next.

Bending on one knee, he fished in his pocket and drew out his mother's engagement ring which he placed on her finger.

Men, women and children were on their feet again as Seb kissed her hand and rising to his feet he walked offstage to the accompaniment of the wedding march hastily decided by the band. By giving the audience something romantic Seb was assured it would endear Tilly to them even more and so help to line his coffers.

It took quite a while for the audience to settle down again as Tilley gazed at the ring, then she called out, 'Will you sing along with me?'

Shouts of 'yes' reached her ears and Tilley leaned forward to speak to the leader of the tiny orchestra. He nodded and Tilley stood back a step.

The introduction sounded and virtually everyone in the place sang with Tilley. *'Hello, hello who's your lady friend?'* By the end, some of the audience members were scrambling towards the stage in an effort to meet and congratulate Tilley Green.

Holding up her hands again, silence fell immediately.

'Please take your seats.' Everyone obeyed. The music began again and Tilley called out, 'Thank you for your good wishes. It's been a strange day, but I feel privileged to have shared it with you.' Before the audience could applaud again she launched into her song, picking just the right moment in the music. 'Silver threads among the gold' reached across the auditorium and there was not a dry eye in the house.

Seb clapped Sutton on the back, saying, 'You be careful, Mr Sutton, if you lose Tilley Green, you lose your audience – and your takings!'

When the last of the audience had gone, Tilley and Seb left the theatre. They had the surprise of their lives as they walked through the stage door. People were standing outside in the road, all pushing and shoving to speak to the girl who had entertained them so beautifully.

Condolences and congratulations were called to the couple as they stood surrounded by admirers. As Tilley happily answered questions, Seb stood with his arm around her protectively. *We're on our way, Tilley Green – we're on our way to the top!* He thought that despite not loving her, he was right all along to have proposed marriage.

Eventually the crowd began to disperse and drift away, chatting about witnessing Tilley's special night.

As the couple turned to walk to New Street Station, an authoritative voice spoke. 'Miss Green!'

Turning back, they saw an older man in a dark overcoat holding a silver-topped cane. A top hat sat on his silver hair which glinted in the moonlight.

'I wonder if I may have a moment of your time,' he said, walking towards them. 'George Addenbury at your service, madam.' The man gave a small bow from the waist as he whisked his top hat from his head. Replacing it, he smiled as Tilley gave an instinctive curtsy. 'My card,' he said as he passed it to her.

Glancing at the card, Tilley gave it to Seb as she said, 'Pleased to meet you, Mr Addenbury.'

The man's silver eyebrows raised as he saw Seb look at the card.

'This is Mr Ryder, my fiancé and manager,' Tilley said and watched as the men shook hands.

Addenbury realised this explained why his card had changed hands. 'I have to say how much I enjoyed your performance tonight as well as extend my congratulations to you both.'

'Thanks ever so . . . thank you,' Tilley corrected herself.

'I wonder if I may discuss a little business with you?' Addenbury asked.

'Oh, Seb sees to all that, Mr Addenbury, so if you'll excuse me I think someone wants to talk to me.' Tilley smiled.

Lifting his top hat an inch, the man returned her smile as she wandered away to speak with the few audience members who were still lingering.

'Mr Ryder, I am hosting a small soiree at my house on Saturday evening and I was hoping that Miss Green would be in a position to entertain us.' Addenbury stroked his silver whiskers with a leather gloved hand.

Seb took out a small notebook from his pocket where he listed Tilley's schedule at the theatre. Consulting his list, he screwed up his mouth, 'Hmmm.'

'If Saturday is inconvenient . . .' Addenbury began.

'Tilley has a booking, which I admit has yet to

be confirmed,' Seb said, closing the notebook quickly, lest Addenbury see that Saturday night was actually free.

'Oh that is a shame,' George Addenbury looked genuinely disappointed. 'Are you sure there is no way I can persuade you?'

'Well, I hate to discuss money – it's so vulgar – but Miss Green has been promised a rather large fee,' Seb responded.

'Rightly so, Mr Ryder.' Addenbury was as aware of the game they played as Seb was. 'Look, would it be possible to rearrange Miss Green's previous engagement in favour of my soiree? I will, of course, recompense for the inconvenience, as well as pay highly for her singing for my guests.'

'I'm sure Miss Green would love to sing for your guests, Mr Addenbury. What time will she be expected?' Seb took out his pen and made a note in his little notebook.

'Would eight o'clock be convenient?' George asked.

'Eight o'clock it is. Now we come to the vulgar part,' Seb said.

Their business concluded Seb and Tilley walked quickly to the station. Running along the platform, they jumped on the train as the steam whistle blew. Even before they sat down, the great iron beast began to chug slowly forward. The train trundled along, its steam lost in the fog that hid everything from view.

Seb excitedly told Tilley about the soiree she was

to sing at in a couple of days' time. However, the fee of three pounds he kept to himself.

'That's all well and good, but how much is he paying?' Tilley asked. Seeing the look cross Seb's face, she added quickly, 'He is paying us, ain't he?'

'Yes Tilley, he's agreed to pay us one pound ten shillings.' Seb lied so easily these days he amazed even himself. He had no intentions of divulging the true fee, in fact he'd decided he wasn't going to discuss finance with Tilley at all, but she had pre-empted him and asked outright.

'I'll have to wear my best frock if it's that important.'

'Tilley, it's important enough for you to have a new dress! An evening dress, I think.' Seb laughed.

Tilley clapped her hands like a little girl. 'Oooh, I ain't never had an evening dress – I ain't never had a *new* dress, come to that!'

Seb's heart lurched. He suddenly felt guilty at the lies he told her; at keeping the larger portion of the money for himself. To redress the feeling, he said, 'Well tomorrow you will have one and I shall buy it for you!'

Tilley's eyes filled with tears. 'You'm such a good man to me, Seb, and I do love you for it.'

Seb was taken aback by her words and guilt rose in him once more. Trying to change the subject quickly for fear of Tilley expecting him to reply in the same vein, he said, 'What colour dress will you choose?'

Tilley began to ramble on about colour and style

and where to shop but Seb's mind was elsewhere. His thoughts roamed around the woman who still haunted him. His mind conjured up the picture of Lily in the church about to be married. She did look beautiful, he could not deny, and he smiled inwardly.

'So what do you think?' Tilley's words snapped his attention back.

'Whatever you want is fine with me,' he said non-committally as he forced a smile to his face.

The train pulled into Wednesbury station and the couple alighted. As they walked through the streets, the glow from the gas-fed street lamps cast an eerie yellow glow over the damp fog.

Seb saw Tilley safely home before going back to his room in the lodging house. Once in bed, he thought again of Lily. The girl who had married another, but he was determined she was destined to be his once again before too long.

Throwing his arm over his eyes, his smile turned into a grin.

CHAPTER 35

Lily sat by her daughter's graveside pulling out the odd weed that had struggled to survive. 'I'm so sorry I haven't been to see you, sweetheart, but daddy and I had things to sort out.' Lily arranged the flowers in the vase she'd bought with her and laid it on the grave. 'There, that looks nice now.'

Looking down at the spot where her little girl lay beneath the earth, Lily felt the sob catch in her throat. The tears pricked her eyes for the child she would never see grow up, be married and have children of her own.

One tear escaped and rolled down her cheek and as she felt its cold trail, she gave in to her grief once more. She cried long and hard and felt her heart would surely break. Then, with hiccupping sobs, she muttered, 'I have been busy, what with the Maud Hurst debacle and regaining my job at Webb's, but, Clara, you have never been far from my thoughts, sweetheart.'

As she stared down at the flowers, she thought how talking to Davy about their child was helping keep her memory alive and she was grateful for that at least.

The church clock chimed, bringing Lily's attention to the time. 'I have to go now, my darling, but I'll be back soon, I promise.' Lily kissed her fingers and laid them on the grassy mound. 'I love you so much, Clara Hurst,' she said quietly as she got to her feet. With a last sad look at the flowers, Lily turned and walked from the churchyard.

As she entered Webb's, Jenny was waiting with a cup of hot tea. 'Well, how did it go with the solicitor?' Jenny noticed her friend had been crying and wondered if it was to do with her question.

Hearing the bell over the door tinkle, Stan and the others came through.

'Fine, the house *does* belong to Davy – and his aunt was not amused,' Lily said.

'I'll bet! What did she do?' Jenny asked.

'She disappeared. When we came out of the solicitor's office she was gone,' Lily said with a shrug.

'Blimey!' Jenny gasped. 'You need to watch out for that one, Lily, bad pennies always turn up again.'

'That was more or less what Davy said,' Lily agreed. Then to Stan, 'So what do we have on today?'

Stan sighed and as he was about to speak Fred jumped in with, 'You'm leading a private burial today – it's a cat.'

'A cat!' Lily looked at Stan who nodded. 'Are you serious?'

Stan nodded again, barely able to hide the smile threatening to erupt.

'Stan! For goodness' sake, how can I lead for a cat?!' Lily was exasperated.

Everyone burst out laughing, unable to hold it back any longer. Lily thought they'd been joking with her until Stan showed her the paperwork.

'Oh no . . . Stan, no. Please don't make me do this – please!' Lily begged, much to the amusement of the others.

Jenny snatched the paperwork from her fingers and tore it up. They all howled at Lily's horrified expression. 'Oh Lily, you should see your face! We thought you needed cheering up a bit, so Fred came up with this idea.' Jenny shook the bits of torn paper in her hand.

Lily laughed along with her friends at the joke played on her. As the men retired to the back room, Lily sat to chat with Jenny.

'I've just been to see Clara,' Lily said.

'About time an' all!' Jenny said sharply. Seeing her friend's face fall, she added, 'I'm sorry, love, that weren't called for.'

'It was, Jenny. So many times I've been to the churchyard but couldn't face it until now.' Lily frowned, her eyes still red and puffy from crying.

'Well, good on yer, you've been now, and it'll be easier each time you go. So, changing the subject, I want to know all about the visit to the solicitor.'

Lily smiled and related the whole tale.

'I wonder why she left the town in the first place

though. And why Davy's uncle told him she was dead?' Lily mumbled.

Jenny shook her head. 'Summat ain't right there, I'm telling you.'

'Do you think we'll ever find out?' Lily asked.

'I don't doubt it. At some point her'll drag herself back into your lives, and when her does – you best be ready for it.' Jenny dipped her chin in emphasis.

The day wore on with nothing to occupy them other than idle chatter and eventually Lily slipped on her coat. Stan came through, saying, 'Good idea, Lily. You two get yourselves off home, I'll lock up.'

Waving goodbye, Lily walked home. The fog was lifting slowly and was now just a murky mist. The gas lamps lit her way as she went and the cold dampness made her shiver. Increasing her pace, Lily wanted to have a roaring fire and hot meal ready for when Davy got home from work.

Hearing footsteps behind her, Lily looked over her shoulder but couldn't see anyone through the mist. She continued up into Trouse Lane and she heard the footsteps again. Was someone following her? Chastising herself for being silly and allowing the mist and fading light to spook her, she hurried on.

Turning into the driveway, she ran to the front door, the key already in her hand. Letting herself in and shutting the door, she ran into the living room and peeped through the window.

The dim light of the street lamp showed a

shadowy figure stop at the end of the driveway then move on. She gasped, her hand covering her mouth. She hadn't imagined it – someone had been following her! Lily felt fear grip her in its iron fist. Who was it? What did they want? Why were they following her?

With her heart beating fast Lily drew the heavy velvet curtains, closing her off from the outside world. Carefully feeling her way around the dark room, she found and lit the oil lamp on the table. The gentle light gave her some comfort as she dropped into the chair next to the fireplace. Slowly she began to breathe easier and, rising, she set a match to the fire. Watching the paper burn and the kindling catch, she sighed heavily. A roaring fire would help quell her fears even more. Sitting once more, she watched the flames lick around the coal nuggets and her thoughts turned again to the stranger at her gateway.

Struggling with the image in her mind, she tried to focus. Was it a man or a woman? She couldn't tell; the light from the street lamp was not strong enough to pierce the mist enough for her to be sure.

Suddenly she thought – could it have been Seb Ryder? She felt the panic rising again and fought to push it away. If it had been Ryder, why would he have followed her? It was common knowledge that she and Davy had taken up residence in this house after their wedding. Also, Clara's tragic accident had been splattered all over the newspaper.

Therefore common sense dictated Ryder would already know where she lived, and she'd not seen him in this area before. Ruling out the stranger being Ryder, she considered again.

Like a bolt out of the blue it came to her. It must have been Maud Hurst! But why would that dreadful woman follow her? Was Maud trying to frighten her? If so, she had succeeded. Was Maud bent on scaring her so badly that she and Davy would move away? If that were the case, it would leave the house ripe for Maud to move into. Not if Lily had anything to do with it! If that person was Maud Hurst, and if that was her plan, then she'd have a shock. Lily had no intentions of being driven from her home by Davy's aunt!

Lily was sitting by the fire when Davy came home from the grocery store. There was no smell of cooking and his wife seemed to be in a world of her own.

'Sweetheart, are you all right?' he said quietly as he approached her.

'Oh Davy! Is it that time already?' Lily had been startled as she'd stared into the fire.

'What's wrong, my love?' he asked.

With a loud and weary sigh, Lily explained about the stranger as Davy sat in his chair. She also told him of her thoughts around whether Maud was endeavouring to scare them away. Wisely her thoughts around Ryder she kept to herself.

When she'd finished speaking, Davy said, 'Well,

firstly I have no doubt, from what you've told me, that someone *did* follow you home.'

Lily sighed with relief that her husband believed her and didn't consider her to be foolish.

'Also, I wouldn't put it past Aunt Maud to do something like that. However, without being certain it was her, there's not much we can do. Even if we were to up and move, Lily, Maud wouldn't be able to move into the house, as it would be up for sale and she couldn't afford to buy it.'

Lily saw the sense of his words and nodded.

'Having said all that, I'm taking no chances. Tomorrow morning I will hire a cabbie to take you to Webb's and bring you home in the evenings.'

'Thank you,' Lily said as she smiled. Feeling relieved, she went to the kitchen to prepare their dinner. As she set the kettle to boil, Lily's mind transported her back. She'd had to travel to and from the café by cab because of Seb Ryder, and now she has having to do it again due to Maud Hurst. At least, she *thought* it was Maud who had frightened her so badly.

Making tea, Lily brooded on her life, her friends and her family. Would there ever come a time when she could be truly happy again? She had been so happy with Clara and Davy but that time had been very short. Tears smarted as she saw the image of her little girl giggling madly as Davy tickled her.

Oh Clara, I miss you so much, sweetheart!

Lily dabbed away her tears and carried the tea tray into the living room.

The following morning while Lily prepared breakfast, Davy went in search of a cabbie. Finding one waiting for a fare a little way down Trouse Lane, Davy whistled. He watched through the prevailing mist as the cab approached. The horse halted and the cabbie jumped down. Doffing his cap, he asked, 'Help you, mister?'

Davy introduced himself, as did the cabbie, Joss Timmins. Davy explained his wife needed to be taken to and collected from Webb's six days a week and it was important that the cabbie was punctual.

Joss nodded and said, 'It will cost you, sir, it'll be a shilling a week.'

'Joss, if you do right by me, I'll pay you half a crown every Monday morning,' Davy said, holding out his hand to be shaken on the deal.

Joss spit on his own hand and shook. The bargain was struck. Then he said, 'I'll just hang around for Mrs Hurst when she's ready. Then I'll drive you round to the grocery store.'

'How did you know . . .?' Davy asked.

'Everybody knows Mrs Hurst and yourself. Beggin' your pardon, but it was a bloody shame about your little girl.' Joss shook his head sadly.

'Thank you, Joss. I'll run in and have the breakfast prepared by my wife, otherwise I'll be going to Webb's myself – in a box!' Davy tried to be light-hearted but his smile didn't reach his eyes.

'Righty-ho, I'll be here when you'm ready.'

Although it was only Saturday, Davy pulled out

364

half a crown and pressed it into the cabbie's hand. 'Thank you, Joss, I'm relying on you to keep my wife safe.'

As Davy disappeared into the house, Joss wondered what the man had meant. Shaking his head, he pocketed the money and climbed back up into the driving seat to wait. He hated these dark mornings and the mist didn't help. Thinking of the money he'd just been given, he smiled to himself and patted his pocket.

Rolling himself a cigarette, Joss Timmins didn't see the figure hiding in the dark shadows further down the street.

CHAPTER 36

During the morning Tilley was doing her best to be patient while she waited for Seb to arrive to take her shopping. Her excitement grew with each passing minute, and her eyes darted constantly to the old tin clock on the mantelpiece.

She paced the room and then pulling the drab net curtain aside she peered through the window. Had he forgotten he was taking her to buy a new dress?

Tilley continued her pacing, then shot to the front door as she heard the knock.

'All ready?' Seb asked as he took in her shabby coat and hat.

Tilley nodded and stepping through the door she locked it behind her.

'Where am we going to first?' Tilley asked as she walked beside her fiancé.

'There's a gown shop in Union Street, we'll try there.' Seb kept his eyes forward as he spoke.

'Oooh, a gown shop!' Tilley's voice tinkled.

As they continued into the marketplace, a large woman dressed in black was hurrying towards them. She barged her way between the couple and in her haste she knocked Tilley to the ground. Stopping in her tracks, the woman looked down at the girl lying on the cobbles. 'It's your own fault, you stupid girl! That's what you get for being in my way!'

Tilley scrambled to her feet and squared up to the woman. 'I wasn't in your way! You should mind where you're going!'

'Don't you yell at me, girl! You should be more respectful to your elders and betters!' the woman rasped.

Seb tried to pull Tilley away but she stood firm. 'You're older yes, but better – I don't bloody think so. You'm a rude old woman who needs to learn some manners!' Tilley jabbed her forefinger at the surprised woman.

'I ain't got time for this,' the woman said as she turned to walk away.

'Oi! You need to 'pologise to me first!' Tilley yelled, grabbing the woman's arm.

Yanking her arm free of Tilley's grasp, the woman whirled around. 'Apologise to you? Hell will freeze over first!' The words were heavy with menace as she glared at the young girl.

Tilley looked at Seb who was trying his best to coax her away. Then Tilley's eyes roamed the gathering crowd. 'You all know me?' she called out. Nods and murmurs confirmed they did. 'You all seen what happened here? Was I to blame?'

'No!' The answer resounded around the street.

Turning back to the woman with a smirk, Tilley said, 'Seems to me it *was* your fault after all.'

With her fist bunched Tilley pulled back her arm, which suddenly flew forward. Her fist caught the woman on her jaw as she tried to step back. She had seen it coming but was too late to get out of the way. Although the punch was not particularly hard as it caught the edge of her chin, it was enough to take her off her feet. The woman heard the clapping and laughing of the crowd as she landed hard on the cobblestones.

Tilley brushed her hands lightly together as if removing dust and turning to the crowd she sang out, 'What a mouth, what a mouth, what a north and south, blimey what a mouth she's got!'

The crowd cheered and Tilley smiled and gave a small bow.

The woman dragged herself to her feet and stumbled away as the cheers turned to jeers.

Tilley and Seb walked on through the market as everyone continued to applaud her actions.

'Was that strictly necessary?' Seb asked.

Tilley's smile evaporated and she stood still staring at him.

'Well, was it?' Seb's tone was harsh.

'Yes! It bloody well was! I ain't havin' no fat woman push me around, and if you were anything like a man, you wouldn't either!' Tilley was furious.

'Tilley, you are on the way to becoming a star. This sort of behaviour is not appropriate. You cannot brawl in the street like a fishwife!' Seb's anger showed in his eyes.

'I see. Well, Seb Ryder, it's who I am! And if you don't like it you can bugger off and leave me alone!' Tilley glared at him before she turned on her heel and swiftly walked homeward.

One hand in his trouser pocket, Seb drew the other through his hair. Tilley had such a mouth on her at times; he just wished she'd keep it for singing. He blew through his teeth. *Women!*

Continuing his journey, Seb wondered what Lily would have done in that situation. He shook his head, he guessed she would have done exactly the same thing!

A couple of hours later, Seb knocked on Tilley's door. It swung open immediately and he smiled inwardly. She'd obviously been looking out for him.

'What do you want now?' she snapped.

'I've bought you this,' Seb held out the large box in front of him.

Tilley gasped and softened instantly. Grabbing his arm, she pulled him into the house and slammed the door. In the tiny living room Seb placed the box on the table and nodded to it.

Her breath rapid, Tilley rushed to open it. Inside she saw a bright red silk dress. 'Red!' she gasped. Carefully she lifted the garment from the box and holding it against her she twirled around. 'Oh Seb, it's – beautiful!'

'Go and try it on then because if it doesn't fit . . .' His sentence halted as Tilley bolted from the room. Sitting down, he sighed. At least she wasn't angry any more.

Upstairs in her bedroom, Tilley slipped into the gown which fit her perfectly. Walking over to the long, cracked mirror which leaned against the wall, she felt the soft silkiness of the material brush against her legs.

Looking into the mirror, her hands shot to her mouth. The scooped neckline showed off a small cleavage, and the bodice nipped into her waist. The capped sleeves sat on her shoulders and the full skirt fell to the floor. The light from the window caressed the silk, giving it a silvery glow. Simple in design, the effect was stunning.

Tilley turned this way and that, admiring her look and enjoying the luxurious rustle of the skirt. She looked at her face and hair and her smile faded. She was so plain. Her sandy hair was a mess and her pale skin, although smooth, was almost milky-white.

Taking off the dress and hanging it on the picture rail, she dressed again in her ordinary day clothes and went downstairs.

'It fits lovely, thank you Seb!' she said. He smiled and nodded once. 'Now you can clear off because I got things to do.' She laughed.

Seb left her with a smile. As he wandered away he knew Tilley had forgiven him for being harsh with her. There was another, however, who would never forgive him. Seb's mood was sombre as a picture of Lily formed in his mind. It would take more than a red dress for Lily Hurst to forgive him – it would take a miracle. But forgiveness was not what Seb was after, he was more concerned with getting what he wanted, and he wanted Lily.

At the time Tilley was trying on her dress, the woman she had knocked to the ground sat in the coffee house across town in Pinfold Street. Sipping her coffee, Maud Hurst winced at the pain in her jaw. *Bloody girl!* She considered she had been assaulted for no good reason. Yes, she had bumped into the young woman but she'd been in a hurry – and it was an accident. There was no call to retaliate as she had, was Maud's opinion.

Maud had watched her nephew and his wife climb into the cab and she had followed to see where it led. The mist was lifting and drab daylight had seeped through the darkness. Neither of which was enough to reveal where she hid in a small entryway.

The cabbie kept the horse to a walk and Maud had kept pace easily. All was going well until the altercation at the top end of the marketplace.

Touching her tender jaw, Maud winced again. Now she'd need to get some arnica to bring out the bruise quicker. Widening her nostrils, she drew in air long and slow, before puffing it out through her mouth. She had lost sight of where the cab was headed because of that damned girl! This meant if a cab was used tomorrow, she would have to follow it again.

She knew Davy would be running the grocery store but Maud wanted to know where that wife of his worked – if she worked. Once she had this information she could break into the house and have a rummage around. She didn't believe one word of what that solicitor had told them. She needed to get her hands on the will Davy had, as well as Bertie's death certificate. If what the solicitor had said was true, then she would simply destroy the evidence. Then with the older will in her possession it was Davy's word against hers. If Davy had nothing to support his claim, then even that solicitor couldn't argue against her.

Satisfied she had a good plan, Maud finished her drink and left the coffee house. Shivering in the dampness, she didn't fancy another night sleeping in Davy's garden. She would have to ensure she was up and in hiding before anyone else in the street roused.

Tramping along towards Trouse Lane, she cursed her dead husband for making a second will and causing her all this trouble.

Buying a hot meat pie from a stallholder in the 'Shambles', she continued to walk up through the main market, keeping a keen eye out for the girl who had hit her. Veering off into the High Street, she walked on, then turned into Trouse Lane.

Reaching the house, she strode confidently up the drive. Skirting the side of the building, she marched straight into the tiny summer house at the end of the garden. Sitting on an upturned bucket, she ate her pie.

Maud Hurst sat with her knees together and her toes pointing inwards. She slouched and, with her hands in her lap, she twiddled her thumbs. It was going to be another long night.

Tilley checked through the window before she left the house, she wanted to be sure Seb was nowhere to be seen. Satisfied, she locked up and hurried through the streets with mounting excitement. She had a surprise for her fiancé and she prayed he would like it.

Walking up Holyhead Road, she walked into a tiny shop wedged between two larger ones. She was greeted warmly by the proprietor and was shown to a seat.

'How may I help you?' the woman asked.

Tilley dragged her hat from her head, revealing an unruly mass of sandy hair.

'Ah, yes.' The woman smiled kindly, as she ran her fingers through Tilley's hair. 'Do you have a particular style in mind?'

'I have a red evening frock and I'm to sing at a soiree.' It was all she could say, she had no idea about hair styles.

'Oh, Miss Green! I'm sorry, I didn't recognise you straight away. Come with me, I know exactly what to do for you.'

Tilley was surprised the woman knew her name, it seemed she was being recognised more and more. It gave her a nice warm feeling as she followed the woman towards a sink.

'Firstly I'll wash your hair, then I'll give it a fashionable cut,' the woman bustled about with jugs and a large bowl.

'How much is this going to cost?' Tilley asked tentatively.

'Miss Green, if I may boast about cutting your hair, it will cost you nothing – not a penny!' the woman whispered conspiratorially.

'Sounds like a good deal to me, but why would you want to do that?' Tilley asked innocently.

'Because you are the talk of the town, my dear. You are said to be heading for stardom. When people know it was me who cut your hair, they in turn will come here to copy your style. That will mean more clients for my little shop,' the woman said proudly.

'Fair enough,' Tilley said and settled down to enjoy the fuss being made of her.

Tilley later walked from the shop sporting a new cottage-loaf hairstyle. Praying it wouldn't rain, she held her head high as she walked home. She revelled in the compliments shouted from the market stallholders.

Once home, she looked into the cracked mirror in her bedroom and gently patted her hair, being careful not to disturb it. She loved her new look.

Going into her mother's room, she rummaged on the dressing table. She had not, as yet, cleared out her mother's things and finding what she looked for she was glad she hadn't. Opening a small pot of rouge, she dabbed the tiniest amount on each cheek. Blending it with her fingers, she watched her complexion transform. Being so pale, she didn't want two bright spots on her cheeks and she gently rubbed until it was barely visible. Then to her lips she did the same. Standing back, she gazed into the mirror; she was pleased with her efforts.

Suddenly realising she had no footwear to complement her dress, she opened the door of her mother's tallboy. Being much the same size, she hoped to find something better than her old boots. Tilley gasped as she saw a fur stole hanging from the rail. She didn't know where or how her mother had come by this, never having seen it before, but it would be perfect for her. Taking it out, she was surprised how heavy it was. Draping it round her shoulders, she realised it covered her arms too. She'd be warm in this. Laying it on the bed, she went hunting for shoes. She pulled out a pair of hardly worn black leather side button boots. Slipping them on, they felt a little big, but with two pairs of woollen stockings they would fit better. She spent the afternoon going through her mother's belongings, finding things she never knew existed.

After eating a hot meal of faggots and peas Tilley dressed herself in readiness for Seb's arrival. She slipped on her red silk dress. Stroking the luxurious material, she crossed to the long mirror and could barely believe her own eyes. The transformation was amazing. Gone was the drab sandy-haired plain-looking tavern cleaner, and in its place stood a beautiful young woman.

Dropping the stole around her shoulders and with a few final touches to her make-up, she went downstairs where she sat waiting in nervous anticipation.

The door opened at Seb's first knock and he stepped into the house and gasped. 'Tilley, you look – beautiful!'

Ruby red lips parted to show even white teeth as she smiled her thanks. She did a little twirl in the hallway her joy clearly showing through.

'Come on, first class on the train this evening, I think,' he said.

Tilley grinned, she'd always wondered what the first-class carriage was like.

Outside as she locked the door behind her, Seb whistled loudly. She heard the clip-clop of hooves and felt like a princess as Seb helped her into a cab which had halted before her.

The cab ride to Wednesbury railway station was short and before she knew it she was boarding the waiting train. Looking around her, she saw the plush seats and tiny tables; so different from the wooden benches of third class.

During the journey Tilley asked Seb questions regarding the soiree they were attending and the man who had invited them, George Addenbury.

Seb answered her quietly as his eyes roamed over her in the dim light of the lamps. He was amazed at how different she looked. Happiness shone from her ice blue eyes; her milky complexion with just a hint of rouge high on her cheekbones, and her lips were the colour of ripe strawberries.

Alighting the train in Birmingham, they walked from the station and Seb noticed the admiring glances Tilley received. Hailing a cab once more, Seb gave the address as Tilley climbed inside.

'I don't half feel spoilt!' she said with a giggle.

'You deserve it, Miss Green,' Seb laughed back.

The cab rattled along the cobblestone streets, eventually pulling into a driveway and up a long gravel path. It stopped outside a massive house. Seb paid the cabbie, who doffed his cap before clucking to his horse to walk on.

Tilley gazed up at the house. Everywhere, gas lamps were lit, bathing the whole place in a bright yellow glow. Music and laughter sounded from within; there appeared to be a lot of people attending.

Seb rapped the knocker and the door was answered by a butler.

'Ah, Miss Green, please come in,' the man said, then nodded to Seb. 'Sir.' Closing the door gently behind them, he turned again to the couple gazing around them. 'May I take your wrap, madam, and your coat, sir?' The butler helped Tilley remove her fur stole as Seb took off his overcoat. Passing them to a young maid hovering nearby, the butler said, 'If you will follow me please, Mr Addenbury is in the music room.'

Tilley shot a glance to Seb and mouthed, '*Music room?*'

Seb nodded and grinned.

The butler opened a set of double doors and called out. 'Miss Green and Mr . . .?' He looked at Seb.

'Ryder.'

'And Mr Ryder,' the butler finished.

George Addenbury was at Tilley's side in an instant, greeting his guests politely.

The massive room was filled with rows of padded spoon back chairs and in the bow of the window sat the musicians. A baby grand piano tinkled, accompanied by a violin, a cello and a double bass.

A maid arrived with a tray of drinks and offered it to Tilley, who took a glass, as did Seb. Taking a sip, she giggled, the bubbles tickled her nose.

'Champagne . . .' Addenbury said with a knowing smile, 'has a tendency to do that, Miss Green.'

'Champagne – ooh!' Tilley had never tasted anything like it.

Addenbury led the pair around the room, introducing them as they went. In attendance were high-powered businessmen and councillors with their wives, and the Mayor of Birmingham and his companion. Tilley smiled inwardly wondering where the Mayor's wife was.

Large trays of canapés were carried around by maids dressed in black dresses with white frilly caps and aprons. Slowly people began to take their seats and George Addenbury led Tilley to stand with the quartet.

'Ladies and gentlemen, Miss Tilley Green has kindly consented to sing for us this evening.' A round of polite applause filled the room. Lifting his hands, the host went on as he addressed the musicians, 'Gentlemen, I leave Miss Green in your capable hands.' Then he took his seat next to Seb on the front row.

Tilley gazed at the faces watching her, then drawing in a breath she turned to speak with the pianist. He nodded and she turned back to the patiently waiting audience.

'I ain't sure what you'd like to hear, so I'll be doing a selection. Right, fellas, when you'm ready.' She heard the titters and giggles before the piano and strings took up. Her voice carried out as she sang her first song, 'My Wild Irish Rose'. Looking at the sea of faces before her, she noticed the butler and a line of maids standing at the back of the room; all were smiling.

Rapturous applause greeted her as she finished and she took a small curtsy, a wide grin spread across her face.

Tilley began to relax and enjoy herself immensely. After a couple more songs she spoke again with the musicians. Nodding eagerly, they struck a chord. Tilley stepped around in the space allowed her and then sang out, *'Hello, hello, who's your lady friend?'* as she sat herself on George Addenbury's knee.

The audience laughed loudly as their host enjoyed the attention given by this beautiful young singer. Seb grinned at Tilley's antics – she certainly was a natural-born performer.

Once more standing by the piano, she thanked her audience and asked, 'Any requests?'

Song titles were called out from every person in the room and Tilley threw back her head and laughed. 'Just a few then?'

As the evening wore on, Tilley finished with her favourite song, 'I don't want to play in your yard', which brought everyone to tears.

The applause was incredibly loud and as it died down Tilley said, 'These fellas ain't half bad, what do you reckon?' The clapping began again as she shook hands with each musician, thanking them for their wonderful playing. Smiles abounded as they in turn said what a pleasure it had been to accompany her.

Addenbury held out his hand and led Tilley to a seat, where she was given another glass of champagne. The two laughed and chatted for some considerable time and Seb, although mingling with the other guests, kept a close eye on his fiancé. He didn't want her lured away by the promise of a big house and lots of money by the man who had hired her to sing. Seb had noticed there was no Mrs Addenbury in evidence and he'd wondered why. Was George not married? Was he a widower?

Looking around him, Seb was surrounded by wealthy people. He felt comfortable; he was back where he belonged among the moneyed echelon of society.

A tap on his shoulder caused Seb to turn. George Addenbury said quietly, 'Please accompany me to the study, remuneration is in order, I believe.'

Seb smiled, 'Ah yes, the vulgar part.' Both men laughed as they walked to the study.

At the close of the evening, Tilley and Seb were driven home in Addenbury's carriage and all the way back Tilley gushed about how much she'd enjoyed the evening.

Seb handed over her share of the money and she thanked him, unaware that he had kept the bigger portion of her fee for himself.

Thanking the carriage driver having reached Tilley's house, Seb saw her safely inside before walking back to his room at the lodging house.

He smiled to himself as he recalled speaking with the guests, the rich people of Birmingham. This affirmed they were going up in the world. Seb chuckled as he thought, *It won't be long now before I'm rich too!*

CHAPTER 37

Lily travelled to Webb's that morning by cab and explained to Jenny and Stan why that was as they were extremely eager to know the reason.

'Right Lily, you ready for the off?' Stan asked, tugging the ends of his waistcoat and checking his black tailcoat was in place.

Lily nodded and they walked through to the back yard where the cart and horses waited.

'Where's the casket?' Lily asked.

'On the table in the parlour,' Stan answered.

Lily sighed and climbed aboard.

The horse-drawn hearse travelled along Holyhead Road and turned into Hobbins Street where it stopped outside a small terraced house. All the curtains were closed as a mark of respect, and the neighbours stood outside their identical homes. The street was filthy and the buildings were inlaid with grime.

Climbing down, Lily knocked on the front door of the dingy property. She stood aside as the door was opened by a woman who nodded. Lily winced as the woman's voice screeched out, 'Undertaker's here!'

Stepping outside, the woman waited and eyed Lily standing at the opposite side of the doorway.

The coffin was carried out by four burly young men.

'Mind my bloody door!' the woman screeched again.

Lily's eyes swivelled to Stan still sitting on the cart. He was doing his best not to smile. The coffin was loaded with a bang.

'Bloody hell, boys! Give yer granny some respect!' the woman yelled.

Again Lily smiled inwardly at how often the women used expletives with no care for what others might think of them.

Lily saw the boys snigger quietly. Obviously there had been no love lost between the boys and their deceased grandmother. As the family lined up behind the hearse, Lily took her position as lead.

The entourage moved off, heading for St James' Church just off Holyhead Road.

When they arrived, the boys strained and heaved to get the casket onto their shoulders and walked unsteadily to the plot where the vicar was waiting.

The service began as Lily moved back to stand with Stan. She watched the vicar as he spoke, his eyes on his open Bible in his hands. Suddenly he began to bob and sway. Lily, thinking the man was unwell, looked at Stan who raised a hand slowly. His fingers wrapped round an imaginary bottle and tipped up and down, then his hand stroked his chin to disguise the action.

Lily's eyes widened before they returned to the swaying vicar. Snapping the Bible shut, he took a step forward trying to maintain his balance. Unfortunately the momentum tipped him headlong into the grave. Everyone gasped at the drunken vicar sprawled in the hole that was meant for another.

'Oh for God's sake!' The woman's voice carried out across the quiet graveyard. 'Boys! Stop that laughing and get the vicar out of that hole, and get yer granny in it!'

Stan pursed his lips and lowered his head to stifle a laugh as the four pallbearers struggled to drag the vicar out of the grave. The mourners heard the churchman giggling uncontrollably as he was finally hauled out. Endeavouring to give his apologies from a sitting position on the ground, the vicar failed miserably. His laughter infecting the mourners and, before a minute had passed, everyone was howling at the spectacle. All that is, except for the woman with the raucous voice who was beating a now prone vicar with her handbag.

'You're a bloody disgrace! Call yerself a vicar! A bloody drunkard is what you am!' she berated the still laughing clergyman.

Lily watched in stifled amusement as the woman finally ceased her tirade.

Turning to the four boys, she screamed, 'Don't just stand there, get the box in that hole,' she pointed to the grave, 'then we can all get home for a cuppa!'

The boys scrambled to the straps to lower the casket into the ground. Unfortunately in their haste, the straps were grabbed with a split second difference in timing and the coffin began to tip at one side.

'Quick!' the woman yelled as everyone envisioned yet another calamity. The casket landed with a thud and the woman heaved a great sigh of relief. 'Right, let's get off home.' As they left, the woman cast the vicar a desultory glance then clipped each of her sons over the head.

Lily watched all this trying desperately to maintain the dignity of her station, but like everyone else, she could not suppress her titters at the whole spectacle.

On the ride back to Webb's, Stan laughed as they discussed the never to be forgotten funeral.

'The others won't believe it when we tell them,' Lily said.

'They will when they know it was Reverend Willis! He's well known for his drinking,' Stan countered.

With the afternoon spent discussing the events surrounding the morning interment, Lily quite forgot her worries until she saw the cabbie waiting to take her home.

After letting herself in through the front door, she waved to the cabbie. Lighting the gas lamps in the hall, she then went straight to the kitchen where she again lit the gas lamps and the range before setting the kettle to boil. Feeling a sudden draught, she looked around her in the dim light. She caught her breath as she spotted the broken window. Someone had broken into her house! Her hands flew to her cheeks as she looked around. Panic held her fast as she thought that whoever it was could still be inside. She strained to listen but could hear nothing other than her own heartbeat. Slowly and quietly she crept from the kitchen into the hall and inched her way along to the sitting room.

The door stood open and Lily peeped around it. The small amount of light filtering through the window from the gas lamp in the street told her the room was empty. Slowly she stepped into the room, her eyes straining to see into the shadows in the dark corners. With shaking hands she lit the gas lamps and looked around her.

She gasped in shock as she surveyed the mess before her. Cushions from the comfy chairs were slashed, the stuffing spread all over the floor. The small table had been upended. Ornaments were lying on the rug shattered into hundreds of pieces.

Lily's eyes roamed the dishevelled room and she felt the tears sting. Who had done this to her lovely home? Why had they wrecked everything? What had they stolen?

Dropping into a chair, Lily cried at the destruction surrounding her. A thought hit her like a thunderbolt. Was that person upstairs still? Jumping up, she grabbed the iron poker from the grate. Running silently back to the kitchen, she moved the kettle from the range so it would not boil dry. Then quietly slipping along the hall, she went to the stairs. Peering up, she saw nothing in the inky blackness. Retracing her steps to the kitchen, she lit a small oil lamp kept there for emergencies. With lamp in one hand and the poker in the other, she crept back to the stairs.

One by one she ascended, fear tight in her chest. Holding the lamp high to light her way, she went first to Clara's room. The door she kept closed was open! Lily moved inside slowly and looked around. Thankfully all was as it should be. Next she tried the spare room, where again, nothing had been touched.

Drawing in a deep breath, she tiptoed to the bedroom she shared with Davy.

'Oh no!' she gasped as she saw the disarray. The bedclothes were in a pile on the floor, the mattress lying at an angle on the springs of the bed. The wardrobe door hung open and all their clothes lay in a heap at the bottom. Dresser drawers were perched precariously on their runners, empty of the contents, which were strewn everywhere. Someone had ransacked their bedroom!

Lily began to shake as tears streamed down her face. Slowly turning away, she descended the stairs and moved to the living room. She dropped the poker back into its stand and, lifting the small table to its feet, placed the lamp on its surface. Dropping heavily into a chair, she stared into the dead fireplace.

Why would someone do such a thing? What had they been looking for? Money maybe, or bits of jewellery. Lily's mind was consumed with these thoughts as she sat in the cold living room. This was how Davy found her on his return from work.

Davy was holding her tightly as she sobbed. 'Who would do such a dreadful thing?'

'I don't know, darling. Maybe it was an opportunistic crime; someone finding the house empty thinking to steal anything of value.'

'Oh Davy, our lovely home!' Lily's tears ran free once more.

Sitting her in a chair, he said, 'You stay there while I make you a cup of tea, then I'll take a cab to the police station in Holyhead Road.'

An hour later the Superintendent of police looked around the rooms in the house and shook his head. Then returning to the living room said, 'Looks to me like someone was searching for something.'

Davy groaned and Lily's eyes turned to him. 'What's the matter?' she asked.

'Maud!' Davy snapped.

Lily sighed loudly as the pieces fell into place.

The Superintendent took careful notes as Davy explained about the wills, the visit to the solicitor and how Maud had disappeared afterwards.

'I see, and do you know if the will and death certificate have been taken, sir?'

'I left them with the solicitor,' Davy answered.

'Very wise. It's my guess that if it was Mrs Hurst

who caused all this, and she didn't find what she was looking for, she probably won't be bothering you again.' He tucked his notebook and pencil into the breast pocket of his uniform. 'I would advise, however, that you get that kitchen window mended as soon as possible, if only to keep out the cold. Other than that, without any evidence, there's nothing more to be done I'm afraid.'

Bidding them both goodnight, he was shown to the front door by Davy.

'I'll get one of the lads to pop along to that solicitor and let him know what's happened, on the off chance it was your aunt. Not finding the will here, she may well try the same thing at the solicitor's office. He'll be advised to lock the paperwork in his safe. In the meantime, I'll instruct a constable to patrol this area and keep a keen eye out.'

Giving his thanks, Davy shook the Superintendent's hand and went back indoors to his distressed wife.

Maud Hurst watched the policeman leave the house and stride away in the opposite direction to where she stood in the dark entry. An evil grin spread across her face as she crept quietly to her hiding place in the summer house. Yet another night spent in the cold, but it would be worth it when she had that will and death certificate in her hands.

Settling herself down, she grinned again. By this time tomorrow night she would be in possession of those papers and she would laugh loudly as she burned that will of Davy's. Tomorrow evening she intended to break into Robert Halstead's office, for that was where she now believed the papers to be.

Yes, in a couple of days' time she could take back the house she had once lived in. Then she would send Davy boy and his interfering wife packing.

Chuckling quietly to herself, Maud settled down to sleep.

CHAPTER 38

The following morning Lily Hurst nodded to the policeman who strolled past her house before she climbed into the cab. The Superintendent had kept his word regarding a constable patrolling the street, which made her feel easier about going off to Webb's.

She noticed as she walked into the shop that Jenny was looking a little pale.

'Are you all right?' she asked, thinking the girl's wooden leg might be causing her some pain.

Jenny shook her head. 'I feel that sick, but then pregnancy does that to you don't it?'

'Oh Jenny! How wonderful! Does Albert know? Do the others . . . what about your mum?' Lily threw her arms around her friend hugging her tightly.

'Whoa! Yes Albert knows, and me mother, and Fred and Stan.' Jenny's grin stretched across her face.

'Jenny, I'm so pleased for you both!' Lily grinned.

'I d'aint know how to tell you after you losing Clara,' the girl's face lost its grin.

'Jenny, we both know Clara's death was an accident. I do miss her dreadfully, but this is you and

Albert we're talking about. I'm so delighted for you, I can't tell you! When are you due?'

'Around May time, I think. So, as I'm resting, you can make the tea.' Jenny laughed just as Stan walked through.

'I'm expecting a young lad soon, ladies, he's going to be learning the trade out back with Fred.'

Just then a boy of around fifteen years walked in saying, 'Watchya, I'm Jimmy Bean and Mr Webb said as I was to call in and see him.'

Lily and Jenny exchanged a look as Stan ushered the boy into the back room.

It was a quiet morning at Webb's and, at lunchtime, all gathered in the tiny kitchen. Lily noticed the new boy had no lunch with him and Stan was back to his usual cheese sandwich.

'I'm just running down to the "Shambles",' Lily said as she grabbed her coat.

Reaching the small market, she rushed into the pie shop and bought six pies filled with meat and potato, then asked, 'Would it be possible to have a regular order to be delivered to Webb's?'

The owner readily agreed to her request, asking, 'Different filling each day?'

'Yes please, I'll pay the delivery boy, shall I?'

'Ar, that would be fine,' the woman said, glad of the regular order.

Lily rushed back to Webb's and passed out the pies, explaining about the order. Jimmy's eyes bulged at the pie passed to him – a pie all to himself!

'Well you ain't paying for them all every day, Lily,' Jenny said sharply.

'No she ain't,' Stan said, 'you are!'

Jenny's mouth dropped open in surprise. 'You what!'

'You'll be paying the delivery boy – out of the petty cash box,' Stan grinned.

Jenny picked up a teaspoon from the table and threw it at Stan, who ducked just in time. It bounced off his shoulder and clattered to the floor as everyone burst out laughing.

During the afternoon Stan wandered through to the girls who were chatting about babies.

'Stan, who is Jimmy Bean and where did you find him?' Lily asked quietly.

Stan dragged a chair to the desk and sat down.

'I buried his dad some years ago, before you girls started here. The family lives over in Moorcroft Row by the old colliery. The father died of consumption in the infectious diseases hospital, which left the mother and six kids to feed. We buried the father and I couldn't charge her a penny – she couldn't have paid anyway. I felt bad for them, Lily, they had no money and no breadwinner. Jimmy scavenged in the market and the others picked coal on the slag heaps. I was locking up after you'd all gone the other night when Mrs Bean walked in. I was surprised, to say the least. I prayed it weren't one of the kids that needed burying.'

'Oh Stan! That would have been awful for her!' Lily said.

'Any road up, she asked me if I'd take on Jimmy as an apprentice.' Stan raised his eyebrows in a 'what-could-I-do?' expression.

'Blimey!' Jenny piped up.

'Mrs Bean said as how her husband had bought their cottage years ago from the colliery so they wouldn't be turned out,' Stan went on.

'Well that's something at least; a sensible thing to do,' Lily remarked.

'Oh Lily, that woman was so thin it was a wonder she could stand up, never mind walk across the town! She said she had nothing to feed to the kids and she was terrified they'd all end up in the workhouse!'

'Oh crikey!' Jenny shivered.

'I know, so I gave her some money to feed the kids and said Jimmy should come by today.' Stan shook his head, a sadness showing in his eyes.

'You'm a big softie, Stan Webb,' Jenny smiled.

'I couldn't see them without. Jimmy's a good lad, he'll take care of his family.'

The door to the back room burst open and an excited Jimmy Bean came rushing through. 'Mr Webb, come and see – I've helped make my first coffin!'

Stan smiled and followed the boy out back.

'Poor little bugger!' Jenny said as she watched them go.

'I wonder what we could do to help the family,' Lily mumbled.

'Whatever it is, it can't be seen as charity. Folk

round here are very proud. It would have been really hard for the woman to accept Stan doing her husband's funeral for nothing. Then she came here to beg – it's like the last straw, Lily.'

'The final humiliation. There must be something we can do,' Lily said, a feeling of frustration building in her.

'Let's have a think about it, we'll come up with something, I'm sure,' Jenny said, trying to comfort her friend.

At the end of the working day as they all began to leave, Lily had an idea. Climbing into the waiting cab, she called to Jimmy Bean. 'Come on, we'll give you a ride home, save you that long walk.'

'Ooh ta, Lily,' the boy said as he jumped aboard.

If Lily's idea came to fruition, there could be two people in the Bean household earning a wage very soon.

Maud Hurst had slipped from her hiding place under cover of dawn darkness. Skirting the house, she checked the street was empty before rushing towards the marketplace. She would buy herself a good breakfast with the loose change she had found in Davy's bedroom. Then she would while away the hours until darkness descended once more, when she would search that solicitor's office. She *had* to find that paperwork in order to claim the house. She had convinced herself it rightly belonged to her. Either way, she would have it!

Finding a cheap café, she ate a hearty breakfast. She took her time, after all she had many hours to fill before she could complete her task.

Maud finally left the café and decided to cruise the market. Slowly she walked through the market-place and into the 'Shambles'. Both sides of the street were lined with stalls selling everything from old boots to fruit and vegetables. Starting at the top, Maud stopped at every stall as she wandered to the end of the street. Then, crossing over, she did the same on the other side, ending where she had begun.

Eventually cold and hungry, she went back to the café, where she sat with a pot of hot tea. She read a newspaper someone had left behind and stayed there all afternoon.

Maud left the café as all the shops began to close up for the evening. She shivered in the late chill and pulled her coat tighter around herself. Slowly walking towards the solicitor's office, she smiled inwardly. She didn't want to arrive before he'd locked up and gone home, or whilst other folk were still ambling about. The gas lamps in Holyhead Road were already lit by the time she got there and the street was almost empty of people. Wandering towards the building, Maud glanced around her. She should be able to get in, find the papers and get out again before anyone knew she was there.

Halting on the opposite side of the road, she stared across at the office. The place was closed for the evening and – it was shuttered! *Bloody man!* There was no entryway to reach the back of the building that she could ascertain from where she stood. Looking to her left, she searched for a way which would take her behind the office. There *had* to be a way, she just needed to find it!

A deep voice suddenly made her jump. 'Move along, madam, no loitering.' Turning, she was faced with a tall, burly policeman looking down at her.

Maud tutted loudly and strode away in disgust. She heard the constable chuckle and, glancing over her shoulder, saw him continue his patrol.

Now what could she do? The copper had seen her and he would remember her if asked. The office had shutters up and no visible way to its rear. Maud had been bested and the thought galled her. This meant she would have to sleep in that summer house again!

Cursing the name of Hurst, she strode on, the anger building inside her. At least her fury was keeping her warm, she thought as she increased her pace.

Sidling up the driveway and around the house into the garden, Maud saw the house was still in darkness. Slipping into the summer house, she settled down for the night.

Lying on the cold floor, Maud's mind slipped back to when she was a girl. She had met and married Bertram Hurst who was a wealthy store owner.

Taking a holiday with her brother-in-law's family one summer, tragedy had struck. The couple had been drowned in a boating accident and young Davy, their son, had come to live with Bertie and herself.

Thinking back, she knew in her heart Davy had been a good boy. Davy had turned up and taken all of Bertie's affections which had made her husband aim all of his anger and bitterness at her. Then the spite shown to her by Bertie had made her angry all the time. This anger she took out on the undeserving boy. She knew the lad hated small spaces yet she often locked him in the cupboard in the scullery and in his bedroom. Maud shivered as she heard again the boy's terrified screams.

Then he had started to drink heavily and with that came the arguments. The imbibing of so much alcohol and the disagreements were the result of his discovering his wife's affair with another man. Although he never raised a hand to her, the mental abuse she felt he inflicted caused row after row. Maud fought her corner bravely, but she believed her husband constantly put her down. She had been miserable beyond belief living with this man she had never loved.

The man she had met had swept her off her feet with his good looks and charm. She had started seeing him whilst Bertie was at work in the grocery store. Even though Bertie knew of her liaisons, she could not give up the man she had fallen so hard for. Jack Fortune was aptly named;

he was always trying to make money, no matter who he hurt in the process.

Jack had treated her like a princess, and Maud had fallen for his lies. One day he had told her he was off to London to make his fortune and she could either go with him or stay and live in misery. Maud had seized the opportunity and took off with Jack to the capital.

The smile his memory brought to her lips turned to a scowl when she recalled how her happy life with Jack suddenly turned into a nightmare. Leaving her more and more in their slum in the East End to go to 'work', Maud had realised she'd made a very big mistake running away with Jack Fortune.

She had made up her mind to return to Wednesbury when, on a cold November night, the police came knocking. They were looking for Jack who, they believed, had been robbing the wealthier houses. Maud was shocked, she knew he was up to no good, but she couldn't believe that of her Jack. Nevertheless, the police searched their dwelling. In the attic they found what they were looking for – stolen goods. Jack Fortune was nowhere to be seen.

Maud closed her eyes tight as she remembered them hauling her away, accusing her of being his accomplice. The magistrate sentenced her to one year in Newgate Prison despite her screaming out her innocence. Twelve long months she spent in that dreadful place where she almost starved to death.

Shuddering again, she thought of her release and how she had struggled to survive. Eventually finding work as a maid, she saved every penny of her wages. She ate well, very well, in the house where she worked and gained the weight she had lost whilst incarcerated in gaol.

When she had gathered enough money, Maud had left her employment and caught the train to Wednesbury. She had gone immediately to the grocery store and had seen Davy through the window. Waiting until he had left the store, she had entered and asked after Bertie. The boy minding the place had told her of the man's demise and she'd left quickly before Davy returned.

Maud shook her head in the darkness of the summer house. She'd never heard another word of, or from, Jack Fortune.

Bertie's will she purported had been sent to her in the post had been safely stashed in a box in the London slum. She had taken the will when she left her husband Bertie, and hidden it away from Jack. On her release from jail she had retrieved the will and kept it on her person until she had presented it to that solicitor.

Maud sighed heavily. Her life had been, and still was, a mess. She didn't feel she'd deserved the hardship she had suffered. Once upon a time she had been liked by many in the town in which she lived. Now, she was ignored – she was just another poor soul trying to make a living. She was a nobody. At one time this thought would have brought tears to her eyes, but now it just made her irate.

She felt the anger rise in her again as she thought about Davy residing in the house which should have been hers. He was living happily with that little wife of his, Lily. However, that would not be for much longer. All she had to do now was figure out a way to get into that solicitor's office.

Pulling her coat around her, Maud set her mind to working out how to acquire the paperwork which would see her living in relative luxury, and Davy boy and his wife out on the street.

While Maud had strolled the market, the constable from Holyhead Road police station walked into Robert Halstead's office and, seeing he had a client with him, waited patiently.

'Can I help you?' Robert asked.

'I can wait, sir, until you've finished with the lady.' The constable nodded in the direction of the woman sat by the desk.

'This is my sister, constable, Emily Johnston. We were just taking tea together.' Robert smiled.

The constable stepped forward. 'Ah right. The Superintendent asked me to call on you, sir. It seems you had some dealings with a Maud Hurst recently.'

'Yes, that's correct. Emily was also at that meeting,' Robert said, feeling intrigued.

'Then this may concern you too, madam. It's the Super's opinion Maud Hurst broke into and ransacked her nephew's house.' The constable heard the intake of breath. 'I take it you knew nothing of this?' Seeing brother and sister shake their heads, he continued. 'It is surmised she was looking for a will and death certificate which, we were told, is kept here by yourself.'

'Yes, constable, it is,' Robert answered. He patted Emily's hand, seeing she was upset at the news.

'Then I must warn you to lock all your papers in your safe overnight, sir.' The constable glanced around the room. 'If it *was* Maud Hurst who had caused the break-in, then she might well try the same thing here.'

'I will indeed, constable, but I can go one further.' Seeing the policeman's eyebrows raise, Robert Halstead stood and crossed to the window. Pulling aside the heavy curtain, he revealed a metal shutter. 'This place was once owned by a jeweller who had these shutters installed. I just never got round to having them removed, and now I'm rather glad I didn't.'

'If I were you, sir, I'd start using them at night, or any time you are out of the office.' The constable nodded as he turned to leave. As an afterthought, he added, 'If either of you see Maud Hurst again, please let them know down at the station. The Super would like a word with her. Good day to you both.' With that he left them.

'Oh Robert!' Emily said on a breath.

'Don't worry, the papers are already in the safe.

Maud Hurst won't be able to ransack this place with the shutters locked securely.'

Emily breathed a sigh of relief. 'Good. That woman is a menace! I'll go round to Lily's later to see if they need any help clearing up.'

Leaving her brother's office a little later, Emily walked home thinking about what the constable had said. Had that woman ruined Clara's room too? If so, Lily would be distraught! She had kept that room exactly as it was before her daughter had died. If that damned woman had desecrated the little girl's room . . .! Emily fumed her anger as she stamped over the cobblestones.

Back at the boarding house, Emily sat by the fire in her sitting room with hot tea. Her boarders were chatting quietly together but she heard nothing. Her thoughts were firmly set on Maud Hurst. What could the woman hope to gain from stealing those papers? Robert had proved to them all the house belonged to Davy, so how would the documents benefit Maud if she had them? The answer struck like lightning. She could destroy them and then take the will she'd received to another solicitor!

Jumping up from her seat, Emily walked swiftly from the room. Grabbing her coat, she let herself out into the street, pulling the door closed behind her.

Walking quickly down Church Street, Emily clamped her teeth together. She had to warn Lily and Davy. They needed to know what she considered could be Maud Hurst's plans.

CHAPTER 39

As the cab pulled up outside Jimmy Bean's cottage, he jumped out. 'Come on, Lily, me mum would love to meet you.'

Lily smiled as he helped her alight.

The cabbie nodded, telling her to take her time, he didn't mind waiting.

Walking carefully in the darkness, Jimmy led her down the path to the back of the small building.

'Mum, I'm back!' Jimmy called as he stepped into the tiny kitchen lit only by a small oil lamp.

Lily stepped in behind him, hearing the noise of children's laughter in what she guessed was the living room.

'We'm all in here,' his mother called back.

Jimmy led Lily into a room full of people. A small lamp stood on the large shelf above the fireplace.

'Mum, this is Lily Hurst, she works at Webb's an' all,' Jimmy said with a touch of pride in his voice.

'Hello Lily, bring yourself in, gel. Kids, move over and give Lily that chair.' Mrs Bean grinned.

Lily sat and her eyes surreptitiously took in her

surroundings. There was no fire in the grate and it was colder inside than it was outside. The small glow from the lamp showed old wallpaper peeling off the wall and Lily smelled the damp mould. There was a big rag rug on the floor where the children now sat.

Smiling at the rail-thin woman sitting in the only other chair, Lily said, 'I'm very pleased to meet you, Mrs Bean.'

'I hopes as our Jimmy's been behaving himself,' the woman smiled fondly at her son.

'I helped make my first coffin today, Mum!' the boy said proudly and laughed as his siblings groaned their disgust.

'Jimmy, yer dinner is in the cupboard,' his mother said and the boy walked into the kitchen, returning a moment later with a chunk of bread and a wedge of cheese. From where she sat Lily could see the green mould on the cheese and watched in dismay as the boy tucked in hungrily.

'I can't offer you tea, Lily, I'm afraid – I don't have any until Jimmy gets paid.' Mrs Bean was clearly distressed but proud enough to speak the truth.

'Please don't worry, I can't stay long anyway. I came to ask a favour actually.' Lily watched the woman eyeing her.

'If I can help I will, so ask yer favour.' Mrs Bean smiled as she pushed her straggly hair out of her eyes.

Lily noted the children were all ears now too.

'Mrs Bean, do you knit?'

Puzzled by the question, the woman answered, 'I can knit – when I've got the wool that is.'

Lily grinned. 'I wonder, if I provided the things you would need, whether you might knit some baby clothes for my friend?'

'I ain't sure I'd have the time,' Mrs Bean said, looking at her children. 'I have this lot to get to school and I have to . . .'

'Oh, I wouldn't expect you to do it for nothing, Mrs Bean!' Lily intervened. 'I'm willing to pay you for your efforts.'

'Really?' Mrs Bean's frown turned to a grin.

'How does sixpence a garment sound?' Lily smiled back.

'Blimey!' Mrs Bean gasped.

'I can knit as well,' one of the older girls volunteered.

'Hey you, don't you be so cheeky!' the woman chastised her daughter.

'No, that's good. I'm not bothered who knits I will pay sixpence a garment. I will provide the money for wool, patterns and needles. Is there anything more you will need?'

Mrs Bean shook her head.

'Erm . . . Mrs Bean, please don't take offence but – you will need more light, otherwise it will strain your eyes.'

'That's true enough. I can knit during the day, but our Prudence is at school then.'

'Right then, I will also provide another lamp and

oil. Will that be all right with you?' Lily was afraid the woman would see this as charity.

'It's more than all right, gel – it's bloody marvellous!' The grin Mrs Bean gave looked macabre on the woman's gaunt features.

Taking three pounds out of her bag, Lily gave it to the astonished woman. 'Jimmy can bring the finished articles to work with him and I will give him your money to bring home.'

Looking at the money in her hand, Mrs Bean asked, 'Ain't this payment in advance?'

'No, that is for wool, needles, lamp and oil. It's to get you set up.' Lily shrugged her shoulders.

'Thank you, we really appreciate this.' Mrs Bean's eyes brimmed with tears. 'You'm an angel in disguise.'

Lily blushed and stood to leave.

'Our Jimmy, see Lily out, there's a good lad,' his mother said.

By the back door of the old cottage, Lily pressed some coins into his hand. 'Get round to the coal yard and order some coal, it's too cold in there,' she whispered.

'Thanks, Lily, I won't forget this.' Jimmy suddenly threw his arms around her, giving her a quick hug before leading her back to the waiting cab.

On her journey home a warm feeling came over Lily. She had helped the family in a way that had allowed them to maintain their dignity. In addition, Jenny would have lots of new baby clothes. Then she thought whether the baby woollens could continue to be made and sold on. Mrs Bean could start up a small business from her cottage.

She smiled to herself, she would mention the idea to Jimmy, who would, in turn, suggest it to his mother. Satisfied, Lily sat back to enjoy the cab ride home.

Lily was delighted to see her friend Emily sitting chatting with Davy as she entered their living room.

'Darling, where have you been? We were so worried!' Davy helped Lily off with her coat.

'Hello Emily, how lovely to see you. I'm sorry I'm late, but I went to visit the Bean family. I asked Mrs Bean to knit some woollens for Jenny's baby and I would pay her for her trouble.' Her excitement turned sour when Emily shared her thoughts regarding Maud and the wills.

'We should warn Mr Halstead!' Lily gasped.

'He knows already. The police called on him earlier while I was there. The papers are in the safe and he has shutters on the windows. Maud Hurst won't be getting into that office, I can assure you.' Seeing Lily relax a little, she went on, 'It's you two I'm worried about.'

'There's no need to, Emily. Maud can't hurt us now. With the will safely locked away, there's nothing she can do,' Lily said.

Realising the sense of Lily's words, the three finally relaxed. Emily helped Lily prepare a meal and the evening passed chatting about the Bean family and Jenny's pregnancy.

Davy escorted Emily home in a cab and now sitting at his fireside once more he looked at his wife. He felt a rush of love as her eyes twinkled in the firelight.

'It's lovely news about Jenny having a baby,' he said.

Lily stiffened. She guessed what Davy was thinking. It was his way of telling her they should try for another child.

'Davy, I . . . I'm not sure I would ever want any more children, not after Clara . . .' Her words trailed off on a sob.

'I wasn't saying that, Lily,' he said, trying to hide the lie.

'Yes, Davy, you were. Be honest, that's precisely what you were saying.' Lily's eyes stung as the tears gathered.

'I'm sorry, sweetheart. I was going to suggest we try for another baby, but I can understand why you don't want to.' Davy sighed.

Seeing the disappointment in her husband's eyes, her heart went out to him. Turning her eyes to the flames dancing in the hearth, she thought about her daughter. A picture formed in her mind of Clara's smiling face, she heard again the giggles when she was tickled. A shuddering sigh escaped her lips and as her tears dripped silently into her lap, Davy came to her wrapping her in his strong arms.

'Come on, sweetheart, what you need is a good night's rest,' he said gently.

Lily nodded at his smile and rose from her chair. As she walked from the room she heard him damp down the fire and place the guard in the fireplace.

Changing into her nightgown, she knew she was being unfair to Davy regarding having more children, but she couldn't face it. She could not put herself in the position of loving another child; one whom the risk of losing would bring a sorrow too great to bear.

Climbing into the cold bed, Lily Hurst made up her mind. She would never have any more children.

A few days later Lily saw the early morning fog still shrouded the drab streets. However, by mid-morning it had been burnt off by the sun pushing through. Bright sunshine glittered on the golden leaves of the trees, some of which had already turned a rusty brown. Tiny patches of green leaves showed through the golden canopy in a bold effort to hang on steadfastly. Some trees had already lost their leaves, their bare branches snaking out against the sky. Piles of red, brown and golden leaves lay at the feet of these naked giants as they began to prepare for their long winter slumber. The allotment gardens were a kaleidoscope of glorious colour. Birds flew high on the unexpectedly warm thermals and dipped and dived to catch the last of the insects. Crows cawed their incessant chatter in a cacophony deafening to the ear.

Returning from Webb's in the early evening, Lily entered the scullery for the old tin bath. It was then she heard someone coughing. Stepping out of the scullery door into the garden, she heard it again. Someone was in the old summer house and they had a nasty rasping cough.

Going back to the kitchen, she lit the small oil lamp and carried it outside. Slowly she stepped down the garden. The coughing was louder now and Lily knew it was a woman. Carefully opening the door, she held the lamp aloft.

'Maud!' Lily gasped as she saw the prone figure on the floor.

Placing the lamp on the ground, she rushed over to the woman who, even in the dim light from the lamp, looked deathly white.

'Maud! Oh my goodness!' Lily struggled to get the woman to her feet. Grabbing the lamp, she helped Maud into the house. Sitting the shivering woman by the roaring fire, Lily dashed off to fetch blankets and a nightgown.

Taking Maud's damp clothes off, she slipped a thick cotton nightdress over the woman's head, then wrapped her in a blanket. Tucking another blanket around her knees, Lily rushed to the kitchen to make tea.

As she watched Maud sip the hot liquid Lily thought, *so that's where you've been hiding!*

Maud nodded her thanks as Lily took the cup from her shaking hands as another bout of coughing took her.

'Whatever were you doing, Maud?' Lily asked as the woman's cough subsided.

'I had nowhere else to go,' Maud managed before her cough robbed her of speech.

'You should have come to us,' Lily said. For all she didn't want Maud there, she could not have seen her out in the streets feeling so poorly.

'Cap in hand you mean?' Maud tried to laugh but her cough prevented it.

'Well it doesn't matter now. Davy will fetch the doctor when he gets home. In the meantime you stay there while I heat you some soup.'

Maud gave a perfunctory nod and Lily walked swiftly to the kitchen.

Maud gave a tiny grin. She was back in the house, albeit not the way she had intended, but now she was in – she was going to stay!

CHAPTER 40

Tilley Green's voice had enchanted everyone at the soiree, especially George Addenbury. She had enjoyed singing for such a select gathering and loved the attention showered on her afterwards.

Sitting in her small living room, she recalled the memories of that evening, and she smiled to herself. Mr Addenbury had even given over the use of his carriage for her to travel home. He was such a nice man, in a fatherly sort of way. Not like her own father, who had upped and left when she was five years old. Mr Green had left her mother to raise Tilley on her own, and the woman had worked herself almost to death doing so.

Snorting her disgust at how some people could behave towards others, Tilley thought of Seb.

Her thoughts then moved to marriage. Seb had said they should be wed soon. How soon? He'd made no mention of a date, in fact he'd said nothing more since his proposal. Should she raise the subject with him? Would he think her pushy if she did?

Tilley considered how it would be when they were married. Seb, of course, would move in with her and they would share a bed. A nervous shiver ran down her spine. She knew what this would mean, but was she ready?

Then there was her trousseau, she would have to buy a wedding dress. Spending money that would take all of her hard-earned savings and she'd be left with nothing. She would find herself totally dependent upon Seb. Tilley frowned into the flames of the small fire. Up until now she had always been independent and she enjoyed the freedom it brought. She recalled something her mother had once told her; when a woman married, any money or property she had would automatically revert to her husband. Tilley Green didn't have much – her house and a few pounds – but it was hers. She had worked hard for it and she wanted to keep it. A flicker of uncertainty caused the girl to frown again. Maybe she wouldn't raise the subject of their wedding after all, at least not for a while anyway.

Shifting her thought process back to Addenbury, she heard again his gentle voice. He had told her he could make sure she would live the high life. He could take her to London to sing at the very best theatres. He had promised her a whole new wardrobe of gowns for her singing career and another for her daily wear. He would command the highest of fees on her behalf. He would ensure she stayed in the best hotels on her trips to the capital and she would see all the sights. Tilley would keep her own money in her pocket.

Sighing loudly, she had to admit she was tempted by his offer, but what would he want in return? She'd mentioned nothing of this to Seb and until she had considered this in more detail felt it wise to keep close-mouthed about the whole thing. What he didn't know, he wouldn't grieve over.

Wearily getting to her feet, Tilley walked to the kitchen to make tea. She sighed again as she cast a glance around the tiny room. Her little house was cold and drab; badly in need of a lick of whitewash and new curtains. As it was, it didn't feel homely. If she had more money she could make some changes. Again, George Addenbury's offer sprang to mind. If she accepted, she knew Seb would be furious; he would probably call off the wedding. How would she feel if that happened?

Looking through her tiny kitchen window onto the standpipe in the court yard serving half a dozen houses, she knew she wouldn't be mortified. That in itself spoke volumes.

She thought she loved Seb, she was certainly taken with his good looks, but at times he could be very sharp with her. That was a side of him she didn't much care for. Was she really ready to take him as a husband? Would she ever be ready? Then again, if anybody waited until they felt ready, then nothing would ever get done.

Making the tea, Tilley took it back to the living room, the quandary ringing loudly in her head. Finally she decided to let things lie and see how it went. At present she had her singing job at the

Grand Theatre, a roof over her head and food in her larder. Drinking her tea, Tilley felt a little better.

On the other side of town, Seb sat in the coffee house thinking much the same thing. He wished he had not been so desperate to hang on to Tilley that he'd asked her to marry him. He'd only been able to see her making his fortune, then afterwards realisation had dawned. He would be tied to her for the rest of his life.

He had watched her closely at the soiree; how she had talked and laughed with Addenbury. What had they discussed? Tilley had said nothing to him about what had been said and that worried him. Was George Addenbury trying to entice her away? Had he promised her the things Seb couldn't yet provide?

Staring into his cup, Seb considered his options. He could marry the girl as soon as possible and be assured of his position as her manager, which would also mean being shackled to her for life, or he could call off the wedding and lose the money she would earn for him. What would he do then? He would have to go back to the Market Tavern begging for his old job back.

Shaking his head, Seb sighed. No, he could never go back to being a barman. He had to walk the path he'd chosen, regardless of the consequences. If he wanted to be a rich man, and Seb Ryder very definitely did, then he had to marry Tilley Green.

Leaving the coffee shop, he walked along the street oblivious to everything around him until he realised people were stopping in their tracks. A funeral procession was coming down the street and it was headed by Lily Hurst.

Seb stopped to watch as she walked sedately in front of the horse-drawn hearse. She held her head high and kept her eyes forward. Had she seen him? Oh yes, he felt sure she had. He watched as she slowly passed by and he raised an eyebrow in amusement. He followed her with his eyes until she was no longer in view. It was then that Seb Ryder knew for certain he could never marry Tilley Green!

That evening Seb and Tilley spoke little on the train to Birmingham. Arriving at the theatre, Seb wandered away and Tilley walked to her tiny dressing room, which to her thinking was a converted broom cupboard. On the table shoved into the corner was a large bouquet of fresh flowers, a tiny card tucked inside. Pulling out the card, she read the words on it.

Kindest regards, George Addenbury.

Tilley smiled as she replaced the card and sniffed the flowers. No one had ever given her flowers before and it made her feel very special.

The knock on the door announced Seb's arrival and he walked in saying, 'You ready then?'

He immediately noticed the flowers and picking out the card he glanced at it before tossing it onto the table.

Tilley watched him through the small mirror on the wall over her cosmetics table. Neither said a word about the flowers.

Standing, Tilley strode out of the room past Seb and went to take her place in the wings.

After another quick look at the flowers, Seb followed her sulkily, his hands in his trouser pockets.

From her place at the side of the stage, Tilley looked out at the audience lit by the gas lamp footlights. There, in the centre seat on the front row, sat George Addenbury. Somehow she knew he would be there.

As she turned to return to her dressing room, Seb whispered, 'Where are you going? You'll be announced in a moment!'

Tilley ignored him and sprinted back to her room. Pulling a rose from the bouquet, she snapped its stem. Pushing the rose into her hair, she secured it with a hairpin. Satisfied, she walked briskly back in time to hear her name called. She also saw the scowl plastered across Seb's face.

The applause began as Tilley walked on stage. She saw Addenbury on his feet, clapping loudly. She patted the rose gently and he beamed at her. They were of an accord, she loved the flowers and he was delighted.

Tilley sang her heart out with a song to make her audience laugh before bringing them to tears with another. Her singing spot came to an end and Tilley turned to leave the stage. Then on impulse she turned back and yelled out, 'Would you care for another song?' The audience went wild. Holding up her hands for quiet, she laughed, 'I'll take that as a yes then. This song is dedicated to a special friend, Mr George Addenbury.' The audience clapped again as she smiled down at the man, who blew her a kiss. A quick word with the orchestra leader and Tilley was ready. 'A bird in a gilded cage' delighted the audience, but for three people it held a special meaning. Tilley, George and Seb all knew the significance of her choice of song for her encore.

Seb stood over Tilley as she removed her stage make-up. Glowering at her through the mirror, he rasped, 'What the hell was all that about? Special friend . . . you only met him recently, how can that make him a special friend?'

Tilley had expected this reaction and she wasn't surprised when it came. She spoke no words as she finished her task. Then she turned in her chair and said, 'Mr Addenbury is the only man who ever sent me flowers, and it was my way of thanking him.'

'I could have bought you flowers, you only needed to ask!' Seb was livid.

Tilley sighed.

'What? What's wrong now?' he asked.

'Seb, I should not have to ask! Maybe you should have thought of it yourself.' Tilley's temper was rising. The side of him she didn't like was showing itself again.

'I bought you that red dress! I thought of that by myself, didn't I?' Seb's frustration was evident.

'Yes. Yes you did,' Tilley said calmly, then yelled, 'As an apology! And, because I had nothing else to wear that *you* thought was good enough!'

Seb closed his eyes tight for a second. Then he said more calmly, 'Look, it wasn't like that . . .'

'Yes it was, Seb, so don't you dare deny it!' Tilley cut across him.

A knock came to the door at that moment and Tilley, without taking her eyes from Seb's, called out, 'Come in.'

Seb groaned as George Addenbury walked through the door. Crossing to Tilley, he took her hand and kissed the back. 'My dear girl, you were simply marvellous tonight!'

Tilley smiled her thanks.

Addenbury went on, completely ignoring Seb, 'Would you do me the honour of dining with me this evening?'

Tilley glanced over at Seb who stood with his hands on his hips.

Addenbury's eyes followed hers and then he said, 'Mr Ryder, you are welcome to join us – if you wish.'

Seb knew he'd been asked along as an afterthought. His anger mounted at the gall of the man.

'I'm not sure it's such a good idea for *us*,' Seb said.

'Ah right. Jolly good. Then it's just us two. I

know the place for a splendid meal, Tilley,' Addenbury said deliberately, misinterpreting Seb's words.

'Oh don't mind me!' Seb's anger bubbled over as he yelled out his frustration.

Addenbury ushered Tilley out through the door, then with a snide grin at Seb, added, 'Goodnight, Mr Ryder.'

Seb stood with his mouth agape. Had that really happened? Had his fiancé just gone out to dinner with another man?

Dropping into the chair Tilley had vacated, he looked at himself in the mirror. Suddenly feeling very tired, he rose to go home. As he stood he saw a glint on the make-up table. It was the engagement ring he had given Tilley. Picking it up, he instantly knew the poignancy of it having been left there. She had broken off the engagement. Dropping it into his pocket, he looked again at the flowers and his arm swung out, knocking them to the floor. Roses and lilies were scattered everywhere and were crushed beneath his boots as he strode from the room.

CHAPTER 41

Maud Hurst had eaten the soup provided by Lily and was now tucked up warmly in bed in the spare room. As promised, Davy had fetched the doctor, who said Maud had a nasty chest infection for which he had left a tonic.

Davy and Lily sat by the fire discussing the latest episode in their life.

'I didn't know what else to do, so I brought her inside. She was looking so ill, Davy, I was afraid she might die!' Lily said.

'You did the right thing, sweetheart. Although I'm not happy Aunt Maud is in this house again, we couldn't have left her out on the streets. The winter won't be long in coming and she would have frozen to death had we not taken her in,' Davy comforted his distressed wife.

Lily nodded her acceptance that her husband had agreed with her actions.

'So what do we do now?' she asked.

'Well, we can't turn her out until her health improves. Aunt Maud will realise that, so she'll be in no hurry to get well.' Davy sighed.

'That was my thought too. Davy, I will have to go to work, as will you, and the winter at Webb's will be the busiest time of the year, as you know,' Lily said quietly.

'I understand, but I'm loath to leave that woman alone in our house. I wouldn't put it past her to have the locks changed the first chance she gets!' Davy was on his feet now, pacing back and forth.

'Oh Davy! Do you really think she would?' Lily was shocked at the idea.

'Yes I do! Lily, we have to work around this somehow. We have to ensure Aunt Maud isn't left alone here, at least for the foreseeable future.'

'How can we do that?' Lily was now beginning to panic.

'I don't know as yet,' Davy answered, shaking his head.

Then an idea came to Lily. 'A nurse! Davy, we could hire someone to look after her whilst we are at work! It would, however, have to be someone we trust, someone who knows the situation.'

'But who?' Davy asked.

'I wonder if Emily would be interested. She has nothing much to do in the boarding house during the day when the lodgers are out, and if we pay her, she might consider it. What do you think?' Lily's thoughts rolled through her mind.

'Well we could ask her. In fact, I think I'll pop along and ask her now,' Davy said, giving his wife a kiss.

Lily smiled as she heard him leave the house, whistling a little tune as he went.

Emily Johnston listened as Davy explained his predicament before saying, 'I'm sorry, Davy, but I must say no.' She saw the crestfallen look cross his face and went on, 'That woman and I would come to blows before the first day was out!'

'I did wonder about that, but I told Lily I would ask. Now I'm not sure what to do about the situation.' Davy sighed loudly.

'I'm sure you'll find a solution,' Emily smiled kindly.

Davy gave his thanks and left. On his way home he racked his brains for that solution but he was left wanting. On reaching home, he was no nearer to finding a way around the problem than he was before.

Lily was upset that Emily had not consented to her request for help but she did see the sense of it. She thought about all the people she knew but none would be in a position to help. Jenny was working; her mother was busy with the baby and her other children, and Mrs Bean was now happily knitting – Mrs Bean! Would she help out if she was informed of the reason? She could do her knitting here just as well as at home. Her children were all in school during the daytime and Lily was certain the extra money would come in useful.

Telling Davy her idea, she grabbed her coat. 'I'm going to see her now before it gets too late to visit,' Lily said.

'Go by cab, just in case,' Davy warned.

Lily nodded and left the house.

Hailing a cab, Lily gave the driver the address. Arriving at the Bean household, Lily knocked the door and prayed the woman would be amenable to her suggestion. She was welcomed in and the children were sent to play upstairs. Only Jimmy Bean remained downstairs with his mother.

Lily explained what she had in mind and the reasons behind it, and when she finished, it was Jimmy who spoke up.

'The extra money would help with coal for the winter, Mum, and it would save the others having to pick on the slag heaps.'

Dora Bean nodded her head. 'Ar, all right, lad, I'll do it,' she said, smiling at her son.

Told she should use the woman's given name, Lily said, 'Dora, I must warn you, Maud Hurst is a spiteful, rude and bossy woman, and I don't want you upset by her.'

'Lily, there ain't a woman alive who could upset me in that way. You just leave her to me.' Then she held up a finger for a pause in their conversation, and Lily saw Jimmy plug his ears with his fingers. The noise of the children's falling out upstairs had risen higher as time went on and Dora had now had enough. Taking a deep breath, she screamed out, 'Will you lot shut up!'

Lily winced as the voice boomed around the tiny room but noticed the immediate silence upstairs.

Dora nodded and Jimmy took his fingers out of

his ears. Lily laughed loudly, she was in no doubt Dora Bean would cope admirably with looking after Aunt Maud.

Money was discussed and the deal was struck. Dora Bean assured Lily she would be on her doorstep first thing in the morning. Jimmy agreed to get the other children off to school before going on to his work at Webb's.

Lily returned home feeling happy and fortunate. Dora Bean had nothing in the way of worldly goods but she had a heart of gold and Lily was glad to know her.

As they had predicted, Maud Hurst kicked up a fuss when introduced to Dora Bean the following morning.

'I don't need no looking after, so you can just clear off back to where you came from!' Maud managed before her cough cut off her words.

'You don't have a choice in the matter!' Dora Bean spat back. 'Lily has hired me to look after you, so look after you I will! Now, you can shout as much as you like, but it won't make the slightest difference. So my advice to you is shut yer yap!'

Lily stifled a grin as Maud harrumphed, sending her into yet another coughing fit.

Back in the living room, Lily allowed her grin to show. 'There's plenty of coal for the fire, so don't be sparing with it. There's food in the larder for your lunches if you've a mind to make it and help yourself to tea.'

'Right, now you get yourself gone and don't you be worrying about a thing,' Dora said as she ushered Lily out of the door.

Once Lily had gone, Dora made tea. Taking a cup upstairs to her charge, she placed it on the bedside table. Leaning forward, she said quietly, 'I know all about you, Maud Hurst. I know what a spiteful old cow you are, so I'm telling you right now, don't you be coming it with me. I ain't averse to picking a few mushrooms for yer dinner, if you get my meaning.'

Maud's eyes widened as she did indeed grasp the concept of the woman's words. Nodding once, Maud picked up her teacup. Looking into it and then at Dora, she made to put the cup back.

Dora laughed. 'Your tea is fine, just remember what I told you. Now you have a think about what you want for your dinner and let me know.'

Frightened eyes looked back at her and Dora laughed again. Turning away, Dora went downstairs to do her knitting by the roaring fire.

The weather turned cold that evening and Lily ensured Dora Bean was taken home by cab. She went upstairs to check on Maud, who instantly voiced her disgust at having to be babysat by *that dreadful woman!*

This immediately told Lily that Maud had not had her own way and Dora had kept her in line.

In between bouts of coughing, Maud said her piece. 'I don't need looking after and treating like a child! So you can tell her not to bother coming again!' she harangued.

'Dora Bean has kindly given up her time to ensure you have a hot meal while Davy and I are at work,' Lily tried to placate Maud.

'I don't give a bugger! I ain't a babby who needs my nose wiping.'

'Maud, just take your medicine while I prepare our evening meal. I've bought some mushrooms from the market which I thought would go nicely with a bit of lamb.'

Maud paled visibly. 'I don't like mushrooms!' she rasped.

Lily sighed and left the bedroom.

Davy came home early and after Lily had taken Maud her dinner, they sat together over their own meal.

'I've been to see the solicitor,' Davy said.

'Oh, what for?' Lily asked.

'I've drawn up my own will, Lily.' He smiled.

'I see. May I ask why?' She was taken aback at his announcement.

'If anything should happen to me, I want you to be taken care of. I've made sure this house and the business comes to you if I die first.'

'Oh sweetheart, don't . . .' Lily couldn't bear the thought of being without him.

'It needed doing, my love. Surely you see that, especially with what's happened with Aunt Maud.' He raised his eyes to the ceiling where his aunt was languishing in her bed.

'Yes, I understand the logic, but let's not talk of death – I see enough of that at work,' Lily said, although she was quietly pleased that Davy had had the foresight to ensure she would not be out of a home if the worst happened.

Sitting together on the sofa, they chatted then retired to bed. All was well in their world, for the moment at least.

CHAPTER 42

A few days later the people of Wednesbury woke to see a thick blanket of snow from their windows, which had fallen silently throughout the night. Hot breath on the icy glass was rubbed by cold hands to form a clear view. Gas street lamps threw out a murky yellow light, which caught the ice crystals embedded in the snowy blanket, making them glitter like diamonds. The smooth snow piles lay on rooftops and windowsills. Gradually the darkness of night was pierced by the sharp daylight. Mother Nature had turned the dirty little town into a white winter wonderland. The schools would close and the children, wrapped warmly, would be out playing in the snow. Snowmen would be seen everywhere and those fortunate enough to own one would drag out their sledges. Children's noise and laughter would ring out and echo through the streets as snowball fights would begin. Eventually the cold and wet would drive them indoors to sit by a fire with a bowl of hot soup.

Tilley Green sat in her living room, her mind going over the last few days. She had enjoyed her meal out with George Addenbury, but the memory had been spoiled the following day by Seb.

He had been in a foul mood when he'd come calling. She understood why he had been upset, after all they had been engaged, and she'd been out with another man.

She tried to explain it was only dinner but Seb's temper had flared. He'd shouted at her, 'Do you realise how this has made me look like a fool?'

Tilley sighed loudly into the quiet room. She had called him selfish and that he could not tell her what to do.

'You left your ring on the cosmetics table – do you think so little of it that you forgot to pick it up?' he'd yelled at her as he produced the engagement ring and handed it to her.

'No, I . . .' Tilley began but couldn't find the words to explain she'd left it there on purpose. She'd felt sure he would understand its meaning, but he obviously didn't. It had been her way of trying to call off the engagement. She had been unable to tell him face to face that she had changed her mind about marrying him.

'Don't shout at me – we're not married yet!' Tilley had said.

'I'm not sure now whether we should be!' Seb retaliated.

Tilley's anger knew no bounds now and she had thrown the ring back at him.

'I think it's time you left, Seb Ryder, and don't bother to come back!'

Seb had taken her at her word and had not come to see her since.

She had taken herself on the train to Birmingham to sing at the Grand Theatre and had told George Addenbury of their quarrel. He had soothed her troubled mind and put his carriage at her disposal.

Rising from her seat, she realised it was once more time to ready herself for the journey to the theatre. She wrapped up warm and stepped out of the house and into the waiting carriage. The roads were treacherous but the driver kept the horse to a steady pace, and they arrived without mishap.

Tilley was sad at falling out with Seb, but in her heart she knew it would happen eventually. Walking to the manager's office, she knocked and heard Thomas Sutton shout, 'Come in.' Looking at the girl facing him, Sutton said, 'Ah Miss Green, what can I do for you?'

Tilley explained that she was no longer engaged to Seb Ryder and asked if her wages could be given to her directly.

'I'm sorry to hear that,' Sutton said, 'but of course I agree to your request. In fact, as you are here, I will pay you now.'

Counting out five shillings from a box kept in his desk, he held it out to her.

'There must be some mistake, Mr Sutton, Seb said you agreed to pay three shillings,' Tilley said.

Thomas Sutton's sad eyes looked into Tilley's bright blue ones. 'Tilley, I agreed to pay Seb Ryder five shillings on the nights you sang here. What he then passed on to you, I have no idea, but I suspect it was, as you mentioned, three shillings per performance.'

Dropping into a chair, Tilley's tears welled. 'No, Mr Sutton, he paid me three shillings a week!'

'Oh, my dear girl,' Sutton was on his feet, producing a clean handkerchief. 'I'm so sorry, it seems he has duped you out of quite a sum.'

Nodding her head, Tilley sobbed.

'The absolute cad!' Sutton said and Tilley couldn't help but smile. 'Now then, dry your eyes and take your money. You have a performance shortly. In the future, I will make sure you are paid your fee and if that man is seen here again, he will be ejected from my theatre!'

'Thank you, Mr Sutton, you have been very kind.' Tilley took her money and left the office.

Sitting in his chair again, Thomas Sutton shook his head. Ryder deserved everything that might come to him. Ryder had lost Tilley Green and Sutton wondered what would happen now. He knew George Addenbury was taking a keen interest in Tilley and he was glad. The girl deserved better than Ryder. He felt sorry for the girl who had trusted the man so readily, but he was sure she had learned a harsh lesson. For his part, Sutton would keep to his promise to ensure her five shillings went into her hand, as well as keeping Ryder out of the theatre.

No one in the audience was aware of Tilley's misery as she entertained them, and when she went back to her dressing room George Addenbury was there to greet her.

Over dinner later that evening Tilly tearfully explained what had happened regarding her singing fee. Comforting her, he said she was better off without the blackguard. Inside, however, George was fuming at the way she had been treated. He sincerely hoped he didn't come face to face with Ryder any time in the near future.

'Tilley, I have a suggestion to make, and I hope you will think about it,' George said quietly. Seeing her nod, he went on, 'I have a small house here in Birmingham which would be ideal for you. I would not expect or want you to pay rent, but it would save you travelling from Wednesbury to the theatre.'

'But I have a house already,' she said.

'I know you do, but you could rent that out. I'm sure the money from that would be useful to you, and if at any time in the future you wished to return, it would be there for you.' George smiled reassuringly.

'I don't know . . .' Tilley was guarded, and rightly so after the debacle with Seb Ryder.

'I'll tell you what, why don't you come over tomorrow and I'll show you the house. Then you can take your time to think about it. What do you say?' George asked.

'And what would you want in return?' Tilley asked forthrightly.

Addenbury's laughter boomed out, then he

answered with, 'Just your promise, Tilley – that you will not take Seb Ryder back into your life.'

Tilley grinned. 'There ain't no fear of that!'

'Then we are agreed?' George asked.

'All right, but I ain't selling my home. I'll rent it out as you suggested,' Tilley said.

'Marvellous!' Addenbury poured more wine into Tilley's glass and they toasted her possible move to Birmingham.

The past few days Seb had spent in turmoil. The row with Tilley was awful but as he looked at the engagement ring in his hand, he couldn't help but heave a sigh of relief. He was no longer committed to marrying her. Despite Tilley being his cash cow he had not tried to go back to her. He thought about the money he would lose in the future but compared to having to marry her for it, he felt he'd had a lucky escape and had decided not to pursue her anymore.

Lying on his bed in the boarding house, he wondered about his future. What would he do for money now that Tilley Green was no longer providing for him?

Closing his hand around the ring, he cursed Tilley and Addenbury – but most of all he cursed himself. Had he not been so hot-headed, he would still be earning. He knew his greed would always be his downfall no matter what he did or where he went.

Looking again at the ring, he decided to sell it. That way he would have a few pounds to tide him over until such time as he found employment. An idea came to him and he rolled it around in his mind.

Rising from his bed, he grabbed his coat and left the boarding house. After a visit to the jeweller's to sell the ring, he would visit Honest John at the Theatre Royal. He would present his idea and hoped the man would agree to it. If he did, Seb would be in the money once more.

Walking through the snow, Seb arrived at the Theatre and stomped inside. Finding Honest John, the two men shook hands.

'I have a proposal for you,' Seb said and saw the spark of interest in the other man's eyes. 'Now, I know you travel all over looking for performers for your theatre, and my suggestion is this. What if I took on that burden? I could scout out talented artistes on your behalf – for a small fee of course. That, in turn, would free you up to concentrate on this place.' Seb stretched his arms to encompass the room.

'I see. Tilley given you the boot, has she?' Honest John was known for his forthright speaking.

'Suffice to say, we had a disagreement,' Seb muttered.

The other man nodded, knowing what he'd said was true; it was the gossip shared all over the town, whether Seb was aware of it or not.

'So, you want to come and work for me now? Tell me, what do you know about theatre life? About the acts I seek out?'

'Well I've seen what's on the billing before now, and it is my guess there's another Tilley Green out there just waiting to be found,' Seb answered.

Honest John roared with laughter. 'Seb my boy, there ain't another like Tilley Green in the world! However, I'll take you up on your suggestion. You find them and I'll put them on the boards, providing they'll make us money. Mind you, I don't want no rubbish!'

A handshake sealed the deal and they went to the office to discuss finance and what Seb would be looking for in the way of artistes.

Seb left the theatre a little while later in a considerably better mood than when he entered. Honest John was giving him a second chance and Seb knew he would not be able to cheat this man out of his money. Now all he had to do was find some acts his new employer would be happy with.

CHAPTER 43

As the week wore on Maud Hurst's health improved, although she swore blind it had not. Her belligerent behaviour towards Lily during this time had the girl biting her tongue rather than respond in the same manner, she knew, but she really didn't care. She had, however, dragged herself downstairs to sit by the fire in the evenings.

It was one night after dinner when Davy said, 'Now you're on the mend, Aunt Maud, it's time you thought about moving on.'

The statement took the woman by surprise and she deliberately forced a coughing fit. 'I ain't nearly well enough, Davy boy.'

Davy and Lily exchanged a knowing look.

'Oh I think you are,' Lily said firmly.

Maud glared at the young woman intent on throwing her out onto the snow-laden streets.

'You know perfectly well you were taken in because you were ill, but the time has come for Davy and me to have our home to ourselves again.' Lily glared back at the woman sat opposite her.

'Where do you suggest I go then?' Maud snapped.

'To be honest, Maud, I don't really care!' Lily countered, her patience was finally worn down.

Davy shifted in his chair, feeling uncomfortable at the exchange between the two women. He could see this ending badly. To ease the tension a little, he said, 'Maybe you should look for somewhere, Maud, a nice little cottage perhaps.'

'And just how do you propose I pay for that?' Maud's anger flared.

'Find yourself a job!' Lily drew the discussion back to herself.

'A job! Where? Doing what? You stupid girl, don't you know about the poverty in Wednesbury?' Maud was livid.

'I am not stupid! I know only too well about the poverty and lack of work, but if you don't look, you won't find!' Lily yelled.

The hatred in Maud's eyes for the young woman shouting at her burned clearly.

'I ain't going trawling through the snow looking for work and that's final! Maybe in the spring I'll have a wander out, but until then I'm staying put.' Maud settled herself further into the armchair to emphasise her point.

Lily gasped at the cheek of the woman, then she said, all sweetness and light, 'If you don't remove yourself from this house tomorrow, Maud Hurst, I will instruct the police to remove you forcibly!'

Now it was Maud's turn to gasp. 'Davy boy, am you going to sit there and let her talk to me like that?'

Davy dragged his hands through his hair. He really couldn't face another showdown.

'Davy! Grow a bloody backbone and tell this wife of yours to mind her own business! This is *your* house, or so you say, so *you* make the decisions – not her!' Maud's finger shot out in Lily's direction.

'Aunt Maud please . . .' Davy began, feeling the life draining out of him.

'Don't you *Aunt Maud* me, Davy boy! Just put your foot down and tell her what's what!'

Lily got to her feet and stared down at Maud. 'I have two things to say to you. Firstly, if you call my husband *Davy boy* one more time I will slap you! Secondly, I want you gone from this house by the time I return from work tomorrow, or else!'

'Or else what?' Maud mocked.

'Or else the police will drag you out kicking and screaming, and neither of us will lose any sleep over it. You have been warned, Maud, and mark my words, I *will* see this through!' Lily strode from the room and retired to her bedroom.

Maud looked at her nephew. 'What you got to say about all this then, Davy b . . . Davy?'

Standing, he said quietly, 'She means it, Aunt Maud, and I agree with her, so you best do as she says.' Turning away from her scowling face, he walked quietly away to his bed.

Maud was left staring into the fire, her head pounding with anger.

In the darkness of their bedroom, Lily whispered,

'I'm sorry, Davy, but I can't stand that woman in our house a moment longer.'

Davy cuddled his wife and whispered back, 'I know, sweetheart, now go to sleep.' He knew he was being a coward where Maud was concerned, but the strong memories of his miserable childhood crept into his mind every time she yelled at him.

Lily lay listening to her husband's breathing and soon it changed to a deep sleep rhythm. She heard Maud going to her bed and she prayed it would be for the last time.

Davy groaned in his sleep and Lily was concerned. She had noticed he had not looked well this past week or so and she hoped he had not caught a cold. Her concern grew as she heard him groan again as he turned over. She would suggest he see the doctor tomorrow, which would put her mind at rest. She knew all the worry and stress of Maud staying with them had not helped.

The following morning Lily was tired, she had slept little. Dora Bean arrived and Lily explained about the heated argument the previous evening.

'What do you want me to do if she won't leave?' Dora asked.

'I'm not sure, Dora. I just pray she will leave.' Lily felt exhausted by it all. 'I have to get going, we have two funerals today.' Grabbing her coat and hat, she prepared to leave, then suddenly realised she'd forgotten to ask Davy to visit the doctor. She would have to make her request this evening, but for now she was late for work.

Stepping outside, she walked carefully to the cab. The ground was frozen and icy; it was treacherous underfoot.

Finally arriving at Webb's, Lily was flustered about being so late. She apologised to Stan and over hot tea she related her tale of Maud and their argument.

'Good on yer, girl! It's about time she was gone from your lives,' Jenny said.

Lily nodded, but the uneasy feeling that settled on her remained. What if Maud was still there when she returned home that evening? Would she actually request the police remove the woman from the house? Would the police do that?

Her thoughts were broken by Jenny. 'I'd better stir my stump and get to the lavvy,' she grumbled. They all laughed as the girl tapped her wooden leg. 'Stan,' she said as she limped towards the back room, 'it ain't right having to go out the back in this weather. I'm piddling more now I'm pregnant and I could break me wooden leg on that ice!'

The laughter increased and Lily knew it was her friend's way of lightening the tension in the room.

At the allotted time, Lily wrapped up warmly and climbed onto the driving seat next to Stan for the first funeral. The 'closed' carriage with a roof and long windows was pulled slowly by the two black horses.

Arriving at the house, Lily knocked on the door and stood back. Four burly men carried the coffin to the back of the carriage where Stan held the door open. Sliding the casket inside, the men took up their positions in the line. Stan closed the door and climbed onto his seat. Lily led the procession to St John's church and the service commenced.

The afternoon passed in much the same manner, but Lily's mind was not on her work. She conducted herself professionally but her thoughts were centred on whether Maud had moved on. She wanted to be home but dreaded it in case the woman was still there. By the time five o'clock came, Lily was beside herself with worry.

The journey home in the cab seemed to take forever as the horse tried to gain purchase on the icy cobbles. Finally they reached the house. With a quick thank you to the cabbie, Lily moved carefully over the ice beneath her feet.

In the living room Dora Bean sat knitting by the fire.

'Is it that time already?' she asked.

Lily nodded and drew a breath to speak.

Dora beat her to it, saying simply, 'She's gone.'

Sighing heavily, Lily dropped into a chair. 'Did you have any trouble with her?' she asked, although in truth she didn't really want to know.

Donning her coat, Dora shook her head. 'No, she went nice as pie. So, I take it you won't be needing me here anymore?'

'No Dora, but I thank you so much for all your help. I couldn't have managed without you. I'm sorry it will mean your extra money will stop now.' Lily felt wretched about that.

'Don't you worry none about that, wench, I've some put aside now thanks to you.' Dora smiled.

'By the way, how did you get Maud out?' Lily asked intrigued.

'I'm saying nothing,' Dora said. Despite Lily's coaxing, she wouldn't be drawn on it, so Lily gave the woman a hug before she left.

Dora thanked the cabbie as she arrived at her home. The children swamped her with hugs as she let herself in and Jimmy made her a cup of tea. Now sitting by her own fireside with all the children in bed, and her knitting needles clacking together in the quiet of the room, she smiled at her good fortune at meeting Lily Hurst.

Casting off her last stitch, Dora began to sew the pieces of the knitted matinee jacket together. As she worked, her mind drifted to Maud Hurst. That was one evil woman. Dora had battled with her all week, but today she had been triumphant.

Maud had steadfastly refused to leave the house, and by lunchtime Dora had had enough. Saying she would prepare a hot dinner, she had busied herself in the kitchen. Carrying a tray with the woman's food on it, Dora placed it on the small table.

Smiling now, Dora saw again the startled look on Maud's face as she looked at her lunch – a small plate of mushrooms. Dora had nodded towards the plate, saying, 'Get that down yer while it's hot.'

Dora's smile turned to a low chuckle as her mind showed the moving pictures of Maud Hurst hurriedly leaving the house, her face as white as the snow outside.

Across town, Lily was warming herself by her own fire, wondering how Dora had ousted Maud. Then as she stood to go to prepare dinner she heard a loud banging on the front door. She bristled, if that was Maud Hurst, she would be getting the sharp edge of Lily's tongue.

Opening the door, she gasped as four men carried her husband into the house, followed by the doctor. Davy was laid on the sofa and the men left with doffs of their caps.

Lily rushed to Davy, her heart beating like a drum.

'Davy! Davy darling . . . speak to me. Davy!' She shook his arm but he didn't respond. Davy Hurst was dead.

The doctor led Lily, who was gasping for air, to a chair and began to speak, 'Lily, they sent for me from the store. Did you know Davy was having chest pains?'

Lily shook her head as she stared at her husband.

'Well, he had been having them for some weeks. I prescribed some medicine and advised him to keep stress to the barest minimum. His heart was weak, Lily, and today it finally gave out. I'm so sorry.'

'I . . . I don't understand. I thought he was not right but – a heart attack! Doctor he's too young, surely?'

'My dear, you don't have to be old to suffer a

heart attack. It can happen to anyone – even children.' He watched her trying to take in what he'd said. 'I will go to Webb's and inform them. Will you be all right alone? Is there anyone I can call for you?'

Lily nodded, then shook her head, she just kept staring at her husband's white face.

'I'll see myself out,' he said, patting her shoulder gently.

Lily sat on the floor, holding Davy's cold hand. Silent tears ran down her cheeks as she whispered, 'Why didn't you tell me, Davy? I'm your wife, I should have known. Oh Davy, whatever will I do without you?'

A short while later a hammering on the door brought her back to her senses.

Opening the door in a daze, she saw Stan, Jenny, Albert, Jimmy and Fred. They had come for Davy.

Jenny held her while the men placed her husband in a casket of polished beech, the brass handles on the sides gleaming in the firelight. Lily watched as they carried the casket out to the waiting cart.

Lily had not spoken a word or uttered a sound, and Jenny watched her friend who had lost her child and now her husband.

Jimmy Bean had been despatched to fetch Emily Johnston. The others took the casket to the Chapel of Rest before Albert would return to collect Jenny.

There was a rap on the door and Jenny hobbled to answer it.

Emily Johnston stepped in asking, 'How is she?'

Jenny shook her head. 'In shock. She's neither said a word nor shed a tear. I ain't half worried about her!'

'The shock will wear off soon enough and then she will really need us, Jenny.'

The two women walked into the living room where Lily sat staring at the sofa.

Jenny whispered, 'That's where they put Davy when they brought him home.' Seeing Emily's puzzled expression, she explained, 'Four men carried him back. Apparently, Davy had a heart attack at work and the lad helping at the store ran for the doctor. Then the doctor grabbed four men off the street to help carry him home before he came for us at Webb's.'

'I'll make some tea,' Emily nodded.

'No, I'll do it, you go to Lily. She might respond to you.' Jenny gave a wan smile and limped into the kitchen.

Emily moved to the girl she thought of as a daughter and her heart went out to her. 'Lily sweetheart . . .' she said gently as she touched the girl's arm.

Lily's eyes moved from the empty sofa to meet those of her friend. 'Oh Emily!' The river of tears burst their banks and she sobbed like her heart would break.

Emily held her tight as her own tears flowed. 'Let it go, sweetheart, just let it all go.'

Jenny returned with a tray of tea and burst into tears at the scene before her.

The three women stood in a huddle and sobbed as the tea on the table went cold.

Albert returned to collect his wife and Jenny let him in. Hugging Lily, he muttered his condolences.

'You two get off home, I'll stay here with Lily,' Emily said.

'Send for us if you need us,' Albert said as he led a sobbing Jenny through the door.

'Now, how about we have a nice cup of tea?' Emily asked.

Lily nodded, and Emily went to the kitchen.

Sitting with their tea by the fire, Lily cried again. 'It's so unfair, Emily! First Clara and now Davy, what will I do without him?'

'You will go on, my love, as we all do. It will take time, a lot of time, but you will come to terms with it as you did with Clara. You'll never stop missing them, but you will learn to cope without them. For now, sweetheart, you will grieve; it's all part of the healing process.' Emily spoke quietly and gently.

Lily's tears were streaming down her face and she nodded, knowing her friend was right.

CHAPTER 44

Over in Birmingham, George Addenbury took Tilley in his carriage to see the small house situated in Gem Street. It was bright and clean, the windows gleamed in the weak winter sunshine. The two-up two-down had been white-washed throughout and new curtains had been hung in all the rooms. The furniture was old but serviceable and had been polished to a high shine. In the inglenook fireplace the fire was set, just awaiting a match to have it roaring up the chimney. A coal scuttle was full to the brim and kindling was piled in the grate. There was a small cupboard set into the side of the fireplace – a warming place for the rising of bread. A separate building out the back held a lavatory, with a scullery next to it where a tin bath was hanging on the wall. A dolly tub and a mangle were housed within.

Tilley liked the place immediately; it was a vast improvement on her house in Wednesbury. It was also close to the Grand Theatre which was an added bonus. As she walked around, she wondered what had prompted George to make such a generous offer. What was his interest in her? Was

449

it her singing voice? Did he want to take over as her manager? Or was it something more personal? He had asked for her promise that she would not allow Seb Ryder back into her life – why? Did he have designs on her? Was it in his mind to propose marriage himself?

'So, Tilley, what do you think?' George's words cut through her thoughts.

'It's lovely, but I can't live here for nothing. I would be happy to pay rent,' she answered.

'No, you don't have to,' George looked almost offended.

'Yes I do, George. I'm independent and I want to stay that way. I am in control of my life and my money now that Seb has gone and I have no intention of giving that control up to any man – ever again. Please don't be upset, but I need to be in charge of my own destiny.'

'Rightly so, but will you come to me if you need advice on anything?' George asked.

Tilley nodded and they agreed a nominal figure for rent as they left for a visit to the tea shop.

Over hot tea, George handed over the key to the house.

A worried look crossed Tilley's face as she said, 'I have no idea how to rent out my own house.'

'Would you like me to sort that out for you?' George asked.

Tilley nodded, a relieved smile replacing her frown.

'Good. As soon as it is sorted out, I will make

sure you have all the paperwork – rent book et cetera. Now, I suggest we get your clothes and anything else you'll need moved to the new house as soon as possible. The quicker you rent out, the sooner the money comes to you.'

Tilley relaxed, glad to leave the details in George's capable hands. Despite wanting her independence, renting out her house was way above her head, and she trusted George to do his best for her. 'I'll go home and pack my things today,' she said as only now her excitement began to build.

As they left the tea shop, George helped her into his carriage. He instructed his driver to help Miss Green to bring what she wanted to her new home. The driver doffed his cap, happy to be of service, knowing his assistance would be rewarded come payday.

That evening Tilley was ensconced in her new home, her few precious belongings arrayed around her. The fire was burning brightly and cast a cosy glow around the room. The gas lamps George had had installed shed their dim yellow light, adding to the warm, comfortable feel of the place.

Tilley sat by the fire blessing her good fortune and the man who had brought it about. Still, why George Addenbury was being so kind to her niggled in the back of her brain. She felt all would be revealed at some point and fretting about it would not help, so she pushed the thought away.

Seb Ryder came to mind and she wondered where he was and what he was doing now. She sighed heavily; Seb had hurt her badly. She had trusted him completely both with her feelings and her singing career, and he had betrayed her. She recalled how angry she had been with him when they'd argued. Tilley touched her finger where the engagement ring had been and she sighed again.

Tilley had thought herself to be in love with Seb but as time wore on she had realised it was infatuation. She had begun to see the darker side of the man she had promised to marry; a side she didn't like one bit. She had been duped and she'd fallen for his charm and lies.

As she stared into the fire, she had mixed emotions. She was sad she would not now be married to the good-looking young man, but she was hurt at his treatment of her. She was angry at his stealing her money and he had taken advantage of her trust. Tears stung her eyes as she thought now that Seb had never really loved her. He had wanted her only for what she could provide for him – money and prestige.

George, on the other hand, had provided *for her*. He had given his help, his advice, and found her this lovely house. As yet, he'd asked nothing in return.

Damping down the fire, Tilley retired to bed. This was her first night in her new house and she hoped she would be able to sleep.

Whilst Tilley had been inspecting her new abode, Seb had hired a horse from the smithy in

Wednesbury. He set out to trawl the streets on the lookout for anyone with hidden talent. He made it known he was Honest John's right-hand man and could possibly find work for those who could sing, dance, play an instrument or make others laugh by telling jokes.

He stopped at numerous public houses and taverns to say the Theatre Royal was looking for new acts and anyone interested should present themselves for an audition that afternoon.

He was tired and saddle-sore by the end of the day and returning the horse to the smithy he walked back to the theatre. There had to be an easier way to attract people.

Greeted by Honest John as he entered, he saw the smirk on the other man's face as he rubbed his aching rump.

Walking together to the back stage door, Honest John flung it open to see a queue of people standing shivering in the cold. Leading them into the theatre proper, he took a seat next to Seb as each act took a turn on the stage, showing what they could do. The pianist was on hand to accompany any who sang.

Two young sisters took their places and said they would sing 'In the Shadow of the Pines'. Honest John and Seb both winced as the girls began. Their voices sounded like cats fighting.

Honest John clapped his hands to halt the dreadful caterwauling and shouted, 'Thank you, next!'

A man came onstage and began to speak. His ribald jokes had everyone laughing fit to burst. Honest John called out, 'Hired. Next!'

And so it went on, a few were given work, but the majority were turned away.

By evening Seb was tired and left the theatre for his quiet room in the boarding house. He flopped down on his bed fully clothed, enjoying the silence that surrounded him.

He had completed his first day as a talent scout and he was exhausted. He wasn't at all sure taking on this work was a good idea. It was hard work in exchange for the pittance he was paid, not like when he was with Tilley.

Where was she now? He had ridden past her house earlier in the day and had been shocked to see another family moving in. She'd wasted no time in moving out of the drab little house. Had she moved in with Addenbury?

Shaking his head in the darkness, Seb could not believe that of her. Tilley had her morals and living with a man she was not wed to just wouldn't happen.

So where had she gone? She would still be singing at the Grand Theatre in Birmingham, he felt sure. Should he go cap in hand and beg her forgiveness? Should he promise to be honest with her in the future? Would she take him back as her manager?

Seb sighed audibly. No, Tilley would never do that. He had well and truly burnt his bridges as far as Tilley Green was concerned, as he had with Lily Hurst.

Rising from the bed, he stripped off his clothes and crawled beneath the cold sheets. Drawing the covers up to his chin, he shivered both with cold and with personal humiliation. He had lost Lily Hurst because of his despicable behaviour towards her and now she was married to another man. He had lost Tilley Green to another because of his greed for wealth. Was he destined to live his life alone, without the comfort of a wife and family? Would he always be poor? Was Fate intervening to ensure he would never find happiness again?

Turning on his side, Seb closed his eyes in an effort to force sleep to come. However, it was not to be, as an image of Lily Hurst was conjured behind his eyelids. Squeezing his eyes closed tightly in an effort to rid himself of the picture, he felt a hot tear roll down his cold cheek. He was feeling extremely sorry for himself. His life was all upside down. He should be hobnobbing with the higher echelon of society, and instead he was living in a boarding house scouting talent for Honest John! He had been humiliated by both women who had moved on without him in their lives.

He pounded his pillow with his fist. *Damn, damn and triple damn!*

CHAPTER 45

All night and into the following day Emily Johnston had watched her friend as tears came and went. Lily was desperately trying to come to terms with her loss. Her beloved daughter lay in the cold ground of the churchyard and now her husband would do the same. The only man she had ever loved had been taken from her in the blink of an eye.

The two women had talked in whispers throughout the night, shedding enough tears to drown in. By the grey light of day both looked drawn and pale; exhausted from crying, tired eyes stared out from beneath red puffy eyelids.

'Emily, you should be getting back to the boarding house,' Lily said on a dry sob.

'No, sweetheart, I'm not going anywhere. They can manage without me. I'm not leaving you alone,' Emily replied as she stood to collect the cups. 'I'll make another cuppa, then if you're up to it, we'll go to Webb's.'

Lily's eyes were brimming with tears again as she nodded. She knew it had to be done, she had to arrange Davy's funeral. She saw again the casket that Stan had brought to her house and she silently blessed the man. He had not brought the usual wooden box, but had chosen one of beech for her husband's journey to the Chapel of Rest.

Once at Webb's she would ask Stan to leave Davy in that coffin, it was a good choice. Then there would be flowers to see to and a plot . . .

Lily burst into tears once more as the thoughts overwhelmed her. Jenny had decided all this on her behalf for Clara; would she do the same for Davy?

Emily brought in the tea and drew in a ragged breath as she saw Lily crying floods again. Pouring the tea, she thought how cruel life could be. Her friend had seen so much misery in her young life. Lily had known happiness with her husband and daughter but for only the briefest time.

People were dying all over the town every day from sickness and poverty, Emily knew, but this was her closest friend. Lily had lost everything that was dear to her.

Watching the girl sip her hot tea, Emily wondered if she would ever get over it. When Clara had died so tragically, Emily knew that Lily had buried part of herself with the child. She also knew that another part would be buried with Davy. Would there be enough of Lily left to live a normal life?

Fetching their coats, Emily spoke gently. 'Lily, it's time. We need to get to Webb's. Stan will be waiting for you.'

Lily nodded and donned her coat and hat.

'Thank you, Emily, I couldn't have done this without you.'

The two women walked out into the snow arm in arm. As they strode forward, Lily felt the cold air sting in her nostrils. The weak sunshine reflected off the snow and made her eyes water. She shivered as she thought about how difficult it would be for the gravedigger now the earth was frozen solid and would she have to hold back more tears.

Arriving at Webb's they walked in to be met by all who worked there. Jenny turned the shop sign to 'closed' and locked the door. Jimmy Bean shot into the kitchen to make tea. Albert and Fred stood to the side, shuffling from foot to foot as Stan wrapped his arms around Lily. Tears ran down everyone's cheeks as the grieving widow was shown to a chair, her shoulders heaving under the strain of her misery.

The following hours were taken up with one of the hardest things Lily had ever done in her life after burying her daughter. She sat in the Chapel of Rest saying her goodbye to her husband while Jenny and Emily chose the funeral package.

The brick building sat to the side of the shop and the gas lamps were turned down low. The casket lay on its stand beneath a huge wooden cross hung on the wall. A few chairs were laid out in rows for mourners and it was in one at the front where Lily now sat.

'Oh Davy, why didn't you tell me? You knew, and you didn't say a word! It makes sense now about you writing your will, but I wish you'd told me you were ill.' She wept into the silence of the Chapel. She recalled Davy having been stuck in the middle of her row with Maud the night he died and guilt weighed heavily on her.

Wiping her tears on her handkerchief, she whispered. 'What will I do without you, my love? I can't bear the thought of never seeing you again – I can't bear it!' Her sobs echoed around the small room as she stood and walked to the casket. Placing her hand on the lid, her whispers came again. 'Say hello to Clara for me, give her a kiss from her mummy.'

Stan had stood silently by the partially open door listening and watching. At these last words he was undone. He fled out into the snow where he let go of his emotions. Hiding behind the Chapel, Stan's heart broke for the young woman standing the other side of the building wall.

Jimmy Bean came looking for his manager and found him sobbing by the chapel wall. Not knowing what to do, he walked to Stan and waited. He watched this man trying to bring his emotions under control. He had never seen a grown man cry so hard, and instinct caused him to wrap his arms around the man in an effort to comfort him. Stan's head rested on the boy's shoulder as he continued to sob. Watching this man who had seen so much death reduced to crying like a baby had Jimmy himself in tears.

Eventually Stan straightened and blew his nose

on his handkerchief. Jimmy had taken a step back and wiped away his own tears. Nodding to each other, they walked back into the shop. No words were needed, that special moment had been shared in silence.

Once more sitting in her warm living room, Lily gazed into the fire. She heard Emily rattling around in the kitchen making tea, a remedy for all ills.

Feeling tiredness wash over her, Lily laid her head back and closed her eyes. It had been a harrowing day and she knew there would be more to come. Without realising, Lily drifted into a dream-filled sleep.

Emily sat with her tea and watched her friend as she slept in the chair opposite her. The much-needed sleep would do her good. Finishing her tea, she slipped quietly from the room to the kitchen. Lily would need sustenance when she woke, so Emily looked around for something from which to make a meal.

Lily woke with the aroma of tomato soup drifting through the open door. Rubbing her eyes, she winced; they were still sore from crying.

A moment later Emily bustled in with a tray, which she placed on Lily's lap. 'Good, you're awake. Now, get that down you.' Without waiting for a reply, she returned to the kitchen for her own tray.

Lily looked down at the steaming hot soup and the chunk of fresh bread. A cup of tea sat next to the bowl. She suddenly realised how hungry she was and began her meal as Emily joined her once more.

After the dishes had been cleared away, the two women dozed by the fire. Emily stood wearily to answer a knock to the door. Returning to the living room, she was followed by Jenny and Albert.

'Change of shift. I'll stop with our Lily while you get off home for a rest,' Jenny said in her own inimitable way. Seeing Emily about to protest, she went on, 'Albert will see you home, won't you, darlin'?'

Albert nodded.

After the two had left, Jenny sat herself down on the sofa with a rub to her leg. 'Crikey, this cold weather's playing havoc with my stump!'

Lily looked across at her friend and managed a brief smile.

'This morning sickness ain't helping either, I can't get this leg on quick enough to get to the lavvy!' Seeing another tight smile on Lily's lips, she ploughed on, 'It's all Albert's fault! Blimey I do get myself in a right pickle. One hand trying to strap me leg on, the other over me mouth trying not to throw up everywhere. What does Albert do? He stands there laughing!'

The smile Lily gave told Jenny her ruse was working. She needed to get her friend laughing, it would help to break the morbid tension.

'Oh Jenny! With everything that's been happening I totally forgot to ask how you were feeling!'

'Oh I'm all right, but Albert wouldn't be if I could run after him!' She rubbed her aching leg again.

'Jenny, you are so brave. How on earth do you do it? How do you manage to see some good in every bad situation?' Lily asked quietly.

'I turn it on its head,' Jenny said simply. 'It was the matron at the hospital taught me how to do it.' Lily listened as Jenny talked. 'Do you mind if I take this blinking thing off?' she asked, knocking her knuckles on the wooden leg.

'Please go ahead, it must be awfully painful,' Lily smiled again.

'Right, come here, you blasted thing!' Jenny unstrapped her prosthetic leg and dropped it on the floor. With a relieved sigh, she swung her stump round to lay on the sofa, pulling her thick skirt over it. 'Now then, when this happened to me, I had two ways of dealing with it. I could either lay down and die or I could get up and live.'

'That took a lot of courage,' Lily nodded.

'Yes it did. It was hard work, but I did it, same as you did.' Jenny raised her eyebrows.

'Me?' Lily asked.

'Yes you. When Clara left us, God rest her soul, you could have laid down and died couldn't you? But you didn't. You carried on.' Jenny saw the sadness creep across her friend's face. 'I know how hard that was for you cos I'd already had to do it. Different circumstances, I'll grant you, but it boils down to the same thing. We both had to carry on.'

Jenny gave a single nod, adding emphasis to her words.

'I see what you mean, I never thought of it that way,' Lily mused.

'Nobody does until they're faced with it themselves. It's a matter of living the life you've been given, which you only get one chance at, or turning up your toes.'

'When did you become so wise, Jenny?' Lily asked, her small smile showing again.

'When you said you'd rather have me with half a leg and alive, remember?'

Lily nodded as she recalled Jenny's distress at being told she needed an amputation of the lower leg.

'Now you need to be strong again, you have to carry on once more.' Jenny saw the look of doubt cloud Lily's features and added quickly, 'It's what Davy would have wanted, Lily, and you know in your heart that's true.'

'It is, that's exactly what he would want me to do,' Lily said sadly.

'Right, now that's settled, how about a cuppa? Please don't make me put that contraption on again to make it though.' She kicked the wooden leg with her good foot.

'You'll do anything to get out of making tea,' Lily said and, for the first time in days, she laughed.

CHAPTER 46

Stan had organised Davy's funeral to be as quick as possible and after a couple of days the time had arrived. The snow was falling silently as Lily dressed in her funereal garb. The hat she wore for work was replaced by a small black cartwheel with a black net veil which fell over her eyes and nose.

Standing with Emily in the warm living room, she gazed out onto the blanket of snow. Then she caught a sob in her throat as she saw the hearse, drawn by the horses, come up the driveway.

She turned and checked her look in the mirror before she and Emily walked to the front door. The knock echoed around the hallway as Lily opened the door and nodded at Stan who, hat in hand, stood aside.

Lily was surprised to see Fred driving the closed carriage and she nodded to him as he tipped his hat. Young Jimmy Bean sat beside him on the driving seat decked out all in black, looking very smart.

Emily closed the front door and walked with Lily to the rear of the carriage. Stan took up his position at the front as the lead conductor.

Jenny was in her wheelchair, pushed by Albert, her mother Vera at her side and Dora Bean at the other side.

Stan walked slowly and the entourage followed, carefully picking their way through the snow. As Lily saw men remove their caps despite the weather, she was reminded of the same journey taken with Clara. Tears burned her eyes as she wished her husband and daughter were still with her. Silently her tears fell as they approached St John's church.

She watched as Stan, Fred, Albert and Jimmy slid the casket out of the carriage and hoisted it expertly to their shoulders. As she followed behind, she noted Vera was struggling with Jenny's wheelchair. She made to help, but Emily beat her to it and together the women pushed the chair to the graveside.

Lily looked at the fresh flowers on top of the casket; Jenny had chosen well. Suddenly she realised that Davy's plot was right beside her daughter's and she was undone. Tears streamed down her face and dripped from her chin as the vicar began the service and the coffin was lowered into the ground.

'Ashes to ashes . . .'

Lily's howl of utter despair rang out over the churchyard. Falling to her knees between the graves of her husband and daughter, she cried bitterly at the cruelty of the world. Great sobs heaved her shoulders as she spread an arm out to each side of her.

Emily made to go to her friend, but Stan caught her arm. 'Let her be, she needs to do this,' he whispered quietly. Emily nodded her understanding, her own tears rolling down her cheeks.

Lily rocked back and forth on her knees as she wept for the two people she had loved most in the world.

The vicar crept away, feeling upset at the scene before him, while the other mourners shed their own tears, as much for the living as the dead.

It was a long time before Lily got to her feet. Blowing a kiss to each grave, she turned and picking up her long coat and skirt she ran from the graveyard, heedless of the snow beneath her feet. The others drifted away as the gravedigger stepped forward. They knew Lily had run so as not to hear the clods of earth rattle down on the coffin.

Each went their separate ways and Emily trundled back to Lily's house. Her knock was answered and she moved inside, following Lily to the living room without a word being said.

'Emily, you should be getting home. It's going dark and it will freeze later,' Lily said a little while later, gazing out at the approaching darkness. Seeing her friend about to object, she went on, 'I really think it's time I get used to living alone.'

'Are you sure, Lily?' Emily was concerned it may be a little too soon for the young woman to be left by herself.

'I am, and I thank you for all you've done for me.' Lily forced a smile.

Emily gave her a hug before donning her hat and coat and letting herself out of the house. She had gone no more than two steps when she heard Lily howl again. Swallowing hard, Emily walked slowly down the driveway. Lily was right, she needed to grieve alone now.

The following cold winter days did nothing to help lift Lily's spirits as she rattled around the empty house. She'd needed time away from her work, but as she looked out of the living room window, she felt the need to do something.

Sighing, she sat again before the fire. 'Oh Davy, whatever will I do now?' Her soft voice sounded loud in the silence.

A sharp rap on the front door made her jump. Going to answer the knock, she suspected it would be Emily checking in on her. She couldn't have been more wrong.

Opening the door, the blast of cold air hit her and she gasped at the woman standing on the doorstep.

'Maud!' Lily gasped in amazement.

'I read in the newspaper . . .' Maud Hurst began.

'Come in out of the cold,' Lily urged as she shivered seeing Maud's eyes all red and puffy; Lily had no more fight in her.

Stepping over the threshold, Maud gave a single nod.

'Go through, warm yourself by the fire,' Lily said, taking the thick coat Maud shrugged off. Hanging it on the stand in the hall, Lily followed into the living room. 'Will you take tea?

Maud nodded as she stood by the fire, her hands outstretched towards the flames.

Once the tea was made the two women sat quietly, neither knowing what to say. It was Maud who eventually broke the uncomfortable silence.

'I'm sorry about Davy.'

'Thank you. It's kind of you to come,' Lily acknowledged even as she wondered what the woman was up to now.

'Heart was it?' Maud asked and seeing Lily nod went on, 'Ar, runs in the family. Seems all the Hurst men had weak hearts.'

Both stared into the fire during another uncomfortable pause in their conversation.

'How have you been?' Lily asked.

'Oh I'm all right,' Maud answered.

Lily knew she was lying, her once ample figure was drastically reduced. Maud obviously had not been eating near enough to keep her healthy.

'How are you managing?' Maud asked.

Lily sighed loudly. 'I can't lie to you, Maud, I'm lost without Davy.' Hot tears stung her eyes and she sniffed.

'I can see that, wench,' Maud said.

Lily was surprised at the endearment spoken by the woman who had caused her so much trouble in the recent past.

'What you need, is to get back to work as soon as possible, it won't do no good you sitting here maudlin'.'

Lily knew it to be the truth and again was surprised at Maud's gentle demeanour.

'To be honest, with the work I do, I couldn't face it,' Lily said as her tears fell.

'Well it's the work you chose to do!' Maud snapped and instantly regretted her harshness as Lily burst into tears. 'Look, you've buried your own, now it's time to go bury others. It's what you do, and by all accounts you do it well.'

Lily dried her tears. 'This house is so empty now with Davy and Clara gone. I don't think I'll ever be happy again.'

'You stop that!' Maud snapped, feeling justified in doing so. 'Get a hold of yourself! Look at what you've got . . . a nice house, friends who love you, a good job – stop wallowing in self-pity and get on with your life!'

Lily's mouth hung open at Maud's outburst.

Maud railed on. 'The day will come soon enough when you'm lying next to Davy and your babby! Don't waste your life mourning. I ain't saying you shouldn't grieve, I'm just saying don't let it rule your remaining years!' Seeing the girl nod, Maud knew Lily had taken her words to heart. 'Now then, before I clear off and leave you in peace, how about another cuppa?'

Lily gave a tiny smile and went to the kitchen feeling suitably admonished.

Settled again, tea in hand, Lily asked, 'Where are you living, Maud?'

'I got me a place over in Gospel Oak,' Maud

said quietly. What she didn't say was it was a derelict cottage. 'It ain't no palace, mind you, but it does me.'

Lily looked at the gaunt face opposite her and guessed exactly what Maud was saying. The woman's thin frame was testament to the fact she'd not eaten a decent meal in a while, and Lily suspected she wasn't working. No work, no pay, therefore she couldn't possibly be paying rent on a property. Maud Hurst had been living like a pauper since being thrown out of this house. Guilt weighed heavily on Lily as she watched Davy's aunt sip her hot tea.

Questions and answers whirled in Lily's head as quiet descended again. Then, making a decision, she spoke before she could change her mind. 'Maud, I can see you've had it hard since . . . you left here. Why don't you come back? I'm sure we could get along together if we try hard enough.'

Maud spluttered into her teacup. 'What! You'd have me back after all I've tried to do to you?'

'There's no sense in us both living alone. Besides, we would be company for each other.' Lily said but thought, *providing you can keep your acerbic tongue behind your teeth!*

'Well, if you'm sure. I can't say as I wouldn't be glad to be living here again, but I ain't in a position as yet to be paying you rent.'

So I was right, she is living hand to mouth!

'Maud, I think it's time for some straight talking. I don't want rent, I want company. Now, providing you are civil, I don't see why this can't work. You have to remember, however, that this is now *my* house. I will be the one to make decisions concerning the house, and you, in essence, will be a lodger. Providing we have ground rules and we stick to them, I don't foresee any problems,' Lily said confidently.

'I have to agree there,' Maud acknowledged. 'For my part I could cook and clean while you'm out at work – in place of rent, so to speak.'

'Excellent. You should probably go and fetch your things then.' Lily smiled for the first time in days.

Maud lowered her eyes. 'I ain't got nothing to fetch.'

'All the better, which means you don't have to go out in the snow again!' Lily said.

Maud smiled at the younger woman, saying, 'I thanks you for this, Lily, honest to God I do!'

'I have some faggots in the pantry, what say we have those this evening?'

'Got any grey peas to go with 'em?' Maud asked, her eyes bright at the prospect of a good hot meal.

'But of course!' Lily said.

'Right, you stay by the fire while I go and make us some dinner,' Maud said as she stood up.

Gazing into the fire, Lily wondered if she'd done the right thing asking Maud to live with her. *What would you have done, Davy?* A coal nugget shifted on the fire and she wanted to think it was a sign that Davy would have agreed with her actions.

CHAPTER 47

Seb Ryder sat in the theatre rereading the article in the newspaper that had shocked him. Davy Hurst was dead! *Poor Lily!* First her child, now her husband. It seemed the young woman was destined for bad luck. Seb realised that Davy and he were of an age and shivered as he considered it was definitely time he began to take care of himself more.

Folding the newspaper, his eyes travelled to the stage where a man was desperately trying to get his dog to do some tricks. The dog was having none of it and wandered to the side of the stage and lifted his leg.

'Oh Christ!' Honest John's voice filtered into Seb's ear. 'Where do you find them from?' Seb grinned at the man sat next to him as Honest John yelled, 'Thank you! Someone clean that mess up. Next!'

The following act proved just as disastrous, as a man aiming to imitate 'Little Titch' fell hard onto his face. Clearly the thin wood inserted into make-shift flipper boots had not been strong enough. As the man endeavoured to balance his weight on the tips of the long flippers, there was a loud crack and the wood snapped in half. The man padded off stage holding his bleeding nose.

Seb heard the loud sigh from Honest John. 'Next!'

Yet another man walked onto the stage carrying wooden stilts. He tried and failed to step onto the stilts by himself, then looking around, muttered, 'I'll need a hand here.'

Honest John rubbed his hand over his eyes as a stagehand went to aid the man. 'I'm not sure I can watch this.'

A calamity ensued as two men and two wooden stilts crashed in a heap on the boards.

'Bloody hell and damnation!' Honest John yelled as he watched the men flee, dragging the broken stilts with them.

'That was the last,' Seb tilted his head towards the stage.

'Thank God for that!' Honest John said, feeling relieved. 'You have to do better than this lot; there has to be someone out there with talent, Seb, you just have to find them!'

Knowing his employer was right, Seb nodded. However, at that moment his mind was elsewhere.

Standing, he bid farewell to his employer and wandered back to his room in the boarding house. He didn't feel the cold as he walked swiftly. The temperature was dropping rapidly now and it was set to freeze overnight.

Lighting the fire in the small hearth, Seb warmed

his hands, his mind still on Lily Hurst. He wondered how she was coping with widowhood. The same as any other he suspected. A slight sadness came over him; Lily had suffered so much hardship in her life, and it had all begun because of him.

Seb Ryder, in his arrogance, had taken Lily against her will, and she had left her employment as maid to get away from him. She had lost her friend, the café owner, before the café itself collapsed into a hole in the road. She had buried her child and now her husband. It was a wonder she had not gone mad with grief as his mother had.

He knew it would be improper to call on her at her home, and he guessed she would be having mourning time away from her work. The only chance he might have of seeing her would be if they met by accident, which he felt was most unlikely. The best he could hope for was to see her in the town and then he could approach her to give his condolences.

'Lily, why do you still haunt me after all this time?' he breathed quietly. Shaking his head, Seb knew the answer. It was because he still desperately wanted what he couldn't have.

While Seb headed downstairs for his evening meal, over in Birmingham Tilley Green was preparing to go onstage at the Grand Theatre. Putting on her make-up by the light of the gas lamps, she looked at her reflection in the mirror. Ice blue eyes stared back at her and she thought, *You're no beauty, Tilley, but you can certainly sing!*

A sharp rap on the door gave her a start. 'Five minutes, Miss Green!' a voice called out.

'Thank you,' she called back.

Dressing her hair, she smiled at the respect shown to her. Not so when she had first arrived. The other acts were displeased when she was made top billing. They had complained bitterly to the manager, Thomas Sutton, saying they had been at the theatre far longer than she had. How Mr Sutton had placated them, she had no idea, but she wondered if it was by him giving them a small raise in earnings.

She suspected they all knew about Seb Ryder duping her out of the money she had worked hard for, but none had shown her any pity. Instead they had given her respect for carrying on without the dreadful man. Besides, they knew it was she who drew in the crowds. Tilley had returned that respect, admiring each for their talent, and had soon been accepted into the inner circle of the artisan world.

Happy with her efforts, she left the room and walked to wait her turn in the wings. From where she stood she could see George Addenbury in his usual seat on the front row.

Again she wondered what he expected from her. Unlike Seb, he was earning nothing from her performances. Indeed, he had no need of her money, he had plenty of his own. She had learned, over their time together, that George was a property dealer. He bought up old slums and shops and had them renovated before renting them out or selling them on again. His expertise had seen her old house in Wednesbury rented out in no time and Tilley was grateful for that at least.

She saw him laugh at the comedian's innuendo and she smiled. George was a lot older than she was and had never married. Was that what he had in mind now? If he *did* propose to her, how would she feel about it? Could she marry a man who she had, until now, thought of as a father figure?

She studied him carefully as she awaited her cue. He was handsome, distinguished and treated her like a lady. Never once had he said or done anything improper.

As she heard the applause and saw the comedian take his bow, she thought, *You could do a lot worse than George Addenbury, Tilley!*

'Nice crowd tonight,' the comedian said as he came offstage and passed by her.

Tilley smiled, saying, 'You had them rolling in the aisles.' Then hearing her name, she walked confidently on stage to applause and whistles.

As quiet descended, Tilley called out, 'As you know I usually have a set number of songs to entertain you with.' The audience responded with applause, not quite sure what Tilley had in mind. Glancing into the wings, she saw Thomas Sutton watching her with a worried look on his face. 'However, tonight – I will take any requests you may have.' The applause threatened to rock the rafters and Tilley stole another glance at the manager. He was dragging his hands through his hair and shaking his head wildly.

'Seems the manager ain't happy,' Tilley yelled out over the noise of the audience. Laughter filled the auditorium as she directed her next words to the small orchestra. 'Ready, boys? This is going to be fun!'

Someone called out a title and the musicians scrabbled around for their sheet music. Tilley tipped back her head and laughed loudly. The music began and her pure voice sailed out to reach those at the back. And so it went, the audience delighted in calling out their favourite songs and Tilley sang them, happy to oblige.

As the evening drew to a close, the applause almost raised the roof. Tilley left the stage to face the manager who, she suspected, would be furious with her. She was surprised though when he shoved her back onstage for an encore.

Sitting at last in her dressing room with George at her side, Thomas Sutton stood facing her.

'I cannot condone your actions tonight, Miss Green. You should have first consulted me. However, in view of the positive reaction from the audience, maybe it's something we should consider for once every few months.'

Tilley grinned.

'Jolly good, that's settled then.' Sutton bade them both goodnight and left.

Tilley burst out laughing.

'Tilley, what on earth made you change the programme?' George asked.

'I ain't got a clue, but it worked. I'll have to 'pologise to the lads in the orchestra though, it were a bit of a surprise to them. It was funny seeing their sheet music flying all over the place and them scrambling to find the right piece!'

'Tilley Green, you are a wicked woman!' George laughed along with her.

'Just wait 'til the boys find out we're doing this every few months – my name will be mud!' She laughed then proceeded to remove her stage make-up.

The couple left the theatre and stepped out into the cold night air. Tilley breathed it in, it made her feel alive. She smiled as admirers surrounded her, begging for her signature on their theatre programmes.

George stood back and watched the young woman as she laughed and chatted with those around her. She was kind and considerate, sporting no airs and graces. What you saw was what you got with Tilley Green – just another thing he liked about her.

Eventually the crowd began to disperse and he smiled as Tilley said her goodnight. As they walked, he murmured, 'They love you.'

Tilley grinned, her face lit by the moonlight.

'You are so lovely, Tilley, in every way,' George said quietly.

Fear of what he might say next had Tilley pick up her skirts and dance down the street, kicking up the snow as she went.

Hearing George laugh out in the quiet, she sighed with relief. She needed time to consider how she felt about the man who she thought might possibly propose marriage before too long.

CHAPTER 48

Despite her misery, Lily Hurst returned to her work at Webb's. She was welcomed warmly and began to explain about taking in Maud as a lodger.

'You ain't! Blimey, Lily, after what that woman did to you!' Jenny was horrified.

'Jenny, she was wasting away. She had nowhere else to go.' Lily knew her friends would not approve of her actions and she was right. The only one to voice an opinion, however, was Jenny – forthright as ever.

'Well I think you're a fool! I just hope you don't come to regret it, because it won't be so easy to get rid of her a second time!'

Lily knew Jenny was right in what she said, but still felt she'd been correct in her decision making. Changing the subject quickly, Lily asked, 'What do we have on the books?'

Stan answered with, 'One at ten this morning and another at two this afternoon. Are you sure you're up to it though, Lily?'

Nodding, she said, 'Yes, Stan. I need to do this.

It's time. So much has happened this last couple of years, now I need the stability that working with you all provides.'

They arrived at the house of mourning ten minutes before the allotted time of the service. Lily knocked the door and stood aside. Her eyes widened as the mourners began to pour through the door. Chancing a quick glance at Stan, she saw him give a grin before regaining his composure. Two pallbearers brought out the casket which leaned precariously front to back. Lily held her breath as the tiny man at the rear struggled to hold up his end, albeit being a small coffin. Breathing in relief, she saw the casket slide into the back of the closed carriage.

This funeral was for the family of a travelling circus who were overwintering in Wednesbury. They had all turned out in their bright circus costumes to bid a fond farewell to their friend and colleague. Thick coats were donned over skimpy costumes worn by the tightrope walkers and the clown's overlarge shoes flapped on the snow as he joined the queue of mourners. A man carried a unicycle over his shoulder, unwilling to ride it on the snow-laden road. The ringmaster in his bright red tailcoat emerged, his black top hat on his head. With black trousers and white gloves, he took his place at the front of the performers.

Lily watched as the strongman stepped from the house, followed by a bearded lady. Her heart went out to Stan in thanks; this was exactly what she needed to allay her own misery.

Acrobats were followed by a one-man band. With a banjo over his shoulder, a bass drum on his back, a harmonica attached to a harp rack beneath his mouth, and cymbals tied to the insides of his knees, he would provide music for the funeral march.

Lily took up her position at the front of the horse-drawn vehicle and was surprised when the musician and clown preceded her. She started forward as the clown danced around in the snow to the sound of the big bass drum and banjo.

As they proceeded, she found it extremely difficult to walk in a sombrely manner and before long she was bouncing along to the music.

People stopped in the streets and applauded the funeral cortège. Lily realised then that these people who were burying their friend were not mourning the death, they were celebrating the life led by the deceased.

At the graveside she watched the strongman carry the small coffin and lower it gently into its final resting place. As the vicar began to speak, each person stepped forward and dropped a small memento onto the coffin. From the clown, an old red nose; from an acrobat, a sparkly bow from her hair.

Lily was mesmerised as each followed the last. Then they all turned to leave as the vicar finished the service. Once more the music played and everyone danced their way out of the churchyard.

On the carriage back to Webb's, Lily breathed, 'What a wonderful way to say goodbye!'

Stan nodded. 'For them it's not about death and mourning, it's about life and the giving of joy to others.'

'Yes, I realised that earlier. It's just a shame more people can't think that way,' Lily said sadly.

'We all mourn in our own way Lily,' Stan said quietly.

Back in the shop, everyone listened as Lily enthused about the most extraordinary funeral she had ever known.

Jenny looked over at Stan, 'You know what's coming next, don't you?'

Stan frowned and shook his head.

Jenny tilted her head towards Lily. 'She'll be wanting to do musical funerals now!'

Everyone burst out laughing, then fell about when Lily said, 'That's a marvellous idea!'

The day wore on and the afternoon funeral went off without a hitch, albeit in a more sedate manner. By closing time Lily could not keep her thoughts to herself any longer. As they all donned their outdoor clothes she said, 'Stan, Jenny's idea is a good one.'

Jenny grinned. 'Here we go, I knew it!'

'No, Jenny, I'm not talking about a full-blown orchestra, but maybe a lone piper or a single trumpeter. Maybe a singer – I'm sure people would like the idea! I know it would cost, but by adding a little more to the package price we could cover that!'

Stan rubbed a hand over a chin badly in need of a shave.

Lily ploughed on, 'It could be done in the best possible taste, Stan.'

'What does everyone else think?' he asked as he looked at each in turn. Nods affirmed they thought it was worth a try.

'I suppose it would be up to me to try and sell the idea to clients?' Jenny asked. Stan nodded with a grin. With a sigh, she added, 'I can just see it. *"Good afternoon, modom, can I hinterest you in a musical interment?"'*

Laughter rang out in the small shop as she went on. '*We haves a singer on offer, her ain't very good, but then I'm sure the deceased won't mind. No? Well I can offer a trumpeter, but all he knows how to play is "The Rat Catcher's Daughter"!*'

Tears of laughter ran down Lily's cheeks as she held her stomach. Eventually everyone settled and Stan said, 'I'll have a think on it, but if we go ahead with this we'll need to hire the people we need. I'm not sure how we'd go about that, so let's get off home and we'll discuss it more in the morning.'

Lily set off, happy enough that Stan had not dismissed the idea out of hand. Now she had to see what sort of mood Maud was in when she got home.

Whilst Lily had been at work, Maud had spent the day having a good clean around the house and over their meal of meat and potato pie and fresh

484

vegetables, she listened as Lily told her of the circus funeral.

'The problem is, I wouldn't know how to go about finding people willing to sing or play an instrument at a funeral,' Lily said, feeling exasperated.

'Why don't you go down to the Theatre Royal and ask Honest John for his advice?' Maud suggested.

'Oh Maud, what a good idea!' Lily's enthusiasm began to rise again.

'Just be careful he don't fob you off with any rubbish acts he don't want,' Maud warned.

'I will, thank you, Maud. I'll go tomorrow as we have nothing on at Webb's.' Lily began to get excited at the prospect.

As they sat by the fire and chatted, Lily could hardly believe the change in Maud Hurst. In place of scathing comments came helpful advice. Rather than sitting lazily by the fire all day, she had cleaned and cooked. Now, she went off to the kitchen to make tea, whereas before she would have ordered Lily to do it.

With a sigh Lily was glad she had made that split-second decision to invite Maud to stay. She just hoped it would not come back on her and she would end up regretting it.

The following morning saw Lily banging on the door of the Theatre Royal. Standing in the cold, she shivered, hoping someone was there to let her in. She banged again and heard a voice calling, 'All right, I heard you the first time!'

The door opened and Lily gasped in surprise at the man standing before her.

Seb Ryder smiled, saying, 'Please come in out of the cold, Mrs Hurst.'

CHAPTER 49

George Addenbury had decided to take Tilley Green to London, but as the freezing fog enveloped the town, he knew it would have to wait. Travelling by carriage would be folly. Even in good weather it was a very long way and would take days. The trains would most likely be cancelled until the fog lifted, so he contented himself with visits to the theatre every night to see Tilley perform.

He sat in the dressing room watching Tilley apply her stage make-up, his fingers clutching the small box in his pocket. He was nervous and sweat began to bead his brow. Standing up, he knew it was now or never. Walking the couple of steps to Tilley and bringing out the box, he dropped to one knee. Opening the lid, he pushed the box towards the girl now staring at him.

Tilley's ice blue eyes opened wide in surprise. She had known he would ask at some time, but didn't think it would be yet awhile.

'Tilley, would you do me the honour of becoming my wife?' George asked in a whisper.

Tilley glanced at the man on bended knee then

back to the diamond ring in its box. Looking into his eyes once more, she nodded shyly.

Placing the ring on her finger, George gently kissed her hand. 'I'll do my best to make you happy, Tilley, I swear.'

'You do make me happy, George,' she smiled affectionately. Then sharing a chaste kiss, George got to his feet.

A tap on the door said it was time and Tilley and her new fiancé walked to the stage wings. George then went to take his usual seat in the audience as Tilley strode out onto the stage to rapturous applause.

As the theatre quietened, Tilley held out her left hand and called out, 'The water in our cellar is *this* deep!' She shook her hand and the diamond ring twinkled in the light from the gas lamps. The old saying was known to all and as one they stood to congratulate her with their applause.

Taking a bow with a grin from ear to ear, Tilley nodded to the musicians. As the introduction was played, the audience sat once more.

The beautiful voice of Tilley Green rang out and she walked the boards inviting her fans to join her song. They sang each song with her until the last, which she performed solo.

The evening was yet another success and Tilley and George celebrated with a candlelight dinner in a posh hotel.

* * *

Over in another town Seb Ryder lay in his bed in the lodging house going over the conversation he'd had with Lily. Explaining Honest John was not around, he'd asked if he could help. He saw she was lovelier than ever, although her eyes now held a tinge of sadness. Hardly surprising after everything she'd endured. She had barely come to terms with the loss of her daughter before having to bury her husband. He'd had his share of bad luck, but it was nowhere near on the scale of Lily's.

The woman's inner strength amazed him; no matter what challenges beset her, she overcame them. Now she was doing her best to help the bereaved bury their loved ones and ease the passing over. Lily had asked his opinion regarding having a singer at the graveside. Seb smiled into the darkness. Was this the first step on the road to him finally completing his quest to win her?

He saw again her smile when he agreed that providing it was a good singer and a dignified song for the occasion, he thought it to be a good idea.

In his mind he watched the pictures of their meeting unfold; her sad face as he had apologised so profusely for his bad behaviour towards her. He had given his word to treat her as the lady she was from now on, and vowed never to cause her any more distress. Yet another promise he had no intention of keeping.

Lily had nodded her acceptance but that didn't mean he was forgiven. Far from it, but then he wasn't seeking forgiveness. He only wanted to prove to himself he could get her into his bed willingly.

He smiled again in the inky blackness of his room. Seb turned onto his side and closed his eyes knowing sleep would not come easily. He needed to plan out how he could make Lily fall for his charms.

A few streets away, Emily Johnston called round to see Lily Hurst and was shocked when the door was opened by Maud.

'Oh it's you,' Maud said without a hint of welcome. 'Best come in then.'

Emily strode into the house and went straight to the living room where Lily was sitting reading a book.

'Emily! What a lovely surprise. Come in and warm yourself,' Lily said with a smile.

Maud, who had followed behind, said, 'You'll be wanting tea, I take it?'

'Thank you,' Emily said as Maud plodded off to the kitchen. Then turning her attention to Lily, said, 'What on earth is that woman doing here?'

Lily explained the circumstances of how Maud came to be living with her, ending with, 'I didn't really have much choice. I couldn't see her out in the cold with no money.'

Emily nodded her understanding and voiced her warning, 'Just watch out for her, Lily, please.'

Changing the subject, Lily said, 'I went to the theatre today to see Honest John about hiring a singer for funerals.'

'A singer – at funerals?' Emily said, feeling confused.

'Yes, I thought it might be nice for people to have someone sing a psalm over their dearly departed.'

'And?' Emily asked.

'Honest John wasn't there, but Seb Ryder was,' Lily answered.

'What?!' Emily was shocked.

'It seems he works for Honest John now, scouting for talent for the theatre,' Lily said.

Emily listened as Lily began to explain as Maud joined them.

'He said he could probably help with finding a good singer and he would liaise with Jenny if and when one was needed.' Lily's eyes met Emily's and the unspoken message was passed and received that Maud knew nothing of Lily's secret.

'You want to watch out for that one,' Maud said, settling herself into an overstuffed chair. 'He's a bad 'un.'

'Oh? Why do you say that Maud?' Lily asked feigning ignorance.

'He's got no sense of right and wrong. He don't care what he does as long as it benefits him. All he thinks about is money,' Maud answered.

'I'm sure he's not the only one,' Emily said snidely.

Maud harrumphed and Lily smiled. She knew these two women would never be friends but would tolerate each other for her sake.

It was Emily who now changed the subject to prevent Maud probing too deeply. 'How's Jenny getting on with her pregnancy?'

'Is that the young crippled wench?' Maud put in.

'Jenny lost her leg through septicaemia, Maud, and no one sees her as a cripple,' Lily said pointedly. Turning to Emily, she answered, 'She's suffering morning sickness but she's coping remarkably well.'

Maud took Lily's sharp words as a dismissal and rose to retire to bed. Without so much as a 'goodnight', she left the room.

'So what happened at the theatre?' Emily asked once she was sure they were alone.

'Seb knew all about my having lost Clara and Davy.' The sadness clouded Lily's eyes as she thought about her husband and daughter. 'He told me how sorry he was about . . . you know.' She tilted her eyes towards the door and Emily nodded. There was always a chance Maud had her ear pinned to the door, and the less she heard the better. 'I wonder if he's genuinely sorry, Emily.'

'Does that mean you have forgiven him?' Emily whispered.

'No, I don't think I will ever forgive him, but it's time to forget, if I can,' Lily whispered back.

'Can you – forget, I mean?'

'I doubt it, but I have to move on. I cannot allow him to frighten me anymore and I won't. We are bound to meet on occasion, living in the same town and especially so if the musical funerals come about, so I will treat him as I do anyone else – as an acquaintance,' Lily said.

The two chatted a while longer, then Emily rose to leave. 'Remember what I said about Maud, don't trust her, Lily.'

Sharing a hug, Lily saw her friend to the door.

Lily thought about Seb Ryder and how different he was now as she resumed her seat by the fire. He appeared to be kind and considerate, but had he really changed so much over the past few years? She sincerely doubted it.

Then there was Maud. Another who had seemed to have changed so radically. Or had she? Was she biding her time while she planned something – maybe a way to oust Lily as mistress of the house?

Shaking her head, Lily damped down the fire and turned off the gas lamps before retiring to her own bed. Whatever was to happen would happen, and fretting about it would change nothing. For all that, Lily determined to keep her wits about her where these two people were concerned.

In her room, Lily was contemplating what she and Emily had discussed. Maud was a shady character and nothing should be taken at face value where she was concerned. The woman's sudden change in demeanour didn't fool Lily and she determined to keep a close eye on her.

Her thoughts turned once again to Seb and how much he had appeared to change. He was like a different man. Gone was the cockiness of a few years ago, to be replaced by what appeared to be a caring nature. Lily had told Emily the bare bones of her meeting with the man but had not revealed all. She had not mentioned his kindness towards her. Emily would have said it was a ploy to lull her into a false sense of security. Would she have been right? Would Seb Ryder do that? Or, was he genuinely sorry?

Only time would give her the answers to all these questions and Lily settled with the notion that she would rarely come into contact with Seb in the future. Her eyelids drooped and before long Lily was fast asleep.

Maud had gone to bed in a temper. She had not actually been dismissed but had been precluded from the conversation. Lily and that Emily woman had things they wished to discuss in private, that had been made very clear, and Maud was not to be privy to it. However, she would not be deterred. She would bide her time and eventually she would find out. Something would slip out in conversation and Maud would follow the trail to discover any secrets they were harbouring. It could prove to be beneficial to her in the future. She grinned as she settled down to sleep.

As Lily drifted into much-needed sleep, across town Emily Johnston sat late into the night, her thoughts swirling around Davy's aunt, Maud Hurst.

She remembered Maud from many years ago. Maud Mountford as she was until she married Bertie Hurst the grocer. Even back then she was a gold-digger, her eye constantly in search of a new way to make her wealthy. Her marriage had brought her up to a better standard of living but, beneath the charade, Maud was still the same – a money-grabber. What had surprised Emily was that Maud appeared not to know *her*. Was it that Maud had forgotten her, or was this another ploy? If so, what could she gain from it? Nothing. But then, Maud would not have known her as Emily Johnston, for this was her name from her second marriage.

Emily then recalled the meeting with her brother, Robert Halstead, regarding the wills, and Maud's behaviour at that meeting. Obviously so upset and wrapped up in herself, Maud had not recollected the name Halstead either. She also remembered what Robert had told her about Maud's sudden disappearance from Wednesbury when Davy was a boy.

Robert's colleagues in London had sent him the newspaper clipping regarding Maud Hurst being arrested for handling stolen goods. They thought he would find it interesting that a woman from his home town was serving twelve months in Newgate Prison.

It appeared she had been living with a man called Jack Fortune who had absconded, leaving Maud to face the consequences. Emily felt sure that

Maud was well aware of what her lover had been up to, even if she had not taken part in the robberies herself. Nevertheless, she had served her time and now she was back causing havoc for Lily.

Emily had kept this knowledge from her friend; poor Lily had enough on her mind, what with Seb Ryder always on the periphery of her life.

There was another person Emily didn't trust – Seb Ryder. A leopard never changes its spots and Emily couldn't believe he had transformed into the caring person he portrayed himself to be. It all seemed a little too convenient. Then a thought struck – did Maud Hurst and Seb Ryder know each other? Were they in cahoots over something?

Allowing herself to follow the train of thoughts, Emily's mind raised more questions. What could they be planning, if that were the case? How would it benefit both of them? Maud would love to be mistress of the house she fought hard to acquire, but what would Ryder get out of that deal? Nothing. Was it that they planned for him to eventually coax Lily into marriage and take her away from the area?

Emily wondered if Ryder was in love with Lily and would do anything to inveigle his way into her affections. On the other hand, she knew how Lily still felt about the man who had hurt her so badly. She would never consider friendship with Seb Ryder, let alone marriage.

Giving a loud sigh, Emily shook her head. Maybe she had let her thoughts run away with her, and this was all in her imagination. But as she watched the flames of the fire flicker and dance, she knew there had to be a reason for those two people to have altered so quickly and so drastically. She just didn't know what that reason was – yet.

CHAPTER 50

Slowly the winter began to move aside and howling winds whipped up street rubbish, swirling it high above the ground before it was caught in the bare tree branches. Tiles were ripped from the rooftops and sent crashing to the streets, their sharp shards flying in all directions. The driving rain washed coal dust from the buildings to run as a dirty river down the gullies in the roadways. The inefficient drainage system clogged up quickly with detritus and large puddles formed on the cobbled roads.

The wind still held winter's chill and people wrapped up warmly against its sting. Smoke puffed from chimneys of those lucky enough to have coal to burn. Those too poor to afford the luxury of coal burned their remaining sticks of furniture in an effort to beat off the cold a while longer.

Women continued to wear their long skirts and woollen cardigans over their blouses, which were covered by coats or shawls tied tightly around cold bodies. Their feet were encased in socks worn over their woollen stockings inside worn-out boots. They trudged the wet streets, keeping a keen eye out for any falling debris shaken loose by the raging wind.

The men, dressed in moleskin trousers, old boots, coats or jackets, mufflers and flat caps hurried to their work eager to be out of the cold wind.

It seemed winter was reluctant to release its firm grip of the small town, but after a few days of torrential rain and screaming winds, an eerie silence descended. The wind had dropped as suddenly as the rain had stopped and the sun finally made a brief and watery appearance. It was then that the clearing up began. Roofs were patched, debris was swept away and drains were cleared, allowing the dirty water to finally filter away. The people of Wednesbury heaved a collective sigh of relief – winter was on its way out.

Jenny Blenkinsop was still suffering morning sickness although she was well into her pregnancy. The extra weight was proving difficult and a strain as Jenny tried to walk using her wooden leg. Bending to strap it on in the first place was impossible now and had become Albert's task. She knew eventually she would have to rely solely on her wheelchair, at least until after the birth.

In her excitement of being pregnant she had not thought about how she would manage when the baby was born. However, Jenny would take on this challenge as she did the others – head-on.

She was explaining all this to Lily as they sat in the shop area of Webb's when a client entered. Immediately, Jenny was all business and helped the woman choose a funeral package within her financial remit.

'For a little more we can offer a singer at the graveside,' Jenny said tentatively. Seeing the woman's eyes widen in surprise, she went on quickly, 'Maybe the twenty-third psalm?'

The woman nodded her agreement and the business was soon concluded.

Once the woman had left, Jenny heaved a sigh of relief. 'This ain't gonna be easy, you know, folk think I'm suggesting something from the music hall!'

'I saw. We have to find a way of presenting the idea that suggests dignity rather than bawdiness,' Lily mused.

'How? As soon as I say *"singer"* the client thinks *"knees up"*! It's going to be really difficult to get people to understand what we're offering.'

'We could draw up a list of appropriate songs which could be used – a catalogue of sorts. Then we could show them to the client. Maybe they would understand a little better then.' Lily was pacing as she mulled over the idea.

'Yes that would help, but we still have to sell it to people; to suggest it in the first place!' Jenny was becoming exasperated.

Lily dropped into a chair, feeling just as frustrated. 'I know and that's the problem. How to voice it to the public.'

'Blimey, Lily! You and your hare-brained schemes! We can't exactly say, *"And now the interment of Mrs so-and-so accompanied by such-and-such singing the twenty-third psalm*"!' Jenny's patience was wearing thin.

A few days later the sound of a woman's lone voice rang clearly across the cemetery of St Bartholomew's church.

'The Lord is my shepherd I shall not want . . .'

People passing stopped to listen. Lily watched the onlookers gather and she knew from nodding heads that her idea had taken flight. The news would be spread far and wide very quickly and folk would be requesting a service such as this without being prompted. She smiled inwardly as she watched the mourners; they had shed fewer tears as the singer ended her rendition.

As she and Stan walked back to the carriage, many came to extend their thanks for such a lovely send-off given to their friend.

Riding back to the shop, Stan congratulated Lily on her idea. 'I had my doubts initially, it has to be said, but I have a feeling this will take off really well, Lily.'

She smiled and nodded. 'I know it costs more for the bereaved as we have to pay Seb Ryder and the singer, but I thought it was beautiful.'

'It was gel, my missis would have loved a service such as that,' Stan said sadly.

'So would Davy,' Lily mumbled.

Lost in thoughts of their own dearly departed, they rode back to the shop in silence.

'So how did it go?' Jenny asked when they walked in.

'Oh Jenny, it was lovely! People stopped to watch over the church wall and the mourners came to give us their thanks. It's our thinking we won't need to advertise this now, it will be all over the town already,' Lily said as she dropped into a chair.

'Good. It's bad enough having to ask folk for the money for the funerals, but asking do they want a singer an' all – I didn't like that one bit,' Jenny railed.

'It's a shame we have to go through Ryder to hire a singer though. Maybe we should try to deal directly with the performer. Then we'd save a little money and could charge the family less in the process. Cut out the middle man as it were,' Lily said but her following thought she kept to herself. *'And, there'd be less chance of my seeing Ryder!'*

'Good idea. I'll sort that out next time we have need of a singer, and if Ryder don't like it – tough!'

'Right, ladies, what's next?' Stan asked.

Jenny lowered her voice, saying, 'Suicide. Bloke laid off from the coal pit went and hung himself.'

Lily drew in a breath, then let it out slowly. She knew the man would have to be buried outside the lych-gate as suicides, in certain towns, were not allowed to be laid to rest on consecrated ground.

'That's at three this afternoon, so we've more than enough time for tea,' Jenny said.

'I'll make it then,' Lily answered quietly as she walked towards the kitchen.

CHAPTER 51

It was days later when Lily walked down Trouse Lane in the early morning chill and turned into Union Street where she heard a ruckus. Someone was yelling – a woman was shouting at the top of her lungs. Rushing on, she saw who it was.

Florence Weston stood in front of a shop window yelling abuse at the mannequin in the display. 'Mad Florrie' was known by everyone in the town for her eccentric behaviour. She walked the streets muttering to herself and sometimes yelling complaints at others. She was normally harmless enough and people tolerated her with kindness. The kids, however, would taunt her and laugh in the cruel way of children.

This morning Florrie had taken exception to the dummy in the wedding shop window. As Lily drew near, Florrie caught sight of her.

'Look at this!' Florrie yelled, pointing at the dummy. 'That woman's wearing my wedding frock! Bloody cheek of it!'

'Now then, Florrie, I think you may be wrong there, this is the wedding shop. That's a manne-quin,' Lily said gently.

'Don't you be telling me no lies, Lily Hurst, I know what's what! I asked her . . .' she jabbed a grubby forefinger at the window again, 'how she come by my frock. You know what her said? Nothing! The woman's too hignorant to answer me!'

Lily saw a small crowd gathering at the commotion going on in the street. 'Florrie, it's a dummy, it can't speak.'

'Dumb eh? Well her should be put away then in one of them homes for the idiots!' Florrie continued to rail. 'I'm fetching a copper, her stole my frock!'

'Good idea, Florrie, you tell the constable, I'm sure he will sort it out for you,' Lily said, trying to lead the elderly woman dressed in rags away from the shop. She knew the local police were used to dealing with Florrie. She also knew Florrie Weston had never married. The rumour was, although once engaged, her fiancé had run off with another woman and Florrie had never got over the shock; it had turned her mind.

Florrie turned to Lily and whispered. 'I know you think I'm mad, Lily . . .'

'No, Florrie, I think you're lonely,' Lily whispered back.

'Ar, that's the truth, but you ain't now you have that lodger.' Florrie saw the surprise on the young woman's face and went on. 'Ask Emily Johnston about that one!'

Lily frowned at the woman, who was nodding her head, eyebrows raised, and a shiver ran down her spine.

The crowd began to disperse and Lily and Florrie walked away. No one could have predicted what would happen next.

Turning on her heel, Florrie marched back to the shop. She rummaged in her shopping bag and pulled out an iron poker, which she flung at the window. The glass shattered and flew in all directions. Before the incident could register with onlookers, Florrie was climbing into the shop trying to tear the wedding dress from the dummy. 'I'll bloody teach you to steal from me!' Florrie ranted as the material was torn and the dummy fell to the floor, where she continued to wrench the gown free.

Lily and the others who had gathered again watched in horror. Florrie had never been violent before and they couldn't believe their eyes. Why ever was she carrying a poker around in her shopping bag?

A whistle sounded and the constable came running.

'Oh blimey!' he puffed as he arrived at the scene. He stepped forward and grabbed Florrie around the waist, hauling her back onto the street. 'Come on now, Florrie, don't you go fighting me.'

'Mad Florrie' *did* fight – like a wildcat. She hissed and screamed as the constable was joined by another. Between them they carried her along the street towards the police station.

Lily sighed as she heard someone say, 'She's done it this time, she'll go to the asylum now.'

Watching the woman being dragged away, she heard Florrie's voice yell out. 'You remember what I told you, Lily Hurst!'

Lily had decided it was time to visit the grocery store which now belonged to her. She had neglected to do this; it was just another thing that reminded her of Davy. However, she needed to thank the young man who had kept it running so smoothly after her husband's death. She had wondered about taking it on herself but in all honesty could not see herself selling groceries, so she had reached a decision. She would sell the store.

Lily walked into the store to be greeted by the young man in charge. Quietly explaining her intentions, Lily saw the shock register on the man's face.

'I will ensure your job here is safe,' she said.

'Thank you,' the man said, not at all certain that would be the case.

'It will take a while for the business to sell, I'm sure, so please don't worry I will keep you up to date on the proceedings,' Lily tried to console the man.

Taking her leave, she walked on to her work, thinking again about the words Florrie had said to her.

'Poor old thing, she'll go to the asylum for sure,' Jenny said as Lily related the incident she had witnessed earlier. Lily shivered at the thought of the woman being locked away for merely breaking a window.

'Talking of mad women, how are you getting on with Maud?' Jenny asked.

'It's strange, but we're getting along fine. Florrie said something odd though, she said to ask Emily about Maud,' Lily frowned.

'I wonder what she meant by that? Anyway, I still don't trust her. I'll bet my wooden leg she's up to something, I just wish I knew what it was.' Jenny sighed heavily.

'Funnily enough Emily said the same thing.'

'There you go then, we can't both be wrong.' Jenny pursed her lips and raised her eyebrows.

Stan walked in at that moment and tutted loudly. 'Got no work to do, ladies?'

'Nothing doing as yet, but as you're on your feet how about a cuppa?' Jenny asked.

Stan laughed as he went to make the tea.

'He's a lovely bloke,' nodding towards the kitchen door, 'he's the boss, but he mucks in like everybody else,' Jenny added.

'He's the best,' Lily agreed, but her mind was on Maud Hurst and what, if anything, she could be planning.

Maud Hurst had planned to visit the market after Lily had left for work when a knock came to the front door.

Opening the door, she felt the shock hold her rigid. 'What the hell do you want?!'

'That's a fine way to greet somebody you ain't seen in a while I must say,' the figure on the doorstep answered.

'One I hoped never to see again, Jack Fortune!'

'Ain't you going to invite me in then?' he asked, an excessively insincere smile on his face.

'No! This isn't my house, so I'll not be inviting you in. What's more, I suggest you get yourself away from here before I call the coppers on you!' Maud's shock had turned to fury. 'You are a swine, Jack Fortune! You left me to carry the can for your thieving ways – twelve months I was in jail. Twelve months! For what? Nothing – I did nothing to deserve that!' Maud could feel the red-hot anger flowing through her veins as she stared at the man who had wronged her.

'You went to jail?' Jack asked innocently, but Maud saw the twinkle in his eye which said he knew fine well she had been incarcerated.

'Don't you play games with me! Where the hell were you when I was in jail, eh? Shacked up nice and cosy with another woman I'll bet.'

'I had to get away, Maud, else I would have gone to jail an' all.' Jack shuffled from foot to foot, feeling distinctly uncomfortable under the woman's scowl.

'It ain't like you don't deserve it, is it? I mean, you pinching all that stuff – I suppose the police should have turned a blind eye, should they?' Maud sneered.

'Come on, Maudy, that's all in the past now. Can't we pick up again?' Jack tried his best to charm her but he could see she was having none of it.

'What?! Good grief, man, do you think I'm daft

enough to pick up with you again after all you've done? Clear off, Jack Fortune, and don't come back!' Maud slammed the door in his face.

Leaning her back against the hall wall, she tried to control her rapid breathing. Her heart was beating out of her chest at the shock of seeing him again after so long.

Drawing in a breath, she walked to the living room and peeped through the window to ensure he had left. Seeing no sign of him, she sat down by the fire. Her anger was now subsiding as she thought Jack had hardly changed over the years they'd been apart. He still had charm and he was as handsome as ever. Maud frowned into the fire-light knowing she was still in love with Jack Fortune.

After a couple of restless days thinking about the man she had once run away with, Maud Hurst walked down to the market. She had shopping to do, she had to decide what she and Lily would have for their evening meal. She would find something *she* liked, and if Lily was unhappy about it – tough luck. Absent-mindedly she meandered between the stalls of the 'Shambles'. Eventually she bought a couple of pork chops from the butcher and with other bits and pieces in her basket she wandered slowly home.

Letting herself in with the key Lily had given her, Maud stiffened. Something was wrong. Someone had been here. Was it Lily? Had she come home from work for some reason?

Marching into the kitchen, Maud could find nothing out of place. She checked the other rooms – all was as it should be. Yet the hairs on the back of her neck prickled. Was it just her imagination running away with her? Was she still in shock at having seen Jack Fortune after all these years? Maud went about her business of cleaning the house but the unsettled feeling stayed with her all day. She was certain it was not her imagination – someone had definitely been in the house whilst she was out. A woman instinctively knew these things about her home.

CHAPTER 52

Folding the newspaper, Seb placed it on the bed where he sat leaning his back against the wall. He mulled over in his mind the article about Tilley Green. She had married George Addenbury and they had moved to live in London where she would be performing in the best West End theatres.

Seb was angry Tilley's singing career had taken off and that as he had been instrumental in her success he had now lost the income she would have brought him. He was also disgusted she had married a man a lot of years her senior. There was no question he would have enjoyed the rewards he would have reaped at still being her manager, but relief had flooded him when she had called off their engagement. He could never have loved her the way a husband should and he knew the girl deserved better.

Have a good life, Mrs Tilley Addenbury, he thought sarcastically as he made ready to leave the boarding house. He was due to meet with Honest John and he was already late.

As Seb walked down Addison Terrace towards

the High Street, he cast his eyes around in the hope of seeing Lily on her way to Webb's. He was disappointed; maybe she was taking a day off. He had relished the idea of seeing more of her since the start of the musical funerals and it was only a matter of time now before he made his move.

Lily had, in fact, not gone into work that morning, instead she had gone to visit her friend Emily Johnston. The words Florrie had told her had played on her mind and she wanted to know more.

Sitting with tea, Lily explained about the incident at the wedding shop. 'She told me to ask you about Maud Hurst, she said you knew all about her.'

Emily nodded gravely, she knew the questions would come eventually and she steeled herself to give the answers. 'Maud Mountford as she was before she married Davy's uncle, lived in one of the six cottages in Moorcroft Row at the back of the colliery. The family were dirt poor then; her father was laid off when the colliery closed down.' Emily shook her head and Lily listened intently as her friend continued, 'Her father moved away to find work and the family never heard from him again. No one knows what happened to him.'

'How did the family manage without a bread-winner?' Lily asked.

'When the colliery shut down they wanted to sell off the tied cottages but no one wanted to buy them so the families were allowed to remain living there until such time that they would sell.' Emily sipped her tea.

'That was fortunate,' Lily sighed.

'They lived hand to mouth, as did most folk at that time. Anyway, Maud met a young man and fell in love. Jack Fortune swept her off her feet – so much so in fact he left her pregnant. When her mother found out, she packed her off to Portland House.'

'That big house – the one for unmarried mothers?' Lily was shocked at the disclosure. She'd heard rumours about the place; at the cruelty that went on there.

'She had a baby girl and it was taken away from her and adopted. Maud was thrown out as soon as she was well enough to leave.'

'Oh good gracious! The poor woman!' Lily's hand flew to her chest as her breathing increased.

'Then she met Bertie Hurst. Oh wait, in the meantime Jack Fortune disappeared, he left her high and dry even before he knew she was pregnant. Seeing her chance, Maud married Bertie Hurst as soon as she could. I don't think Bertie ever knew about the child. If he did, it was never mentioned.' Emily sighed.

'Emily, how do you know all this?' Lily asked.

Drawing in a deep breath, Emily said, 'Maud, Florrie and I all grew up together. My brother and I lived next door to Maud, and Florrie Weston lived the other side of her.'

'Oh Emily, I didn't know!' Lily gasped.

'Well you already know about Maud and Bertie taking in your Davy as a boy after losing his parents. It was around that time that Jack Fortune turned up again. Maud must have forgiven him abandoning her because she ran off with him.' Emily raised her eyebrows as she breathed deeply.

Lily recalled her knowledge of this part of the tale. 'Where did they go I wonder?'

'London. According to my brother's colleagues in the capital, Maud was arrested as an accomplice to her lover's thieving. The stolen goods were found in their house and Jack absconded again, leaving Maud to face the music alone. She served twelve months in Newgate Prison.'

Lily was shocked to her core; her mouth hanging open at the revelation. 'Good grief!'

'When she got out of jail she came back here. Discovering Bertie had died, she decided to go after his property,' Emily added.

'I can't believe it!' Lily flopped back in her chair.

'It's true, Lily, every word. As God is my witness,' Emily emphasised.

'Oh I believe you, Emily, it's all this about Maud I'm having difficulty with. Did she ever find her child?' Lily asked quietly.

'The girls from Portland House who gave up their babies were never told where the children went. I suppose being unmarried they would just want to forget and get on with their lives,' Emily mused.

'I wonder where this Jack Fortune is now,' Lily said, still shaking her head in disbelief.

Neither of the two women could know that the man in question was virtually on their doorstep.

'Didn't Maud ever try to find her daughter?' Lily suddenly asked.

'Lily, if you had given birth to Seb Ryder's child and given it up for adoption, would you have searched for it later?' Emily saw her friend shudder. 'Exactly. However . . .'

'You know where she is don't you, Emily?' Lily regarded the woman sitting next to her on the sofa.

'Yes. When my brother qualified as a solicitor, I asked him if he could find out where the child was placed. Robert threatened to sue the staff at Portland House for their slapdash way of handling their affairs. Naturally, afraid of being closed down, they gave him the address,' Emily said in a matter-of-fact way.

'Where did she go? Who was it who adopted Maud Hurst's daughter?' Lily felt the excitement build in her as she became embroiled in the intriguing story.

'She went to Mr and Mrs Green in Russell Street. Mrs Green couldn't have any children of her own so they adopted. They named their little girl Tilley.' Emily watched the reaction from her friend.

'Tilley! Tilley Green – the singer?' Lily was astounded.

'The very same,' Emily nodded.

Lily blew through her teeth before they both fell silent.

Throughout the day Lily's thoughts centred on what she'd learned from her friend and that evening she sat lost in her thoughts, Maud doing the same.

Lily had agreed to keep the secret of Tilley Green being Maud's daughter; there was nothing to be gained from revealing it. Besides, she thought it would only cause the woman more heartache.

Maud's thoughts surrounded Jack Fortune. That man kept turning up like a bad penny, yet her heart ached for the man she had loved all her life. If he asked, would she go with him again? He had left her twice before and both times she'd had to sort out the mess he left in his wake. If she went with him and he left her again, how would she cope?

Both women sighed in unison as they gazed at the fire in the hearth. Both carried burdens and neither could share their load with the other. Their secrets would weigh heavily on them, maybe for the rest of their lives.

CHAPTER 53

It was the following day in the kitchen at Webb's that Jenny was pushing home the point of her leaving work.

'I'm not far off my birthing time now, so by April I will finish here. You need to find someone to replace me, Stan.'

'Well we'll be sorry to lose you, but I can see as how you'll be busy with the little 'un. I'm not sure I fancy taking in a stranger though,' Stan shook his head.

'Then don't,' Lily said as all eyes turned to her. 'What about Jimmy's mum? All your siblings are at school now aren't they, Jimmy?' The boy nodded. 'Dora Bean has been doing a lot of knitting these last months and selling on her garments.'

'How do you know that?' Jenny asked.

'Because it was my idea. I gave her a little money to get started and now she has a nice business going with orders coming in. She began with these, which I asked her to knit for you, Jenny,' Lily rummaged in her bag and brought out the tiny matinee coats, hats, mittens and bootees.

'Oh Lily! They're beautiful, thank you!' Jenny pawed over the small garments all knitted in different colours.

'If we could persuade Dora to mind the shop in the daytime, she could still knit in the evenings if she chose to do so,' Lily smiled.

'What do you think, lad?' Stan asked the young apprentice.

'I think her'd love it!' the boy answered.

'Right then, I'll come home with you later and ask her,' Stan said; the young boy beamed his pleasure.

'I was also thinking . . .' Lily put in, 'Albert, do you think it would be wise to have a telephone installed at home? Jenny won't be able to run for the doctor when her time comes. I know it's an expense you probably could do without, but I'm sure you'll agree it will be very useful.'

'I do agree, Lily, and I'd thought about it myself the other day, so it's all arranged.' Albert smiled his appreciation at her concern.

'When you've all finished discussing what's best for me . . .' Jenny began.

Jimmy Bean cut her off with, 'We ain't worried about you, it's the babby we're concerned with.' He gave a cheeky grin and stood back a pace.

Jenny burst out laughing and grabbed her walking stick, swinging it in a small arc in the boy's direction. 'Cheeky young devil.'

Everyone enjoyed the display of affection between the two. They had formed a close relationship, akin to sibling rivalry, in the time Jimmy had worked there.

'We'd best get ourselves ready then, Lily, we've got the drunken vicar to deal with this morning,' Stan sighed.

'Oh no! I wonder what will go wrong today!' Lily groaned.

Albert, Jimmy and Fred filed out to the back rooms and Jenny wheeled her chair back to her desk. Stan and Lily donned hats and gloves, ready for the off.

All went well with the collecting of the coffin from the house and the entourage made it safely to the graveside. The vicar stood waiting for them. Lily saw immediately the clergyman was having difficulty standing upright and was swaying gently. She also saw another horse-drawn hearse approaching from the opposite direction.

Peate's Funeral Directors obviously had an interment today too. Lily watched as the rival company drew nearer, and her heart sank. There was going to be trouble now. Instinctively she knew what had happened. There were two bodies and only one grave dug. The vicar had confused his times of service. The gravedigger took off his flat cap and scratched his head before replacing it and leaning on his shovel.

The vicar giggled like a girl as he realised his mistake.

'What's going on here then?' someone yelled from the other party of mourners. 'This is our plot!'

A woman from Webb's entourage called back, 'It ain't! It's for our mum!'

Before Lily knew what was happening, an all-out battle was underway. Women were yelling abuse at each other, men were fighting and children were crying. Stan pulled her away from the graveside and out of danger as they watched the melee before them.

The vicar was sitting on the ground by the grave swinging his dangling legs in the hole. He grinned as he watched the families at war over who should bury their deceased in the grave.

Lily was shocked at the behaviour taking place in the churchyard.

Charlie Peate walked over to join them and said, 'Best leave them to it I think, Stan, don't you?'

Stan nodded. 'Whoever wins the fight gets the plot,' he answered Lily's enquiring gaze.

'Stan!' she gasped. She couldn't help the smile forming as he merely shrugged his shoulders and turned back to watch the fight.

It was over as quickly as it had begun and the mourners from Webb's were the victors.

Lily watched in utter disbelief as both parties shook hands and invitations were extended verbally to join the wake at the Joiner's Arms pub in Camp Street.

Peate's mourners loaded their coffin back on the hearse and turned to leave the graveyard. That funeral would have to be rearranged for another day.

Webb's mourners dragged the vicar to his feet in order to conduct a swift service. The beer was waiting and the fighting had given them a mighty thirst.

Back at the shop Jenny howled as Lily explained the goings-on at the cemetery. 'I've never seen anything like it! Fighting one minute, best of friends the next!'

'It's a way of sorting it, you'd be surprised how often it used to happen – not so much these days though,' Fred chimed in.

Laughter resounded as Lily huffed, 'It's all so . . . undignified!'

That evening saw Dora Bean delighted at being asked to replace Jenny at the shop. She said she would attend every day to learn how to conduct business from Jenny.

'Mum, when we'm at work you have to treat me as a colleague, not your son,' Jimmy said tentatively.

Dora smiled at her boy. He was a young man now; how had that happened so quickly? 'I know, son,' she smiled at her eldest child.

'I love working there, Mum, everyone is so kind. They're good to me,' Jimmy said.

'I'm proud of you, Jimmy Bean. Your dad would have been an' all,' Dora said, a small tear forming at the corner of her eye.

Jimmy grabbed his mother in a big bear hug. 'I love you, Mum, you've done this family proud.'

Dora choked back a sob as she hugged her son to her.

Jenny and Dora got on like a house on fire over the following weeks and all too soon Jenny's leaving day arrived. Tearful goodbyes were said, although Jenny promised to visit once the baby was born.

On her next day off Lily walked up Church Street and noted the dirty buildings on either side of the road looked no better in the weak sunshine. The smell of smoke from the household chimneys filled her nose and she heard young children laughing as they played. Passing a house, she wrinkled her nose; someone was boiling meat. Then she smiled to herself, at least that family would eat well tonight.

Turning to walk up Church Hill, she passed St Bartholomew's Church and gazed across the grave-yard. As she continued, the open spaces were more apparent, with fewer buildings lining the road.

Lily walked into the allotment gardens and she breathed in the fresher air. These gardens had the appearance of a small park and as she ambled along, the sound of birdsong was loud in her ears.

Sitting on a bench beneath the trees, she sighed contentedly. She watched the birds perform their dance of courtship high in the branches. She was surprised to see a squirrel scamper up a tree trunk, its bushy tail twitching as it went. New grass pushed up to meet the sun at either side of the narrow cobbled walkways and leaves and buds were in evidence everywhere.

Lily sighed loudly as she thought how Davy and Clara would have loved this. A sob caught in her throat as grief mounted in her yet again. A lone tear escaped and trickled down her cheek. The feeling of loss weighed heavily still and she recognised how a thought, sound or smell could trigger her grieving at any time. Taking a deep breath, Lily stood and walked slowly away from the bench.

Home once more, Lily opened her front door and heard raised voices. Stepping inside, she closed the front door quietly and tiptoed towards the living room door which stood ajar.

Maud was arguing with someone, a man. Lily knew she should announce her arrival and that to eavesdrop was rude, but she couldn't help herself. She listened intently to the argument raging in her living room.

'Oh Maud, come on, don't be like that,' the man cajoled.

'You what! You left me – twice! And now you think you can come back here and I'll forgive and forget. I don't damn well think so!' Maud's voice held an anger that made Lily shiver.

'I didn't mean to, Maud, you know I wouldn't have knowingly . . .' The man was now trying to charm his way out of whatever hole he'd dug for himself.

'Jack, don't lie to me anymore!' Maud was having none of it.

Lily caught her breath as she heard the name. Jack – was this the Jack Fortune that Emily had told her about? The man Maud had run away with all those years ago?

'Maud, I ain't lying to you, I swear!' Jack's silky tones grated on Lily's nerves as she listened; more so when she heard Maud's next words.

'You swear on the Holy Bible, Jack Fortune, and I might believe you.'

Lily sighed and thought, *'Don't fall for it, Maud, whatever it is – don't fall for it!'*

'I swear!' Jack went on, his voice almost an octave higher than before.

'Jack, you took off and didn't even stop to find out I was carrying. I went through the birth and everything alone and I was no more than a child myself. Why Jack?' Maud's voice pleaded for answers. It held a vulnerability Lily had never heard before.

'I didn't know you was carrying, did I? I went to find work, Maud, so I could feed us. So you wouldn't want for anything but . . . but when I came back for you, you was gone.'

The hesitation in his speech told Lily he was lying through his back teeth.

'I had to go away to have the child,' Maud said sadly, 'it was a baby girl, Jack. We have a daughter out there somewhere.'

Lily swallowed the sob which threatened to expose her. Even knowing it was wrong of her, she wanted to hear more.

'I'm sorry, Maud, but you could have had more kids when you married Bertie Hurst.'

Lily could imagine his swagger as he spoke.

'No, Bertie couldn't have any kids, that's why he doted on young Davy, his nephew.' Maud's voice was hardly more than a whisper.

Lily's hand flew to her mouth at the mention of her late husband's name, and she strained to hear more of the conversation.

'Anyway, what about London, Jack? What about you stealing all that stuff and leaving me to take the blame as well as going to jail for it? What about all that then, Jack, eh? How are you going to explain your way out of that?' Maud's anger was rising again as was her voice.

'Maud, I was tipped off about the bobbies calling round the house and when I went to get you out – I saw the coppers leading you away. Maud, I couldn't do anything then, could I?' Jack's lies slipped from his lips.

'You're a liar, Jack Fortune! Besides, you could have given yourself up. You could have told the police of my innocence,' Maud shouted.

'Maud – Maudy . . . do you really think they would have believed that? No, they would have put us both away, gel; you know that to be the truth.' Jack's voice oozed like honey.

'I suppose you're right,' Maud conceded.

'Of course I'm right, my Maudy. Now then, how's about you make us a nice cuppa tea?' Jack said.

Lily quickly retraced her steps and opened the front door. Banging it shut, she called out, 'Maud, I'm home.'

Striding into the living room, she saw Maud standing by the fire, a nervous look on her face. Then her eyes travelled to Jack Fortune who had made himself quite comfortable in Davy's chair!

CHAPTER 54

As Lily had been strolling around the allotment gardens, Emily Johnston was re-reading the note she'd received in the post that morning, hardly able to believe the words.

Dear Mrs Johnston,

I'm sure this will come as a surprise to you, but I wondered if you would be kind enough to take tea with me this afternoon. I will be at the Victoria Tea Rooms in Albert Street, next to the Art Gallery, at two o'clock.

I hope you will accept my invitation as there is something I wish to discuss with you.

Kindest regards,

Seb Ryder.

Folding the letter, Emily wondered what the young man wanted with her. To find out, she would have to meet with him.

Donning her hat and coat, Emily left her boarding house and walked down into the town.

Immediately she walked into the tea shop, she

saw Seb waiting for her. He stood to greet her as she walked towards the table.

Giving a nod to the waitress, Seb said, 'Mrs Johnston, thank you for coming. Please take a seat. I have taken the liberty of ordering tea and cake, I hope that meets with your approval.'

Emily sat at the table and took off her gloves. Folding them neatly, she placed them in her draw-string bag, then her eyes met his.

'What is it you want, Mr Ryder?' she asked pointedly.

'Mrs Johnston, I am a man in torment!' he said dramatically on a hushed breath.

The maid brought the tea and cakes and Emily watched her linger a moment with a smile only for Seb. She also noted Seb did not return the smile but merely nodded his thanks. The maid sauntered away clearly disgruntled the handsome young man had barely acknowledged her.

'Mr Ryder, whatever it is that is causing your torment, why do you think meeting with me could ease it?'

'I wish to ask you a favour, Mrs Johnson, a very big favour,' Seb said as he poured tea for them both.

Emily sighed loudly. She knew straight away what this young man was about to ask her.

'No,' she said flatly.

'Mrs Johnston, you don't know yet what it is I would ask of you.'

'Mr Ryder, I know exactly what you would ask and my answer is and always will be – no!' Emily

528

sipped her tea, her eyes never leaving his. Replacing the cup on its saucer, she went on, 'If this is about Lily, which I suspect it is, then you must know she will never forgive you.'

Seb's eyes widened in surprise.

'Oh yes, young man, I know all about it. I know what you did and why Lily left her employment at your father's house.' Emily kept her voice low so no one else could be privy to their conversation. 'She went to hell and back, Mr Ryder, and I wonder if you realise the enormity of the crime you committed.'

Seb dragged a hand through his hair and he cast a glance around the room to ensure their speaking was not being overheard. Seb's acting skills were award-winning.

'Yes, Mrs Johnston, I do realise,' he said as his eyes returned to hers. 'I wish I could turn back the clock and . . . but I can't! I need Lily's forgiveness before I can even think about forgiving myself.'

'You selfish little swine!' Emily rasped. 'You have absolutely no idea what Lily has suffered in her short life, and it all began with you! Now all you want is her forgiveness so you can be free of the guilt you carry. Mr Ryder, you committed the worst possible crime against a woman, and now you think you've carried the burden long enough. Let me tell you, young man, you will carry this guilt for the rest of your life regardless of whether Lily forgives you or not. It will haunt you for all of your days. It will raise its ugly head to remind you each time you think it's forgotten, and the pain of it will drive you mad.'

Seb saw the hatred in Emily's eyes as she stared back at him. The venom from the sting of her words seeped into his brain and he knew, no matter how much he begged, Emily Johnston would never help him gain Lily's trust.

With a last disgusted look Emily stood and stalked away.

Once back in her living room, Emily silently fumed at the gall of Seb Ryder. He had actually thought she might be instrumental in him gaining favour with Lily. The cheek of the man!

Her tea having gone cold in the cup, Emily stared into its milky depths and pondered her dilemma. Should she tell Lily of her meeting with Ryder? Or should she keep it to herself? If she kept close-mouthed and Lily should find out, then she could be accused of, in effect, consorting with the enemy. Nodding, Emily decided Lily should be told exactly what had occurred. Then she was at liberty to draw her own conclusions as to why Ryder had written that letter.

Feeling there was no time like the present, Emily grabbed her bag, coat and hat and set off for Lily's house in Trouse Lane.

Whilst Emily was making her way to Lily's, Maud was introducing Jack Fortune as a friend from when she was a girl. Lily knew all about the charmer but kept her counsel.

The three had chatted amiably for a while, but Lily was aware of Maud's nervous demeanour. She also noted the looks Maud gave Jack; looks of longing. The woman was still in love with the man who had abandoned her twice.

Casting a glance around the room, Jack said, 'You've done well for yourself, Lily.'

She bristled at his familiar use of her name, but she nodded once; her smile lifting only the corners of her mouth.

'What is it you do, Mr Fortune, for work I mean?' Lily asked.

'I am an entrepreneur, I buy and sell – mainly antiques, but I have a good eye for anything that has a value.' Jack gave her what he considered to be a charming smile as he pushed his sandy hair back from his face.

Lily saw it as a sickly grin and watched his ice blue eyes roam over her furniture.

'So do I, Mr Fortune – and before you ask, no.' She saw his eyes flick back to hers and she held them steadily. 'There is nothing in this house that is for sale.' Raising an eyebrow, she added. 'My house is under constant watch from the police, as Maud can attest to.' She heard the other woman draw in a breath. 'You see, Mr Fortune, some time ago someone was watching the comings and goings from this property. However, the very presence of the police patrol evidently scared the person away.' Lily turned her head towards Maud; her eyes confirming she knew it had been Maud all along.

531

The woman squirmed under Lily's firm gaze. 'Should I put the kettle to boil again?' Maud asked in an effort to dispel the guilt she was feeling.

'Good idea, gel,' Fortune said as he crossed his legs and watched Lily from hooded eyes.

'Not for Mr Fortune, Maud, he is leaving – now!' Lily stood and walked to the door.

Jack grinned and followed.

At the front door which Lily held open, Fortune gave a greasy smile and muttered, 'I'll see you again, Lily.'

'It's Mrs Hurst to you, Mr Fortune, and I'll thank you to stay away from my house. Whatever is between Maud and yourself is none of my business, but heed my warning – stay away from me and my house!' Lily was about to slam the door shut when she saw Emily standing behind Fortune.

'Well said!' Emily clapped her hands and as the man faced her, she added, 'Well, well . . . Jack Fortune!'

'Emily. Nice to see you again,' Jack said, his voice once more like dripping honey.

'I can't say the same. Now, excuse me, I have business with my friend.' Emily pushed past the man and stepped indoors. It was she who slammed the door in his face.

Maud rounded on Lily the moment she re-entered the living room. 'How did you know it was me who watched the house?' She ignored Emily who sat down on the sofa.

'I saw you. I wasn't sure at first, but later I saw you through the fog,' Lily said simply.

Maud harrumphed, then dropped into the chair Fortune had so recently vacated. Seeing Lily's face scowl, she stood and moved to another chair.

'Why didn't you say anything?' Maud asked.

'Why did you trash my house?' Lily answered with her own question.

'I was searching for Bertie's will,' Maud bristled.

'That's all water under the bridge now,' Emily interjected, 'you both have other things to worry about.'

'What things?' Lily asked.

'Jack Fortune for one. He's trying to ingratiate himself with you again, Maud, and my advice would be not to let him. Just remember what he did to you before.' Emily saw Maud's eyes widen with shock. 'Oh Maud, for God's sake! We both know all about that man and what he put you through.'

Turning to Lily, Emily then related the bare bones of her meeting with Seb Ryder, keeping her words veiled as Maud's ears pricked up.

When she'd finished speaking, Maud said, 'Bloody men!' The tension was broken a little and all three women smiled.

CHAPTER 55

Vera Pickard felt the need to visit her daughter, and as she left her own house in Camp Street, the uneasy feeling she'd had all morning deepened. Something was wrong. Vera hurried along, her long skirt swishing about her legs. Clutched tightly in her hand was the key Albert had given her. Turning into the street where Jenny lived, Vera ran to the house.

Letting herself in, Vera called out, 'Jenny love, it's only me.' Vera walked into the living room where Jenny sat in her wheelchair.

'Oh thank God! The baby's coming, Mum, you'll have to telephone for the doctor,' Jenny said breathlessly.

Vera threw her shawl onto the sofa and, shaking her head, said, 'I ain't using that thing – I don't trust it.'

'Mum! It's only a telephone – I need the doctor and I need Albert! I can't get up the stairs on my own, Mum, he has to carry me!' Jenny drew in a deep breath and let it out on a moan as pain rolled over her. Seeing Vera wringing her hands, Jenny's voice was stern as she said, 'Mother! Stop dithering and ring Albert – NOW!'

Vera ran to the telephone and following the instructions from Jenny she made the call. She was told Albert was on his way and he would bring the doctor with him.

'Right, my nightie is on the bed, Mum, I think it would be a good idea to get into it before Albert gets back.'

Vera shot up the stairs and grabbed the nightgown. Rushing back to the living room, she helped her daughter undress and don the voluminous white cotton gown, then Jenny lay back on the sofa.

'Mum, I've never seen you like this, you're pathering around,' Jenny smiled lovingly.

'I ain't never had a daughter in labour before!' Vera laughed. 'I knew this morning something was up, but I weren't sure what it was.'

'Albert will be back in a minute, Mum, and I'm sure he'd love a cup of tea,' Jenny nodded towards the kitchen.

'Oh right yes. I'll get the kettle on then,' Vera muttered, glad of something to do.

She heard Jenny moan again as she fumbled with the tea things. *Oh God, let all be well for our Jenny. Please watch over her and the babby. My wench has enough on her plate, please don't let her have to deal with an infant death as well. Amen.*

Vera shuffled in with the tea tray and plonked it on the small table, setting the cups rattling. A tea towel soaked in a bowl of cold water sat on the tray and Vera used it to mop Jenny's brow.

'You're doing really well, my wench,' Vera said, looking into her daughter's frightened eyes. Gently wiping away the beads of sweat on Jenny's forehead, she added, 'Hard work, ain't it?'

Jenny nodded and a tear escaped her eye. 'Mum . . . I'm . . . scared!' Her words were punctuated by short sharp breaths as she felt the pain building once more.

'Ain't nothing to be frightened of, sweetheart, look how many times I've done it. What I will say though is I bissent doin' it no more!' Vera laughed and was glad to see Jenny's grin.

The young woman gripped her mother's hand so tightly it stopped the blood flow. After a howl, Jenny relaxed as the pain subsided.

'Blimey, our Jenny, you nearly broke my fingers!' Vera said with a smile as she rubbed the life back into her hand.

'Sorry, Mum. Where's Albert got to? He should be here by now.'

'He'll be picking up the doctor on his way – oh, he's here now,' Vera said, hearing his key in the door.

'Jenny! Jenny, oh my love, my darling!' Albert rushed to his wife.

'I'm all right, where's the doctor?' Jenny said, looking over her husband's shoulder.

'He was out on a call, but he'll come as soon as he's finished. A midwife is here though, she was at the surgery fortunately.' Albert stood aside to reveal a stern-looking woman in a dark uniform.

'I am Nurse Fletcher and I will be taking care of things until the doctor arrives,' the woman said with her hands folded over her apron front. Looking at Vera, she asked, 'And you are?'

'I'm Jenny's mum, Vera Pickard.'

The nurse pushed past Vera with a nod of her head. Looking down at Jenny lying on the sofa, she said haughtily, 'Right, my girl, you shouldn't be lying there. You should be moving about to allow the baby to get into its birthing position.'

It was then that Jenny let out another agonising howl. Albert was on his knees at his wife's side in a second, holding her hand and willing her pain to pass quickly.

Nurse Fletcher winced and then said sharply, 'Stop that noise! Come on, let's have you on your feet and walking about!'

Albert glared at the woman standing over him. With a swift movement he clutched the hem of Jenny's nightgown and pulled it up to her knees, revealing her stump.

The shock on the midwife's face was evident, but she quickly hid it. 'Does she own a prosthetic?'

'Yes I do! And no, I'm not putting it on, it's too painful!' More pains rolled over the girl and she began to pant.

'Well she can't stay there!' the nurse snapped.

'Don't talk about me . . . as if I'm . . . not here!'

Jenny managed. Then as the pain eased, she said, 'Albert, please will you carry me to bed?'

Instantly on his feet, Albert swept his wife from the sofa and headed for the stairs.

Nurse Fletcher turned to follow but Vera caught her arm, swinging the woman to face her. 'Where do you think you'm going?' she asked.

'To do my job,' the midwife glared at Vera.

'Oh no you ain't. You get your coat and get out – now! I won't have you treating my girl like that, you stuck-up cow!' Vera's temper was boiling now.

'You can't speak to me in that manner,' Nurse Fletcher said as she made for the door.

'I just did!' Vera said with a sarcastic smile.

'Please be advised I will be reporting this to the doctor,' the nurse said huffily.

'You can report it to whoever you like, frankly I don't give a bugger!' Vera yelled as she pushed the woman out of the front door. Wiping her hands down her skirt, Vera then slammed the door shut.

A scream brought Vera running up the stairs, where Albert was in a blind panic.

'Where's the nurse?' he asked, looking around.

'I chucked her out!' Vera spat, then moved to her daughter. 'Come on, my gel, let's have a little look at you.' After a moment of checking on Jenny, Vera yelled, 'Albert – sharp knife, hot water, towels, swaddling cloth – the babby's almost here!'

Albert ran round like a scalded cat fetching and carrying, then he was despatched to make tea. As he stood in the kitchen listening to Jenny's screams, he whispered his own prayer to the Lord to keep his wife and child safe.

By the time he returned to the bedroom, his child was being wrapped in a swaddling cloth.

Albert stood gazing down at the baby in his mother's arms and the cup rattled on the saucer as his shoulders heaved great sobs of joy.

'Albert, put that cup down and help me over here.'

Doing as he was bid, he moved towards Vera who was placing the baby in the crib Albert had made and put next to their bed.

'Now, when I say I want you to place your hands here on Jenny's belly, then lean all your weight down.' Seeing the look of horror on his face, she went on, 'The afterbirth needs to come away, Albert, so come let's get our Jenny comfortable.'

Turning to Jenny, she said, 'Ready yourself, gel, then it will all be over.'

Jenny braced herself and Albert leaned down. She felt the breath pushed from her lungs as the afterbirth slid from her body.

'Good girl. Albert, go get your son out of the crib – I'll just burn this out the back.'

She took the towel wrapped afterbirth and left the happy couple with their newborn.

As she attended to the burning in the garden, Vera sent up a silent thanks to the Almighty for taking care of her baby and in turn *her* baby.

CHAPTER 56

Lily was walking home from seeing Jenny and the new baby a couple of days later and her thoughts were full of her own daughter Clara, cruelly lost to her in a tragic accident.

Stepping in through the front door, she heard voices. Sighing heavily, she removed her coat and hung it on the stand in the hall. Standing a minute, she listened as Maud's voice rose.

'I've told you, Jack, this is Lily's house and I don't think she'll be too happy to find you here when she gets home!'

Too right she's not happy! Lily thought as she continued to listen. The man was in her house yet again!

'Maudy, it'll be all right. I can get round her don't you worry,' Jack replied.

Lily stiffened. Drawing in a breath, she straightened her posture and walked into the living room.

Two pairs of eyes shot in her direction.

'So, Mr Fortune, you grace us with your presence yet again, even though I specifically told you to stay away.' Lily walked over to the fireplace and confronted the man.

'I just called in to speak to Maud,' Jack said confidently.

'I see. Well now you have spoken to her, I wish you to leave. Oh and Maud, you are not to let this man into my house again. Should you do so, you will find yourself leaving with him – for good!' Lily sat in her armchair and, eyeing the man once more, said, 'Goodbye, Mr Fortune.'

Maud ushered Jack out of the door and after a moment she returned. 'He's only been here a couple of minutes Lily. I don't see what all the fuss is about.'

'Maud, you should not have let him in. What did he want anyway?' Lily asked sharply.

'He was going to ask if you had a room to rent,' Maud said.

'What!' Lily was dumbfounded at the gall of the man.

'I told him it wasn't a good idea . . .' Maud began.

'Definitely not! The man has the cheek of the devil!' Lily cut across.

'He is a charmer,' Maud smiled.

'Well he won't charm me!' Lily retorted.

Lily sat thinking about how much the woman had changed in such a short time. From a blustering termagant, she had become almost a servile lackey. What had caused this sudden change? Was it because she knew Lily would not stand for her bombastic ways anymore? Or was it all an act? Did Jack Fortune have anything to do with it?

Lily sighed and shook her head. She could not figure it out, no matter how she tried.

Maud brought in the tray and poured tea for them both, her lips clamped tightly shut.

'Maud, whatever has come over you? I can't believe you are the same person that came into my life like a bull in a china shop. What's happened to you?'

Maud dropped her head to her chest trying to think quickly. 'That wasn't the real me, Lily. I've had some bad luck over the years and – well it made me hard. I had to be, otherwise I would never have survived.' It would never do to let Lily think she hadn't changed at all. Maud's compliance was her way of endeavouring to find a way to oust Lily and reinstall herself as mistress of the house.

'You and I have both had our fair share of rotten luck, Maud, so believe me when I say I understand that,' Lily softened her demeanour.

'Ar, I know. You lost your child and your husband and I'm sorry for that.' Maud lifted her eyes to Lily's. 'Now Jack's back and . . .'

'You can't get him out of your system, can you?' Lily asked. Seeing Maud shake her head, she went on. 'I understand that too. I could never love another like I loved Davy. He and Clara were my world. It all seems so empty without them.'

'I know Jack's no good, Lily, God knows I realise that, but for all the world I still care for him.' Maud's words caught in her throat at the truth of it.

'Maud, I see that in your eyes, but please, don't be taken in by him. He will only break your heart.'

Maud nodded slowly in agreement. 'I think he's in trouble again. I think he needs money – a lot of it – and quickly.'

'Why do you say that? Has he said as much?' Lily asked, feeling intrigued.

'I know him well, it's only a matter of time before he asks me for it. Then again, I ain't got it to give, so it's anybody's guess what he'll do then.'

'Oh Maud, I'm sorry. I wish for your sake he was a good man,' Lily tried to comfort with her words.

'Me an' all, but he's rotten to the core and he'll never change.'

Both women lapsed into silence as they drank their tea.

It was after their evening meal that Maud broke the silence by asking, 'How's your friend and her new baby?'

'They are both doing well, but how she will manage with her wooden leg I have no idea.'

'I'd be happy to do a bit of shopping for her, or any odd jobs she needs doing,' Maud said tentatively.

'Maud, that's kind of you, I'm sure she'd appreciate it, although I would warn you, she's very outspoken. I will mention your offer the next time I visit.' Lily was surprised and her instinct told her the two women would very definitely not get along. Nevertheless she would keep her word and mention it to Jenny.

The two women spent the evening chatting about the new baby and the problems Jenny would encounter with taking care of him.

Lily began to yawn and retired to bed, leaving Maud sitting by the fire alone. Her thoughts of Jack Fortune swirled in her mind. He *was* bad but she *did* still love him. Then she smiled, Lily had fallen hook, line and sinker for her sob story. She was finding it difficult to play the poor relation role, but she would carry on until she saw Lily Hurst out on the streets.

Jack Fortune grumbled to himself as he walked back to the ramshackle hovel on the heath behind the railway line. He knew Maud Hurst's feelings for him had not changed despite what he'd put her through over the years.

Flinging the door open to the old abandoned cottage, he sat down heavily on the crate that served as a chair.

He had been relying on Maud to stump up the cash he was so badly in need of. He owed a lot of money to some men in London and, unable to pay, he had fled the capital. He lived in fear of his life should they discover where he was now. He knew they would not hesitate to make him suffer before they sent him to meet his maker.

His mind took him back to when he was living hand to mouth. Maud was in jail and he was scratching out a meagre sum, stealing and selling anything he could lay his hands on. In desperation he had gone to the underworld moneylenders. That was his first mistake.

Jack sighed and spat on the dirty floor. His second mistake was living the high life on the money he had borrowed without a care for having to repay it. He had been so sure he could pay when he had burgled that large house. The goods he had set his sights on would have repaid the moneylenders, with enough left over to enable him to retire from a life of crime.

He shook his head as he remembered how it had all gone wrong. He saw again the pictures unfolding in his mind. He had gained entry to the fine big house by way of a back window left open. Fortuitous, as it meant he didn't have to smash it. He was pushing the gold jewellery and silver trinkets into a hessian bag when the front door opened. The owners were back! He had mistimed everything in his greed to gather as much as he could. He had stayed far longer than he'd planned. Then there was a shout; a scream as he was discovered. Before he knew what was happening, he had barged past the owners who had entered the parlour and he ran for his life, dropping everything in his haste to escape.

Then Jack Fortune was on the run. The police undoubtedly had been informed, so he had to keep his head down. He had no goods to sell and no money. Unable to repay the money he had borrowed and knowing the consequences, Jack had left London in double quick time.

Coming back to the 'Black Country', he had sought out Maud in the hope of relieving her of any cash she had. However, those hopes had been dashed when he saw she was a lodger in what had once been her own house. This spoke volumes; Maud Hurst was as penniless as himself.

Kicking a booted heel against the wooden crate he sat on, Jack wondered what he should do next. Maud had nothing – but that other one, Lily, she had money and a nice house. If he could get in there, he could swipe a few things, which would tide him over until something better came along.

An evil grin spread across his face as he began to formulate a plan. Lily worked, so that meant she'd be out all day. Maud, on the other hand, was at home, so he would have to wait for her to go out then he would nip around the back of the house, smash a window and let himself in. He could grab a few bits and pieces and leg it out of there. In and out in ten minutes and Bob's your uncle, he'd be in the money again!

CHAPTER 57

The meeting with Emily Johnston had been a waste of time, Seb thought as he sat in the music hall listening to Honest John complaining.

'You ain't doing at all well finding new acts for this place,' the man grumbled. 'Your heart's not in it, lad. You'll have to do better or else we'll both be out of work!'

Seb nodded and cringed as the singer auditioning missed her note, sounding like the scraping of a glead under a door. He watched as a juggler took the singer's place and proceeded to throw apples in the air. He shook his head as the fruit crashed to the floor and rolled away.

'Next!' Honest John yelled.

Seb left the auditorium and stepped out into the morning sunshine. Leaning against the wall, his mind was consumed with thoughts of Lily. He had to find a way of seeing her as he only ever saw Jenny or Dora when singers were booked for the funerals

Closing his eyes, he lifted his face to the warmth of the sunshine and sighed. He heard the steam train whistle in the near distance and, opening his eyes, he saw a flock of birds fly past startled by the sound.

He nodded a greeting to an older woman as she passed him.

'All right cocka?' she asked.

He smiled at the friendly endearment. He recalled on his travels how people in different areas used such greetings. Here in Wednesbury it was 'cock' or 'cocka'; further afield it was 'me duck'. In London they used 'darlin' or 'sweetheart'.

Again he thought of Lily and how he wished he could get round her. How could he manage to see her? Should he wait for her leaving work? No, it may frighten her, thinking he was trying to accost her. Should he visit her home? Maybe. That would at least give her the choice of either letting him in or slamming the door in his face. He doubted she would allow him access into her house without someone else being present, however he could think of no other way to speak to her. Reaching a decision, he marched back into the music hall. He would visit her and hang the consequences.

Later that same afternoon Lily began to feel unwell. Her throat was on fire, her head pounded and her whole body ached.

'Get yourself off home, Lily, and get some rest. Stay home until you feel better,' Stan told her.

The weather was fine but Lily shivered as she

walked home. She hoped it was just a head cold and not influenza.

It was quiet in the house, she noted as she let herself in. Maud must be out at the market. Leaving her coat on, she walked into the living room and stopped dead in her tracks.

'What the . . .!' she gasped.

Jack Fortune stood by the fireplace, a silver snuffbox in his hand.

'Oh dearie me, you're supposed to be at work.' He shoved the box in his pocket as he grinned.

'Put that box back! It doesn't belong to you!' Lily croaked.

'It does now!' Jack sneered as he stepped towards her. 'You have a few nice things here, things that will do me more good than you.'

'Get out of my house!' Lily's anger rose despite her feeling ill. 'You think you can steal from me, Jack Fortune? I'll see you in jail for this!' She backed away from him towards the hall. She felt the old familiar fear rising as she remembered being cornered once before. Would the same thing befall her a second time? Or would he knock her senseless and make his escape? Either way, Lily knew she had to get away – and quickly.

'I'm warning you!' she threatened as she backed into the hall and towards the front door.

Fortune stepped slowly forward, an evil grin forming as he snapped, 'You're warning me! Ha! Am I supposed to be scared? Believe me, Lily, I'm not afraid of a woman.'

At that moment Lily turned to open the front door, and instantly she felt his arm snake around her neck. She was pulled backwards and felt his body against her back. Her hands flew to her throat in an effort to drag his arm away.

Fortune whispered in her ear, 'Now then, Miss High-and-Mighty, let's you and me discuss this, shall we?'

Lily threw her body from side to side, trying to release herself, but his vice-like grip held her fast. Her fingers tried to push between his arm and her neck to lessen the pressure she was feeling as he started to drag her backwards down the hallway. Lily was struggling to breathe, but she persevered with her fight to escape. She felt his other arm slide across her waist at the front; he was about to pick her up.

'Let me go!' she mumbled through clenched teeth.

Fortune tightened his arm around her throat for an instant and Lily gagged. Releasing the pressure a tad, he whispered, 'Oh no you don't! I've got things to do and you're getting in my way. So be a good little girl and stop your wriggling.'

Lily saw red at the denigrating way he spoke and her anger flared once more. With renewed vigour, she twisted her body, then raising an arm she reached back over her head. Her nails dragged down his cheek drawing blood and he yelped in pain.

'You little . . .!' Fortune rasped and tightened his grip yet again.

Lily's eyes bulged as her breath was stopped.

She saw green blobs floating before her eyes and her hearing became muffled. Her strength evaporated and her limbs felt heavy as her arms dropped. Her knees buckled and she began to collapse slowly down into the blackness which beckoned her. She was going to die.

A sharp sound echoed in her ears and suddenly the pressure lessened and she dragged in a great lungful of air. Her senses rallied as the oxygen reached her brain and she heard the knock again. Someone was at the front door.

'Keep quiet!' Jack whispered.

The knock came again.

Lily's eyes widened as she searched her mind frantically for a way out of her predicament.

'Stay quiet and they'll go away.' Jack said in hushed tones.

No! They mustn't go away! She needed help!

'All right, Jack, you win,' Lily whispered back as she suddenly remembered she'd left the door on the latch for Maud's return. Feeling his arm slacken a little more as the knocking continued, Lily slowly drew in a deep breath. Then she let it out with a loud yell, 'Help! Help me!'

Jack yanked her back a step and his arm tightened yet again about her throat, cutting off her air supply once more.

All of a sudden the door burst open and Lily's last thought was *thank God* as she descended into blackness.

★ ★ ★

Across town, Jenny Blenkinsop was having tea with her mother Vera.

'So what you going to name him?' Vera asked, nodding to the crib by the side of Jenny's bed.

'We haven't decided yet. Albert wants to call him Algernon, but I ain't having that!' Jenny laughed.

'Bloody hell, I should think not!' Vera returned. 'You'll have to get him registered soon, so think on.'

'I like Edward, after the King,' Jenny said thoughtfully.

'Have you thought how you'll manage once your confinement time is up?' Vera asked.

'Oh I'll be all right, Mum. Albert's here to help at night and in the daytime Edward and I will be downstairs. We'll be fine.'

'If you're sure,' Vera smiled at her brave young daughter.

'Lily popped in again yesterday and said Maud Hurst was happy to help out if I needed it,' Jenny said, glancing over as her baby snuffled.

'Did she now? That's a turn-up for the books, I must say. I remember her from years ago.'

The next few hours were spent with Vera telling what she knew of Maud running away with another man, and then suddenly reappearing again.

A lusty cry told Edward was hungry and Vera lifted him and passed him to his mother for a feed.

'You know, gel, I'm so proud of you. You've overcome some huge obstacles and given me a beautiful grandson.' Vera wiped away a tear then said, 'Oh blimey! I almost forgot the kids! I'd better go and fetch the little 'un from the child minder. I bet she's tearing her hair out! Will you be all right on your own until Albert gets home?'

'Yes we'll be fine, Mum. You get off and don't worry.' Jenny laughed.

Vera left feeling on top of the world.

Lily came to as the sound of fighting pounded in her ears. Dragging herself to her knees, she shook her head to clear it. Once on her feet, she leaned her back to the wall and gasped as the two men stumbled out through the front door and onto the driveway.

Punches were being thrown and she heard the grunts from Jack Fortune as blow after blow landed. Then she realised who it was that was hitting her attacker. Seb Ryder! She watched as Seb stood in the stance of a boxer. With fists clenched, his weight was on the back foot, giving him a solid grounding. His left hand was up protecting his face and he jabbed his opponent, making contact each time.

Fortune was tiring and his lip was bleeding.

'Getting tired? Come on, let's have you!' Ryder rasped. Then he pushed onto the front foot and punched Fortune's cheek, knocking him off his feet.

Scrambling to his knees, Fortune held out his hands in surrender, dragging air into his lungs.

'Get up, you swine!' Ryder said as he slowly lowered his guard.

Fortune saw his chance. Slowly he got to his feet

and in an instant he had turned and was running down the driveway.

Ryder sighed as he turned to face Lily who was white and shaking with shock. 'Oh Lily! I think you should sit down.'

Lily nodded, her brain still whirling from the whole affair.

'May I come in? Just to see you settled – I give you my word,' Seb said quietly.

Lily nodded again slowly. Still in her outdoor coat, she sat by the fire as Seb threw on more coal and poked the flames into action.

'Tea?' he asked.

Lily pointed to the kitchen, then sneezed three times in succession.

Ryder went to make the tea while Lily sat snuffling into her handkerchief. She couldn't believe what had just happened even as she went over it again in her mind. Jack Fortune had somehow got into her house and was in the process of stealing her things when she had disturbed him. Suddenly it all became too much for her and she burst into tears.

Seb came through with the tray which he laid on a small table. At the sight of Lily's tears he wondered whether he should try to comfort her. Seeing Lily at risk had stirred in him something unexpected, a need to protect her, to help her. This strange feeling was alien to him and as he tried to understand it he sat and waited, pouring the tea for when she calmed.

After a moment Lily dried her eyes and sniffed. 'Thank you, Mr Ryder.' She realised then that Seb was sitting here having tea with her and that he had saved her from the clutches of Jack Fortune. A melange of feelings swept over her; total disdain for the man who had attacked her, and also dislike for the one who stepped in to rescue her.

'Lily, who was that man and what was he doing here? I thought . . . .' He let the words hang in the quiet of the room.

Lily drew in a breath and explained, between sips of tea, about Jack Fortune and Maud Hurst, omitting the part about their having a child together. She told him only the bare bones as she felt it was not her place to discuss another's relationship. However, the man had come to her rescue and deserved some an explanation of some sort.

'Good grief!' he said on a breath as she drew the tale to its conclusion.

Lily sneezed again.

'I can see you are not at all well. You should get yourself to bed.' Seeing the fear spring into her eyes, he quickly went on, 'I'm going to inform the police about the incident.' She nodded. Lily was still afraid of him for all her bravado. He was certain then she would never forgive him.

'Mr Ryder, why did you come here in the first place?' she asked as he stood to leave.

'That doesn't matter for now, what's important is that the police be informed of this man attacking you and trying to steal from your house. Now, if you're sure you are all right, I'll be on my way.'

'Thank you again,' she said as she followed him to the front door.

Closing the door behind him, she made sure she locked it securely.

As Seb walked away he smiled. Another feather in his cap as far as Lily was concerned – saving a damsel in distress albeit by coincidence that he should have called at that particular time.

CHAPTER 58

In the meantime, Maud was shopping in the marketplace. Looking up, she saw the man coming towards her. Jack Fortune was looking dishevelled and sporting a split lip. She sighed, it looked like he'd been fighting.

'Maudy,' he said, taking her arm and leading her away from prying eyes.

'What have you been up to now, Jack?' she asked as she looked at his battered face.

'Nothing, but I've got to get out of Wednesbury,' he said as he gingerly touched his lip and winced.

'More trouble?' Maud asked in an exasperated tone.

'I'm going, Maudy – and I want you to come with me,' he whispered as he glanced around for anyone listening.

Maud stopped in her tracks and stared at him. 'You what! Where are you going?'

'I don't know yet, but I've got to be away. Now, are you coming with me or not?' Jack's head swivelled on his neck, his eyes searching the marketplace.

'The coppers after you again, are they?' Maud asked as she too glanced around.

'Not yet, but they will be,' Jack grinned and winced again as the cut on his lip cracked open and began to bleed once more. 'Maudy, come on, wench, let's me and you bugger off somewhere. It could be like it was years ago – remember?' Jack continued to look around him as he spoke.

'How could I ever forget?!' Maud spat.

'All right, but it will be better this time, I swear,' Jack mumbled his reply.

Maud stared at the man she still loved with all her heart; the man who had left her twice before. Would he leave her again if things went wrong? How could she trust him? She had another chance to be with the love of her life, and the choice hung heavy in her heart. She could go with him and risk being hurt by him again or, she could stay here without him in her life. If she stayed, would she ever see him again? The thought was like a barb in her chest, its sting harsh and relentless. Regardless of what the future held for her, she knew she could face it as long as she had Jack Fortune.

Nodding, she saw him smile then grimace as his lip stung again.

Maud had set out to win back the house she still maintained belonged to her, but constantly being seen as Lily's lackey had worn her down. Now she had the chance to be out of there and she decided to take it. Besides, she could always come back for the house at a later date.

The two walked swiftly from the market amid the stares of people passing by.

Excitement built in her chest as she strode along. Maud was setting out on another adventure, but where it would take her was a mystery. All she cared about was being with Jack, wherever they might end up.

When Maud didn't return that evening, Lily became worried. It was not like Maud to be late back from the market, but then she was a grown woman and could do as she pleased. Lily chastised herself, but the worry remained.

Coughing and sneezing, Lily climbed the stairs to bed. She felt sure Maud would be home before morning. Sitting in bed, she sipped the drink she'd made earlier, hot water, lemon, honey with a touch of brandy. Then she settled down hoping for a good night's rest.

As she lay in the darkness, she wondered where Maud was which led onto how Jack Fortune had got into her house. There were no broken windows, she'd checked. Therefore he must have had a key. How had he come by a key to her property? Maud! The question now was, had Maud given him her key or had he stolen it? Did Maud know it was missing if she'd not given it to him? One after another, queries raced through her mind. Were Maud and Jack together? Why had Seb Ryder turned up on her doorstep? It was fortuitous he had, but what did he want?

Lily turned over and closed her eyes, all this thinking was making her head ache.

The following morning Lily heard the sharp rapping on the door. Opening it cautiously, she saw a policeman standing before her.

'Mrs Hurst?' he asked.

Nodding, she invited him inside.

As they sat by the fire she listened as the constable explained about Seb's visit to the station. Lily confirmed that everything he'd been told was correct and true. She said also that Maud had not returned home and she was now very concerned.

'Well it seems Mr Ryder gave Fortune a bit of a hiding and it's my guess he's taken off. I wouldn't be surprised if Maud has gone with him,' the constable said finally.

Lily sighed, this was something she hadn't thought of. Something inside her made her feel sorry for Maud falling for Jack's charms yet again but also she felt angry that the woman had duped her all along. Maybe it would be the last she saw of either of them.

'Would you mind if I took a look around, Mrs Hurst?'

'Please go right ahead, although there are no broken windows, I've looked already,' Lily said.

Nodding, the policeman did a quick tour of the house, and once more back in the living room he said, 'As you say, no broken panes – no sign of forced entry that I can see, which means he had to have had a key. Who else has a key to your house, Mrs Hurst?'

'Maud,' Lily said glumly.

'I see. May I suggest you get the locks changed as soon as possible?' The constable stood to leave.

Thanking him, she saw him out, making sure the door was locked behind him.

Lily stayed indoors nursing her head cold and feeling sorry for herself. She was surprised Seb Ryder had not called again to check on her welfare, but she was very relieved he had not although she still wondered why he'd called in the first place.

Everyone was pleased to see her when she returned to work the following day, her health much improved. She decided to keep the debacle of the break-in and attack to herself not wishing to worry anyone or have them asking questions she wasn't sure she had answers for.

At the end of the day she wandered up to the churchyard to tend the graves of her husband and child. She talked to Davy in her mind as she tidied around the gravestones. She told him all that had happened. Telling them both she loved them dearly, she picked her way out of the cemetery and returned home to an empty house.

It was always slow at this time of year at Webb's regarding burials. It was usually the elderly that passed over, unless a virus or disease ravaged the town. Lily was glad that they were not busy, it meant more people were enjoying life.

When the working day drew to a close, Lily sauntered down the street towards the locksmith in Lower High Street to arrange for her locks to be changed. Then she continued on to the estate agents in Union Street. She explained her reason for the visit to the man behind the desk and he assured her he would do his best to sell her grocery business. She said once a buyer was found, she could be contacted at Webb's.

Walking up the High Bullen, Lily was enjoying the early evening sunshine. She heard the laughter of children as she watched them kicking a ball around. The shout went up, 'Goal!' and the cheers sounded. Their football match was going well, it seemed. Lily smiled as she walked on.

Stepping aside at the sound of a trumpet blow, she waited for the horse and cart to rumble past her. The rag-and-bone man yelled out, 'Any old rags?

Reaching home, her thoughts turned to Maud and where she could be. She was still angry at being deceived by Maud, but couldn't help a pang of worry springing to her chest that the woman would be safe with Jack. Sighing, she let herself in through the front door. The house was silent and again loneliness wrapped itself around her.

On the other side of town, on the heathland known as The Coppice, Jack and Maud stood in the kitchen of a ramshackle cottage.

'Is this where you've been living?' Maud asked as she glanced around.

Fortune nodded, his hair bouncing and his eyes blinked rapidly.

Maud had paid for lodgings for them both for a couple of nights with the money Lily had given her for food shopping. With that money now gone, Jack had brought her to the cottage.

'Bloody hell, Jack!' Maud gasped in utter frustration.

'I know, Maudy, but I thought we could do it up a bit.' He knew he was clutching at straws.

'Well you thought wrong! I ain't living in this pigsty for all the tea in China!' Maud turned on her heel and walked out into the sunshine.

'Maudy . . .' Jack pleaded as he followed her.

Sitting on an old upturned bucket, she said, 'Look, Jack, I think it's time you told me what's going on. First you say you're taking off and ask me to go with you. Then you bring me here!'

Dropping onto the dirt beside her, he nodded. Drawing in a deep breath, he began. He told her of his owing money in London and being unable to repay it. He explained about his injuries caused by a caller at the house and how and why that had come about.

'What! You tried to rob Lily's house? Christ Jack!' Maud was aghast. 'How did you get in?'

Jack wriggled his fingers. 'There ain't a house I can't get into, Maudy.'

Maud shook her head and snorted.

'I borrowed your key the first time I called on you and got another cut, then I put yours back in your coat the second time I visited,' he said sheepishly.

Maud heaved a great sigh as she shook her head. She wished Jack had been with her all along then they could have got their hands on the will and now be living the high life themselves in Trouse Lane.

'So what shall we do now?' Jack asked quietly as he laid his head in her lap.

'First of all we need money,' Maud said, stroking his hair like he was a child.

She had considered leaving him to his fate and going back to Lily's, but seeing him looking so forlorn she hadn't the heart. If Jack Fortune was to avoid going to prison, he would need her by his side to guide him.

After an uncomfortable night at the cottage, Maud kept a keen eye out the following morning as she trudged through the streets. It was mid-morning so Lily should be at work. However if Lily was at home for some reason, Maud would say she wanted to return to live there after seeing Jack off once and for all.

Turning the key in the lock, Maud heaved a sigh of relief; at least Lily hadn't thought to change the locks. Quietly moving through the house, she ascertained she was alone.

In Lily's bedroom, she made a methodical search of all the drawers and the tallboy.

Maud's eyes lit up when she eventually spied what she'd been looking for. Picking up the item, she clasped it to her breast with a broad grin on her face. Ensuring everything was in place and looked untouched, she scurried out of the house locking the door behind her. Hurrying down Trouse Lane, she wondered if her plan would work. If it did, she would be a rich woman. If not, she could well end up back in jail.

CHAPTER 59

Lily supervised the changing of her house locks that afternoon, and with her new keys in her hand she walked up to the marketplace. She felt better now that task was complete; all that was left to do was pay the locksmith.

Walking into the London & Midland Bank, she stood before the teller. Looking into her bag she suddenly realised she had forgotten to pick up her bank book. 'I'm afraid I've forgotten to bring my bank book, but I need to withdraw some funds,' she said.

'I'm sorry, madam, but without your book I cannot release any money,' the snooty teller replied.

Lily studied the young man carefully. She had not seen him before and she surmised he must be new to the Bank. 'I understand,' she said brightly, 'I wonder, may I speak with the manager?'

'He's busy,' the teller held his nose in the air.

Lily drew in a frustrated breath. 'Sir, I have a bill to pay which cannot wait, so I'd be obliged if you would ask the manager if he will see me.'

'I'm sorry, madam, but I can't possibly disturb

him,' he said without the courtesy of even looking at her.

'Now you listen to me, young man!' Lily's voice was like a rasp. 'I need to see your manager right now!' Anger mounted in her chest as she stared at the arrogant man before her.

Just then a door opened and out walked the manager.

'Mrs Hurst, how very nice to see you,' he said, walking towards her.

'Mr Fredrickson.' Lily inclined her head. 'I wonder if you could assist me, I need to withdraw a small amount from my account but I have forgotten my bank book . . .'

'Of course, dear lady,' the manager nodded to the teller who stood scowling.

Checking through the paperwork the teller gave a small smile. He coughed politely to interrupt the quiet conversation between Lily and Mr Fredrickson.

The manager looked at the young man, his eyebrows raised in question. 'Is there a problem?'

The spiteful teller raised his voice as he said, 'Mrs Hurst has virtually no funds in her account, sir.'

Lily's eyebrows drew together in a frown. Fredrickson sighed audibly and showed her to his office. Leaving her a moment, he returned to the teller to check the paperwork for himself. He frowned as he returned to his office.

'I'm afraid what the teller said is true, Mrs Hurst. Your account was almost emptied of its funds early this morning.'

'What! How can that be?' Lily felt her world crumble around her.

The manager called the teller to bring in the paperwork for Lily's account.

The teller stood in the office, giving a sobbing Lily a snide look while Mr Fredrickson cast an eye over the accounts.

'Mr Phillips, these are your initials alongside this transaction, I see.' The young man looked across the desk and nodded. The manager continued, 'So can you tell me who you gave all that money to – without consulting me?'

'Mrs Lily Hurst, sir, she brought in her bank book and requested to withdraw nearly all the funds.' Still the man's superior tone remained.

'What did she look like?' Lily managed to ask.

Phillips looked down his nose at the woman drying her eyes. 'Older than you. Brown hair, but she had the book, which you do not have.'

'Are you accusing me of being a fraud?' Lily asked heatedly.

The teller raised one eyebrow and looked down his beaky nose. 'I'm not accusing you of anything madam, but you see how it looks.'

'That's enough, Phillips!' the manager rounded on him. Mr Fredrickson intervened sharply. 'This lady is Mrs Lily Hurst and this bank has conducted business on her behalf for many years!'

The teller's confident smile evaporated in an instant. 'Then who . . .?' he babbled.

'Maud!' Lily gasped under her breath.

Mr Fredrickson paled. 'Oh dear. Oh dearie, dearie me!'

Phillips looked at his boss, his stomach lurching.

'Mrs Hurst, may I suggest you check to see if your bank book is missing. I will telephone the police station in the meantime and request they send a constable.'

As Lily stood she saw the teller's face turn a sickly shade of green at the mention of the police.

Phillips jumped as the manager said to him, 'As for you, I suggest you stay in this office until this mess is sorted out!'

Lily ran back to her house, oblivious of the stares of passing people. If her bank book was missing, then the only people who could have taken it were Maud or Jack. The account had been almost emptied early that morning, leaving only a small amount to keep the account open which would raise no red flags for a while. This all meant Maud must have taken the book.

Making her way back to the bank, Lily sat in the office once more with the manager, teller and a police constable.

'Mrs Hurst, you are not having a very good time of it lately,' the constable said.

Seeing it was the same policeman she had spoken to previously, she answered, 'It would seem not.'

'Mr Fredrickson has given me the details, so can you tell me anything more?' the constable asked.

'My bank book is definitely missing. The only

other person to have a key to my house is Maud Hurst.'

'Ah yes – Maud Hurst,' the constable said. 'I remember you telling me about her when I called to see you.'

'Well I took your advice and had the locks changed, however it appears I was too late.' Lily was close to tears once more.

'Is this your signature?' he asked, passing a slip of paper to Lily.

'No. May I?' she asked Mr Fredrickson, pointing to his fountain pen. At his nod, she took the pen and paper and signed her name.

The constable compared the two signatures and passed them over to the manager to scrutinise before taking them back as evidence.

'Well, Mrs Hurst, I'm very sorry but it looks like Maud has had it away with your money. We will of course make a search for the woman in question, but I'm not holding out any hope of her still being hereabouts.' With a sad look, the constable shook his head.

Lily burst into tears again.

Fredrickson glared at the teller, who was quaking in his shoes. 'This is your fault! Get your things and get out of my bank – you're sacked!' he bellowed.

Phillips almost fell over himself in his scramble to leave the office.

'Mrs Hurst, I'm so very sorry. I really don't know what else I can say.' The manager felt bad for the woman, but also at the back of his mind was the bank's reputation. If this got out, folk would be coming to withdraw their money left, right and centre – the bank would be ruined!

'May I make a suggestion?' the constable asked.

'Please do,' Lily responded.

'Firstly you need to open a new account and have a new bank book – which you need to keep in a more secure hiding place. I think this account should be left open as a lure,' he said, shaking the paper with the signatures on it.

'A lure? I don't understand,' Lily said with a sniff.

'The staff should be informed anyone trying to withdraw money from this account should notify us immediately.'

'Oh I see, but there's not much left to draw upon,' Lily said sadly.

'I understand that, Mrs Hurst, however Maud will be unaware that you've discovered the loss. So, I'm sure she'll be expecting you to add to what is left, being none the wiser.'

Lily was confused, her brain was still in a whirl at the events taking place.

'If Maud thinks you don't know she's stolen your money, she will expect you to put your salary into that account. She may try again to withdraw and then we'll have her!' Fredrickson said, slapping his hand on the desk.

'Exactly,' the constable said as he rolled his eyes at the man's theatrics.

'But what about the money I've lost already?' Lily asked.

'Unless we come upon the lady in question with that money still on her, I'm afraid you will have to kiss it goodbye.' The constable shook his head in dismay.

Fredrickson, by way of compensation, agreed to pay the locksmith from the bank's own funds and promised to look into their policies regarding situations such as this.

The constable left and Lily and the manager completed paperwork for a new account – one which would hold all Lily's future wages and Maud would know nothing about.

CHAPTER 60

It was the following week when Webb's received a telephone call from the bank requesting Lily's attendance as soon as possible.

Wondering what had happened now, Lily rushed along to the bank. The sun beamed down full and hot and she was perspiring beneath her funereal garb when she arrived.

Entering the bank manager's office, she was stunned to see not only the constable, but also Maud sitting uncomfortably by the desk.

'Mrs Hurst, as you can see we've caught this lady trying to withdraw monies from your account – again,' the constable said.

Lily stared at the woman who sat with a bowed head. 'Maud, why?'

Looking up, the woman said simply, 'I needed the money, Lily.'

'Maud, if you had asked me I would have provided . . .' Lily began.

'It wasn't for me,' Maud cut across her sentence, 'it was for Jack.'

Lily sighed. *That man again!*

The constable took up, 'She's given back most of the money she stole from you, Mrs Hurst.'

Fredrickson added, 'We can put it in your *new* account if you'd like, Mrs Hurst.'

Maud flinched at the emphasis on the word. Had she been thinking clearly, she would have realised Lily would open another account at discovering she'd been robbed.

'Also, we have officers about to arrest Jack Fortune now we know where he's holed up,' the constable added as he nodded at Maud.

'If I'm to do time for this, then he can as well!' Maud spat venomously. 'He ain't getting off so easily this time! He got off scot-free before, this time he can pay the price himself!' Maud's anger flared again.

A tap on the door sounded and it opened a fraction. A nervous voice said, 'They're here.'

The constable, with a hand under Maud's elbow, drew her to her feet.

Lily watched as Maud was led to the Black Maria waiting by the front door. A sob caught in her throat as the back door of the police wagon was closed and locked. Maud stared out sadly through the bars on the window. Try as she might Lily could find no forgiveness in her heart for the woman who had deceived and robbed her.

The constable climbed beside the driver, who clucked to the horses and the carriage moved off.

Fredrickson called for tea as Lily re-joined him in the office. He explained the events; how Maud had boldly tried to claim further funds from Lily's old account but a teller was wise to her. Saying he needed to get the money from the office, he informed the manager. Between them they had manhandled Maud into the office where they kept her until the constable came. Having telephoned the station, he had arrived in short order.

Lily sat listening, the shock of it all keeping her silent.

Maud had told the policeman where Jack Fortune was waiting for her. He had, in turn, telephoned the station and the hunt was on. The police were confident Fortune would be in their custody very soon. They felt sure Maud would serve a prison sentence for theft; as for her lover, no doubt he would go to jail too for being an accessory as well as attempting to rob Lily's house and intent on causing her physical harm.

Lily wandered slowly back to Webb's as if in a daydream. Everything had happened so fast it had left her mind in turmoil. She was pleased to have most of her money returned, but she felt sad for Maud.

Once she'd related the tale back at Webb's, Stan sent her home for the rest of the day. Lily needed to rest and they could manage without her for one day.

Lily, rather than going home to an empty house, walked over to Church Street to visit Emily Johnston. Over tea, she told the story yet again.

'It's sad, but at least that pair are out of your life now,' Emily said.

'I still can't believe Maud would do what she did for that man,' Lily said, shaking her head.

'She's in love, Lily. She will love him until the day she dies. Love such as that comes but once in a lifetime.'

Lily's thoughts turned to Davy, her deceased husband. She'd loved him more than life itself and so Maud's actions made more sense. Inevitably her thoughts moved to Clara, hoping she was happy with her daddy in heaven.

'Good morning, I'm looking for Lily Hurst,' the honeyed voice said.

Dora Bean showed the man to a seat in Webb's shop before going to the kitchen. A moment later she reappeared with Lily in tow.

'Good morning, you asked to see me?' Lily said as she stood before him.

'Ah yes. Mrs Hurst, I am Benjamin Addenbury and I'm interested in buying your store.'

Lily studied the man with the twinkling blue eyes. His fair hair was cut fashionably and his clothes were tailor made. His riding boots shone in the light and showed to be of the very best leather.

'I'm sorry I'm unable to leave my work, but if you would care to come into the kitchen, we could discuss it more there,' Lily said as she racked her brains. Addenbury – where had she heard the name before?

Following behind her, they entered the kitchen and sat at the small table.

'Mr Addenbury, I seem to know that name, but I can't remember where from.' Lily flushed in embarrassment.

'Please call me Ben. My uncle is George Addenbury who married the singer Tilley Green.'

'Oh but of course!' Lily said. 'I recall now reading the newspaper article.' Her mind brought forth a picture of Tilley singing in the music hall and then the memory of Emily's words. Tilley was Maud's long-lost daughter.

She watched the man as he chatted away about purchasing her store. He was very handsome and she found herself wondering if he was married. She pushed away the thought as a blush rose to her cheeks.

'Mr Addenbury – Ben – my only stipulation is that the staff who work there are kept on in their present positions,' Lily said eventually.

'You have my word, Mrs Hurst. May I call you Lily?' He smiled.

'Please do,' Lily felt the heat rise in her as he said her name. It flowed off his tongue like honey from a dipper.

'Then if you are agreeable, Lily, I will conduct my business with the estate agent and leave you to your work.' Ben stood to leave.

'How are your uncle and Miss Green?' Lily asked quickly. She didn't want this man to leave just yet.

'They are well, thank you for asking. Are they

friends of yours?' he asked, surprised by her question.

Lily shook her head, feeling uncomfortable. 'No, I heard Miss Green sing at the music hall some time ago.'

'I see. Well I believe she will be revisiting very soon to sing there again. It will be for one night only, so if you wish to see her I suggest you purchase a ticket early.' Ben grinned, clearly proud of his aunt-by-marriage.

Lily shook her head. 'It's unlikely I will be going, Mr Add— Ben.'

'Oh, is it not to your husband's taste?' he asked.

Lily gave a grim smile. 'I'm a widow and women alone don't go out to the music hall.'

'I'm sorry to hear that,' he said. 'Forgive me, but I must be away to the estate agent and seal the deal. I hope we meet again, Lily Hurst.' Taking her hand, he bent forward and kissed the back.

Again the flush rose to the roots of her hair as she mumbled, 'So do I, Ben Addenbury.'

She sat by the table as the man left and a tingle ran down her spine. It had been a long time since she'd had feelings of this sort and she tried to push them away feeling guilty towards Davy. Chiding herself, she set about making tea for everyone as lunchtime approached.

Dora and Lily spent the afternoon giving the shop a good clean. The sun was still warm as she left Webb's and Lily decided to enjoy the good weather and go for a walk. She sauntered up Squire's Walk and past the reservoir and Water Works Co., heading for the allotment gardens. She heard the birds twittering in the distance as she ambled up Church Hill.

Sitting on a bench, she watched the men working their plots of land. She smiled as they doffed their caps to her. Listening to the sound of hoes striking the soil, Lily's thoughts wandered.

Ben Addenbury came instantly to mind. He had the bluest eyes she'd ever seen, which held a mischievous twinkle. His smile, which she had found to be infectious, lit up his whole face. He had a mild manner and an easy confidence, showing he came from good stock. Lily smiled inwardly at this thought – she made him sound like he came from a line of cattle. He appeared savvy in the ways of business – and he had set her heart aflutter.

Lily frowned as she thought of her deceased husband Davy. Was she betraying him with her thoughts of another man? Was she disrespecting his memory and that of Clara? She sighed heavily as her mind swirled. What would Davy say? Would he tell her to live her life and find love again? Or would he expect her to honour his memory and stay widowed and single for the rest of her life? The thoughts swung in her head like a pendulum, until, unable to bear it a moment longer, she rose to leave, hoping the walk would clear her mind.

Waving to the allotment workers, Lily retraced her steps towards home. As she walked, she realised she needed someone else's opinion, so she decided to call in on Jenny. If she was quick she might be able to cuddle baby Edward before he was settled for the night.

Jenny was thrilled to see her friend and while Albert prepared the baby's bottle, Lily enjoyed her cuddle with their baby boy. Taking Edward upstairs to feed him, Albert left the women to chat.

'I thought you were feeding Edward yourself,' Lily said.

'I was, but I ran dry!' Jenny laughed. After a moment she rubbed the stump of her aching leg and asked, 'So what's occurring?'

Lily told her friend about Ben Addenbury wanting to buy her store. Jenny listened as Lily prattled on.

'You think he's genuine?' Jenny probed.

'Oh yes!' Lily exclaimed just a little too quickly. Her blush gave her away in an instant.

'Our Lily, I do believe you've got your eye on this man,' Jenny grinned.

'Jenny, I've only met him once!' Lily said in mock horror.

'Once is all it takes. Is he married do you know?'

'I have no idea,' Lily's voice held a sadness as she looked at her friend.

'Well you'd best find out!' Jenny grinned again. 'How?'

'Ask him,' Jenny said forthrightly.

'Jenny! I couldn't possibly . . .' But already Lily's mind was working as to how she could find out if Ben was indeed married or single.

'You seeing him again?' Jenny asked.

'He did say he hoped we'd meet again,' Lily blushed.

'There you go then,' Jenny lifted her stump onto the sofa. 'Lily – get in there and dip your bread!'

Lily laughed loudly at her friend's expression as Albert joined them.

'The nipper is fast asleep,' he said.

Lily watched as he gently rubbed ointment on his wife's stump before pulling on the woollen sock and covering it with her long skirt.

'I'll just wash my hands, then I'll make some tea,' Albert said.

'Oh Jenny, that man adores you,' Lily gushed.

'I know, bless him. You could have that, you know, if you and this Ben get together,' Jenny nodded.

'Jenny, these feelings – it's as though I'm being unfaithful to Davy.'

'Look, Davy's gone – God rest his soul – but you're still here. The question is, for how much longer?' Seeing the shocked look on Lily's face, she ploughed on regardless, 'None of us know when our time will be up, so you have to decide how to use what time you have.'

'I'm not an old woman yet,' Lily laughed.

'True, but when you are, do you want to be on your own? Or do you want to meet old age with someone you love? It's my opinion that Davy would want you to be happy and if that means marrying again, so be it.'

'For all we know Ben could be married already

or betrothed,' Lily said, angst written all over her face.

'If he is – find someone else!'

After tea and updates on the baby, Lily left the family and made her way home. It was still light as she walked quickly back to Trouse Lane. She had a lot to think about now she'd heard what Jenny had said on the matter, and she hoped she would be meeting Ben Addenbury again in the near future.

CHAPTER 61

Jack Fortune couldn't believe his bad luck. The police had surrounded the dilapidated cottage where he waited for Maud, then they had pounced. He'd had no chance of escape. He was hauled off to the station on Holyhead Road.

Sitting in a room with the Superintendent of police and the constable, he was told Maud Hurst had given him up and she was already in the cells awaiting her turn before the magistrate.

Fortune had blustered that it was all Maud's idea and that he'd had no part in it. Then the constable reminded him that they knew about his attack on Lily. The man who had fought him off was their witness.

Jack was told he was going to jail – for a very long time.

The following day Maud Hurst and Jack Fortune stood before the Magistrate in the Petty Sessions court room and listened as the charges were read out by the court clerk.

Maud hung her head as the Magistrate glared at her, shame colouring her cheeks. She heard the words – twelve months in gaol! Turning to Jack standing next to her in the dock, Maud's anger boiled over. She began to land punches and kicks, screaming at the top of her lungs, 'May you rot in hell, Jack Fortune!' Maud was dragged away still kicking and screaming her fury at the man left behind.

Jack Fortune was sentenced to five years in Stafford jail for his crimes of burglary and assault on Lily Hurst at her home.

The magistrate banged his gavel down and Jack was led away. The whole process had taken less than fifteen minutes.

The newspapers the following day reported the outcome of the Fortune/Hurst court case and Lily's heart was saddened as she read the article.

Drinking her morning tea, she reflected. Anyone meeting Black Country women for the first time might consider them to be hard-faced, but beneath that gruff veneer lay hearts that could be shattered as easily as a pane of glass. Lily thought Maud would be showing her hard exterior whilst in jail in order to survive, but she felt the woman's heart might have finally broken. She doubted Maud would ever get over this last cruel blow struck by Jack Fortune. Lily sighed, two lives destroyed by one man's greed.

Lily walked down to the churchyard to tend the graves of her husband and daughter. Arranging the flowers she had bought in the market on her way, she whispered into the quiet of the cemetery, 'Hello you two, I've come to visit. I miss you both dreadfully.' Sitting on the ground between the graves, she laid a hand on each which were now covered with grass. 'Davy, a nice man, Ben, is buying the grocery store. I felt it was time to sell it on and I'm sure you would agree. I think I'm ready to move on with my life now, so I needed to let you know. I would hate for you to think I'm betraying you, but Ben has stirred feelings in me I thought had died with you. No matter what the future holds for me, I will always love you both. Davy, take care of Clara until it's time for me to join you.'

Getting to her feet, Lily sighed as she looked down at the grassy mounds. It was then that a sparrow flew down and perched on Clara's headstone. Its head jerked from side to side as it eyed Lily before flying onto Davy's headstone. Lily smiled as it took to the wing and soared up into the sky. She thought it a good omen; she had their approval to find happiness again.

The smile stayed on her lips as she left the cemetery and made her way to Webb's. As she neared the parlour, she saw Ben Addenbury alight from a cab. Turning to pay the driver, he noticed her coming towards him. Lily felt fate was intervening and her smile was broad as she approached him.

'Good morning, Mrs Hurst,' he said with a smile.

'It is indeed, Mr Addenbury,' she returned.

'I'm glad I've caught you before you begin your work, I have something to ask you.'

'Is there something amiss with the store?' Lily asked.

'No, no. Everything there is proceeding nicely. I wondered if you would care to join me in a visit to the Theatre Royal this coming Saturday.' He gave her a beaming smile which completely disarmed her.

'This is a surprise,' Lily said, feeling the blush rise to her cheeks.

'Yes, I know it's short notice and I'm sorry for that, but Aunt Tilley will be singing there and I thought you might enjoy an evening out. Forgive me if you think I'm being presumptuous.' Ben's eyes moved to his shoes as if checking they were clean.

'I cannot deny I would love to hear Miss Green sing again,' Lily said.

'So will you come?'

'Thank you – Ben. I will.' Lily's heartbeat quickened as she watched the grin spread across his face.

Ben said he would collect her by cab, but she thought it better to meet him at the theatre at eight o'clock.

With a nod, he turned and walked away. Lily entered Webb's and was bombarded with questions from the staff who had watched the exchange through the window.

For the next couple of days Lily went through the process of being conductor at the funerals booked, although her mind was firmly fixed on the handsome young Ben Addenbury. She questioned her rash decision many times about accompanying him to the theatre. After all, they were relatively new acquaintances, but her counterargument was she would be safe enough in the crowd and she wanted to go.

As the time drew nearer, her excitement grew until she was hardly able to think of anything else. Then she found herself preparing for her evening out with Ben. Checking her look in the mirror one last time, she grabbed her coat and left the house.

Walking towards the theatre, her mind was in turmoil. Was she doing the right thing? Would he be there waiting for her? What should she do if he wasn't, should she wait or return home? In her angst she realised her pace had quickened, so she slowed her step. She didn't want to seem too eager.

Her worries disappeared, however, when she saw Ben strutting back and forth outside the building. He was looking around for her and when he caught sight of her, he waved.

'Here you are, I was afraid you may have changed your mind,' he said as she walked up to him.

'Had I decided against this – outing – I would have informed you. I would not have left you standing.' She smiled.

'Shall we go in?'

Lily nodded and felt a rush of heat consume her as he placed his hand beneath her elbow.

Taking their places on the front bench, Lily remembered her previous visit to the place with Davy. She felt a pang of sadness, then smiled at Ben when he asked if she was comfortable.

They laughed at the comedian who was first to come on stage. They winced as the juggler dropped the balls, which rolled away out of his reach. The evening wore on until it was time for Tilley Green to sing. Everyone applauded and whistled as the sandy-haired girl took to the boards with a loud laugh. They loved her for staying true to her roots and not adopting airs and graces.

The audience clearly adored her as she coaxed them to sing along with her. At the close of her set, the whole of the audience were on their feet shouting for more.

Tilley returned to the stage and stood waiting for the noise to die down.

'Ain't you lot got homes to go to?' she yelled out with a laugh.

'Nooo!' came the reply.

'Well I ain't had my dinner yet,' Tilley bellowed. Laughter filled the auditorium as she went on. 'So, one more song then I'm away.'

The applause was deafening as Tilley finally drew the evening to a close and Lily was caught up in the excitement of it all.

People filed out of the room exchanging opinions on the performances. Lily stood to leave also and Ben said, 'Would you have dinner with me, Lily – along with my aunt and uncle, of course?'

'Thank you, I would enjoy that very much.'

Ben led her backstage to a small room which Tilley was using as a dressing room. Knocking on the door, he walked in as a voice bade him enter.

'Aunt Tilley! You were wonderful, as always.' Ben gave the young woman a warm hug. Despite there being little difference in their ages, Ben had maintained his respect by referring to Tilley as 'aunt'.

'Uncle George,' Ben said, shaking hands with the much older man. 'I'd like you both to meet Lily Hurst.'

Shaking hands with them both, Lily smiled her greeting. She found herself searching Tilley's face for any likeness to Maud. There was nothing to say the two were related. However, the young woman was the spitting image of Jack Fortune, and for a moment Lily was transfixed.

'I think I know you,' Tilley said, 'didn't you once have a café in the town?'

'Yes, until the road collapsed taking the café with it.' Lily shrugged her shoulders.

'Lord yes! I remember that.' Tilley turned to the men saying, 'I need to get this make-up off and change my clothes, so you two can wait outside. Lily, stay and talk to me.'

George and Ben snapped out a smart salute, turned on their heels and marched out military style. Lily laughed.

'They always do that. Have a seat, Lily, and tell me about yourself,' Tilley grinned.

Thinking there wasn't much to tell, Lily condensed her life story, giving only the barest facts. She omitted to speak of Seb Ryder. She thought the singer wasn't taking much notice as she wiped the stage make-up off her face, but Lily was mistaken. Tilley Green had taken in every word.

'I take it you ain't got a mother then?' Tilley called from behind the screen where she was changing her clothes.

'No,' Lily replied.

'Me neither, never knew my real mother. I was adopted.'

Lily sucked in a breath. She knew who and where Tilley's real mother was. Should she say? Should she tell the famous singer her birth mother was in jail? No, she couldn't bring herself to be so callous. It would most definitely bring upset and possible anger at what might be seen as an intrusion into the girl's private life.

Tilley returned to her seat before the mirror. 'It would have been nice to know who she was and why she gave me up.'

'I can understand that, but what if you found her and she was not what you hoped she would be?' Lily probed.

'At least I would have my questions answered,' Tilley replied, her tone matter-of-fact. 'Right, let's go, I'm famished!'

Lily breathed a sigh of relief that the conversation had ended.

A little while later the four sat at a table in the restaurant of a hotel. Wine was served and food ordered and the conversation was flowing nicely.

Suddenly the colour drained from Lily's face as

she saw Seb Ryder walk in. Averting her eyes, she prayed he would not see her.

'Tilley!' The voice boomed out as Seb strode towards their table.

Lily's heart sank.

'Well hello, Seb,' Tilley returned his greeting. 'You remember George? This is his nephew Ben and this is . . .'

'Hello Lily,' Seb cut across. Now he was glad he had chosen this particular restaurant to eat in. Lady Luck was most definitely on his side tonight.

All eyes moved to the young woman looking distinctly uncomfortable, then back to Seb.

'Lily and I know each other very well, don't we?'

'We have crossed paths a few times, yes,' she answered.

Lily could feel Ben's eyes on her and she scowled at Ryder who seemed hell-bent on disrupting her life.

'Forgive my intrusion, but I just wanted to say hello. Enjoy your evening.' Seb turned and walked to a table, where he sat facing Lily.

The conversation resumed with Ben asking how Lily knew Seb Ryder.

'I was in service at his parents' house years ago,' she explained, then shifting the onus to Tilley, she asked, 'How is it you know him, Miss Green?'

'The name's Tilley, and he was the one who got me on the stage in the first place. I have to say he weren't best pleased when George came on the scene though.'

'Indeed, Tilley was engaged to him at the time, but she chose me in the end, for which I will be forever grateful,' George put in. He grasped his wife's hand and gave it a quick squeeze.

Lily became more and more uncomfortable beneath Ryder's overt stare as the evening wore on. Eventually, unable to stand it any longer, she gave her apologies and stood to leave.

'I'll take you home,' Ben said.

Bidding the others goodnight, Lily and Ben left the dining room. Outside, Ben hailed a cab.

On their journey, Ben said quietly, 'I get the impression you don't like Seb Ryder overly much.'

Lily tensed. 'You are correct in your assumption, Ben. He is a pretentious, acquisitive prig. I have no time for the man.'

'Goodness! I hope you never see me that way.' Ben was surprised.

Lily burst out laughing, releasing the pent-up tension of the last hours.

The cab stopped outside her house in Trouse Lane and Ben helped Lily alight.

'Please say you will see me again, Lily,' he said quietly.

'I would very much like to, Ben.'

'Then tomorrow I suggest we take a walk in the park,' he laughed at her surprised look. 'I will be here at ten o'clock in the morning to collect you.'

'Thank you for a lovely evening, I will see you tomorrow,' Lily grinned before turning to walk up the driveway.

Later as she lay in bed, Lily thought again about the earlier events. Tilley Green wanted to know who her mother was, but Lily was not going to be the one who enlightened her. Seb Ryder had once again spoiled her evening, despite his having saved her from the despicable Jack Fortune, and she still lived in constant dread he would divulge her secret. Residing in the same town meant there was no getting away from him. She wondered if he would try to come between Ben and herself sometime in the future.

Lily sighed into the darkness. She would cross that bridge when she came to it. For now, she would enjoy Ben's company and see whether the relationship developed further.

Seb was also lying on his bed in the boarding house thinking back over his life. An only child born to wealthy parents he had been thoroughly spoiled. His mother had indulged his every whim, seeing no wrong in him. His father had lost all patience with them both and thrown himself into his work.

As soon as he was able, Seb had taken up with the wrong crowd who had led him into drinking and debauchery.

Encouraged by his mother to be a 'cut-above' all others, his arrogance had increased to a ridiculously high level until he felt he was untouchable.

His thoughts again returned to Lily. Why had he abused her so badly that day? Trying to analyse the question, an answer evaded him. He didn't know other than it had brought him immense excitement and satisfaction.

Only now after all this time, and knowing his quest had finally failed, did he feel a little ashamed. It was a totally new emotion for him and he hoped that he had not hurt the girl too badly. He also realised he had developed feelings for Lily Hurst – was this what they called love?

With a sigh, Seb saw again Lily with the Addenburys and he had noted she'd found herself a new love.

He felt he had wasted so many years of his life trying to act like a gentleman, when in fact he had been a spoilt brat.

Turning his face to the wall, Seb did something he hadn't done since he was a child. He cried himself to sleep.

CHAPTER 62

Lily and Ben enjoyed many walks in the park and evenings out at the Theatre Royal. He had bought the grocery business and it was running smoothly, having kept to his word of maintaining the current staff. Lily continued to work at Webb's, which she loved. She saw her friends often both in work and socially and life was sweet.

Some months after their initial evening spent with Tilley Green and her husband George, Lily had a shock.

Over dinner in a hotel with Ben one evening, he spoke to her in a whisper, 'Lily, will you marry me?'

Her mouth dropped open and her eyes widened. Although in her private moments she had dreamed of this, she had not expected it to come so soon.

'Ben, I . . . we . . .' As she faltered, she remembered something said to her previously, the gist of which was – grab happiness while you can!

Looking into his eyes, she saw the love shining out at her. Ben Addenbury loved her with all his heart, and she felt the same. He made her happy and she realised there and then it was what she wanted more than anything else in the world.

'Lily . . .?' he asked.

'Yes,' she said, suddenly feeling very shy.

Ben stood up and tapping his wine glass gently with his knife he watched all eyes in the dining room turn to him. 'Waiter, wine for everyone please. Ladies and gentlemen, please join me in a toast to Lily Hurst who has just consented to become my wife!'

Applause rang out before glasses were raised. Lily flushed to the roots of her hair as waiters scuttled around opening bottles and refilling wine goblets.

As Ben retook his seat he laughed with his blushing bride-to-be. Occasionally people wandered over to pass their thanks for the wine and give their congratulations to the happy couple. The evening was a complete success and Lily was on cloud nine as they travelled home.

A couple of days later Lily saw Ben had announced their engagement in the newspaper. She had already told her friends of the forthcoming wedding and they were delighted for her. Although they had not, as yet, set a date, Lily was already testing out her new name in her mind. Mrs Lily Addenbury. It had a nice ring to it.

The following morning Lily was reading the newspaper before going to Webb's. She almost dropped her teacup as she read the headline.

Man found hanged in Wednesbury. Coroner rules it was suicide.

Her hand shot to her mouth as she read on. The

man had left behind a letter in which he said he was desperately unhappy. To all intents and purposes his life had ended years ago when he lost the love of his life to another man. He wished her well in the future. He requested to be buried by Webb's Funeral Parlour. His landlady had found him hanging from the balustrade of the stairs. Seb Ryder had strangled himself with a washing line.

Lily was shocked to the core; she knew it was her he referred to in that note. She also knew he would not be buried in consecrated ground; suicides were buried at the other side of the lych-gate.

Gathering her things together, she shot from the house. Once at Webb's it was confirmed they would be carrying out the funeral. Seb had left enough money behind to cover the cost, it seemed.

Lily said she had an errand to run and wouldn't be long. Stan nodded, saying to bring back cake to have with their mid-morning tea.

Striding out, Lily went straight to St John's Church where she found the vicar. Explaining why she was there, she asked if there was any way he could help.

Shaking his head, the vicar thought on the matter.

'I know he took his own life, but I'm sure he would want to go to heaven,' Lily was distressed.

'My dear, you must know in your profession that suicide is a sin against God and the law,' the vicar said sadly.

'Yes I do, but I also know some clergymen ignore

the church rules. Now, I'm not saying you are such a man, I'm merely asking if you could give this particular person a blessing before he's laid to rest.'

'I suppose I could do that,' the vicar said, 'I can't see how it would hurt.'

'Thank you!' Lily shook the man's hand.

Feeling better, she walked back to Webb's remembering to buy cake on her way.

She thought, *I couldn't make you happy in this life, Seb, but I've tried to ensure you'll be happy in the next.* She realised that though what Seb had done to her was very wrong, his letter showed he was misguided and alone. This had given her some sympathy for him, although she could still never forgive his act against her.

Now, at last Lily felt she could completely leave her old life behind and embark on a new one with Ben Addenbury.

Two days later she led the carriage to St John's Church. The vicar stood by the lych-gate and as they approached Lily nodded to him.

Leading them around the outside of the wall, the clergyman halted beneath the trees.

For all it was not consecrated ground, Lily thought it was a nice spot and Seb Ryder would have been pleased.

Stan frowned when Lily did not step away from the casket immediately as protocol demanded.

The vicar gave a blessing over the coffin and Lily

dropped a handful of dirt onto its top. Other than his landlady, there were no other mourners at Seb's funeral.

Lily stepped back to join Stan, who eyed her suspiciously. She shook her head and continued to watch the proceedings.

On their way back to the parlour, Stan asked, 'What was all that about then?'

'There was only one mourner there and I knew the man from years ago. I was once a maid to the family,' Lily responded.

Stan nodded his understanding and seeing Lily's mouth clamped tightly shut he kept quiet for the remainder of the journey.

Lily spent that evening with Emily Johnston, where she explained about the funeral.

'That was a kind thing to do, Lily, especially considering who it was you were burying,' Emily said.

'I felt he did me wrong Emily, but he didn't deserve to die alone. He must have been so desperately unhappy to have taken his own life.'

'You have had a lot of misfortune in your own life, Lily, but God has seen fit to relieve you of those burdens and set you on the path to happiness once more,' Emily said with a smile.

'It's Tilley Green I feel a little sorry for though. She has so many unanswered questions about her parentage.'

'It's not our place to tell her what we know, Lily,' Emily said.

'I know that, Emily. It would only cause her distress.' Lily sighed again as she thought about Maud locked up in prison.

'You have to concentrate on yourself now, sweetheart,' Emily said.

'Yes, so I was wondering – will you come with me to choose a wedding outfit?' Lily asked with a grin.

Emily jumped up from her seat and grabbed her coat.

Lily laughed at her friend's excitement as she also got to her feet.

'*Come on!* We have a wedding to plan!' Emily said all in a rush.

The two women wrapped their arms around each other before they headed off for the town.

Later that day, Ben and Lily took a walk around the park. Coming to the bandstand, Lily smiled inwardly as she remembered Davy.

Ben took her hand and looking into her eyes, he said, 'I will do my utmost to make you happy, Lily.'

'After I lost Clara and Davy, I thought I'd never be happy again, and then I met you. You stirred feelings in me I thought had died with my family.' Lily smiled up at him.

'Oh Lily! I love you so much it hurts,' Ben said as he pulled her into his arms.

'I love you too, Ben, and I know we'll have a wonderful life together . . .'

Lily's words were lost as his lips closed on hers and she felt herself melt against the man who was to be her husband. Then as she looked up into the sky she saw two butterflies flutter past and it was, she thought, Davy and Clara's blessing on the union.